H. R. HOWLAND

# ASHES

BERKLEY BOOKS, NEW YORK

**THE BERKLEY PUBLISHING GROUP**
**Published by the Penguin Group**
**Penguin Group (USA) Inc.**
**375 Hudson Street, New York, New York 10014, USA**
Penguin Group (Canada), 10 Alcorn Avenue, Toronto, Ontario M4V 3B2, Canada
(a division of Pearson Penguin Canada Inc.)
Penguin Books Ltd., 80 Strand, London WC2R 0RL, England
Penguin Group Ireland, 25 St. Stephen's Green, Dublin 2, Ireland (a division of Penguin Books Ltd.)
Penguin Group (Australia), 250 Camberwell Road, Camberwell, Victoria 3124, Australia
(a division of Pearson Australia Group Pty. Ltd.)
Penguin Books India Pvt. Ltd., 11 Community Centre, Panchsheel Park, New Delhi—110 017, India
Penguin Group (NZ), Cnr. Airborne and Rosedale Roads, Albany, Auckland 1310, New Zealand
(a division of Pearson New Zealand Ltd.)
Penguin Books (South Africa) (Pty.) Ltd., 24 Sturdee Avenue, Rosebank, Johannesburg 2196,
South Africa

Penguin Books Ltd., Registered Offices: 80 Strand, London WC2R 0RL, England

This is a work of fiction. Names, characters, places, and incidents either are the product of the authors' imaginations or are used fictitiously, and any resemblance to actual persons, living or dead, business establishments, events, or locales is entirely coincidental.

ASHES

A Berkley Book / published by arrangement with the authors

PRINTING HISTORY
Berkley mass-market edition / June 2005

Copyright © 2005 by Holly Newstein and Ralph W. Bieber II.
"Love Is the Answer," by Harry Nilssen and Perry Botkin, Jr. © 1980 Black Molasses Music and Perryvale MC Co. All rights on behalf of black Molasses Music Administered by WB Music Co. All rights reserved. Permission Warner Brothers Publications, U.S. Inc., Miami, FL 33014
Cover design by Rita Frangie.
Interior text design by Stacy Irwin.
Cover photo by David Hiser.

ISBN: 0-425-20353-0

BERKLEY®
Berkley Books are published by The Berkley Publishing Group
a division of Penguin Group (USA) Inc.
375 Hudson Street, New York, New York 10014
BERKLEY is a registered trademark of Penguin Group (USA) Inc.
The "B" design is a trademark belonging to Penguin Group (USA) Inc.

PRINTED IN THE UNITED STATES OF AMERICA

10  9  8  7  6  5  4  3  2  1

# ACKNOWLEDGMENTS

The authors would like to thank the following people for their help:

Rick Hautala, whose wisdom and experience with the world of publishing is invaluable, and whose love and support is indispensable; Ralph Bardwell Heavens, for his assistance with Coast Guard SAR procedures; our beta testers Trent Greschuk, Judi Madsen, Kathleen and the Palmyra Readers; Connie Foster, for helping us step into a new world; Brian Keene for insisting this book see print; and Louisa Edwards for making it all come true.

IN MEMORIAM

DARREN C. ZEHRING
September 8, 1960–March 31, 1996

*For Cheryl Bieber*
*and Rick Newstein,*
*whose patience and tolerance*
*made it possible*

Dr. Paul Crane, professor of archaeology at the University of Pennsylvania, emerged from his tent. He yawned and stretched, surrounded by the lush green of the Honduran mountain valley. A drop of sweat trickled down his forehead and into his eyes. He mopped his forehead with an old bandanna and ran a hand over his thinning brown hair.

"Damn it, eight in the morning and it's already eighty degrees in the shade," he grumbled. January was the height of the dry season in Honduras, and it was hot. "Worse than Philly in July." He could still remember, years later, how the air felt so heavy that it was like suffocating inside a hot wet sponge.

He walked over to his student assistants, who were sitting on a grassy patch at the edge of the dig site. They exchanged glances as he approached them.

"Some coffee, Professor?" one student asked slyly and held out a white ceramic mug. The bittersweet fragrance of steaming Honduran espresso was thick in the humid morning air.

"Hell, no," he snorted and walked down the path toward the lake. He heard them laughing and smiled to himself. They were good kids. They represented the best of the best in the archaeology program at Penn. He had personally hand-picked each one to aid in his Mayan research. For most of them it was their first time at a real dig. Their excitement was catching—except on days like this, when even thinking hard made you sweat.

For the millionth time in his life, he wondered why the hell he ever got into this business. He had had no real plans when he was young, except that he would someday own a beach house at Avalon, down on the southern Jersey coast. His family had always rented a place for the summer when he was a kid, and he vowed that someday he'd live there full-time. It was cooler there, and the air was fresh and tangy with salt. And the beaches, with their tall grassy dunes, went on forever.

The sun's glare on the lake stung his gray eyes, and he fumbled in his pockets for his sunglasses. His mother used to say that he spent so much time on the beach that his eyes took on the color of the water. When he was eighteen, he went to Penn because he was accepted there, he didn't know what else to do, and his parents were willing to pay for it. Plus he'd have his summers free to go down to the shore.

In the second semester of his freshman year he took an Introduction to Archaeology course for no other reason but that the girl he was in love with was taking it also. When the professor began teaching about the Mayan civilization, Dr. Crane finally found the thing that would ignite his imagination and become his lifelong love. Second only to Avalon, of course.

He was enchanted by the story of the Mayans, by the fact that they had a sophisticated, brilliant civilization while Europe was deep in the Dark Ages. Their religion and cosmology were complex and beautiful. He liked the idea of the multi-layered world, that the world they lived on was just a thin crust over another, equally real world below. And up above were the gods, watching over them, controlling every aspect of their lives.

They developed astronomy, an accurate solar calendar, and abstract mathematics. They also had a system of writing—one of only five civilizations in the ancient world to have one—and a rich language. Dr. Crane even liked their art and architecture—the step pyramid temples, the fortress walls, and the stylized bas-reliefs illustrating daily Mayan life carved into the walls.

He was intrigued by the mystery of how such an intelligent nation could be so warlike, so obsessed with blood and death and killing. Most of the Mayans were farmers, growing their corn, bound to the earth and the rain and the sun in a deeply elemental way. He was curious about what it took to turn such a peaceful, intellectual people into warriors, and to drench their belief systems in blood.

Dr. Crane threw himself into the study of archaeology. He displayed a real talent for the work, fired by his near-obsession with the Mayans, and was eventually recognized as one of the leading experts in the study of the Mayan civilization. He became a professor and was offered tenure by the University of Pennsylvania and happily accepted it. Not only was it a prestigious Ivy League school, it was only an hour and a half from Avalon. He finally realized his dream of a beach house when he was in his early thirties. He purchased a duplex overlooking the dunes and the beach. He found that the ocean had a galvanizing effect on him, and he wrote his best articles and two definitive books on the Maya while living on the beach.

He was a familiar sight in town and on the beaches. Early in the morning, no matter what the season, he would walk along the edge of the surf, lost in thought, his short, thin body a dark outline against the lightening sky and the rolling gray waves. Nearly every day he would drive into town in his old blue Jeep Wrangler and have a few beers in the Shore Thing Bar and Grill, mingling with the crowds in the summer and chatting up the barmaids in the off-season. He was content with his life, but there were still questions about his life's work that he wanted desperately to solve.

The Chorti Maya civilization of western Honduras had flourished and then mysteriously vanished over a thousand years ago. Dr. Crane had chosen the remote site of Los Naranjos because its small size and difficult access discouraged tourists and their souvenir hunting. It was also some distance from Copan, the ceremonial center of the Chorti Maya. Los Naranjos was a smaller city-state, the Mayan equivalent of a small town. Dr. Crane and his students planned to spend a month collecting artifacts, and then bring them back to Penn for identification and cataloguing.

The dig site had already yielded some mildly interesting artifacts, bits of ceramics and some stone implements that might have been used in maize farming. There were a few broken obsidian blades, which were used as weapons. The most interesting discovery was the apparent remains of a stela that had been destroyed. The way in which the pieces were shattered suggested that it had been hacked apart, not eroded by natural events. The Mayans often erected beautifully carved stone stelae to commemorate a ruler or a victory. They would be covered with pictures and glyphs depicting the occasion to be immortalized.

Dr. Crane thought it seemed a little strange to find this ruined wreck, when so many other structures were wonderfully preserved at Los Naranjos. The only readable glyph from the stela they had recovered so far was a glyph for Chac Mol, the name of someone important.

"It also means 'jaguar'," Dr. Crane told his students. He turned the rock shard over in his hand and ran his thumb over the carved name. "You know, if circumstances changed for a king or a priest, the stelae that was put up in his honor would be destroyed."

"So this Chac Mol could have been a king who lost a battle, maybe? And the conquerors tore down his stela?" asked Andrew Wright, his graduate assistant. Andrew took the shard from Dr. Crane and gently rubbed another bit of dirt from it with the tail of his Metallica T-shirt.

"Could be. It could also be that his own people turned against him and wanted to obliterate every trace of his existence. It looks like we have a mystery here ," said Paul Crane. "Now we'll have to see into the past instead of the future and find out where we've been." That'll give them some incentive, he thought. Something to work for.

A few days later Dr. Crane was called back to the dig pit. Beth Boynton, a petite young woman who still managed to be attractive even in a dirty tank top and cutoff jeans, was crouching over a section of the dig, not far from where they found the Chac Mol fragment. She was carefully easing another fragment out of the dirt. She brushed some of the dirt off with a soft sable brush and looked at it. "Could be another piece of our mystery stela, Professor. It has a name on it."

Dr. Crane walked over to Beth and picked up the piece as she charted the find in a notebook. He rubbed the stone fragment with his dirty fingers and looked at it again. Sweat trickled into his eyes and burned. Digs were hot, dusty, often tedious work, and for a moment he longed for the crying gulls and the roaring gray ocean.

"It's a woman's name. Xochitl." Dr. Crane pronounced it So-chee. "Looks like there may have been more written here, like a title or something, but it's unreadable now. Good job, Beth. Keep looking, people."

It had been nearly a week since the Xochitl discovery and nothing terribly interesting had turned up since. Well, this day had barely begun. You never knew what might turn up, thought Dr. Crane.

He gave up the search for his sunglasses and turned to look down toward the site where the village stood long ago. The Maya had occupied Los Naranjos for nearly two thousand years, and it was easy to understand why. It was on the edge of a lake, which supplied fresh water for drinking and for their corn and fish. The forests would have been full of game for hunters. Previous archaeologists had unearthed the ball courts that the Maya had built for recreation, often life-and-death games with captives taken in war. A small pyramid temple was carved with lovely, intricate glyphs depicting religious ceremonies. Even though it lacked the grandeur of Palenque or even Tulum, set as it was along the turquoise Yucatan coast it was a beautiful, peaceful place to live out your life.

Dr. Crane closed his eyes for a moment and imagined the thriving village, men fishing on the lake, children playing and laughing, the delicious smells of food cooking over open fires, the songs of the priests. He decided to take a look at the temple again. At least it would be shady and cool in there.

He entered the dim recesses of the temple. As his eyes adjusted to the darkness, an indefinable sense of fear came over him. He found himself wishing he'd brought a flashlight.

"Shit, there's no such thing as ghosts," he muttered. He took a step farther into the temple. The cool air felt good. He took a deep breath of the coolness and told himself to relax.

His sandaled foot caught on something poking through the dirt floor. He lost his balance and fell against the temple wall. He got up, rubbing his shoulder.

"Goddamn it! What the hell was that?" He bent down to look at his foot. His big toenail was torn and bleeding a bit, but nothing else seemed damaged. From the corner of his eye he saw a glint of light on a smooth, rounded shape between two stones along the wall. He knelt and carefully pulled the stones from the earth. Then he began pushing the dirt aside with his fingers.

His hands began to shake with excitement. He had found a stunning artifact—a beautifully preserved, intact pottery jar, fitted with a lid sealed with some kind of pitch. He eased it out of its earthen tomb and stepped back outside, blinking against the glare. The jar was in perfect condition and elegantly painted with glyphs and pictures. He stared at it, turning it over in his hands. In the shadowy gloom of the temple it had seemed almost to glow with a cold gray light. It was a magnificent find and he wondered why he wasn't overcome with excitement. The sense of dread he'd felt earlier oppressed him for a moment.

"What's so scary about a jar, for Christ's sake? Straighten up, Crane."

Again, he was able to brush away his fear. Then elation came rushing over him in a wave.

"Come over here!" he called to the students. His voice was high-pitched with excitement. "Someone bring tools." The students scrambled over to him. One of them handed him a screwdriver. They circled around him as he held up the jar as proudly and tenderly as a father holds his newborn child.

"Look at the painting on this jar! Gorgeous! It looks like it was done just yesterday." The students murmured with awe and wonder. They crowded closer to get a better look at the jar. "Someone better chart where we found this," warned Dr. Crane. Beth Boynton grabbed a notebook and stood next to Dr. Crane to detail the find. "What do the glyphs say, exactly?" she asked.

Dr. Crane frowned. "Apparently they tell of a sacrifice of some royal figure. This jar held—holds—the heart. Look here, this is the priest pulling it, still beating, from the poor sod's living chest. Then they sealed the jar." Dr. Crane turned the jar gently, studying the glyphs. "What puzzles me is that the Maya usually did not go to such elaborate lengths to preserve body parts. They were usually burned as a sacrifice to the gods." As he turned the heavy, exquisite piece in his hand, it thrummed like a rapidly beating heart. Suddenly he was overcome by an irresistible urge to open it. He carefully placed the jar on the ground and knelt next to it. Without a word he took out his pocketknife and began picking at the ancient pitch seal at the mouth of the jar.

Beth's eyes widened. "Professor Crane, what on earth are you doing? You're not supposed to do that until the object's been catalogued!" The other students pressed closer, trying to see what was going on.

Dr. Crane ignored his students. They watched, wide-eyed, as he put his fingers under the lid and pried it off.

As he did, they all heard a roar like a rush-hour subway train. Dr. Crane's body jerked convulsively. With catlike speed Crane jumped to his feet, pivoted, and picked up a huge piece of stone that was lying on the ground next to him. The pottery jar rolled away, coming to rest several yards away against a gnarled tree root. A small green object fell out of the jar.

Dr. Crane brought the heavy stone down squarely on Beth's face. The blow crushed her face into a bloody pulp. As she toppled over, Crane grabbed the sides of her head and twisted it violently. Her neck snapped with a ghastly crunch. Death was instantaneous.

All of the students backed away instinctively, horror-stricken.

"Dr. Crane! Have you gone crazy?" Andrew Wright, his face pale with horror, started moving toward Dr. Crane. Crane lifted his right hand and pointed at the closest student to the approaching young man. That student happened to be holding a pick. The pick swung through the air and embedded itself into Andrew Wright's back. Andrew screamed once, and then fell face down into the dirt.

What had been a group of eager students a moment ago became a mindless mob intent on killing one another with axes, picks, shovels, rocks, and even bare hands. Screams of rage and pain echoed in the heavy air. Gouts of blood and chunks of gore flew through the air. Flies began buzzing around the fallen even as the survivors kept at each other with crazed intent. Crane stood back to watch the carnage with a peculiar expression. His eyes glowed with satisfaction.

When all were dead but one, Crane retrieved a broken axe handle and beat the man to death. When he had finished, he took the axe handle and stuck it through the young man's throat. Then he turned his attention back to the once-beautiful Beth. He rolled her onto her back, stripped off her clothing, and raped her corpse. He took an unholy relish in the rubbery feeling of the limp, fast cooling body and the taste of blood and brains mingled on her ravaged face.

After he had finished, he surveyed the bloody carnage and was pleased with what he saw. The bright sunshine and warm air intensified the coppery aroma of the rivulets of clotting blood. Flies gathered in dense clouds, and he could see birds circling overhead. He smiled, and for some reason he didn't understand, the heat no longer bothered him. A feeling of intense satisfaction filled him. He turned and strode briskly off into the forested valley.

The forgotten jar was left resting in the crook of the tree root. The green object next to it was a carved and polished jade ring. A shaft of sunlight illuminated its delicate, leaf-green surface. A fly landed on it to investigate. Finding nothing of interest, it flew off a moment later to dine on Beth Boynton's bloody and ravaged corpse.

After several hours of hiking rapidly and easily through the forest, Dr. Crane began to feel fatigued. A sense he could not understand told him to sit down under a large, spreading oak tree. As he did so, an almost inaudible sound made him look up and into the greenish-yellow eyes of a jaguar. The big cat, its sleek bronze fur intricately spotted with black, was obviously considering whether it should put Dr. Crane on the lunch menu.

Crane held the cat's eyes with his own. He raised his hand and beckoned.

"Here, kitty, kitty," he called softly.

The cat's eyes fixed on Crane's. Slowly it descended from the tree as if an invisible leash was pulling it down. Shudders rippled under the glossy fur. The jaguar's eyes were fixed on him. It panted anxiously, its pink tongue speckled with white foam.

Like reeling in a bluefish, Crane thought. He smiled and reached out, stroking the trembling animal's silky head.

The jaguar snarled. The snarl became a shrieking yowl. Its body arched backwards in a spasm of pain. It turned and streaked off into the forest. Crane watched it go. Suddenly he screamed, then choked on his own body fluids as they gushed from every pore and orifice. Crane's flesh burst into flames, a white-hot flash of light that consumed him almost instantly. Finally nothing was left of Dr. Paul Crane but a fine gray ash.

**2**

Well, hello, little girl. Come in, come in. Forgive
me for not getting up. Legs, you know. Nothing works like it
used to anymore. Damn shame, too. Give me a hand here.
These bony old fingers can't squeeze a tea bag or a lemon
wedge any more. I only get one cup a day, so I like to make it
count. Now, push me over to the window. That's a nice place
to have a chat.

So what's this thing you wanted to talk to me about? Shawn
Williams asked you to talk to me? Whatever for? Why does he
want you to talk to your gabby, old great-grandpa? Oh, I see.
Shawn's in charge of the Founders' Days Committee this year.
Needs some stories from Aronston history. Well, you came to
the right place. Stories are about all I have anymore.

Pass me that lap robe there, would you? This is the northeast corner of the building. Coldest room in the house always
faces northeast, right? Damn cinder-block walls are no help
either. Painted 'em that awful color, too. Mudslide beige, I

*call it. Hey, I saw you smile! There's another blanket in that closet there if you're cold. No? Well, help yourself if you need it.*

*I read someplace that beige is supposed to keep people calm and relaxed, a neutral color, they call it. Need to keep all us old folks calm, I guess. Who are they kidding, anyway? This is not my home, this is my prison. A prison with a view. A waiting room for death. Thank God for my window and my old Westinghouse radio.*

*Even looks like a prison. Nothing homey about this place. Just a big, cold rectangle. Except for the chapel they left. See, they built the ElderCare Center where the old Presbyterian church used to be. Demolished the whole building. Shame, too. It was a real pretty red brick building, built around 1875 or so. Gorgeous stained glass windows. But for some reason they decided to leave the chapel standing and connect it to the Center with a walkway. So here you have this big modern building with this lovely little old chapel sticking off the side of it. Wonder whose fool idea that was. But chapel's a nice place to go when you need to forget for a while.*

*How old am I? Boy, you are conducting this like an interview, aren't you? Well, I turned one hundred and one last October. October thirty-first. Halloween. Your great-grandma Kitty always said that's why I was different. Why am I different? Well, sometimes I get a feeling about something, kind of a premonition. Haven't been wrong yet. For instance, when the Cross Keys Tavern burned down eighty years ago. My father and I passed by it the day before and I looked over and saw flames coming out of the windows and smoke rising in the air. I said to my father, "Look, look! The Cross Keys is on fire!" My father looked at me and looked at the Cross Keys and said, "Levi, the sun must be in your eyes. Nothing's wrong over there."*

*Well, I rubbed my eyes and blinked but I could still see the flames and smoke. Then a few seconds later the flames were gone. Next day we heard that the Cross Keys had burned the night before. Father looked at me real hard but said nothing. First time that ever happened to me but it wasn't the last.*

*Never told anyone about my premonitions again, except Kitty. And now you.*

*Oldest man in Aronston, that's my claim to fame. I tell you, living to be this old is no fun. Too many good-byes. Too many people to miss. Body gets tired and won't listen to you anymore. You have a tape recorder? Shawn wanted you to get me on tape? You need to plug that thing in or do you have batteries? And you're going to take notes, too? I remember you used to be a Girl Scout, honey—you came prepared. There's a smile.*

*Yep, owned a feed and grain store for fifty-five years, till I was seventy-five. You see, I was never cut out to be a farmer. Never liked being out in the fields or mucking out the barn. My older brother, Matty, he was the one who enjoyed all that. My father died when I was sixteen. Then Matty went over to fight in World War I and died in the trenches there. Few months later, spring of 1918 it was, Mother died of the influenza. Her heart was broken over Matty and my father and she had no will to fight. Think she actually looked forward to joining them in the Promised Land.*

*I was sick with the flu, too, and for a while they thought I was going to die, but I didn't. I sold the farm and used the money to buy the lot on the Gretna Road. I built the store and did pretty darned well with it, if I do say so myself. Made enough of a living to have a nice home, good food, and saw two of my boys through college.*

*I was going to retire at sixty, but my wife, Katharine, she got the cancer and died thirty-five years ago. Still miss her. Prettiest girl I ever saw—big sparkling brown eyes, long brown hair, almost down to her knees. She wore it up all the time. Took it down only for me. She was a big girl, too, the way I like 'em. No skinny Minnies for me. Oops, guess I shouldn't be talking like this to my great-granddaughter, eh?*

*You're pretty when you laugh there, Tracy girl. Don't hear too much laughter around here. Retirement homes are sad places. Places where you wait to die. At night it gets lonely. Scary, too. This window is my salvation during the day, but at night I can't see a damn thing except for the lights. And the crazies come out of the damn woodwork. In here you can hear*

people moaning in their sleep. Sometimes someone'll get the
heebie-jeebies and wake the whole damn building up screaming. Feel like screaming myself half the time.

I didn't really know what to do with myself after Kitty—
that's my name for Katharine—died, so I just kept on working.
There were folks who'd been coming to my store for years,
and their kids and grandkids came when they had farms of
their own. Kind of like family to me, helped fill the hole Kitty
left behind. Finally got too damn old to run the place. None
of my kids wanted the business, so I sold it. The new owners
tore down the store and put up an antique mall. Probably
made more money in six months than I did in two years. But I
made friends, and that meant the most to me.

After I sold the grain store, I retired. Went on bus trips to
Atlantic City, New York City. Played penny-a-point poker with
my friends. On a real good night I might make all of twenty-
five, fifty cents. But then they all started dying on me. I tried
to keep busy with church and all, but pretty soon I was alone
most of the time. Everyone I was close to was six feet under.
Then I had that stroke a couple of years ago, and my legs went
on me. Everyone wanted to help, I know, but nobody in the
family had a place where they could keep me, or someone to
take care of me. So here I am. I'm glad Kitty didn't live to see
me like this.

Yep, met Kitty here in Aronston. Katharine Moyer. I told
you she was pretty. Smart as a whip, too. Went to Normal
School down in Lancaster, was going to be a teacher. Met her
at church one Sunday and that was that. Nobody else like her.
She loved to have real conversation. She'd go pick up a book
in the morning and bone up on something and surprise me at
dinner with lively chatter. And the five kids would join in, too.
A regular debating society. We had five, but one died. My eldest
daughter, Mary. Peritonitis, it was. From a ruptured appen-
dix. Few years later they came out with penicillin and that
would have saved her.


So, you want to know about Aronston? Don't you remember the dry stuff from your schoolbooks? Oh, I have to say it

*for the tape recorder, eh? Well, Aronston was founded in 1767
along the Harris' Ferry Road. About two-thirds of the way between Reading and Harris' Ferry—that's Harrisburg now. My
Kitty could trace her line back to the founding father, Ezekiel
Moyer. Zeke Moyer, now there was a smart man. Not very
friendly, but he knew land when he saw it. Came up here from
Lancaster. His family was pretty wealthy, as farmers go, and
lent him the cash for the land as a wedding gift.*

*You have to admit that this is some of the prettiest land in
Pennsylvania. You've got these rolling hills and broad val-
leys. Here, come stand next to me and I'll show you around.*

*Yep, got a nice view of the town. Right down there's the
town square. This corner room lets me see almost all the way
to Reading. And the town looks almost like it did fifty years
ago, thanks to Emma Bardwell and her preservation society.
Real pretty place, this is. Keep looking east and you'll see
Bardwell's factory and the meatball place, Mama Angelina's.
Over on the right, there's the hospital there, and if you keep
looking to your right you can just make out Gretna and a couple of the college buildings.*

*'Course, back then, there was nothing here but the creek
and the trees. There were lots of deer and fish. Plenty of
water, little streams and lakes. Lots of timber, too. My father
used to tell me in the fall, the hills were just blazing with
color. Even wolves lived in those woods. Haven't heard one
since I was a boy, but I still remember. It was a moonlit January night, and I was snug in bed with Matty and heard this
eerie howl. Chilled me down to my soul. I got out of bed and
looked out the window. The snow was thick and white on the
ground and it reflected the moonlight. Turned everything
bright silver. Up on the ridge behind the house there was a
wolf. I could see him clear as day, black against the silver sky.
He pointed his nose in the air and howled again. No other
sound on earth compares. Never heard a wolf howl again, but
I'll never forget that sound.*

*Even grouchy old Zeke must have smiled, looking over his
five hundred acres. It made him a good living. One thing I do
know is that when his son Aaron was born, he must've had an
ear-to-ear grin. You see, old Zeke was the seventh son in his*

family. When Leah, his wife, had their seventh son, Zeke thought it was a good omen. Even though he had nine other children, good and strong ones, too, Aaron was his folks' spoiled darling.

Now, some say Aaron Moyer was the devil's son. I don't know as I believe that, but I've seen old engravings of Aaron and he had a cruel face. Handsome but cruel. Hand me that book over there, Tracy. Got all these books here. Kitty collected them. She was a real bug on history, especially since her family founded the town. I just like to have the pictures. Let me find the page . . . See? I saw you frown, young lady. You know what I mean. That twist to the mouth. Would've been a pretty mouth on a girl, but it just looks mean on Aaron there.

I've heard tell that after Aaron was born, his mama moved out of Zeke's room and in with the three girls. She decided that ten kids was enough, and Aaron was about all she could handle. Anyway, says here in this book that Aaron Moyer was born in March of 1784. Not long after that, old Zeke sold some land facing the Harris' Ferry Road to someone who built an inn. Can't remember the name, but you can look it up. He built the Cross Keys Tavern. Building used to be right there, facing the square. Already told you what happened to that. Zeke sold a couple of other parcels to some others looking to start up in business, and put in the sale papers the condition that the settlement be named Aaron's Town. He figured that being a seventh son of a seventh son was a lucky thing. Besides, it was catchier than Moyer's Farm, which was what it used to be known as. The name got changed over time, with some bad spelling, to Aronston. My store was on the Gretna Road, like I told you, which crosses Harris' Ferry Road— Harrisburg Pike it is now—right here at the square. You can just see the roof from here, a quarter mile east of the square.

Anyway, this town grew and prospered through the years. See how pretty it's set here in the valley? You got the Swatara Creek over there, and these hills rise up on the other three sides. Come around the bend on the Harrisburg Pike and there it is, like a jewel. They built the railroad over there, and you could go east to Philadelphia and New York, or west out *to Pittsburgh. People came from all over and settled here. Plenty of transportation, coal, water, and good, good farmland. Even had some kind of religious colony living in the hills there, right near the college. You know about that? Yes, like the Oneida colony, or the Shakers. Never know it now, Gretna's all full of those artsy-craftsy tourist stores, but it was a big scandal in town.*

*See, those Gretna colonists hatched all kinds of loony utopian ideas up there. Thing that got everyone going was that they didn't believe in marriage. Or rather, they believed all of 'em were married to one another. Took turns, I guess you could say. There I go, talking randy talk again . . . dang fool I am. But it's truth, Tracy girl. Half the people here in Aronston said leave 'em alone; it's none of our business. The other half said they were evil fornicators and it was the town's duty to run 'em off. Didn't matter in the long run anyway. They left and a bunch of bohemian types moved in and now it's a college town and an artist's colony. If you want to call that overpriced junk art.*

*Of course, what iced the cake for the town was Bardwell. But you know all about that, working for Bardwell's Chocolates like you do. But you want me to tell it anyway? Well, all right. William Ewing Bardwell. Him and that candy factory put Aronston on the map. Bill Bardwell made this town what it is today, what with the factory and all the money he spent on the town, all the cultural stuff and the hospital. He wanted to be sure people would want to live here so they would keep on working for him. He was almost as smart as you are—and he sure would be proud if he knew you were his customer service manager, or whatever you are these days.*

*Anyway, Bardwell was as canny as old Zeke Moyer. He knew how to market his products, and he treated his people right. Didn't take long before everyone on the East Coast knew of Bardwell's Chocolates. Then came World War II, and Bardwell's became world famous. All our GI's giving that chocolate to the half-starved kids in Europe. Great publicity. Smart as a whip, that man.*

*No, I'm not tired. I want to finish Aaron's story for you. Yep, there's lots more to tell about him. Pass me that book again. See, here's an old portrait of Zeke and Leah. Dark they were, and their faces look like someone carved 'em from rock. They wouldn't win a beauty contest on a hog farm. The other nine Moyers were all dark, too. Like my Kitty. But let's go back to Aaron here.*

*Aaron grew up to be tall and slim and fair. Looked nothing like anyone in the family. His mama's spoiled darling and the apple of his father's eye. But he was mean. Sadistic, they'd say nowadays. The story goes that when he was two, he was pulling wings off flies. At three he was stabbing toads down at the creek with sharp sticks. No cats lived in the barn for fear of Aaron. But they never had a problem with mice or rats, no, ma'am. Aaron'd spend hours catching them and doing his perverted experiments on them. Only respect for his father's buggy whip kept Aaron away from the livestock.*

*Every kid in town was afraid of Aaron, even his brothers and sisters. They'd try to play with him and he'd blacken their eyes and bloody their noses. Even the big boys didn't want to be near him. He fought like a kid twice his size. Aaron had enough meanness in him for twenty people.*

*Kitty told me that he liked liquor, too. Not too many people know this. Big secret, you know. God-fearing Christian families back then thought liquor was the tool of Satan. They weren't too far wrong on that one. Never saw any good come out of being drunk. One time when Aaron was drunk he set fire to his family's barn. Zeke and the boys worked like madmen to save all the cows and horses. And they did, no thanks to Aaron. Kitty said Aaron stood off to one side, half-hidden in a stand of trees, just watching the fun with a look of pure evil on his face. Zeke and Leah believed him when he denied it, but his brothers and sisters knew better.*

*As Aaron got older, he got worse and worse. Finally, at seventeen, Zeke gave him fifty acres and helped him build a house on it. Then Leah set about finding Aaron a wife. Guess they figured marriage and a family might settle him down. There was a Mennonite family come into Aronston from near to Reading, the Reifsnyders, and they had a daughter named Zipporiah. There aren't any pictures of her, but Kitty said she was a real pretty girl—curly strawberry blonde hair, big* bright green eyes, wide warm smile. A lively, happy girl, but pious and religious. Well, the Moyers and Reifsnyders made up a match and Zipporiah married Aaron when she was just sixteen.

Aaron had seemed pretty taken with Zipporiah when they were courting. He acted real respectful and kind. Zeke and Leah were delighted. They figured the problem was solved. Zipporiah, poor child, actually fell in love with her handsome husband.

Well, Tracy, on their wedding night Aaron knocked out her front teeth. Yes, it was horrible and it got worse. He beat her once a week, and then he'd rape her. Even after she was pregnant. Never let her out of the house. Made excuses for her at church. Told her family she didn't want to see them anymore. She had two brothers, Mark and Tom, who thought the world of their baby sister. They figured Aaron was up to no good but what could they do? A wife was her husband's property back then. If he wanted to treat her like a dog, or worse, so be it.

You see, I'm no Sigmund Freud or anything, but I think Aaron knew Zipporiah was pretty and happy and good and he wanted to marry her so he could destroy her. I see from your face you're pretty disgusted. Grossed out, isn't that what you say these days?

Yep, Aaron was something all right. Something not human. Ten months after the wedding, Zipporiah gave birth to a little girl. According to Kitty, the midwife said that Aaron stayed in the room the whole time, watching. He'd get a real evil look every time Zipporiah screamed. Well, Zipporiah waited until Aaron got liquored up and passed out. Then she got up, bundled up the baby and herself and walked fifteen miles to her parents' house in the bitter January cold. Mind you, she'd just had the baby less than twelve hours earlier. She must have been crazy with fear for herself and the baby.

Her family took one look at her—missing teeth, broken nose, bloody eyes, scars all over—and knew they weren't sending her back to Aaron. Her brothers were furious. Wanted to go out to Aaron's place and horsewhip him. Eye for an eye, they said. No, their father said. Vengeance is mine, saith the

Lord. Zipporiah named her little girl Angel. Angel was Kitty's cousin.

What's in that bag you're rattling around with? Cookies, eh? That's sweet of you, Tracy. Oatmeal raisin, my favorite. And homemade to boot. Now all I need is a big glass of ice-cold milk, but they won't let me have that. Bad for the digestion, you know. To be blunt, young lady, I don't want to get an enema any more than they want to give me one. So, we'll do without the milk.

Delicious! I can taste the cinnamon in here. I may be old, but thank God I can still enjoy my food. Some man's gonna be real lucky to get you, Tracy girl. Pretty, smart as a whip, and cooks, too. Just like my Kitty. Except you need some more meat on your bones, young lady. No, no. I know all you see on TV and in the magazines are these starved little girls, but trust an old man.

Let's see. We were talking about Aaron Moyer. Well, after poor Zipporiah came home with the baby girl, Mark and Tom Reifsnyder were fit to be tied. They were good boys, too—kind and respectful, honored their parents, helped on the farm. Never in trouble. Everyone in town liked 'em. They were eighteen and twenty, I think. Mark was the older and he'd just got himself some land because he was fixing to get married. It broke their hearts to see what their little sister had gone through. For no reason except she married Aaron Moyer. Look, here's an old engraving of the two of them. Nice looking boys, weren't they? Both of them were big, strapping, healthy fellows.

About two weeks after Zipporiah came home with her daughter, Aaron came riding up in a wagon to bring her home. Like I said before, a wife was a husband's property. They didn't have any laws to protect women like they do now. Me, I think any man who hits a woman is a cowardly dog. I'd have rather had my hand cut off than raise it to your great-grandma.

So anyway, up comes Aaron Moyer to the Reifsnyder place, as cool as you please. Mark and Tom were in the front yard when he got there. Aaron told them, in a real arrogant tone of voice, to go get Zipporiah so he could take her home.

*Well, Mark and Tom had a few things to say about that. Property or not, they were not going to let their sister and their baby niece go back to Aaron Moyer. No, sirree. The three of them were arguing there in the yard and the noise brought Zipporiah to the window. As Kitty told it, something inside Zipporiah snapped. She wasn't afraid anymore. She knew that she would kill Aaron Moyer before she would ever let him come near her or her daughter again.*

*She went into her parents' room and picked up her father's shotgun. She loaded it as she had seen her father and Mark and Tom do many times, tamping down the powder, carefully putting in the shot. She walked down to the front door with the gun and opened it. Mark and Tom and Aaron were just about ready to let fly with fists when she came out. She lifted the gun up to her shoulder, pointed it at Aaron and told him, in a level, calm voice to get off the property or she'd kill him. Seems like hate either makes you see red or makes you go stone cold. Zipporiah was cold as new-fallen snow as she stared Aaron down, along the barrel of her father's gun. He looked at those green eyes and knew she was deadly serious. She'd pull the trigger in a heartbeat.*

*Aaron looked at her and then that evil, twisted smile spread across his face. Guess he figured his work was done. He'd taken a happy, trusting, pretty young girl who loved life and turned her into a reclusive, bitter woman with a smashed-up face. He'd destroyed her worse than if he'd just killed her.*

*Mark and Tom saw that smile and their blood boiled. They knew what that smile meant. They told Aaron to go. And if he ever set foot on their farm again, well, they'd treat him like they would any other trespasser or horse thief. So Aaron left. Didn't even ask about his little daughter. Zipporiah kept pointing the shotgun at Aaron as he went down the road, long after he was out of range, until she couldn't see him any longer. Then she fired the gun. She turned and walked into the house and never set foot outside again.*

*A couple of months later, Mark and Tom were out doing some late-winter hunting. They had two friends with them, Zachary Leicht and Joseph Keller. The four of them came upon Aaron in the woods, just sitting and singing between big* swallows of liquor. There were some words exchanged, which I am sure concerned Zipporiah. Aaron, being drunk, must have said something terrible because Mark and Tom went plain berserk, I guess. Beat Aaron senseless. They say his face was so badly smashed you couldn't recognize him. Then they dragged him home and left him there. Leah Moyer found him there that night when she came over with some hot supper for him. That woman was still spoiling him after what he did to his wife. 'Course she probably only heard his side of it, but they all knew what Aaron was capable of. He died a few days later, but not before he came to and told who did it.

The constable came out and arrested the boys. Now, in 1802, Aronston didn't have a jail. No need of one. So they put the boys up in the clerk's office. Brought in cots and a table and chairs. Mark and Tom helped out with clerk's business during the day and slept there at night. Never caused any trouble; they were patiently waiting for justice to be served. And believe me, everyone except the Moyers thought justice had already been done. All the ladies of the town kept them well-fed, bringing them hot suppers and rich desserts. They also brought their daughters to flirt with them—while their mamas watched, of course. Everything was proper in those days. No backseats of cars for young people back then.

You see, Miss Tracy, no one in town liked the Moyers. They were all scared of Aaron. A lot of people really thought he was the devil's own. Figured he got what was coming to him. Eye for an eye, you know. And the way Zeke and Leah had tried to protect him didn't sit well either. Zeke and Leah were not friendly folk, either. Kept to themselves and asked for no help and gave none.

The Reifsnyders, on the other hand, were good, down-to-earth farming folk. Helped out their neighbors. Everyone in town thought it was a dreadful shame for Mark and Tom to be locked up just when spring lambing and plowing was about to start.

Back then, murders like this didn't happen real often, so they were big news. The Philadelphia and New York papers had reporters here. Called Mark and Tom the "Murdering Mennonites." Nowadays stuff like this happens all the time

*and people are used to it. More's the pity. Lucky if it gets men-
tioned on the back page of the paper. But the Murdering Mennonites were front-page news for months. You can borrow my
books here if you want to, Tracy girl, and read up
on it.*

*They finally went to trial before Judge Cyrus Buchanan.
Old Cyrus was irascible—a cranky old fart, as they would say
now. Fair minded and all, but stuck to the letter of the law like
it was Holy Writ. Mark and Tom didn't hire a lawyer. Felt that
they were in the right. They argued that they never wanted to
kill Aaron Moyer. Only wanted to show him how it felt to be
treated as he had done their sister. Many of the townsfolk
came to testify as character witnesses for the Reifsnyders.
How they were an asset to the community and all.*

*What did them in, though, were their friends. Zack and Joe
didn't want to say anything to get Mark and Tom in trouble.
They were friends. But the Moyers had hired some hotshot
lawyer out of Philadelphia. Lawyers were scum of the earth
even back then. Anyway, this lawyer wore 'em down. Nowadays it's called browbeating the witness, I think. Zack and Joe
had to tell that Tom held Aaron while Mark beat his face in.
And Tom kicked Aaron after he passed out, over and over.
That's what caused the internal bleeding that killed him. I
know it's not a pretty story, Tracy, but it's important for history. And that's what you and Shawn want, right?*

*Everyone wanted to call Zipporiah to testify. Figured that
her terrible story would sway the judge. Well, Mark and Tom
wouldn't allow it. Little Zipporiah's face was so ruined and
broken she couldn't go out without being stared at. She never
left her family's farm again, ever. The town was crawling with
reporters doing drawings of the trial and all the people there.
The thought of their poor sister's face splashed on every
newspaper between New York and Baltimore made them sick.
So they lost their best chance for acquittal, protecting their
sister to the very end. Well, they say that if you plead your
own case, you have a fool for a lawyer. Guess that was right
in this case.*

*Old Cyrus Buchanan's decision rocked the town. He al-
lowed that Aaron Moyer was a cruel bully and a drunk. The*

*Reifsnyder boys may well have been justified in their feelings. However, murder was murder. Zach and Joe's testimony convinced the judge that it was not exactly an accident that Aaron died. Since the penalty for murder back then was death, Mark and Tom must hang for it. The people in the courtroom cried, Tracy. The whole of Aronston cried.*

*Get me a drink of water, would you? The worst part of the story is still coming and my throat is dry. Aaah, that's good. Best water I ever had. There, I got you to smile. Let's finish this up, shall we?*

*Back then, what with no TV and most people not being able to read, you got your fun where you found it. Public executions were a big thing back then. And this one was a dandy— double execution and all. People dressed up and came all the way from Reading Towne, as it was called back then, and Harris' Ferry to see the poor souls hanged. It was like a picnic or a festival. And everyone had heard of the Murdering Mennonites.*

*Anyway, it was a beautiful June day when they executed Tom and Mark. Right down there in the town square they built a gallows. Perfect day for a picnic. But it got real bad real fast. You see, the hangman had got drunk over at the Cross Keys. Told you nothing good ever came of being drunk. He was too drunk to figure out the drop needed to break Mark and Tom's necks. The reverend came and heard their last words, and the hangman put black silk hoods over their heads. They say he had the shakes real bad, plus those in the front could smell the whiskey on him. Mark and Tom must have known what was coming.*

*So the hangman pulls the lever and opens the trapdoor. The Reifsnyder boys, instead of having their necks broken, slowly strangled to death. You saw that they were big strong boys, so it took a long time. Strangling is a horrible way to die. Worse than being in this damned warehouse waiting to die. And there ain't much worse than that. Your great-grandma said one of the boys got the hood off his face and the crowd watched his eyes pop out and his tongue get all big and black and his face turn purple. Couldn't scream though—not enough air. They took ten minutes, writhing and kicking, to die. At the very end, they peed and shat themselves. Sorry, Tracy, but it's true. A lot of ladies fainted. No, Zipporiah wasn't there. Thank goodness.*

The people were so disgusted with the hangman for botching everything up—don't forget now, most people were on Mark and Tom's side—anyway, they chased down the hangman and beat him up pretty bad. Left him half-drowned in the Swatara Creek. Never saw anything like it until Susanna Cox was executed a few years later in Reading. Crowd almost killed the hangman there, too.

Not long after this, Zeke and Leah Moyer sold their land, for a handsome profit, mind you, and moved back to Lancaster County.

Now, I told you Angel, the baby girl, was related to my Kitty. Zipporiah had named her Angel to kind of ward off her father's evil. It was a very strange name back then. Nowadays she wouldn't stand out in a crowd. Every other kid these days has a strange name. Anyway, Angel grew up to be a raving beauty. Reddish blonde hair, green eyes, fair skin. Had her mother's lively temperament, too. Broke every man's heart between Aronston and Reading, and a few from Harris' Ferry and Lancaster, too. Look at that picture of her on this page. Old daguerreotype, that is. Taken after she was married. Yes, Tracy, she had an hourglass figure. Lots of handhold. You're laughing at me now, aren't you, young lady?

She waited until after her mother died to marry. Angel was close to forty when she married a man fifteen years younger— see, that's how pretty she was. They say she was still pretty when she died at the age of eighty-seven. Her husband, Seth Reed, made a fortune for her. Owned a hosiery mill in Reading. She had one son and one daughter. The son, Otis, thought he was some kind of society boy there in Reading until he lost the family fortune in the crash of '29. Shot himself after that. Kitty's fourth cousin six times removed, or some such nonsense, is a boy named Roger Phillips. Met him at one of Kitty's family reunions years ago. He was in the Army then— 82nd Airborne, I think. Good-looking young man—has the Reifsnyder strawberry hair and green eyes. I do know that he lives here in Aronston and is Aaron's only living descendant.

*Don't know as he'd be much help to you, though. Angel told Kitty that she never told Seth or her children about her father. Zipporiah was gone and so were Angel's grandparents.*

*I'm about talked out. Come back again real soon. I'll try to think of some other tales for Founders' Days. I love you, too, Tracy girl. Take care of yourself now.*

# 3

Captain Jesus Perez stood on the bridge of his ship. "Head zero-four-zero, north-northwest at twenty knots, Mr. Sanchez," he commanded his first officer.

"Twenty knots, aye, sir," Sanchez responded.

The bow of the cargo ship *Empreza* cut cleanly through the Atlantic, leaving the warm blue Caribbean behind. A wake of white foam spread behind the ship. Perez had made the trip from Honduras to Philadelphia more times than he cared to remember during his twenty-five years at sea. He knew he had to make good time with the holds filled with coffee beans and frozen meat. Spoilage was costly; besides, the shipping company paid him a handsome bonus for arriving on time. He knew the *Empreza* was a good ship, having captained her for nearly ten years. She was a bit rusty and could use some fresh paint, but she was fast and reliable.

He looked again around the bridge. The crewmen were busy at their stations but also relaxed, sipping coffee and chatting softly in Spanish. A lot of the equipment on the bridge, such as the radio, was less than state-of-the-art, but it all worked. Something was missing. Ah, Poseidon, his big white tomcat. Usually Poseidon followed Perez everywhere, like a puppy. When the captain was on the bridge, Poseidon would curl up on a coil of rope and watch the activity through his half-closed blue eyes.

"Mr. Sanchez, have you seen Poseidon today?" Perez inquired.

"No, sir. He is probably down in the hold doing what cats should do."

"Goddamn worthless furball better be," grumbled the captain. Poseidon generally preferred Perez' company to rat-catching. Perez wasn't sure whether he was pleased or disappointed that Poseidon might actually be earning his keep. He had been in a melancholy mood since the voyage began a week ago, and the cat's temporary desertion did not improve his temper much.

Sanchez watched the captain's face. "He's probably got a nice fat rat right now, sir."

"I hope you are right, Mr. Sanchez. I'll be in my cabin. You have the bridge."

"Aye, sir."

Sanchez was correct. At that precise moment, Poseidon lay between two refrigerated containers in the cargo hold. Blood flecked his snowy fur as he ripped the skin off a lifeless, mutilated rat. The cat had tortured the creature for an hour before actually killing it and had enjoyed every second.

On his way to his quarters, Captain Perez passed by the galley and mess room. A few of his crew were in there, discussing what had been big news in Honduras when they left. There had been a jaguar attack two months ago at Copan. A busload of American tourists had been visiting the ruins. The jaguar had emerged from the forest like a bolt of lightning. It had leaped upon an unsuspecting American tourist and killed him. But not in the usual way that jaguars killed their prey. This attack had happened in broad daylight. The jaguar, instead of swiftly dispatching its victim, had killed the man slowly, almost sadistically, peeling his skin off like a grape. The poor gringo had struggled and screamed while the other tourists were frozen with terror.

Finally, the tour operator found his legs and ran back to the bus. He had grabbed a rifle he kept on board and ran back to the big cat. He shot the cat, killing it instantly. Almost immediately the gringo's wife had run over and grabbed the jaguar, apparently trying to pull it off her husband. She was thrown to the ground with what seemed like a seizure. A split second later the jaguar's body had burst into flames, becoming a small pile of gray ash in an eyeblink.

They loaded the bodies of the dead man and his unconscious wife onto the bus. The other members of the tour boarded and they left Copan. The tour operator, the lone survivor of the trip, had told the police that the bus had been jouncing down the rutted road when suddenly the dead gringo's wife had stood up and screamed. Then she had savagely attacked the woman who had been sitting next to her, biting and clawing. Someone else had picked up the rifle and all of a sudden the whole bus went mad with gunshots and screaming and flying fists.

The tour operator, who was driving the bus, ran off the road into a ravine. Having used up his small stock of courage killing the jaguar, he leaped from the bus just as another passenger had grabbed him. He shook off the frenzied man's grip, jumped and ran a few yards into the woods, and passed out.

When he awoke the bus was burning. It was burning with an intensity he had never seen before. The metal was glowing white-hot and there was almost no smoke. Everything inside the bus had been vaporized. The trees nearby were beginning to burn. He made his way back to the road and ran for miles before being picked up.

The police were a little skeptical, but the bus wreck showed that it had burned with incredible intensity. Then the tour operator appeared to go insane, ranting about the other voice in his head and the evil living in his heart. He disappeared and was never found.

There were stories of vicious murders and freak attacks by animals. Bright white fires consumed entire villages. The scenes of violence marked a trail from Copan to Puerto Cortes, the port city that the *Empreza* had left a few days ago. Two neighborhoods on the outskirts of the city had burned to the ground; the fires burning so hot that the firefighters could not get close enough to the flames to contain them.

There was much speculation—rabies, witchcraft, arson, terrorists, aliens, ghosts, even the Apocalypse—but nothing definite pointed to the cause of the terror. Captain Perez paused and listened for a moment, then continued on to his cabin. The story did not interest him much at the moment.


Captain Perez sat at the small mahogany table in his cabin, resting his elbows on the tabletop and holding his chin in his hands. In front of him were charts, logs, and duty rosters but the captain just stared out the porthole, pensively. The realization of how much he valued Poseidon's company forced him to realize that the cat and the *Empreza* were the only family he had.

He grew up in Puerto Cortes, the major port city of Honduras. He used to go down to the waterfront and watch the ships for hours on end. He would dream about the cities they would visit, the sights they would see, even the storms they would brave on their voyages. He loved to play pirate and sailed the seven seas in his imagination, using an old, galvanized metal washtub for a boat. He had dreamed of the day he would captain a ship and travel the world. And here he was, his dreams realized. Here he was, at fifty-four, all alone except for a useless feline and an aging ship that was in the same shape as the old washtub he once played in.

His thoughts turned to Sarafina, the wife of his youth. When he was sixteen, his father had bought a farm in a village near San Pedro Sula. There he had met Sarafina. A sultry beauty with sun-kissed skin, long inky black hair, and fiery brown eyes with a temper to match. He had been enchanted with her from the moment he saw her. After a stormy courtship they married when he was eighteen. He had bought a little farm and worked hard at growing beans and corn, to make a home for his Sarafina. He put aside his dreams of the sea to please her. But they never really left him, and one day an opportunity presented itself. He remembered how she had thrown every plate in the kitchen at him when he told her he was joining the crew of *La Nuestra Señora,* a freighter on the European route.

"You will be gone for months! How dare you leave me like this, *cabrón*! I won't have it!" Sarafina's screaming could be heard for nearly a mile. He ducked just in time as the last plate whizzed past him and shattered on the wall behind him.

"Sara, *querida,* listen to me! The money is good, very good. I will send it all to you, my wife, for our home and our children."

"How do you expect to have any children if you are never here?" Sarafina's eyes flashed as she looked around for something else to throw. Perez took advantage of the opportunity to take her in his arms. She struggled fiercely, stamping painfully on the tops of his feet, but he held on, partly in self-defense and partly because he found her tremendously exciting when she was in a rage.

"You know I have always loved the sea. This is something I must do. For both of us, *carina.* Wouldn't you like a nice house in Puerto Cortes, a maid to work for you, a garden full of flowers? On my new salary, we can afford it." He used his most soothing, wheedling tone, knowing she found it hard to resist.

"There is no home without you, Jesus. You will have to choose—me or your precious sea." Sarafina's voice had gotten small, like a hurt child's, and her lips trembled. He had bent down to kiss her and she locked her arms around him in a deathgrip. Tears streamed down her cheeks as he made love to her on the cool tiles of the kitchen floor, amidst the shards of broken crockery.

He woke up the next morning and she was gone. She had taken nothing but her clothes. He was never able to find her. It wasn't until many years later that he realized she had made the choice for him. A choice he would have found impossible to make. *Ah, Sara, you knew me so well,* he thought.

There was never anyone else. Not ever. Just ships and crews and, finally, Poseidon. Sad when a man finds the pinnacle of a dream to be so lonely.

An insistent meowing roused the captain from his unhappy thoughts. He rose from his chair and opened the door.

"So, you finally wish my company, eh?" Irony changed to alarm as he looked at the bloody cat. "*Mi gato,* what is wrong?" He bent down and picked Poseidon up under his front legs, bringing the cat face to face with him. As Captain Perez studied Poseidon's face for injuries, Poseidon's china-blue eyes stared into his. Perez's head snapped back as if struck by a blow to the chin. Instinctively the captain dropped the cat but it was too late. A rain of bone and ash and fur fell all over the captain's shoes.

An eerie, inhuman howl reverberated through the ship.

**4**

The bright orange United States Coast Guard Dolphin helicopter sliced through the clear morning sky. Commander Craig Kaufman gazed out over the ocean, his eyes searching. Early this morning the Air Station at Cape May, New Jersey, had received a report from the tanker *Amoco Cheryl B.* The tanker was heading for Philadelphia, and had spotted a freighter apparently adrift at the edge of the shipping lanes fifty miles southeast of Cape May. The *Cheryl B.* attempted to make radio contact but was unsuccessful.

Well, at least it was a beautiful day, he thought. SAR operations were a piece of cake when the weather was good. Almost made it a pleasure flight. Only thing missing was food and beverage service. He glanced over at his copilot, Lieutenant Amy Gordon, and amused himself with imagining what she'd do if he asked her to fetch him some coffee. She was small, dark-haired, and tough, and an excellent copilot. And she would probably get the coffee, if he asked, and pour it into his lap. He gave a little shudder.

Like Dr. Crane, Commander Kaufman had grown up with a love of the Jersey shore. He was born and raised in Stone Harbor, New Jersey. The rolling Atlantic had been a constant presence in his life. It affected the weather, the recreation available on a given day, and the hordes of tourists that arrived every summer. With the ocean as backdrop, Craig Kaufman had grown tall and lanky, with blue eyes and a shock of light brown hair. He was an intensely focused young boy who rarely smiled, but when he did, his grin seemed larger than his thin face.

He used to stand at the water's edge as a child and watch the planes skim across the horizon, pulling advertising banners: *coppertone—for a deep dark tan*. He watched helicopters taking tourists on expensive sightseeing flights, and occasionally searching for pleasure boaters who'd overestimated their expertise. He knew he had to fly someday.

One November, when he was thirteen, a vicious nor'easter blew in. The tides were running four feet above normal and the sea was black and boiling with white foam. A fishing boat had been swamped off the coast and broken up. Craig Kaufman had gone down to the beach and watched through binoculars as the Coast Guard copters pushed through the wind and rain, hovering precariously over heaving seas to rescue the fishermen as they clung to their orange life raft. They had looked so tiny and helpless out there, and he breathed a sigh of relief as he watched them lifted one by one to the swaying helicopter, clutching the harness of the hoist as if it were the hand of salvation. The copter, not much larger than the fishing boat that broke up, turned and headed south toward Cape May. Craig took down his binoculars and wiped the rain off the lenses.

"Wow," he said into the howling storm.

From that moment on, he knew exactly what he wanted to do with his life.

When he graduated from high school, he enlisted in the Coast Guard. He reported to the Cape May Air Station on his eighteenth birthday, and discovered that flying was even better than he'd dreamed. The feeling of power and control, of being completely in command of an activity humans were never meant to do, gave him immense satisfaction. As his training progressed, he enjoyed the adrenaline rush of piloting SAR missions, especially when the weather was foul.

The Dolphin helicopter he learned to pilot was a marvelous flying machine. Its twin Lycoming engines cruised at 120 knots and it had state-of-the-art everything. It was very stable in rough weather. It could even fly itself when programmed with a search pattern, so that he could concentrate on searching instead of flying.

"Are we there yet? Sir?" A good imitation of a child's whiny voice came from the back door of the cockpit. Airmen Mark Miller and Lou Paganiello grinned at Commander Kaufman. He pretended to ignore them, but he smiled inwardly. They were a good crew, so he allowed them their fun. As long as they didn't get out of line. So far, they never had. The medic, Susan Ellison, a serious young woman whose glasses made her look older than her twenty-four years, was in the back rechecking the oxygen tank.

"We'll get there when we get there. What was the heading, Lieutenant?"

"Our present heading is one-five-zero," replied Lieutenant Gordon.

"Should be visual any minute."

"There it is, sir." Gordon pointed at a gray smudge on the horizon.

"Radio base and tell them we've spotted the freighter and we're going in for recon," ordered Kaufman.

The helicopter bore down on the freighter, turned and hovered over it at 100 feet. The decks were empty. No signs of life. The copter's rotors made oscillating ripples on the water's surface but there was no wake from the freighter. She was adrift. All lifeboats were in place and secured.

Kaufman was not terribly surprised yet. The freighter had to be twenty, thirty years old and looked to be badly in need of maintenance. He could see rust and peeling paint. Radio was probably broken, but that was unusual on commercial

ships. He could make out the word *Empreza* painted on her
stern.

He picked up the mic and switched the radio to hail.

"*Empreza,* this is the United States Coast Guard. Do you
need assistance?"

His electronically altered voice boomed in the morning
air. Nothing moved aboard the ship. He tried again. Still no
response. He sighed and lowered the copter to a fifty-foot
hover.

"Lieutenant, radio base and tell them the freighter appears to be abandoned. No sign of foul play. Request permission to search."

You couldn't be too careful these days, he thought
grimly. Drug runners were a vicious bunch of animals. Had
a way of turning up just where you didn't want them to. He
could see the word "Honduras" painted in peeling white let-
ters under the name *Empreza*. He wondered if he should request backup. Still, the morning was clear, the seas were
calm, the ship appeared absolutely lifeless, and he could
hear Miller and Paganiello in the back over the engine roar.
They were strapping on their M-16's and helping Ellison
prepare the hoist. They were ready to go when he gave them
the word.


Paganiello went first. He struggled out of the harness
and waved to Miller, who brought the hoist back up to the
copter. The roar of the Dolphin's engines was almost deafening, but under his feet he felt . . . nothing. No vibrating
throb. The ship's engines were definitely dead.

He looked up, one hand shielding his eyes. He saw the
sun glint off Ellison's glasses as she leaned through the open
hatch. She was watching Miller as he descended. As he
looked back at her, a cold shadow passed through him. His
superstitious Italian grandmother claimed that such a feeling
meant someone just walked over your future grave.

Paganiello suddenly hoped Ellison's services would not
be needed.

"Better luck next time, Suze, I hope," he muttered. "And if I'm lucky I won't be there."

Miller landed on the deck with a thud. When he got out of the harness, they both waved to Gordon, who waved back and began bringing up the hoist. Paganiello lifted the radio to his mouth.

"We're here, Commander. Beginning search with the bridge. Over."

Commander Kaufman's voice crackled back. "Roger. Report back to me every three minutes whether you have anything to tell me or not."

"Aye, sir. Approaching the bridge now."

The ship rocked almost imperceptibly as Miller and Paganiello looked around the bridge. The sun streamed in through the forward windows. Two half-empty coffee cups were the only indication that anyone had been there recently. That, and some curious piles of dust.

"Think they forgot a broom, huh, Lou?" Miller asked jokingly. He poked one of the dust piles with the toe of his boot.

"Don't do that, you moron! Could be evidence." Lou walked over to the radio console and flipped a few switches. He picked up the mike. "Paganiello to Commander Kaufman. The bridge is clear. Radio appears to be functional."

"Roger. Keep looking." Commander Kaufman's reply came from the ship's radio.

"Well, the radio works, anyway. Weird," muttered Paganiello. He felt a gnawing fear in the pit of his stomach. He couldn't explain it. After all, it was a clear day, the seas were calm, no evidence—yet—of any real problems on the *Empreza*. Still, it was there, and not getting any better.

They searched through the eerily silent ship, flashlights at hand and guns at the ready. There were no signs that the crew had abandoned ship in any hurry. In the crew quarters, personal effects were stowed neatly or scattered about, depending on the habits of their owners. The captain had charts carefully spread over the table in his tidy room. In the galley they noticed that the cook had been in the midst of preparing breakfast. Eggs were congealing on the griddle, and the faint smell of burned bread still lingered.

At the mess tables, more coffee cups. Some had been knocked over, their contents flowing over the floor, where they had dried into brown stains. A few of the chairs were overturned and one was broken.

"Like there was a fight. But no blood or anything," said Paganiello, puzzled.

"Maybe they didn't like the food."

"Jeez, Miller, cut it out with the jokes."

"What's your problem?" snorted Miller.

"I don't know . . . this is just creepy." Paganiello was a veteran of quite a few SAR missions and figured he'd seen it all. From nailing drug runners in their fast, sleek boats to pulling drunken, dumb-ass weekend sailors out of situations that they had no business being in. Usually he felt exhilarated by these missions. And usually he roared with laughter at Miller's stupid wisecracks. But this . . . this was a ghost ship. The heavy silence, the clank of their boots in the empty corridors, those little piles of ashy dust—even the air seemed dense and brooding.

Paganiello's growing panic was held in check only by his sense of duty and pride.

Occasionally they would see another dust pile and carefully step around or over it.

"Doesn't look like any coke powder I ever saw," muttered Paganiello.

Miller resisted the temptation to say no, it was Pepsi powder. "Got me, Lou. Maybe it's some new thing. But then why would they have it in little piles here and there? That stuff's usually in Baggies or something."

They reached the cargo hold. Refrigeration units hummed. The cargo was intact.

"There's a chewed-up rat over here, Miller, but that's it." Paganiello's neck hairs stood on end as he looked at the skinned and mutilated carcass. Miller looked at the dead rat and feigned retching sounds. Paganiello quickly turned toward the ladder.

"Well, let's get back," he said, trying to sound calm.

"Guess this is a job for the salvage tugs. Wonder what happened here? How the hell did everyone get off the ship?"

Not twelve inches from the back of Paganiello's neck, in the vent of one of the refrigeration units, a fat spider slept, sated. It was the only living thing left aboard the *Empreza*.

**5**

What a surprise to see you again so soon, Tracy! And you brought me lunch, too. Mmm. Minestrone soup. Let me turn down my old Westinghouse here. Oh, no. I wasn't listening to anything important. I like to listen to classical music. Helps me remember things. And it's pretty peaceful to listen to, most of the time. At my age I need all the peace I can get.

What's that? You played the tapes of me for Shawn? And he's going to write a play about Aaron Moyer for Founders' Days? Hmmm . . . I can tell by your face that you thought I'd be real pleased about it. Let me think a minute and I'll try to tell you why I'm not. Takes a while to get this old brain working. Like I said, nothing works like it used to anymore. Anyway, about Aaron. I told you some people thought he was the devil's own son. He was tall and fair, while his parents and brothers and sisters were dark and plain. He had strange blue *eyes, cold as ice. And you already know what he was like. What he did.*

*Founders' Days is a happy time, a time to be proud of Aronston. And rightly so. Lots of people worked real hard to make this town what it is. My family, Kitty's family, many other families built this place into a wonderful home for themselves and others. Guess I just don't care for the idea of such a horrible story put on for everyone to see. Send your tapes to that King fellow, the one that writes those trashy horror stories. Let him write about Aaron Moyer.*

*There's another thing, too, Tracy girl. I just have a bad feeling about this. Like you should let a sleeping dog lie. It's one thing to have it written down in dusty old books full of pictures and stories no one cares about. It's another thing to have it brought to life again in a play.*

*Shawn said that was the point, eh? Living history? Young pup always had big ideas. Too big sometimes. What's that? What's so funny? He's fifty years old and bald on top? Not such a pup anymore? Well, that's too bad about his hair. Least I made you laugh. Tell him he can have my books, but I don't like it. He should write about the Gretna colony or Bardwell, or just a simple tale of the folks who built Aronston. I'm sorry I disappointed you. You and Shawn may think that this is a good story. I think it's a horrible story. Like tempting fate, or the devil. Don't know exactly why I feel this way but I do. Wish your great-grandma was here. She always had me figured out.*

*Well, here's my tea. My daily cup of caffeine. Oh, you're a good girl to squeeze the lemon in for me. Glad you're not too mad at me, young lady. Oh well, I suppose Shawn will do what he wants to, so may as well give him the books and have him do it right anyway.*

*If it wasn't for you I'd starve to death. I love the way you bring me real food, like fried chicken or pot roast of beef. Or some of your mama's Eyetalian food. Not that overcooked tasteless slop they serve here. By the time they get it up here to the ninth floor it's cold anyway. Lost twenty pounds in this place. Of all my kids and grandkids, you take such good care of me. The rest of 'em visit now and then, and I feel like it's*

just to be polite, and then they go. Just waiting for me to die,
I guess.

What's that, Tracy? I'm sorry, it isn't a nice thing to say, is
it? Maybe it's this place got me spooked. Everyone comes
here to die. Death lives here, like a big old barn cat stalking
us little broken-down mice. Every now and then, he takes one
of us. Sometimes he just sends us dreams. Can't decide which
is worse. Tell Shawn I want to read the thing when he's done
writing it. I can't say as I'll like it, but guess I should read it.
After all, he's Aronston's famous playwriter.

Next time I'll tell you more about the Gretna colony, or
anything else you'd like to know. Let's leave Aaron alone for
a while. We need to hear some funny stories. A good laugh is
a wonderful thing. Clears the mind and cheers the soul.

**6**

Other than the huge factory housing Bardwell's Chocolates, Aronston's main industry was tourism. The town was blessed with lots of Victorian architecture, natural beauty, and easy access to Philadelphia and New York. The Aronston Chamber of Commerce promoted its many attractions with slick ads in travel magazines, and newspapers in five states. Aronston had plenty of charming antique stores, art galleries, and upscale gift shops featuring handcrafted pottery, textiles, and jewelry. There were charming bed-and-breakfasts to stay in, and two or three really good restaurants. And of course, the fragrance of fresh chocolate suffused the town on warm, still days.

The neighboring village of Gretna was similar, but with a more intellectual and artistic air. The antiques were more apt to be Art Deco, the paintings post-modern. Gretna College's quaint brick buildings surrounded by steel sculptures in the style of Brancusi and Calder contributed to the atmosphere of the tiny town, as did the town's bohemian history.

As Aronston grew, it was decided that most of the streets should run one-way to decrease traffic flow on any one street. The Harrisburg Pike became one-way westbound, and an eastbound lane was constructed two blocks south. The Gretna Road was similarly divided.

Since these two streets roughly marked the center of town, it was decided to create a town square between the Harrisburg Pike roads and the Gretna roads. The town square became a pretty park one block long and two blocks wide. Chestnut Street, one of the few two-way streets in town, was constructed with a wide, grassy, tree-lined median strip separating the two lanes. It would have bisected the town square, but the planners decreed that the road be closed to vehicle traffic through the square. The median strip had the effect of extending the town-square boundaries, and a Victorian bandstand was constructed on the western median strip just beyond the square.

Pedestrians loved the arrangement, and indeed Aronston was a wonderful town to walk in, to window-shop, and admire the beautiful old architecture. Drivers hated it—the one-way streets and divided highways made it hell to get around in. Every few years there would be rumblings about constructing a bypass on the Harrisburg Pike, so that only people who really wanted to would have to negotiate the rat's maze of Aronston streets. But it never came to pass.

As well as strolling and shopping, there were other attractions. Bardwell's offered tours of the factory, ending with enough free samples to delight even a hard-core chocolate addict, and of course there was the requisite gift shop. In the summer, the Gretna College theater department sponsored a summer drama series in an open-air theater that Shakespeare would have found familiar. Aronston's proximity to Reading and its shopping outlets for the diehard bargain hunters, and Harrisburg and Gettysburg for the more historical-minded, added to its already manifold charms.

Aronston kicked off the summer season in early May by celebrating Founders' Days, originally an opportunity to appreciate the town's history and its people's contributions. There would be a parade put on by the various civic organizations, house and farm tours, even lectures by local historians. Bardwell's would devote some space at the factory complex for a museum display about William Ewing Bardwell and his effect on Aronston.

Over the years, interest in history had deteriorated and Founders' Days had become a commercialized retail orgy. The house tours, rather than being a lesson in period building, became an interior-decorating showcase, with each exquisite antique carefully labeled as to which store it came from and the purchase price. The bed-and-breakfasts took out ads in the Sunday papers from New York to Washington, and west to Pittsburgh, touting package deals. The Founders' Days festivals enjoyed increasing attendance, but there were some in Aronston who felt that the point was being missed.

The Aronston Historical Society (dubbed the Hysterical Society by some who had been inconvenienced by its activities) worked closely with the planners and the zoning board. Anyone planning renovations, additions, or new construction had to get approval from the Society or they faced being voted down by the zoning board. Emma Bardwell, the granddaughter of William Ewing Bardwell, headed the Society. She was the closest thing Aronston had to a grande dame and, since she controlled the Bardwell money, the most powerful woman in town.

Miss Emma Bardwell was an imposing and terrifying figure. She stood nearly six feet tall and carried herself like a queen. She wore her blue-rinsed hair in a tight French roll, which emphasized her small, thin mouth and large, crooked nose. She had lost an eye in a childhood accident, but Emma Bardwell had no need of two eyes. When she wanted something, she would pin her victim to the wall with a laser-beam stare from her good eye. It was a rare person who could resist that direct and piercing stare.

She never married, and devoted her life to the improvement of Aronston according to her own views. She vigorously supported the Aronston orchestra, tried vainly to create an opera company, and was a patron of the Gretna College theater program. She also busied herself with the Aronston County Hospital Ladies' Auxiliary and dabbled in town politics, always behind the scenes. She found that it was easy to impose her will on the elected officials, blessed as she was with the Bardwell name and the Bardwell money—and her icy one-eyed stare.

The main focus of her life, however, was the preservation of the lovely Victorian-era buildings that her grandfather had helped construct. Aronston was dotted with churches; almost all built between 1860 and 1900, in styles ranging from Gothic intricacy to New England plainness. Beautiful beaux-arts office buildings surrounded the town square. And there were quite a few gabled, turreted, and gingerbreaded homes in town, which were crying out to be preserved from vinyl siding, louvered windows, and other modern insults. Emma Bardwell's efforts made downtown Aronston a picturesque open-air architectural museum and a delightful tourist draw. Even the homeowners and businesses she inconvenienced with her inflexible preservationist zoning and regulations had to admit that the end result was worth it.

Word got out that the Historical Society (meaning Emma Bardwell) would make sure that the street fair along Chestnut would not be given a permit this year. Too honky-tonk. Besides, whatever did it have to do with the history of Aronston? The fireworks display at Cumberland Park, at the west end of town, was threatened, also. Not historically accurate, decreed the Society.

Faced with the loss of two major attractions, the retailers and restaurateurs formed a Founders' Days Committee, with the idea of providing Emma Bardwell with enough history to allow the profitable, if lowbrow, street fair to continue.

Professor Shawn Williams, a critically acclaimed play-wright with several off-Broadway productions to his credit, was on the staff at Gretna College. He loved New York City and the literary life there, the noise and the excitement, the bargaining, maneuvering, and aggravation of having his plays produced. But he preferred the familiar and gentler pace of Aronston.

"I was born here, I'll die here, and they'll bury me here," he was fond of saying.

He agreed to a certain point with the aims of the Historical Society. He wanted to bring some of the sense of history back to Founders' Days. But, being no fool, he also realized that this might present an opportunity to promote his own work, and the summer theater season at Gretna College.

He volunteered to write an original play, to be presented in the town square and performed by Gretna drama students, as the high point of the weekend celebrations. The play would dramatize an actual event in Aronston history. The committee, which consisted mostly of shop owners and a few civic leaders, thought this was an absolutely wonderful idea. After all, a new play by a well-known playwright would bring the tourists to the town in droves. Especially the highbrow New Yorkers with all their disposable income.

When the play idea was presented to the Historical Society, along with all the other more commercial activities, the Society was so pleased with it that it approved the celebration without a murmur. They were not fools, either.

The only stipulation was that they—Miss Bardwell— would have to approve the subject matter for the play.

Now Professor Williams needed something to write about. William Ewing Bardwell, the founder of the nationally known chocolate conglomerate, was the obvious choice, but Shawn Williams rejected it. He knew that anything he wrote would have to practically canonize Bill Bardwell in order to please his granddaughter. He wanted something that would appeal to everyone, not just history and biography buffs. He did some research, but found nothing terribly inspiring or interesting. Then he consulted his old friend Philip Faber, who taught history at Gretna. They had been friends since they were children. On Phil's advice, he called Tracy, Phil's daughter. Tracy was happy to take a tape recorder with her on one of her visits with Phil's grandfather, Levi Faber, the town's oldest living resident. She knew Levi loved to tell stories, and he told them well. When Tracy came back with Levi's tale of Aaron

Moyer, Shawn knew with a showman's instinct that it was the perfect story for Founders' Days. It had everything: violence, sex, revenge, and retribution. There was enough myth and uncertainty to allow a little creative liberty, and enough actual documented fact to qualify it as a genuine piece of Aronston's history.

Shawn wrote a synopsis of the play, which he titled *The Devil's Own,* and gave it to the Founders' Days Committee. A few objected, feeling that Aronston might become notorious as the home of the devil. Some felt that dramatizing a hanging was no way to create a festive mood, in order to encourage people to part with their money. But most agreed with Shawn that it was a sensational story. It was decided that it would be staged at the end of the festival, on Sunday afternoon, after most of the tourists' dollars were spent.

Shawn made an appointment with Miss Bardwell to present *The Devil's Own* personally to her. On the chosen day, he put on his only suit, found a tie, trimmed his beard, and pulled his long, graying hair neatly back into a ponytail. He slicked a few strands back over his bald spot. He even forsook his beloved Birkenstock sandals in favor of real shoes. He had never met Emma Bardwell, and he wanted to make the best impression possible. The better to sell the play, of course.

He looked at himself in the mirror and laughed. "Geez, I look like I'm going on a goddamn date. Hope the old battleaxe appreciates it." Shawn laughed again and drove off in his antique Volkswagen Beetle, arriving at the Bardwell estate, named Shady Maples, punctually at eleven o'clock in the morning.

Shady Maples was situated on a rise in the northeast part of Aronston. A long, curving driveway ended in a circle in front of the house. The house itself was built of gray stone, exquisitely pointed, with marble steps leading up to the white-columned front portico. Large black double doors formed the entrance, and the black-shuttered windows were tall and narrow on the first floor.

The grounds were perfectly manicured. True to its name, tall spreading maple trees grew near the house. Late tulips and lilacs bloomed along the foundation. As he came up the driveway, Professor Williams could see the white picket fence that enclosed the formal gardens behind the house.

He parked the Beetle in front of the house and ascended the stairs. There was a large brass knocker on the front door. Shawn Williams knocked and almost jumped at the booming sound.

An ancient man with rheumy blue eyes opened the door. He was impeccably dressed in a crisp white jacket and black pants with a knife-sharp crease. Shawn could not help glancing down at his own rumpled suit and carelessly knotted tie.

"Shawn Williams to see Miss Emma Bardwell," he said, answering the unspoken question in the old man's eyes.

"She is expecting you, sir." The man's voice was expressionless and polite. Shawn suspected he was a local fellow who had worked for the Bardwells since he was a teenager. "Miss Emma will be right down," he said, unsmiling, and left.

He looked around the room, storing details with a writer's memory. They might come in handy someday. Old, polished curly-maple paneling. Cream-colored satin damask curtains at the windows. Shawn noted tiny tears in the fabric, as the curtains slowly disintegrated after almost a hundred years of service. Ornate and shabby old leather and velvet Victorian furniture that was probably purchased by old Bill Bardwell himself. Lamps with frosted and painted glass globes. Ceramic and crystal knickknacks everywhere.

A musty smell, a smell of old age and rotting leather and dust accumulating in corners overlaid everything. It's something out of a Dickens novel, thought Shawn. A real time capsule. When Emma Bardwell finally entered the room, Shawn was examining the leather-bound, gold-tooled books that filled the dusty bookcases.

"Are you a bibliophile, Mr. Williams?" she asked in her cold, precise voice.

Shawn turned to face the formidable Miss Bardwell and her laser-beam eye. "To some extent, yes. Several of these books are first editions." He kept his voice level and his eyes steady.

Miss Bardwell was even more intimidating than he expected. She was dressed in an expensive but worn silk dress that might have been fashionable fifty years ago. Her bluish hair was pulled so tightly away from her face that he could see the delicate veins throbbing under the pale, papery skin at her temples. She gazed coldly at him with her good eye, as if sizing him up. Her left eyelid was a dark-purple tab of skin covering her dead eye. Then she walked, tall and erect, to the slippery old leather sofa and sat down. Her back was ramrod straight and at least six inches from the back of the sofa.

"You are perceptive, Mr. Williams. Please sit down." Shawn took the nearest chair, which happened to be old, small, and extremely uncomfortable. It wobbled under his weight ominously, and he prayed it wouldn't break under him.

"You wished to discuss the play you propose for Founders' Days?" she asked, looking hard at him. Shawn felt the effects of her piercing stare and met her eye resolutely.

"Yes, Miss Bardwell. It's called *The Devil's Own*. It tells the story of Aaron Moyer, for whom this town is named." He handed her the two-page synopsis.

She read it, slowly, while Shawn tried not to fidget in his chair. Her thin mouth curled downward. She put the papers in her lap and folded her hands on top of them. Then she lifted her eye to his.

"I am familiar with the story. Do you think it appropriate to dramatize such an unsavory tale? Have you not considered other subjects? The founding of Bardwell's Chocolates comes to mind." She smiled thinly.

Shawn took a deep breath. "Yes, Miss Bardwell, I did consider that, but the factory always puts on such a good display of Bardwell's history that I thought it might be redundant." *Hope that satisfies your ego, Emma Bardwell*, he thought. "I wanted to have a subject that might not be familiar to everyone in Aronston, and probably not familiar to the out-of-towners. From a strictly dramatic point of view, it is a good story. It has vivid characters and a strong storyline. The Gretna students are eager to stage it." He hoped the reference to the students might soften her. She was an avid supporter of the theater program.

Emma Bardwell stared at him for a full minute. Shawn Williams was in an agony of suspense but was determined not

to show it. He tried to appear cool and relaxed. At least as relaxed as he could get in that awful chair. Finally she spoke.

"You are correct, Mr. Williams, in that it is a very dramatic
tale. However, I feel it is more suitable for a New York audience." He thought he detected a faint sneer on her lips. She
turned the papers face down in her lap. "But I will say this.
Founders' Days have become a frivolous and meaningless
spring rite that benefits no one but the shopkeepers. Perhaps
a serious play on a serious subject will amend this." She
picked up the papers and the corners of her mouth turned up.
"Also, I am not unmindful of the attention an original play
written by you will attract." Her mouth turned down again
and she fell silent. Shawn thought, She's going to say that she
needs to think it over. Let's see if I can talk her out of it.

He spoke. "Miss Bardwell, if you are concerned about the
violent nature of the story, let me tell you that much of the violence will take place offstage. I don't have the money to
stage the play in a New York style." He smiled into her eye.
"And I agree that it is hardly a cheerful story, yet I think it is
a important one. It helps us to remember that there is a dark
side to history. Even in the history of a beautiful old town like
Aronston."

"Will you be staging the hanging?" she asked.

"Yes, for two reasons. One, because it presents an interesting production problem for the students to solve. Two, because public hangings were spectacular entertainment back
then. As it will be in the play."

"Very true, Mr. Williams. Perhaps we are not as civilized
as we think." She appeared lost in thought again. After another interminable minute, she spoke. "I have no doubt that in
your capable hands, and the eager ones of your students, that
it will be a memorable event." She rose and gave Shawn another thin smile. "I will present this for approval at the next
Historical Society meeting. I have no objection to *The Devil's
Own* as long as it is enacted as you have told me. There is
enough pandering to baser instincts during Founders' Days as
it is." She held out her hand to Shawn. He took it, unsure
whether he should shake it or kiss it. He opted for a gentle
shake.

"Good day, Mr. Williams." She rang a small brass bell that was on a side table. "Walter will see you out."

"Good day and thank you, Miss Bardwell." Shawn was escorted out of Shady Maples and the door firmly closed behind him. As he stood on the marble steps that led to the front door, he grinned. It's a done deal, he thought.

He hurried back to his office at Gretna College. He had a play to write.

# 7

Colette Walls stepped out of the shower and dried herself with a big, fluffy, white towel. As she combed out her long, tawny blonde hair she smiled at the reflection in the mirror, her full mouth curving into a smile.

"Not bad for a small-town girl," she said to herself. Her blue eyes gazed back steadily from the mirror. "And not small-town for long, either. New York is calling me."

She was an adventure-seeker who loved hiking, camping, hang gliding, and skydiving. She had learned to scuba dive on her last vacation in Cozumel, and her next goal was to explore a shipwreck. Learning to pilot a plane was another plan of hers. There was something deeply affirming about pushing your abilities and your luck to the edge of the precipice, and living to tell the tale. Personal power was a rush. All kinds. Including the power she had to attract people.

It had been like that ever since she was fifteen and had discovered the power and pleasure of sex.

The captain of the football team had maneuvered her into the backseat of his father's Cadillac. She remembered lying on the smooth, cold leather seat, her blouse undone and her skirt hitched up around her waist. She stared at his face in the filtered moonlight from the steamed up windows. The urgency, bordering on pleading, was a revelation to her. Deep kisses and warm skin could reduce a man nearly to tears. She immediately decided to use this effect to her best advantage.

Through careful use of her body, she was able to keep her football captain devoted to her all through high school. On graduation day, she dumped him. Going steady was for kids, and certainly she didn't want to get married and stay stuck in this podunk town forever.

But even while she dreamed her big dreams, there were urges to satisfy.

She glanced at the clock and realized that she would be late for work.

"I know how to deal with that," she said, grinning. She walked over to the closet and selected a dress that she affectionately called her "fuck me" dress. It was black, tight, and short. She slipped it over her naked body.

Then she put on her lipstick and left for work.


The Delaware River flowed sluggishly past what was probably the ugliest section of its journey to the Atlantic. The Philadelphia/Camden waterfront was a solid phalanx of old industrial buildings, oil refineries, and Superfund sites. The remains of the naval shipyard rotted quietly away. Small and medium-sized cargo ships and tankers cruised ponderously on the oily brownish-green river, loaded with everything from crude oil to Chilean fruit.

The truck pulled into the Packer Marine Terminal. The driver looked up and down the rows of huge cargo cranes and ships until he saw the rusty black and white cargo ship named *Empreza*. He stopped his rig nearby and walked over.

A heavyset, dark and balding man was standing near the ship, examining a manifest. He looked up as the driver approached.

"You from Davis Freight?"

"I am Davis Freight. Dave Davis. Owner and operator."

"Hell of a name, son. Al Di Maio, Al's Marine Salvage. We got your container over there. Going to Aronston, PA. Meat passed inspection but I sure as hell wouldn't eat it."

"What's the story?"

"See that ship?" He pointed to the *Empreza*. "She's a ghost ship, son."

Dave Davis snorted. "Whaddaya mean, a ghost ship?"

"Coast Guard found her drifting. Nobody aboard. Lifeboats, life jackets all in place. No distress calls, no nothing. Crew just disappeared."

"Drugs?"

"Nah. No sign of any struggle, no bullet holes. Just piles of dust and crap all over the ship. Lucky for us the paperwork was all in order, or you wouldn't have no meat to take to— what's this place—Mama Angelina's?" He handed Davis papers to sign.

"Agent paying you or you sell this yourself?"

Al laughed, a deep wheezy chuckle. "Agent's paying good money to make sure this stuff gets there before it goes bad. I been in this business too many years. I hate sellin' stuff that's gonna spoil."

Davis watched as the crane lowered the refrigerator container down onto the flat trailer of his truck.

"We'll get it there," he said.

"You better."

"Later, Al."

As Davis walked away, a fiftyish woman with jet-black hair and heavily pencilled eyebrows leaned out of the trailer that served as headquarters for Al's Marine Salvage.

"Yo, Al!!" she screamed in a harsh South Philly voice. "Cops wanna talk wit' you!"

Davis swung up into his cab and started the engine. He felt vaguely uneasy as he pulled out of the parking lot, but decided it was nothing a good cup of coffee wouldn't fix. Better yet, a cup of coffee at one of the strip joints that dotted Delaware Avenue. He had some time to kill.

**8**

Mama Angelina's Specialty Meats was housed in a large, red brick building on the east end of Aronston, Pennsylvania. The building had been constructed in the Early Industrial Park style of the 60s—flat roofed, utilitarian, and nondescript. Behind the plant, the back lot was enclosed with a six-foot chain-link fence. It kept the local teens from using the lot as a place to experiment with sex, drugs, and alcohol. It also prevented the occasional tire-slashing rampages on the trucks. Bardwell's factory was a quarter-mile away. As Bardwell's was the first large manufacturing operation in Aronston, other industrial concerns sprang up in that end of the town. The zoning board, under Emma Bardwell's watchful single eye, made it official by proclaiming the east end of Aronston an industrial/commercial zone.

The Aronston County Boys Home and Vocational School was built there, so that the students would be close to places where they could gain practical experience. The east end was also dotted with machine shops, tool-and-die makers, garages, and other small businesses. Next to Bardwell's, Mama Angelina's was the second-largest employer in town.

Mama Angelina's made hamburger patties and Italian-style meatballs, which were sold in bulk to restaurants or packaged for sale in supermarkets. Business was good. So good that Corporate had recently begun importing Central American beef for Mama Angelina's to process. The larger section of the building housed the plant. There was a loading dock, where sides of beef and pork were unloaded into a refrigeration chamber. There the sides were cut and trimmed and reduced to manageable chunks. The chunks were tossed into wheeled carts and taken to be ground.

Two shifts of forty-three workers each fed the meat grinders and the other machines that made Mama Angelina's fine products. The grinders were large, gleaming steel machines that rumbled ominously. Meat chunks were placed on a conveyor belt, which led to a chute at the top of the machine. On the other side, through a spout about two-thirds of the way down, spiraled out red-and-white coils of freshly ground meat. The piles of hamburger went down another belt and into a cloth cart.

The meat was taken to another machine to be pressed and formed into hamburger patties, which were packed and quick-frozen in a freezer the size of a living room. Or it was dumped into a large steel vat, where steel paddles mixed it with spices and breadcrumbs and Parmesan cheese. The mixture was formed into balls by yet another machine, quickly steam-cooked, packed, and frozen.

Everything in the plant was scrupulously clean. The machines gleamed, the floor was spotless. The workers wore white coats with the brown traces of washed-out bloodstains, paper caps on their heads, plastic gloves, and rubber boots. If you picked up a piece of meat off the floor and put it back into the machine, you were immediately terminated. The plant was kept at a year-round fifty-five degrees to retard spoilage of the meat during processing. Every night, the machines and the floor were scrubbed and disinfected. Rodents, insects, and bacteria never lived long enough to die of old age at Mama Angelina's.

Darren Keller, the general manager, wanted no surprises when the USDA inspectors came around on their semi-annual visits. He also wanted no tainted meat traced back to Mama Angelina's.

To get to the offices from the plant, you walked through metal double doors, down a long hallway, and through another set of doors. The general manager and the president/owner had their own offices. There was a tastefully decorated reception area with posters of Ansel Adams' wildlife photographs. Colette Walls had hung them there eight years ago when she came to work as the secretary. Her desk was at one end of the reception area, backed by a row of cream-colored filing cabinets.

The president's office was rarely used. Mama Angelina's had been a family enterprise for many years. When there were no more Fritzinger family members interested in running Mama's, the plant was sold to a food conglomerate based in New York City. Four or five times a year, someone from Corporate would come down for a few days, take over the president's office, pore over the books, stare at Colette, get taken out to dinner by Darren, and then go back to New York.

Darren Keller sat at his desk, scanning the front page of the *Philadelphia Inquirer*. One story in particular caught his eye:

## UNIVERSITY OF PENNSYLVANIA ARCHAEOLOGISTS FOUND SLAIN

### Penn Professor Missing

HONDURAS, AP—A team of thirteen Penn archaeologists were found brutally murdered at the Mayan site of Los Naranjos.

The students appeared to have been hacked to death with their own tools. One female student's body showed evidence of sexual assault. Dr. Paul Crane, head of the archaeology department at Penn and leader of the expedition, was nowhere to be found. . . .

There was a knock at the office door. Darren set the paper aside. "Come in," he called. Where was Colette anyway? He shifted in his chair, thinking about what would happen when she finally arrived.

Byron Mirkowski worked in maintenance. He was heavy-set, moon-faced, and balding, with vacant pale eyes. Byron had a third-grade-level education, and was very slow to understand anything. But he kept the machines clean, the plant immaculate, cut the grass, and was thrilled to work for not much more than minimum wage.

"Hi, Mr. Keller. Just goin' to empty the wastebasket." He shuffled around the desk and picked up the wastebasket, emptying it into a large trash bag. His movements were slow and deliberate, as if it cost him a great deal of thought.

"'Morning, Byron," Darren smiled. "When did you get here today?"

"Uh, I couldn't sleep too good so I came in about five. Mr. Phillips gave me some cookies his wife made. He's a nice guy."

"Byron, what have I told you about these long hours? I can't pay you the overtime," Darren sighed, exasperated.

"Uh, that's okay, Mr. Keller. You don't have to pay me. I like it here. Gotta go empty Miss Walls' wastebasket now." He walked slowly out of Darren's office.

As if on cue, Colette entered her boss' office and closed the door as Mirkowski left. Darren looked over at her with an expectant expression. She sat down in a chair and crossed her legs. Her skirt rode up to the tops of her thighs. The *Inquirer* article was quickly forgotten.

A tractor-trailer marked Davis Freight pulled into the loading dock behind Mama Angelina's. Even with the forty-five minute detour Dave Davis had taken to the Doll House on Delaware Avenue, he had still made good time to Aronston. He smiled, very pleased with himself.

Dave Davis was an attractive enough man, with thick brown hair and a luxuriant mustache. His air of confidence bordering on conceit was a hit with certain insecure women.

He had watched the nearly naked girls at the Doll House
writhe around brass poles and strut across the bar, but their
staged lustful expressions could not conceal their boredom.
Still, he had seen enough to kindle his desire. He was hoping
to get back to Philly soon enough to make a date.

Scott Herr, who worked in shipping and receiving, opened
the dock door and came out to see what was coming in.

"Got some frozen meat from Central America here for
you," said Davis, pulling up the door to the trailer.

"About time you showed up," grumbled Herr. "This stuff's
about five days overdue."

"Hey, man, ain't my fault. This stuff came off of a ghost
ship they found off Jersey."

"Whaddaya mean, a ghost ship?" Herr lit a cigarette, taking an unauthorized break.

"Coast Guard found this ship with nobody on board. Al's
Marine Salvage towed it into Philly. Me, I ain't eating no
meat off a ghost ship, so remind me not to buy your stuff for
a couple of months."

Herr shrugged. "Hey, if it passed inspection that's good
enough for me. Hey, Pete, get out here with the forklift!"

Davis' eyes fell on a gleaming red Corvette in the parking
lot. He let out a low whistle. "Damn, that's a beauty. Whose
is it and are they selling?"

Herr grinned. "Belongs to our secretary, Colette. She's the
only thing in this town prettier than that car. Better not even
breathe on it if you value your life."

"Pretty's one thing. Is she fast?"

"The car or Colette?"

"Both, man."

"Well, I can say the car is for sure. Not like I ever took it
out for a spin, though, 'cause nobody drives it but Colette.
And she's . . . Well, go check her out while we get this unloaded. She's gotta sign the papers and then my boss has to
sign, too."

"Might have an excuse to stay a night in your fair city,
huh?"

"Go for it," Herr said with a laugh.

As the refrigerated container was unloaded onto the dock,

a spider crawled out of the vent. It spun a small parachute-like web. The spring breeze picked it up and carried it through the air and over to the fence. It caught one of the links and settled down. Hunger was beginning to gnaw at it, but it was willing to wait. Something would turn up. Soon.


Colette sat on Darren's lap, facing him. Her dress was pulled down and up, forming a cummerbund around her waist. A spent Darren leaned back in his chair and admired the view.

"Feeling better now?" Colette smiled. She put her arms around his neck and kissed him.

"I hate to say it, 'Lette, but you really need to get here on time more often. There, I've done my boss thing." He grinned at her.

Colette rearranged her dress and finger-combed her hair. "If I do manage to get here on time, will you recommend me for the outside sales job?" Her tone was light but there was no doubt that she was serious.

"But that's at Corporate, right?" Darren, caught by surprise, went with his first reaction. He roared with laughter. "You? 'Lette, if it's money you want, hell, I'll give you a raise. Might cost you, though." He slid his hand up her leg, in exaggerated lechery.

Colette stared hard at him, her eyes cold as glaciers. "What is the problem?" she asked. "You know I could do the job."

"Now don't get an attitude, 'Lette. I know you think New York is the place for you. But it's not. Well, for one thing, I thought they wanted someone with a college degree."

"But I know this business inside and out. All of the details that they'd have to train someone else to do. If there's anything I need to learn—you know I'm a hard worker. I could learn in no time"

Darren patted her shoulder. "You're a great worker—when you're here, that is—and I need your smarts here in Aronston. Plus, this is not exactly the time for a job interview. For one thing, you're not dressed for it."

Without a word, Colette got off Darren's lap, stalked to the door and slammed it behind her.

"Hey, get me some coffee, okay?" Darren called through the door.

She sat down at her desk, furious. How could she possibly expect to be taken seriously after they'd just screwed their brains out? That bit of bad timing was her own fault. But he didn't have to have such a paternal attitude about her. He was just being selfish. She knew that she was smart enough and tough enough to work and live in New York.

"What the hell did he expect?" she muttered. "That I'd come in a suit with a blouse up to my chin and skirt to my ankles? A copy of my résumé and a list of my corporate achievements? If he doesn't know what I can handle by now . . ."

She looked at the photographs on her desk. There was the one taken after her first parachute jump a few years ago. She was the only woman she knew who liked skydiving. What a rush it was. Then there was the one in Yosemite where she had gone hang gliding (illegally) off the top of Half Dome. The next day she'd climbed up the side of El Capitan. There were a couple of pictures she'd taken deep off the reefs of Cozumel—some jewel-like fish and a moray eel, just about to strike at her. No one could say Colette Walls didn't have guts.

If she could jump out of planes, dive deep in the ocean, and climb up cliffs, she could handle New York. It would be a piece of cake. She knew it, and so did Darren.

She'd been at the plant ever since she got out of high school eight years ago, and always as the goddamn secretary. She knew she deserved a promotion. But nobody in Aronston was going anywhere. Everyone here seemed to stay here. Get a job working at Bardwell's or Mama Angelina's, or a nice cushy job with the state over in Harrisburg. Get married, have kids, raise kids. Mate, spawn, and die.

"Not me," she muttered under her breath. "I am so outta here. I just need a job to go to."

Colette turned on her computer and stared at the flickering screen. If she were honest, she thought, money was not the only issue. There was another, and that was Darren Keller. Somehow they just fit together well. The sex was good, surprisingly so. He was funny, and occasionally he had a wonderful, expectant smile that made her wonder what he was thinking. He never bored her and never wanted to change her. He appreciated her exactly as she was—even if he didn't support all her goals. He was one of her best friends. But he was extremely married. And wasn't that how she liked it? No commitment, no strings, and her Saturday nights free for herself. Right?

Oh, well. Anyway, what she did on her own time was her own business. She was twenty-five years old and Darren had no right . . .

The door opened and a uniformed driver came in. Dave Davis walked into the lobby and nearly stopped dead in his tracks. Sitting at the reception desk was one of the most gorgeous women he had ever seen. The little black dress she was wearing left almost nothing to the imagination. The fact that her stare was icy and her cheeks flushed with anger did not slow him down.

"I got a delivery out back. Frozen meat from Central America. Got these papers that need a signature."

Colette sighed and took the papers. The driver looked her over, again. "Hey sweetheart, the name's Dave. I saw your car outside. Nice vehicle. If you're having a bad day, I can make it better. Let me take you for a ride tonight. What do you say?" He grinned down at her, feet apart, thumbs in his belt.

Colette looked at him. Her eyes narrowed ominously. She was definitely not in the mood for flirting just now. Besides, his overconfidence was obnoxious.

"My car is busy for the rest of your life, okay? And so am I," she snapped.

"Sorrry." His grin became almost a leer.

Colette handed the papers back to him. "Here. Get the plant manager to countersign after the meat's unloaded. Then go back to whatever slime pit you came from."

He seemed unperturbed by the insult. "Maybe next time,

babe. I know we could have a good time. Especially with that dress." He winked at her and walked out the door.

Colette bit her lip and began the day's work.


Darren stopped chuckling to himself when he heard Colette's angry voice and the driver's insolent one in the outer office. The scent of Colette's perfume and the earthier aroma of her sex still filled the room. He turned to his desk, picked up a pencil and drummed it on the desktop. He knew that with her brains and ambition she could do anything, but . . . His eyes fell on the picture on his desk. A small, slender woman with pale, perfect skin, short dark hair, and dark eyes.

Fine-boned, fragile-looking Andrea was a good wife and mother. She worked hard, both at home and at her job as deli manager at the ShopRite. His house was always clean, the garden tended, the kids well-behaved. She had supported him through seven years of night school and the long hours at the plant while we worked his way up to the manager's job. She had been both mother and father to his daughters. In ten years of marriage they had almost never fought about anything. He knew he had a lot to be grateful for.

Except that she absolutely and utterly bored him. The things she cared about seemed petty to him, and anything that interested him—well, he could practically hear her mind snap shut when he tried to discuss them. The only things they had in common were Katelyn and Corrine.

"It wasn't always that way, Andrea," he muttered, and reached over to turn the picture toward the wall.

Colette, on the other hand . . . He had been attracted to her when she had first begun working at the plant as a teenager. She had a wonderful throaty laugh that always made him smile when he heard it. Even at seventeen, she was exactly the opposite of Andrea in every way—tall, curvy, with long, dark blonde hair and those amazing baby blues. Still, he was a married man, so he contented himself with befriending her.

As she grew older, her looks matured and she became stunningly beautiful. She had a real eagerness to live, to experience things, to enjoy the moment. He had been appalled but a little jealous when she told him she had gone skydiving. Her eyes had glowed as she talked about the rush of free-falling, the thump and jerk when the chute opened, and the slow drift toward the ground. Darren would never let his daughters do something like that. But a small part of him almost envied the way she took risks like some people took aspirin.

'Lette did all the things he longed to do but couldn't because he was a responsible husband and father. She was able to live her dreams in a way he could not. Lately she had been chattering about getting her private pilot's license. He had given up on his dreams long ago.

He remembered the day she got her car. He was still plant manager then and the Fritzinger family still owned Mama Angelina's. She had come back after lunch with glowing cheeks. He had just come out of Kurt Fritzinger's office—the one that was now his—as she breezed through the door. He could not help noticing that her blouse was cut very low and her skirt was slit to her upper thigh.

"Oh, Darren, come see!" she exclaimed.

"See what?" he had asked, a little confused. Then he grinned wickedly at her. "Couldn't help noticing what you're wearing. Is that what I'm supposed to see?"

"Dar-ren," she groaned, then returned the smile. "I want you to see my new baby, of course. Just picked it up half an hour ago." He had followed her out to the parking lot, stealing glances at her ear-to-ear grin. She stopped proudly in front of the reddest, shiniest Corvette Darren had ever seen. She stroked the car's hood affectionately.

"I saved forever to buy this. Then I needed this outfit to close the deal." She shot him a sidelong glance. "Cleavage will get you exactly what you want. But Darren, it's a dream come true. What do you think?"

"It's great, 'Lette. Wow, stickshift and everything."

She laughed. "I never drove a stick before today. Nothing like learning by doing." She looked at him and noticed a slightly wistful expression on his face. The phrase "dream come true" had resonated within him deeply and unexpectedly.

"Is something wrong, Darren?"

He quickly smiled. "Nothing. When do I get to check it out?"

She frowned at him. "I'll give you a ride anytime, but I'm the one who drives the car. It's mine."

Darren laughed. In spite of his own disappointments, he enjoyed Colette's pleasure in her car, and, later, in her adventures. She told a story well, and he found her tales of vacation action and derring-do much more interesting than the gossip Andrea brought home from the ShopRite.

When the plant was sold and he was promoted, he made sure she stayed on. She smoothed the transition for him and for the others in the plant, ran interference with Corporate, and Darren found that her opinions were usually worth listening to. She was a good partner and he respected her. She was warm and alive and caring in a way Andrea could never be.

Her only flaw was her total inability to get into work on time. This had led to a profound change in their relationship about a year ago. He had brought her into his office and closed the door. Another lecture on her lateness. He was thinking of giving her a formal warning.

" 'Lette, this has got to stop. The plant office opens at eight A.M. You can't waltz in here at eight-thirty or nine three days a week. I need you here on time."

"Darren, you know I make up the time. I stay until seven or eight at night. I finish my work."

"That's not the point. I *need* you here."

Colette's face suddenly broke into a sly grin. "Do you need me, Darren?" she said in a low voice. She stood up and leaned over the desk. The V-neck of her blouse fell away from her body. Darren could smell her perfume, warm and musky. Her face was about six inches from his, and her turquoise eyes glowed with desire and amusement. It was as if she was half-teasing, but also half-serious.

"I can think of a way to make it up to you for being late. Can you?" she murmured.

Suddenly all memory of Andrea and the girls and of being responsible vanished. He completely forgot about the formal warning. All he knew was that he wanted her, fiercely. Blood pounded in his temples. Abruptly he stood up and walked around the desk to her. Colette, surprised, turned to face him. He took her face in his hands.

"God, yes, 'Lette," he had said hoarsely. He had kissed her and run his hands all over her body, feeling those supple, soft curves of hers. She pressed against him, molding her body to his. That particular closed-door session had gone on for another hour at least. And there had been many more. In a way, it *was* a dream come true for him. He was married and a father who took his obligations seriously, but he could not imagine life without Colette.

And that was the problem. Darren suddenly wondered if perhaps he was jealous of Colette. He pictured her working in another city, another office, with another boss who looked at her with the same longing he felt, and knowing that he was nothing but a memory in her life. A wave of anger flooded him. He was surprised at its intensity.

Am I in love with 'Lette? he wondered.

He rocked back in his chair. He picked up the *Inquirer* and began rereading the article about the slain archaeologists. A good murder mystery could take his mind off anything. So could a busy day at the office. And it would be busy, now that the meat had finally arrived from Honduras.

# 9

The fat spider on the chain-link fence watched as the late afternoon shadows lengthened over the squat brick building and the parking lot. It watched the people leaving and entering the plant. They chatted and laughed and waved at cars driving in and out of the lot. No one passed close enough for it to reach. It saw a tall man with wavy brown hair and a dissatisfied expression come out of the plant office, get into a dark blue minivan and go. It saw a lovely, angry woman in a very small black dress drive off too fast in a low-slung red car. Darkness fell.

After thousands of years shut away in a pottery coffin, it had fully indulged its hunger for blood and violence, jumping from host to host to satisfy its desires. It had aimlessly wandered through Honduras, going where its hosts took it. At the end of its bloody journey it found itself on a ship bound for North America. Now it was in a little town in south-central

Pennsylvania. It was time to find a permanent host, someone with whom it could find a purpose, a way to exist.

The Mayan civilization that had supported it so comfortably was long gone. It had been so easy, then. Hosts had been most generously provided for it by the Mayans.

Long ago, temple priests would lead a Mayan prince into a small, windowless room below the temple, deep underground. There the priests would pierce the future king's tongue and penis, letting the blood flow onto paper as an offering to the gods. The priests would burn the papers and then seal the young prince in the room. There, in pain, trembling in the darkness, the prince awaited the living god-presence. The presence would linger in the absolute blackness, feeding on the rising fear of the young man. Finally it would enter the new host. The boy would scream and faint, usually, and then the priests performing the ritual would enter the room to revive their new god-king.

That feeling of otherness the hosts experienced was simply the divine presence within them. Its wishes and desires became commands from the gods. It had gone on like this, comfortably, for hundreds of years. Until, finally, a mistake was made.

Now, centuries later, there were no cultures so accommodating. No matter. It would find a new host. After that . . .

At 10:00 P.M. a white car drove up and parked near the loading dock. The fat spider felt a spark of interest as it watched a man get out and light a cigarette. In the flame from the lighter, the creature saw that the man had reddish hair, tired eyes, and slumped shoulders. He seemed to be beaten down. Yet there was something . . . The creature focused on this insignificant man. Under the defeat and self-pity it felt an anger, a powerful rage, and a love of cruelty that the man feared. Feared so much that he hid it deep inside, away from his own knowledge. But it was there, and had been there forever.

This man was not a Mayan prince, but the creature knew he was a kindred spirit, a powerful ally. It might take time to develop his potential, but the creature had the luxury of time.

Pulling a silvery silk thread from his spinneret, the spider dropped lower on the fence and waited patiently for him to come.

It was 1:13 a.m. and colder than it should be for early May. Time to walk that damn fence again, thought Roger Phillips. He stubbed out his cigarette and sighed. He wanted nothing more than to be home in bed right now, next to the warm body of his sleeping wife, with his kids snoring down the hall. A hot cup of coffee was a poor substitute. He ran his hands through his strawberry blond hair, pulled on his blue jacket with the security guard badge, picked up a flashlight, and walked out into Mama Angelina's parking lot.

He hadn't always been a security guard. No, he had been an upwardly mobile corporate type with the suit and the briefcase, happily working for Bardwell's Chocolates in Aronston. Until Lawrence Downey came along.

Roger Phillips was born and raised in Reading, Pennsylvania. He had a fairly tranquil, happy childhood, playing with his friends along the quiet tree-lined streets of West Reading, racing their bicycles in the alleys behind the neat and well-kept twin homes. Roger was a handsome child, with thick reddish-blond hair and green eyes. He had a full, almost sensual mouth, which was nearly always grinning. He had an engaging personality and made friends easily. This quality helped him get along with his teachers, though he was no scholar. At eighteen Roger enlisted in the Army. He served in the 82nd Airborne and loved the exhilaration of parachuting from the sky, ready to face the enemy. He earned the rank of lieutenant, was popular with his men and his superior officers, and cheerfully served his country for eight years.

Roger was seemingly destined to become one of the many anonymous, unsung heroes who did their duty and lived their lives in service to the country, the community, and to God. People who loved their spouses and their children, supported them well, neither drugged nor drank to excess, and died quietly, missed by only a few.

What kept Roger from normalcy and obscurity were the nightmares. For as long as he could remember, he had suffered from intense, terrifying dreams that woke him up screaming, icy sweat pouring off his body. He was unable to find any pattern to them or even to remember them clearly. He could recall only broken, disjointed images. Images of pain. Of blood. Of unspeakable horrors. What made the dreams so ghastly was that, while he was dreaming, he enjoyed every minute of them. Only when his consciousness reasserted itself did the terror and the panic set in. Not just fear of what he saw in the dreams, but more deeply, his own reaction. The dreams seemed to spring from some dank abyss deep within him. It was disconcerting to think that such horrors could be contained within good old normal Roger Phillips.

He came home to Reading with an honorable discharge. He married Wendy Larson, a petite, attractive girl he had dated off and on in high school. They promptly began a family. When his son Bryan was on the way, he accepted a job at Bardwell's Chocolates in Aronston and bought a neat, little, white cape house on the edge of the town. He liked being just an hour's drive from his family, in-laws, and friends in Reading. Wendy and Roger thought Aronston was a pretty town, a lot like West Reading. A nice place for a family, they thought. And Bardwell's was a good company to work for.

Roger Phillips worked in the customer service department at Bardwell's and he was good at it. His army training came in handy when he worked with inventory management. His efficiency saved the company several hundred thousand dollars and earned him a promotion. Believing that small accounts were no less important than big accounts, he broke cases and a few other rules to supply his small mom-and-pop store accounts. His customers liked him and his coworkers valued him. Bill Bardwell would have appreciated him.

When William Ewing Bardwell visited Aronston a century ago, he was quick to realize that Aronston was a perfect location for his plant to manufacture candy. Aronston was far enough out in the country to attract a stable, English-speaking workforce in search of lots of fresh air and green hills for their families. Yet it had excellent rail and road transportation to supply the major East Coast cities. Bardwell was a farsighted man who cleverly invested not only in his company, but also in Aronston itself. He was the first to provide Gretna College with a significant endowment. He established and supported civic and cultural activities, such as the Aronston Symphony Orchestra and the Aronston County Hospital. Bardwell knew that the better Aronston was, the better the people living there would be, and be better employees for his sprawling candy factory.

When the process of producing shelf-stable milk chocolate was discovered, Bardwell's was fortunate enough to be surrounded by numerous dairy farms, providing the factory with an ample supply of milk. Bardwell was a shrewd marketer. He manufactured novelty chocolates for the holidays, such as chocolate Santas for Christmas, bunnies at Easter, and chocolate roses for Valentine's Day. His salesmen were the best in the business. Bardwell personally hired them and retained them by respecting their business sense and compensating them extremely well. The sales force responded by being persistent, devoted to their customers, and absolutely ruthless to the competition. It was not long before Bardwell's Chocolates were sold in almost every store from New York to Washington, D.C.

Bardwell also sold candy to the military nearly at cost, and the young soldiers became lifelong consumers of his chocolate. It did not take long before Bardwell's was a household name.

The man who would become Roger's nemesis, Lawrence Downey, was a tall, imposing man with horn-rimmed glasses and an M.B.A. from the Wharton School. He was the spoiled only child of newly affluent parents on Philadelphia's Main Line. He grew up to become an arrogant, selfish man with a tendency to be verbally abusive when thwarted. He was also very good at manipulating people and situations to his advantage.

He alternately charmed and threatened his way through school. He chose only Fortune 500 companies for his senior-year interviews. He wanted to be able to say that he worked for a company people had heard of. The personnel representative for Bardwell's mistook his arrogance for confidence and strongly recommended young Mr. Downey be hired as a high-level management trainee. More perceptive firms declined to extend Downey any offers that suited his ego, so he accepted the job in Aronston.

Rather than appreciating the beauty and history of Aronston, Downey regarded the town as an ignorant backwater burg and frequently escaped to Philadelphia for the culture, so he said. He married Harriet Seltzer from Gladwyne, a rich girl with equally inflated notions of herself, and built an elegant, slightly overdone house for her in the most upscale subdivision in town.

Downey was transferred from department to department. Bardwell's had grown management-heavy over the years, as many large and prosperous firms will. Corporate inertia had set in. It was this lack of any involvement by anyone with the ability to make changes happen that allowed creatures like Downey to survive.

Nobody seemed to understand what the problems were. After all, Downey had an Ivy League degree and great credentials and he was a consummate apple-polisher. In reality, Downey was incompetent enough to make his subordinates miserable but not incompetent enough to be fired. Orderly, profitable departments of the company would be in chaos after Downey joined them. So the brass kept moving him, looking for a "good fit". His reputation preceded him, and Roger felt a chill of fear when he learned that he was coming to "reorganize" the customer service department according to the latest in management theory.

Downey was not blessed with imagination, except when it came to his abilities as a manager. He took an unreasonable and immediate dislike to Roger Phillips. Perhaps it was because Roger was easygoing, well-liked, and good at what he did without the aid of a college education. It didn't help that his wife, Harriet, had been very impressed by Roger at the company Christmas party. Roger had made sure her drinks were fresh and that she was introduced to her husband's new coworkers. Downey had left her awkwardly alone while he was off in another room chatting up the brass.

On the way home from the party, Harriet delivered a sizzling lecture on proper party behavior when accompanied by one's wife. She compared Downey's behavior very unfavorably with Roger's attentive politeness, and could not resist a few comments on Roger's personal charm. Harriet rarely found anyone to be charming, and certainly never her husband. She made that plain, loudly and often. Downey, enraged, resolved to get rid of Roger in the quickest and most humiliating way possible

He began by trying to intimidate Roger. Downey was six feet four inches tall and a screamer, and he knew how to use those gifts on his employees. One day, about two weeks after Downey's arrival, Roger's phone intercom crackled.

"Phillips, come to my office. Now." Downey's surprisingly high-pitched voice had a nasty edge to it.

Roger entered the office. "Close the door," barked Downey. He did not ask Roger to sit down. Roger took note of that and sat down anyway.

"What the hell do you think you're doing, Phillips?" Downey asked icily.

"What do you mean?" Roger was taken aback.

Downey picked up a sheaf of orders and slapped them down on his desk. "This is what I mean. Since when do we break cases?" He stared balefully over the tops of his glasses at Roger.

"Ever since I've been here," Roger replied evenly.

"This company has never broken cases and we're not going to start just because Roger Phillips wants to do it." Downey's voice began to rise. "If you would take the time to familiarize yourself with the procedures, you'd be aware of that. Or haven't you read the manual yet?"

"I've read it. But the majority of my customers can't handle full cases of product."

Downey worked himself up to full roar. "Don't be stupid, Phillips. We have contracts with the armed services. We have contracts with all the major supermarket chains. I am not going to break company policy because some corner grocer comes crying on the phone to me. They have to buy full cases just like anyone else. They're not fucking special."

Roger felt the veins in his temples begin to throb. "They

may not be little closet stores forever. Isn't it better to win their loyalty and get a bigger share of the pie as they grow?"

Downey stood up behind his desk and leaned over, looking down at Roger in his chair. "Are you questioning my authority, Phillips? If you are, get your ass out of here now. If not, then you will play by *my* goddamn rules. You got that, Phillips?"

Roger got up and walked out of the office.

"You better change that stinking attitude or I'll make sure you never get promoted again," shrieked Downey as Roger walked down the hall.

The ashen faces and averted eyes of his coworkers told Roger that they had heard every word. Just as Downey had intended they should.

Every day became a battle, with Downey screaming at him at least once a day. Roger had never been this stressed, not even with the reserves during the worst of Desert Storm. His blood pressure rose. He began smoking cigarettes. He began to suffer from stomach cramps and frequent colds that never seemed to go away. His hair began to gray rapidly at the temples. The nightmares came much more frequently and intensely. Roger was almost afraid to go to sleep anymore. His case figures, the only proof of productivity that mattered, declined markedly. Still, he soldiered on out of pride in not being known as a quitter. There was also a part of him that refused to believe that this was happening to him.

His wife Wendy urged him to quit. This made him more stubborn and determined to win Downey over. Roger put in nights and weekends at the office, trying to improve his performance, trying to play by the new rules. No matter what he did, it was going to be wrong. Corporate politics had Roger tightly in its nasty leghold trap.

Roger obsessed over his job and the situation at work. He tried to forget, but he couldn't. Sundays, which used to be peaceful days sacred to his family and church, now became dreadful because the next day was Monday. He'd have to go back to work and Downey would be there, just waiting for him.

He no longer enjoyed the things that used to delight his

soul. Watching Bryan at hockey practice, chatting with the other hockey fathers, including his friend Eddie Haas. Taking long walks with Wendy early in the morning, holding hands and talking as they did when it was just the two of them. Looking forward to the time when it would be just the two of them again. Watching his daughter, Sarah, begin to blossom into a young woman, and not quite sure what to do about it. None of this held any magic for him anymore.

At first his coworkers tried to rally around him. Roger's immediate supervisor, a young and ambitious woman named Tracy Faber, sent Downey a performance overview showing that Roger had exceeded the standards and objectives for his position. Downey sent it back to her downgraded. Then he began to court Tracy, alternately praising her and giving her new responsibilities, and blaming her for her lack of vision in supporting Roger Phillips. Tracy realized which way the winds were blowing, and silently and regretfully withdrew from Roger. Others did the same, fearful of Downey's wrath and of the loss of their own jobs. Roger felt their support eroding but still refused to give up.

Then Lawrence Downey took to belittling Roger to the company brass. Over expense account dinners (Downey being careful never to order a meal more expensive than the boss') he would fulsomely praise everyone in the customer service department, except that deadwood deadbeat Roger Phillips. I can't work with him, he would sigh. The poor man simply doesn't get it. Too bad. So promising in the beginning. Downey's boss listened. Roger's figures did not improve. Downey's political smear campaign was magnificently effective.

Finally, defeated, Roger applied for a transfer. But the damage had been done. Tracy Faber tried to put in a good word for him, but no transfer was forthcoming. Instead, Roger Phillips was "let go," which meant that he was fired but would be able to collect unemployment insurance. A meager severance was also included—a small tribute to Roger's past successes.

Downey had grinned when he handed Roger his pink slip. "Sorry about this, Phillips, but now I can hire someone who knows what they're doing." Roger could have sworn the bastard was licking his lips. So ended the corporate climb and the bright future of Roger Phillips. Roger later found out that Downey had been promoted, after a number of the customer service staff had left.

Roger was almost shell-shocked from the stress for over a year. The nightmares did not let up for a long time. A good night's sleep became a distant memory. Even Wendy's tea, made with herbs she grew herself in the garden, was no help. He spent his days endlessly rehashing conversations he had had with Downey, second-guessing himself over and over. Self-pity deepened into depression. Wendy went to work as a part-time secretary at Gretna College.

In Aronston, executive level jobs were hard to come by unless Bardwell's employed you. Most of the other companies in town were small, family-owned businesses, or retail stores geared toward the tourist trade. Finally, with two teenagers to support and unemployment about to run out, Roger applied for the security guard position at Mama's. The salary, $8.45 an hour plus benefits, was not too bad and the stress level promised to be low. Roger still felt a need to heal. The company treated him well, and Darren Keller had promised him first shot when there was an opening in the plant. Got to start somewhere, he thought. Even if it is at the bottom. Again.

He did a good job at Mama's—he was conscientious, careful, and always there, even on days when it seemed like an effort just to get up out of bed. He made friends among the few people he saw, notably Byron Mirkowski. Roger found Byron's childlike simplicity refreshing after his cutthroat experience with office politics. He took pleasure in being kind to Byron. But the depression and the sense of powerlessness never really left him. He felt life had beaten him like a dog, when all he had done was his best.

As he walked along the fence line, he had an eerie feeling that he was being watched. He had felt that in Iraq. It meant the enemy was near. Something was going to happen.

The hairs on his neck rose. It was overcast, and the night was utterly black. The yellow beam of his flashlight pierced the inky blackness. He saw nothing but a big spider crawling on the asphalt, near his foot. Must be nerves, he thought, and lit a fresh cigarette.

Suddenly he felt a surge of something dark and powerful pass into his body. As if he'd stepped on a live wire. His head exploded with excruciating pain. And then he knew no more.

He didn't even have time to scream.

**10**

When Roger came to, he realized he was walking. He had no idea how long he'd been walking. His head ached with a stabbing pain, and his belly felt hollow from hunger. There was a strange heaviness in his chest. There was no perimeter fence in sight. The creepy feeling of not being alone was more intense than ever. Why wasn't he at work? Where was he, anyway? Was he dreaming? His hands trembled as he lit a cigarette.

He looked around. He was in an upscale neighborhood of new homes. They were big, brick-fronted Georgian colonials, with Palladian windows and pedimented doors. All the lawns were manicured and professionally, expensively landscaped. The street looked slightly familiar, as if he'd seen a photograph of it somewhere, a long time ago. He tried to think, but the pain in his head overwhelmed him.

His steps slowed and he stopped in front of one of the homes. There was an island garden in front of it, with Japanese dwarf maples beginning to leaf out. A riot of pansies, daffodils, and tulips circled the little trees and crowded around the shrubbery along the house's foundation. One of the garage doors had been left open and he could see a Mitsubishi 3000GT. It looked so familiar. Roger could feel that there was something he had to do, something with the house, but he couldn't focus on what it was. He shook his head, trying to clear it once more, but a sharp stabbing pain jolted through his temples.

He walked over to the prettily stenciled mailbox and read the name in the pale gloomy light.

### 310 THE DOWNEYS
### WELCOME

"Son of a bitch," he whispered. All at once the pain and the fog were gone. In its place was perfect clarity. He was going to avenge himself on the man who had blasted his career and ruined his hopes. The one who had grinned as he fired him. The one he had worked hard for, tried to be a team player for, given up so much time for.

His moment of clarity also brought the knowledge that he was definitely not alone. There was a presence, an Other within him. Half-formed thoughts came into his consciousness and broke up, like radio static, before he completely understood them. A red tsunami of rage rose up within him and Roger let it wash over him. He was going to let the Other help him wreak his revenge.

"You incompetent asshole! You're gonna get what you deserve. Welcome to hell, you fuck!" Roger roared at the dark and slumbering house.

Moving with an unknown instinct, he raised his arms up over his head. The cigarette fell to the ground as his palms turned toward the house. He felt a wave of indescribable power pass up from his chest and out of his hands. The house began to shake as though an earthquake had struck. Every window in the house imploded with a jangling crash. Within thirty seconds, the interior of the house was engulfed in white-hot flames, so intense that they burned without smoke.

Roger stared at the house, his mouth agape. He brought down his arms, stared at his hands, and looked back up at the house. Just then a burning body tumbled out of a hole where a second-story window had been. The reek of burning flesh assailed Roger's nostrils. He recoiled instinctively, but to his amazement he found the scent curiously pleasing. The body thudded to the ground, shooting blazing orange sparks like a Fourth of July firework.

Another blazing body staggered out the front door, a thin scream issuing from its charred lips. As the bubbling skin melted and fell away from the skull, Roger recognized the features of Lawrence Downey. Downey lifted his blackened arms toward Roger and shambled a few steps toward him, his gray-filmed eyes staring right at Roger as though he recognized him. Then he pitched forward and fell face down in a black, smoldering heap on the brick walkway.

A feeling of triumphant satisfaction filled Roger's heart. He exhaled, a deep contented breath. Then, abruptly, his humanity reasserted itself. He recoiled at the incredible violence of the scene and he whispered, "How? How?"

With a roar that issued from the very gates of hell, the roof of the house collapsed onto the inferno. Sparks and flames shot everywhere, igniting the dwarf maples and charring the daffodils and tulips. Lights began appearing in neighboring homes. Roger detected the shrill wail of a fire siren in the distance. Overcome with terror and panic, yet somehow renewed, Roger turned and fled.

Two hours later, Fire Marshal Marcus Turner looked down and noticed a cigarette butt near the curb, half-hidden in the faded brown of last year's leaves. He pulled out a plastic bag, the kind used for evidence collection, and carefully picked it up. The fire had been so intense that there was precious little evidence to collect. Turner sighed and put it in his pocket. It would be sent to the crime lab and analyzed for fingerprints.


Roger ran blindly through the woods for a long time. He had no idea where he was going, just that he had to run. He tripped over a large, twisted tree root and fell flat. He lay there, sobbing for breath, while the image of Lawrence Downey's black and blistering skin and sightless gray eyes danced before him.

I don't understand, he thought. What the fuck happened back there? Did I do that? *How* did I do that? The pain in his head returned and his heart beat heavily inside his chest.

His mind turned back to the Downey's house and the bodies. He shuddered with horror. It was one of his dreams, his awful dreams. But he also remembered the feeling of peace and contentment that filled him when he saw Lawrence Downey scream in unimaginable agony. The feeling stole over him, almost against his will, and he felt clean and warm. The sense of the Other, a feeling that somehow it had come home, flashed through Roger's mind.

I don't know . . . but it feels good.

He felt irresistibly drowsy, like a tired child. Roger closed his eyes and slept, his head pillowed on a tree root.


It was getting dark when the first drops of rain woke Roger from an almost comatose sleep. For a moment, he was confused. Why am I out here in the woods? Another bizarre dream, I guess. Really weird this time. Then he was aware of an insistent throbbing in his head, and he realized that it was not a dream.

Shit, what do I do now? he thought.

The rain began to fall faster and harder. Roger looked around and realized he was about three miles from Mama Angelina's, at the other end of town. Guess I'd better go back there and get my car. Probably I'm fired for taking off in the middle of my shift. Not like I had a choice. But they'll never believe that.

He sighed, got up and started walking toward the plant. The rain began to pour down in sheets.

**11**

It was 6:30 P.M. Colette heard the rain as she shut down her computer and opened her file drawer to put away the remaining papers on her desk. Darren came out of his office and walked up behind her. She had barely spoken to him since their argument yesterday. Today, she had come in on time and gone immediately to work. She hadn't even made coffee. In a fit of spite, she had even worn Darren's favorite dress. It was made of a silky royal-blue fabric that made her eyes look even larger and brighter.

He had watched Colette seethe all day, and he wanted to make it up to her. He still believed he was right, but maybe the dress-for-success crack was out of line. And then for her to have to deal with that jerk of a delivery guy . . . He had overheard the entire exchange. He walked over to her desk and stood behind her.

"Still mad, 'Lette?" He started to put his hands on her shoulders. She grabbed his hands and threw them back at him.

"Yes, I'm still mad. I can't believe you won't put me up for the promotion. You know I could do that job."

Darren's face hardened. Her angry rejection of his peaceful overture stung. "Well, Miss Walls, if that's how you want to play it, fine. But you'd better get your butt in here every day on time. And you'd better study the company manual, especially the parts on dress code and employee fraternization. Corporate won't let you get away with the shit that I do. See you tomorrow at eight A.M. sharp or you'll get a written warning." He strode out the door. Just outside, he hesitated. Part of him wanted to go back inside and apologize again. But, damn it, he was right about keeping her in the front office with him. Wasn't he? He squared his shoulders and walked away, ducking his head against the pouring rain.

Colette watched him through the double glass doors. Stubborn pig, she thought. Then she sighed. Sulking all day really wasn't much fun. She considered apologizing to Darren for snapping at him. Then she shook her head. Not this time, she thought.

She took her keys out of her purse and looked around for an umbrella. Finding none, she knew she'd just have to run for it. What a perfect ending to a rotten day. She'd go home, take a hot bubble bath, and crawl into bed alone. Maybe a nice glass of wine for company.

She stepped outside and locked the door behind her. Her car was over at the end of the lot. Her little red Corvette, just like in the song. She had saved for two years to make the down payment after she started working at Mama Angelina's. She cared for that car almost tenderly, keeping it tuned and maintained. She always parked at the end of the lot, far from other cars and their careless owners. She wanted no dings or scratches in the cherry red paint.

Driving the 'Vette was like flying. She loved cruising at eighty miles an hour, hearing the roar of the engine and the screech of the tires as she cornered on the winding back roads. So what if she drove too fast? Apparently she did everything too far and too fast, for Aronston anyway. Stop whining, she told herself. Forget New York. Maybe it was time to move out west to Colorado or someplace. Where there was lots of sky

and air and mountains to climb. Throw caution to the winds
and just go—get in the car and drive and see what turned up.
She'd plan it all out tonight. The idea pleased her and she
began to feel better.

She took off her ankle-strapped, high-heel pumps and
began to run to her car.


Roger approached the parking lot. He was soaking wet
and tired. He was also feeling a little hungry. Wonder what
Wendy's made for dinner? Wonder what I'll tell her when I
get home?

Roger looked over at the office entrance. He saw a female
figure bend down, slip off her shoes, and begin to run barefoot across the parking lot. In a split second his mind was no
longer his own. With the mindless instinct of a predator he
pursued her at top speed. Images flashed through his mind—
beating her, feeling her agony as she writhed beneath him, her
fear as she cringed away from his blows, feeding on her pain.
Finally, his hands locked around her throat, breathing in the
last breath to escape from her lips. The images were revolting
and stimulating at the same time.

He drew close enough to her to recognize her as the secretary. He had met her only once, when he interviewed for the
job at Mama Angelina's. Her warm beauty and easy friendli-
ness had relaxed him and given him some needed confidence
when he sat down with Darren Keller. Now he was going to
kill her. The small piece of consciousness that still belonged
to him cried out against this atrocity, but the hunger and the
images overwhelmed him. The Other wanted her dead. So be
it. He ran faster, toward his victim.

The rain was too loud for her to hear his splashing footsteps
coming up behind her until it was too late. She reached the car
and fumbled with the keys for a moment. Suddenly someone—or something—pulled her off her feet with tremendous
speed. Before she could react she found herself flat on her
back beside her car. Her head hit the ground hard and she saw
stars. Wet gravel ground painfully into her skin. She was
pinned down by a man's bulk. She tried to claw at his face but

he grabbed her wrists and held them in an unbreakable grip.
She flailed her legs, trying to shake him off, but he locked his
legs over hers. He was incredibly strong. For the first time in
her life she felt totally powerless. Fear overtook her.

"What do you want?" she said in a quavering voice.

As if in answer, the man wrapped his hands around her
neck and squeezed, hard. She couldn't speak or breathe. She
tried desperately to pull his hands from her throat, digging her
nails into his arms, but he was too strong. The arteries in her
neck pulsed. She struggled convulsively, to no avail. She could
hear her dress tearing. She was losing consciousness. Please,
God, I don't want to die, she thought. Not like this.

Roger felt Colette's strong animal vitality beating against
his hands. Her heartbeat was audible. He watched her
turquoise-blue eyes stare into his for a moment, then roll back
into her head as she began to lose consciousness. The drum-
beat splash of the rain faded. Suddenly it was a blinding
sunny day. A priest-king of some ancient civilization stood
atop a stepped pyramid. The sun beamed down on the elaborate feathered headdress he wore and made his pearl-and-jade
jewelry gleam. The king bowed before a large stone slab that
seemed to be an altar. He held a huge curved sword in his
right hand. The obsidian blade had been ground to razor
sharpness. Two men were pulling a struggling, slender, naked
young girl up the steps of the pyramid. They forced her to
kneel in front of the priest. The girl was a royal princess, a
prisoner captured in a war with a neighboring city. She was to
be sacrificed to the gods. While living, she would be disemboweled on the altar. Her still-beating heart would be held
high for the gods to inspect, then thrown into a glowing charcoal brazier, the smoke making an offering.

The girl stared up at the king, her face ablaze with hate and
defiance. Her body was painted with red cinnabar, signifying
her status. She wore a small jade ring in her right nostril. The
king looked at her, his eyes wide. Her features were perfect,
her neck graceful, her shiny long hair gleaming in the sun.
But that was not what struck him so deeply. The prisoner's
eyes were a deep turquoise blue, contrasting strangely and
beautifully with her black hair and coffee-colored skin. The

blue eyes enchanted the king. He knew beyond doubt that he had to have her, no matter what the cost. He reached down and took her hand.

"What is your name?" he asked.

"Xochitl," she spat. She looked into the priest-king's face. The king looked intently at her. It was as if he possessed a strange power, for suddenly she relaxed, her anger and fear gone. Their eyes held for a long moment. Then he pulled her to her feet and took her face in his hands.

"I am Chac Mol, ruler of the City of Warriors. You will be mine."

He reached down and took her hand. They turned to face the priests and the crowd below. Chac Mol spoke in a powerful, deep voice.

"This woman has been chosen by the gods. Her eyes are the color of the sky above us and the lake below us. I will take her for my wife, so that I may be closer to the gods." The men who had brought Xochitl up to the altar scowled and whispered "Sacrilege!" The crowd murmured, confused and apprehensive.

The king turned to his priests. "Be silent! Do not interfere!" They dropped their eyes respectfully, but their faces still scowled. Prisoners were sacrificed to please the gods, not taken for man's pleasure. Chac Mol reached out and grasped Xochitl's face. "Put out your tongue," he commanded. As she did so, he lifted the sword and cut her tongue with the gleaming blade. Then he did the same to himself. He and Xochitl stepped to the altar, hand in hand, and allowed the blood from their tongues to run onto a piece of paper made from tree bark. Then Chac Mol placed the bloody paper into a hollowed stone filled with glowing charcoal. The paper burned, sending a dark puff of smoke skyward. The priests murmured apprehensively, worried by the black smoke. The king ignored them.

"Our blood, mingled, is a gift to the gods. May they bless our union and give us victories!"

The rain beat into Roger's face again. The name Xochitl echoed in his head. Roger realized that he had just seen a memory. A memory possessed by a being within him, an

Other whose powers Roger could not yet comprehend. He looked down at Colette, half-dead, her face mottled, eyes closed. The eyes . . . the eyes were the same. Exactly the same.

Roger dropped his hands from around Colette's throat. She was no longer struggling. He pressed his hands over her heart, beating very slowly now, starved for oxygen. A white light burst in his brain. Her entire being filled him. He realized he knew her name, where she lived, who she was. He was joined to her in a way more intimate and final than death. He kissed her wet face and neck gently, almost possessively. Then, slowly, savoring the anticipation, he unzipped his pants and pulled her skirt up around her waist. He entered her.

Colette gasped for air, a ragged, tearing breath. The mists cleared from her mind abruptly. She realized she was being raped. The rain beat down on her face, blinding her. She sensed an energy filling her, something elemental, a pure force sweeping her away like a raging torrent. It rose inside her, to the hollow place that nothing else was ever able to reach. She arched her hips up to take him in deeper. She could not see Roger's face change as he felt her respond to him. Her body began to tremble with cold and wet and desire. He kissed her hard, his tongue probing far into her mouth, feeling her heat. She returned his kiss with an equal frenzy, as though she were starving for him. She could taste that same strange energy, hot and exciting. She wrapped her arms and legs around him in complete surrender.

He pulled her tightly to him and held her as they lay together on the wet gravel of the parking lot. Colette felt utterly fulfilled for the first time in her life, heedless of the many cuts on her back and the bruises on her neck. She sighed. Roger pushed her wet hair out of her face and looked at it. The rain had washed away her makeup and she looked innocent and fresh and beautiful. Like the girl on the pyramid. He wanted her alive. So did this thing inside him.

He picked her up as though she was a precious, fragile object and opened the passenger door on her car. He placed her tenderly on the seat, got in on the other side and drove off.

Neither said a word for a long time.

# 12

Darren pulled into his driveway. His modest two-story home was one of the best-kept in the neighborhood. A profusion of newly planted geraniums and marigolds bloomed by the walkway, along down the driveway, and surrounded the mailbox. The shrubs were neatly trimmed and the lawn mowed. A home to be proud of, and it was all his wife's doing. Darren tried to feel grateful affection for Andrea's hard work and failed. Sighing, he walked into the house.

The savory smell of spaghetti sauce mingled with the fragrance of furniture polish and potpourri. The house was spotless, as usual. It was exquisitely decorated in a comfortable country motif with soothing shades of blue and white. It looked like something out of a magazine, which it was. Andrea had meticulously studied dozens of home magazines, carefully selecting and cutting out pages of glossy photographs. Then she scrimped and saved, purchasing each piece of furniture, carpet, draperies, and accessories as they could afford it. Darren looked around the cool, serene, perfect rooms and felt like an intruder in his own home. Heaven forbid he might drop a newspaper on the white carpet or spill a drink on the cerulean-blue sofa.

Andrea came downstairs to greet him. Her hair was combed and her makeup was perfect. Her lips brushed his cheek.

"Hello, dear. How was your day?"

Darren knew the script. "Busy. How was yours?"

"Oh, Corrine had gymnastics practice today and her coach says she's getting better every day. All her hard work and practice is really paying off. You should see her on the uneven bars. Don't forget, she has a meet this Saturday and I know she'd like you to come." Andrea moved gracefully around the blue-and-white kitchen, making the final preparations for dinner. "Katelyn's still at choir practice and then she's going to Jenny's house for dinner. She has a solo in the spring concert, you know. I just hope she doesn't get too nervous. And Michelle at work—you know, the one with the pregnant sister in Pittsburgh—well, she said . . ."

Darren interrupted Andrea's monologue. "Did you see the article in the paper about those archaeologists who were murdered in Honduras?"

Andrea looked surprised. "No, I didn't, dear. You know I don't read the papers. Anyway, Michelle said . . ."

Corrine came leaping downstairs. Tall and wiry at seventeen, she resembled Darren at the same age.

"Hey, Daddy-O, how's it going?" she said affectionately, and kissed him.

"Great, Queenie. Mom says you're all ready for your meet Saturday."

Corrine put her arms around his neck. "Oh, Popsie, please say you'll come. They can live without you at work for one day, can't they?" Her pleading tone melted him, as it always did. He reached up and patted her arm.

"For you, my little Queenie, anything."

"Oh, how cool! I'm going to do the uneven bars. Coach says . . ."

Andrea interrupted. "Corrine dear, I could use some help

with the salad. Don't forget the croutons. As I was saying,
Michelle said . . ."

Darren heard the edge in Andrea's voice. He felt as though
he were suffocating.

# 13

Tracy Faber struggled to open the heavy doors to the ElderCare Center. Her hands were full with an umbrella, a shopping bag, and a tray of lasagna and salad for her Pop-Pop. For some reason she could never think of Levi as her great-grandfather—he was forever her Pop-Pop. Silly for a thirty-five year old to think that way, but there it was.

Finally she got through the door. She signed in at the front desk, silently cursing at the bored receptionist who had watched her wrestle with the doors and never offered to help.

"What am I, the evening's entertainment?" muttered Tracy under her breath.

"You say something?" asked the receptionist, rocking back in her swivel chair.

Tracy locked eyes with the insolent girl until she looked down. "Not to you," Tracy said coldly. She stalked into the elevator and pressed the button.

The doors slid open on the ninth floor. Tracy wrinkled her

nose at the smell of the hospital disinfectant, with the unpleasant aromas of spilled bowel contents and pureed institu-
tional food lurking underneath it. She hated coming here and
wished there was a better place for Pop-Pop. But he needed
constant care and nobody in the family was able or willing to
provide it. She knew Pop-Pop hated it worse than she did, and
that kept her coming back every week with good hot food for
him.

She entered Levi's small, dark, cold room. He was staring
out the window at the deepening twilight. The old radio was
on, tuned to a classical station. The pensive strains of
Chopin's *Nocturne* played softly. The scene moved Tracy. It
seemed so . . . mournful, so empty.

She took a deep breath and smiled. "Hey, Pop-Pop!" she
called cheerily.

Levi's gnarled, arthritic hands shot out from under his lap
robe. With surprising spryness he wheeled the chair around to
see his great-granddaughter.

"Tracy, my Tracy! Hello, pretty girl. How are you? Come
and give your Pop-Pop a big hug." Levi's voice was cracked
and tired, but his pleasure in seeing her was obvious. Tracy
was a tall woman, with big dark eyes and lots of brown hair.
She had come straight from work, so she was dressed in an
expensive, beautiful suit and tasteful jewelry. She grinned at
Levi as she bent down to hug him.

At one time, Levi had been a burly man, used to hard work
and heavy lifting. Now, at one hundred and one years of age,
he was withered and wheelchair-bound. He wore a blue
chambray workshirt and navy slacks, neatly pressed. He still
had a thick shock of silvery hair on his head, which at one
time had been blond. His blue eyes had sunken a bit and were
red-rimmed now, but they sparkled joyfully when he was
happy. His great-granddaughter could still see the handsome
man he used to be.

She pressed her face against his wrinkled and weathered
cheek. "Pop-Pop, it's so good to see you," she whispered. She
straightened up. "I've got some of Mom's lasagna here for
you. Just let me warm it up."

"One thing about your mother, young lady. She sure can

cook. My grandboy was smart to marry her. Even though he doesn't appreciate it now."

"You're so right about Mom. It's a wonder I'm not fat," laughed Tracy. She put the lasagna in the microwave Levi kept in a corner and busied herself unpacking the shopping bag, which was filled with napkins, salad dressing, and fresh Italian bread. Levi had a tiny table in his room, with two chairs. She set it for two and put some flowers she had bought in a waterglass on the table. Levi watched, delighted.

"Did you talk to Shawn Williams again? What's going on with the play for Founders' Days?"

"Dad told me that Shawn took the idea to Miss Emma Bardwell herself, and she approved it. I think Shawn was more surprised than anyone else. Dad says Shawn's been working like crazy on it to get it all done in time. So, the play will be about crazy Aaron Moyer who was murdered by his wife's brothers. I think the paper is going to do a big article on it soon."

Levi shifted in his chair. The uncomfortable, apprehensive feeling was back. "I don't know as Aaron Moyer was crazy, little girl. Think he was just plain mean. Evil."

Tracy glanced over at him. "What is it, Pops?" she asked.

Levi was agitated. "I don't know. I just don't know. To me it seems like Pandora's box—some things are better left alone. Kind of like writing about Aaron will bring that evil back. Aaron should be left alone to rot in hell." Levi's voice scaled up angrily.

Tracy was astonished. She had never seen Levi so worked up about anything. He was frowning, his cheeks were red, and his fingers drummed restlessly on the arms of the wheelchair.

"Pop-Pop, I don't understand why you feel this way, but this Aaron guy died almost two hundred years ago. It really is a good story, even if it is a little gross. Don't worry yourself about it. Come over and eat. It's all ready."

Levi wheeled himself to the table. The room was filled with the scent of Italian herbs, tomato sauce, and fresh bread, temporarily crowding out the other, foreboding nursing-home odors. He breathed it in deeply, and smiled. He still had all his teeth, and surprisingly well-preserved they were.

"Well, what's going on at the chocolate factory these days?" he asked, taking a big bite of lasagna.

"Do you remember that jerk who was my boss? The one who drove everyone crazy with his stupid power games? Well, he's dead. His house burned down early this morning, with him in it."

"So it was your boss, eh? That Downey fellow?"

"Not my boss anymore, Pop-Pop. They transferred him out to Purchasing after he turned Customer Service upside down and fired half my people. I still miss one of them. Roger Phillips, now he was a good worker and an all-around good guy. He's been gone over a year now and some of his old customers still ask me about him." Tracy sighed.

"Roger Phillips, eh? Funny. I wonder if it's that same Roger Phillips who's the only living descendant of Aaron Moyer. Knew he still lived here in Aronston but didn't know he was working for you."

"Well, I don't know if it's the same guy but he's not working for me anymore. I think he's working over at Mama Angelina's now."

Levi nodded. "They make good meatballs there. When the wind is just right and I have my window open, sometimes I can smell 'em cooking."

Tracy continued, "Anyway, this afternoon a secretary from upstairs came around collecting for flowers for Downey's funeral on Sunday. Bardwell's will send an official arrangement, but she wanted to see if anyone wanted to chip in personally. Not a soul in the department contributed anything. Finally she comes around to me, and I could tell she was kind of embarrassed.

" 'How much did you collect?' I asked her.

" 'Nothing, except a bunch of cold stares. It's been like this in every department where he worked. I don't understand. He seemed like such a nice guy.'

"I said, 'You didn't work for him. The guy was a total asshole'—sorry, Pops—'and maybe now the brass will finally understand how hated he was. I'm not giving anything either.' And she left. All I have to say about Lawrence Downey is, ding dong the witch is dead."

"Watch your language, missy," said Levi with his mouth full. "Your great-grandma always said that people who used curse words had very limited vocabularies. Besides, it just doesn't sound right, hearing a pretty girl cuss."

Tracy laughed. At that moment, a small, thin woman, with light brown, very curly hair and glasses poked her head in.

"May I come in?" she asked in a soft voice.

Tracy looked over. "May I help you?" she asked in her most professional voice.

"I'm from Gretna College. Professor Williams sent me down with a copy of the play he just finished. It's for Levi Faber."

"Well, you found him all right." Levi pushed himself back from the table and executed a perfect ninety-degree turn.

The young woman took a binder out from under her arm.

"Here you are, Mr. Faber. An autographed copy of *The Devil's Own* by Shawn Williams. I hope you'll come and see it. After all, you inspired it." She placed it in Levi's hands.

Levi was silent for a few moments. He looked down at the gray binder, with its neatly typed label. As he looked, his eyes blurred. The cover seemed to glow with a strange phosphorescence, almost ghostly, and somehow evil. He pushed the binder onto the floor abruptly. It landed with a thud.

"What is it, Pop-Pop?" asked Tracy.

Levi's hands shook with agitation. "Don't mind me, ladies. Guess I'm seeing things. But Tracy, take that play away. I don't want to read it. Something is very wrong with all this, and I'll be damned for a fool, but I think Aaron has something to do with it."

"Well, I really have to be going now," said the young woman hastily. "I'm Professor Williams' grad assistant and he's so busy right now . . . Thanks again, Mr. Faber." She turned and quickly left. Tracy thought she heard her mutter something about a "crazy old coot", but her first concern was for Levi.

"Don't be silly, Pop-Pop," chided Tracy, trying to keep her voice light. "Here, have a cannoli. I'll go out to the nurses' station and see if I can sneak us some coffee."

Levi turned to her. "Hold my hands, little girl." She got up and put her hands in his. His hands were cold and trembling. "I don't understand," said Tracy. "Why are you so upset?"

"I don't know exactly, but I'll tell you this. Remember the premonitions I told you about? The fire at the Cross Keys? Well, I didn't tell you about the other ones I've had. When Mary came down with appendicitis, I'd taken her into the store just the day before. She was nine years old, and she just played while I worked. She made a house out of some crates and called me to see. I looked at her, cuddled up in a bed she'd made of crates, all snug in her little playhouse. Suddenly the crates turned into coffins and I saw Mary lying in one of the coffins, dead. Her face was white as a sheet and she had white roses in her hands. I froze and just stared at her. She must have seen something in my face because she got real quiet and scared, like. Scrambled out of the playhouse like it was on fire. A week later she was dead." He took a deep breath.

"And Kitty. My dearest Kitty. About a year before she got the cancer I was out in the yard, working in the garden. It was twilight, that time of day when everything's a kind of purply-pink color. My Kitty came out to give me a glass of cold ice water. Well, she handed it to me and all of a sudden it wasn't clear, cold water anymore. It was hot and bubbling and dark and nasty-looking stuff. I looked at Kitty and was going to ask her what the hell did she bring to me when on her chest I saw this black ugly thing. It was alive. It had these arms—like tentacles, they were—and they were wrapped all over Kitty's chest and around her body, squirming and squeezing her. It had this bloody red mouth and it was hanging onto her breast sucking her life out like a damn leech. Well, I dropped the glass and went to grab for that thing on Kitty and she cried out 'Levi! What are you doing?' And then, poof! It was gone, and on the ground was a broken glass and spilled water.

"I knew something was inside her, something going to kill her. All I could do was look at her. Kitty looked at my face and she knew I'd seen something and it wasn't good. She never asked what it was I saw. Just turned around and went in the house and brought me another glass of water. Few months later the doctors said she had cancer of the breast and there wasn't much they could do. And I couldn't tell Kitty what I'd seen. It would have taken the last bit of hope away."

Levi shifted restlessly in his chair. "But Kitty knew something was up. Knew it that night I dropped the glass. She told those doctors, 'Don't cut me open. Just make me comfortable.' And they did. My Kitty died at home, in my arms." Levi's voice broke.

Tracy's hands tightened on Levi's. He went on, not noticing. "Ever since this play business started, I've been seeing things. Just flashes, mostly. Of terrible fires, of people dying. People I don't even know. Aaron Moyer, alive and well and laughing at us all. It gets a little worse every day. Something's coming, something bad. I hope it's just an old man's fancy. Or even that Alzheimer's.

"But I haven't been wrong with these feelings yet, and I'm a hundred and one years old. Take that play away with you and tell Shawn . . . tell Shawn I said thanks, but no thanks." Levi hung his head.

Tracy felt an icy stab of fear in her chest.

"Pop-Pop, you're scaring me. Isn't there anything I can do to help? Do you want me to talk to Shawn?"

Levi looked up at Tracy and forced a smile. "No, he'll think I'm just touched in the head lately, and he very likely could be right. Don't you worry about me. You have enough to worry about down at Bardwell's. Hope you don't get in trouble for not chipping in for the flowers."

Tracy frowned. "So what if I do? And you can't tell me you're touched in the head if you can remember what we talked about before that grad student got here." She looked at Levi's pale, blue-veined cheeks and wide eyes. "Maybe I should call the doctor."

*"No!"* Levi exploded. His face suddenly flushed an angry red. "You know what they'll do to me? They'll pump me full of sleeping pills and tie me to my chair. I'll spend the rest of my life in Never-Neverland like all the other zombies in here you see watching TV and drooling all over themselves. They won't give a tinker's damn what's wrong with me. All they care about is having everything run smoothly. No time for a

crazy old man and his crazy old ideas. I'll thank you to keep
this to yourself, Tracy girl."

Tracy was taken aback by Levi's vehemence. She found
her voice after a few moments. "If that's what you want, Pop-
Pop, so be it. Nothing will be said to anyone. But do me a
favor. Call me, talk to me if you don't feel better tomorrow.
Wait, I'll stop by and check on you anyway. Now, here. Let
me fix you a cannoli and I'll go get some coffee"

Levi grinned weakly at her. "Make it a big cup, little girl.
You know how much I love coffee—almost as much as I do
you."

Tracy smiled and shook her head. She said, "I just hope
I'm doing the right thing by not fighting you on this, Pop-
Pop." Her tone was light but her dark eyes were serious.

"I'll be fine, little girl. At least as soon as this business
about Aaron Moyer is over and done with." He looked into
Tracy's eyes with equal gravity.

Tracy sighed. "Well, then that's it, I suppose." Then she
grinned mischievously. When I come tomorrow, I'll stop by
the Coffeeteria and bring you a mocha latte, Pop-Pop."

"A what?" asked Levi. "Not one of those fancy new *Eye*-
talian coffee drinks?" He sounded dismayed. "If that's all
they've got, I'll stick with my tea, thank you."

Tracy laughed. "You'll love it. Trust me."

She stayed for another half hour while he drank his coffee
and ate his cannoli, making sure he was calmed down. Then
she picked up the play in its binder and tucked it under her
arm, kissed Levi goodbye, and walked out.

At the elevator, Tracy pondered Levi's secret. Pop-Pop
never told anyone about the premonitions but great-gran and
me. I'm not going to tell anyone, she decided. He seems to
think that putting on a play about Aaron is like . . . summon-
ing a spirit in a séance, I guess.

She sighed and said to herself, "Well, he's doing wonderfully for one hundred and one. But I guess even his time is
coming. I was just hoping that his mind wouldn't go before
his body. Damn, I can't imagine a world without Pop-Pop."

The elevator doors slid open and Tracy got on. They closed
in front of her with a swish-thunk, and she suddenly felt

boxed in, as if she were in a coffin. She felt the walls closing in around her and the air was cold and stale. Her chest tightened and her lungs burned as she struggled to breathe. It seemed an interminable time before the doors opened again, and Tracy almost fell out of the elevator in her hurry to get out.

The receptionist raised an eyebrow, watching Tracy as she took deep whooshing gulps of air.

"Place is creepy sometimes, ain't it?" she said. "Looks like you saw a ghost."

Tracy stared at her for a moment. Then she turned and ran out. She raced to her car, flung the door open and got in, locking the door behind her.

"It's just the heebie-jeebies, that's all," she said, trying to believe it.

# 14

Colette's first coherent thought was that she must be out of her mind. She was letting a stranger drive her car. Not just any stranger, either. A stranger who had tried to kill her. A stranger who had raped her. She shifted slightly in the passenger's seat, remembering that marvelous feeling. She thought, *If he wanted to kill me, why didn't he just kill me there? I don't think he's going to kill me at all. I don't know how I know, but I do.*

She gazed at his profile, illuminated by the greenish light from the dashboard. *Not bad, actually nice-looking. Reddish hair and beard. Green eyes. Full, soft mouth. Nice hands. Strong, sturdy build. About forty or so. He looked somehow familiar, but then so did a lot of people in this one-horse town. Yet obviously there was something different about him. Yeah, he's different, he's a goddamn rapist,* she told herself. She shifted again in the seat, uncomfortable in her clammy wet clothes. Her throat ached dully, and she could feel the sting of countless gravel scratches on her backside.

*I must have known him somewhere before,* she thought. *A long time ago.*

The wipers made a creaky swishing sound as the rain spattered on the windshield. She watched his face, the way the flickering shadows and wet reflections changed it as they drove. The idea struck her that she might be dealing with something beyond her knowledge. Beyond her common sense. She wondered again why she was not afraid. *Maybe I'll be afraid when I get the answers to my questions,* she thought.

"Who are you?" she asked softly. Her voice was hoarse from the rough treatment her neck had recently received.

Roger glanced at her, curled down in the seat. Her wet hair hung in strings around her face. Her dress was torn off her left shoulder, exposing her breast. Blood from the gravel scratches on her shoulder had trickled down over it, mixing with the rain and making the pale flesh look like pink-veined marble. Her eyes, huge and dark blue in the dim light, searched his, seeking answers. He reached over and gently picked up her hand.

"Roger," Roger said simply.

"Okay, Roger, tell me what the hell is going on here."

Roger felt something flowing from his hand into Colette's. She gasped. "You are very special, Colette. You have been chosen." He turned right on Gretna Road North, drove past the town square, and turned down a narrow street lined with tall maple trees.

On either side of the street were Victorian-style homes, built a hundred years ago for the owners and managers of the up-and-coming Aronston industries. Over the years, some had been converted to twin homes or apartments, and some had had their charm and character erased by layers of aluminum siding and awkward additions. The Aronston Historical Society had put a stop to such modernization years ago. Several had been lovingly kept in the family for generations, their tall narrow windows and gingerbread trim intact. Roger pulled the Corvette up in front of a huge house restored in the Painted Lady style. The porch light illuminated the carefully painted trim, in shades of purple, blue, and mauve. Three brass mailboxes showed that the home had been converted into apartments.

A young couple, Jason and Emily McDevitt, bought the home five years before. It was termite-infested, the paint was peeling, and the slate roof leaked. They painstakingly brought it back to its former glory and more, with the full approval and guidance of the Society. To cover the tremendous expense involved in the restoration, they converted the second and third floor to apartments while they lived on the first floor. Colette lived on the second floor. A student, Lee Hsiang, lived on the third floor.

"How do you know my name? And how do you know where I live? Chosen for what?" Colette asked, her voice soft and distant. She was unable to think clearly. Speech was an effort. She was lost in a sea of pure sensation.

"That's my secret." He got out of the car, walked around to Colette and lifted her out as though she were a feather. He carried her onto the porch, opened the mahogany-and-etched-glass front door and walked up a narrow flight of stairs. He put her down in front of her apartment door and she began fumbling for her keys. Roger pulled her close to him and kissed her, that same deep probing kiss he had given her in the parking lot. He drew his hand gently down over her exposed flesh. Colette felt a power surge through her body and her mind went blank. All she knew was that she wanted nothing more than to melt with Roger. To become one with him and belong wholly to him. He completed her.

Finally her released her. She swayed for a moment, then unlocked the door. Roger picked her up again.

"Carrying me over the threshold, eh?"

"Yes."

They made love for the rest of the night.

**15**

After a delicious, nutritious dinner, spiced with dull conversation, Darren escaped to the den. Andrea only half-humorously referred to it as "Darren's room." It was the only room in the house that she hadn't been allowed to decorate in the current House Beautiful style. Darren had taken it over shortly after they bought the house, and refused to have anything done to it. It was his private refuge from the world, from his job, and from his marriage.

Floor-to-ceiling bookshelves were crammed with mystery novels, music folders, and staff paper scribbled over with compositions in progress. The walls and floor were bare. In the center of the room stood a beautiful mahogany baby grand piano with a photograph on it. The only other piece of furniture in the room was a battered, overstuffed recliner. When she was young, Katelyn called it a "Papa Bear chair."

Next to the recliner was an untidy pile of newspapers and magazines. To Darren, the room had every comfort he could want—a soft chair, lots of things to read, and of course the magnificent piano.

Years ago, before Andrea and the girls, Darren had played keyboards in a succession of local bands. The photograph on the piano was a publicity shot of the last and most promising band, called Myth. It graced the cover of *Street Runner,* the one and only album he had ever made. A much younger version of himself—wavy brown hair below his shoulders, a soft brown moustache and beard—was grinning and standing next to a tall, blonde, willowy girl in jeans and a tank top. She was the lead singer. Two other young men stood in the background, equally mustached and bearded. In the photo Darren's hazel eyes were bright and alive with youth and dreams. Now, seventeen years later, his wavy brown hair was cut short and touched with gray. He was twenty pounds heavier, a little out of shape, and years of hard work had netted his eyes with fine wrinkles. Still, he was a handsome man, especially when his face came alive again with that expectant, youthful grin. Colette had seen that grin many times.

He passed his fingers lightly over the keyboard, sounding random chords. They sounded melancholy and subdued. He looked down at his hands, not really seeing them as his mind turned inward.

He remembered the beginning of the end of the dream—the night he met Andrea. They had just finished a set, and Darren looked down into the audience. He had seen a pretty, almost ethereal girl with dark eyes and hair. She returned his stare and smiled. He got a beer and sat down at her table. By the time the bar closed, he had her phone number.

He was intrigued by her fragile looks and her cool, analytical mind. They dated for a while. Darren was absorbed in promoting his album and making his music. Andrea was fun but he had other things on his mind. He knew she was serious about having a life with him, so he supposed he should have seen what was coming next. Andrea got pregnant.

She tearfully announced this development to Darren and refused to consider any other option but that he marry her and give the child his name. After the initial shock, Darren thought it over and decided marriage was not so bad, and he could do a lot worse than Andrea. So they married, Andrea's white gown stretching tight over the growing bulge that was Corrine. Andrea gently but persistently suggested that the late hours and sporadic money a struggling musician made were incompatible with being a good husband and father.

So he got a day job at Mama Angelina's, working in the plant. He thought that perhaps he could continue to play on the weekends, but Andrea argued that night school was a better idea. Then Andrea became pregnant again. The night Katelyn was born was the night he gave up Myth and music for good, and enrolled in night school.

He worked hard to support his family, pored over his books and earned his degree, played with his daughters, and became the general manager at Mama's. Along the way, he slowly realized that he had been forced to set something precious aside before he was ready to. The dream died hard, and along with it any love for his wife. Yet he was still able on occasion to appreciate her good qualities, and could admit that the life she chose for him was not a bad one. He loved his daughters, and divorce was not an option for him. Not now, anyway.

The random chords Darren was playing settled into a pattern, and the first few bars of "Love Is the Answer" filled the room. The old piano had a rich, full sound that did justice to Rundgren's intricate melodies. Darren smiled to himself, remembering how he'd acquired the piano.

When Darren saw the piano in the window of an antique shop in downtown Aronston, he cheerfully and uncharacteristically parted with the money earmarked for Corrine's education in order to possess this work of art. It had ornately carved legs and the bench was topped with dark green silk velvet. The finish was aged and polished to a deep reddish-brown patina. The yellowed ivory keys felt warm and alive under his fingers.

Andrea had disapproved. "You don't play in a band anymore. Why do you need a baby grand, for heaven's sake?" she said in her soft, even voice. There was only the slightest perceptible edge to it. Darren knew her well enough to know she was frustrated with his stubbornness. He had been unable to explain to her exactly why, except that he just had to have it. It had been part of the dream, and he was suddenly and utterly determined to have at least a small piece of it.

This time Andrea could not come up with a pregnancy to thwart his plans. He'd gotten himself a vasectomy after Katelyn.

Andrea, knowing that this was a battle she would not win, tried to convince him to buy a digital piano instead. "They're perfectly good for what you need, Darren, and they're a tenth of the price. Think of your daughters' education, dear." He was not going to consider anyone else's wants or needs. Not this time. Andrea did not say one word to him for several days after the piano was delivered.

The old piano soothed the emptiness inside and helped him to focus his thoughts. His fingers began to play the song in earnest, and he was back. Back in time. Back in a club. The stage lights were bright, the air was smoky, and he could hear Ed's drums, Tommy's guitar, and Laurie's strong contralto singing:

> *Light of the world*
> *Shine on me*
> *Love is the answer . . .*

Darren remembered the time when anything was possible. He felt good again.

In the kitchen, Andrea and Corrine exchanged glances as they finished drying the dishes.

"Your father and that damn piano," Andrea sighed, shaking her head. Corrine just smiled.

**16**

Thank God. Thank God. Here I am, in my own bed, in my own room. What a dream I had! Is that me screaming? No, it's Esther down the hall. Wonder if she had a nightmare, too? Well, we'll never know. Poor soul can't talk since she had her stroke a year ago. Think if I couldn't talk, I'd scream, too.

Dreamed I was picnicking in the town square, only it must have been ninety years ago. I was a kid again. It felt so real. All the ladies in their lace-trimmed shirtwaists and long skirts and big hats. Men with big moustaches and celluloid collars and cuffs on their shirts. It was a beautiful summer day, a peaceful quiet Sunday afternoon.

We were all sitting on the grass in the golden sunshine, enjoying our fried chicken and rhubarb pie. Mother kept filling my plate with chicken. She had a smile on her face, under her hat with the white ostrich feathers on it. I remember so clearly that sweet smile of hers. There were biscuits, too. Mother's biscuits were light as a feather. Not like those heavy things they call biscuits nowadays. Mouth waters, just remembering. Matty and I were sitting right over near the Civil War memorial, waiting for more of our friends to show up so we could get a stickball game going.

All of a sudden, someone grabs my shoulder. Tight, like to hurt. I turn around and who's got hold of me but Aaron Moyer! Tall and fair and just the soul of evil. He looks at me with those ice-blue eyes of his and my stomach turns to Jell-O. Stay out of my way, he says. Whispers it, like, with a nasty hiss. Those lips of his pull back from his teeth in a grin like I've never seen before. Like a wolf's snarl. His teeth must have been six inches long, and all bloody like he'd just torn someone's throat out. Then poof! He was gone. I look around and everyone's smiling and minding their own business.

Matty, I cried, Matty, did you see that?

No, Levi, what was I supposed to see?

He was standing right next to you, you idiot. Had his hand on my shoulder.

Levi, I didn't see anything. Is this a joke or something?

Nobody saw Aaron Moyer but me.

I wish Kitty were here. When I had nightmares, she'd wake up and just hold me close. Sometimes, we'd make love in the middle of the night. I remember her long, long hair so silky soft, and her warm smooth skin and her loving kisses. Kitty, guess I'll never stop missing you until I'm with you. Hope it won't be too much longer. Don't know how much more of this place I can stand. There, Esther's finally quiet. Probably gave her a shot of something. She'll be dopey all day tomorrow, poor soul.

And, Aaron Moyer, stay away from me. Stay out of my dreams. Stay dead.

# 17

The master bedroom in the Keller home was decorated in shades of cream and white, with gold and royal blue for accent colors. The linens, bedspread, and drapes were elegant yet feminine. The only sign that a man occupied this room also was the wallet, watch, and pocket contents strewn untidily over the bureau, and the tie adorning the bedpost on the Shaker-style headboard.

Darren was reading in the snowy-white king-sized bed he shared with Andrea, propped up comfortably with pillows. He had the latest Dick Francis novel, a gift from Corrine. Darren was deeply engrossed in the story, and thought he'd figured out who the killer was, when Andrea came into the bedroom from the bathroom. He looked over at his wife.

She was wearing a high-necked, long-sleeved cotton nightgown that made her look as chaste as a nun. She smelled of soap and night cream. She frowned at Darren's mess, as she did every night, and shook her head. She got into bed with

Darren and picked up her book, the latest Danielle Steel. As he studied her profile, with its delicate nose, high cheekbones, and sharp chin, he noticed that her inky hair had become threaded with gray. He became thoughtful.

Darren could not remember the last time he and Andrea had made love. After Katelyn was born and he'd gotten clipped, Andrea's interest in sex had declined precipitously. Darren got tired of the rejection and withdrew from Andrea, spending his energy on his work, his daughters, and what was left of his music. He noticed, bitterly, that Andrea didn't seem to care that he no longer asked. Then, a few years later, Colette Walls had made him an offer he couldn't refuse. If Andrea suspected anything, she never said a word.

Physical contact with Andrea was limited to the cool cheek-brushing kiss she gave him when he came home, and an occasional quick hug, usually in front of the kids. He remembered a time when it had been different.

Practical, logical Andrea had been passionate in bed. She had been open and loving with him, sharing his dreams. Or so he thought. At least, she had been warm and caring until she had achieved her own goal of two daughters and a thoroughly domesticated husband. Then, all at once, she became reserved, almost formal with him.

Darren sighed. Andrea glanced at him.

"Is something wrong, dear?" she asked. Her voice was neutral, as if she were asking the question of one of her deli customers instead of her husband.

Darren thought for a moment. "Andrea, do you remember the good old days? In the beginning, when it was just you and I? I was just thinking about how much fun it was."

Andrea's eyebrows went up. She did not look up from her book. "I don't remember it as being fun, exactly, Darren. I remember throwing up every ten minutes when I was pregnant with Corrine. I remember following you around to those smoky dive bars you used to play in and staying up till all hours while you and your hippie friends did your thing. I remember not knowing where the money was going to come from, for rent and food and diapers and formula. No, Darren, those were not the good old days." She shook her head. "Now we have a nice home and you have a good job, and the girls are grown up enough that I can work. These are the good old days, Darren."

Darren pressed on. He had to know. "But don't you remember when we used to stay up all night just talking and making love? We'd talk about everything—music, the meaning of life, aliens from Alpha Centauri—and then we'd just hold each other and love each other until we were exhausted. And then we'd sleep together, nestled up like spoons." He took Andrea's face in his hands and turned it towards his. He looked directly into Andrea's brown eyes. "When Corrine was on the way, I used to put my hands on your belly and feel her kick. You'd laugh and laugh and tell me she was going to be a soccer player. It was so simple back then, and we were happy. Don't you miss those days, Andrea?"

"No," came the quick, cold answer. "That's kid stuff, Darren. We're not twenty-one anymore. I don't miss those days at all."

Her eyes were like dark pools. He could not see anything in them. They narrowed slightly as, deliberately, she added, "I have everything I want—my house, my girls, my husband. I don't need anything else. Now let me finish this chapter." She turned her face back to her book.

Darren thought he was past the point where she could hurt him, but her short, emphatic rejection stung. No, Andrea, you don't want me, he thought bitterly. You need my paycheck and you needed me to be a sperm donor and you need me to be your husband and play Ozzie to your Harriet. But other than that you could give two shits about me.

He looked at her again. "Well, dear, it's so nice to know that you're happy now," he said, trying for the same neutral tone she used with him. But he could not keep a slight edge out of his voice. "Goodnight, Andrea." He rolled over with his back to her and turned off the light, alone with his emptiness.

Andrea read her book. Her face was expressionless.

## 18

Colette was drying her hair early the next morning. She felt as though she had slept for days even though she hadn't slept at all. In the morning light her skin looked fresh, her hair shone like burnished bronze, and her eyes sparkled. She had never looked so lovely. She tossed her hair back and began to braid it.

She started and clutched the edges of the sink. Her knees suddenly turned to rubber as she stared into the bathroom mirror.

The bruises on her neck were gone. Completely healed. Her skin was unmarked.

She ran her hands over her lower back and her flanks. No gravel scratches, either.

Roger came into the bathroom and put his arms around her from behind her. She stood stiffly in his embrace.

"Who *are* you?" she breathed, studying his reflection in the mirror.

"Roger," he smiled back at her in the mirror. "How could you forget? You've been moaning my name all night."

Colette felt a small clutch of fear. "Look. Last night you bruised the hell out of my neck. Plus my back was all scratched and cut from the gravel in the parking lot. Today it's all gone. What's going on here?"

"Love heals all," he said. His smile became a grin, as he released her from his embrace.

Colette bit her lip and finished braiding her hair. She secured it with a black velvet ribbon. "Speaking of moaning, who or what is Sochee? You called me that at least twice last night."

Xochitl, the voice had said. "Just someone I used to know. She was a very special woman, proud and beautiful. You remind me of her."

Colette studied him with a direct blue gaze as she pulled on her skirt. "This whole thing is too weird. There is something about you . . . I just don't know." She bent her head down as she buttoned her blouse, sunlight from the window making reddish-gold glints in her hair. Roger watched her in silence. Things he did not understand were happening to him so quickly. He felt as if he were in free fall, with no parachute. It was a welcome, if momentary, respite just to watch a pretty woman get dressed. He sighed.

She looked up and saw the pensive expression on his face. Feeling a rush of tenderness, she walked up to him and put her hand on his cheek. Roger turned his head and kissed the palm of her hand. She felt the now-familiar oceanic sensation galvanize her entire body. It carried with it a tide of new and uncomfortable emotions.

*What is happening here?* she wondered. *This is beyond weird, and I have no idea how to handle this. And I don't like not knowing. But this man . . . is he the One?*

She said in an unsteady voice, "I have to go now, but we have *got* to talk. See you tonight, then?"

Roger released her hand and grinned. "Till then, beautiful." He turned on the water and stepped into the shower.

# 19

Darren Keller pulled into Mama Angelina's parking lot at 7:30 A.M. He saw Colette's car in the lot but that was not unusual. She had left it there before when she went out after work. Nobody ever drove that Corvette but her. He wondered if she'd had a date, and tried to ignore a twinge of jealousy. He picked the newspaper up from the passenger's seat, locked his car and walked to the front door, keys in hand.

The door was open. Byron must have unlocked it, he thought.

He walked into the reception area and stopped dead in his tracks. Colette was standing by the filing cabinets, riffling through several days' worth of paperwork. She was wearing a tailored white blouse and knee-length black skirt. Her hair was neatly braided. She looked stunning. And very professional.

" 'Morning, Darren," she smiled. "How are you?"

It took Darren a few moments to find his voice. "Fine,

'Lette. You look great this morning." He was still staring at her.

"Just following the boss' orders," she said.

Byron came in from the plant. "Hi, Mr. Keller. Miss Walls here got here before me this morning. She even got me some coffee."

"Great, Byron. How's it going?"

"Okay." Byron paused, a troubled look on his face. "Listen, Mr. Keller, d'you find out what happened to Roger Phillips? He didn't come in here last night and nobody knows where he went to. Miz Phillips has been callin' here every hour or so."

Out of the corner of his eye, Darren saw Colette jump as if ice water had been thrown on her. She spun around and looked hard at Byron. "Roger? Roger who?" Her voice scaled up a notch.

Byron dropped his eyes and shifted his feet, surprised by the force of her reaction. "He's our night guard, Miss Walls. I found his cap by the fence. I put the cap on your desk." Byron paused as if collecting his thoughts. "He left the night before last without punching out. Mr. Keller told me always to punch out when I was done." He looked over at Darren. "Is Mr. Phillips in trouble?"

Couldn't be the same Roger, Colette thought. Or could it? He had looked familiar. She hadn't noticed what he was wearing. She knew nothing about him except how he made her feel.

"Oh, an' by the way, Miss Walls, I found these here shoes in the parking lot this mornin'." He held up Colette's high-heeled, ankle-strapped shoes. The ones she took off last night. The ones she must have dropped when Roger . . .

"Thank you, Byron." She took the shoes from him, her expression troubled.

Darren spoke to Byron without taking his eyes from Colette. "No, Byron, I haven't heard anything about Roger Phillips, but I'll let you know soon as I do. Come in my office, 'Lette."

They entered the office. Colette did not close the door, as she usually did. Darren saw this and his curiosity was piqued further. "'Lette, do you know something about this guy? I saw how you reacted."

Colette looked at his face. He was genuinely concerned. And she had to tell someone, if only to organize her own thoughts by saying them out loud.

"Well, I just met someone last night named Roger. I don't know anything about him, really. Not even his last name. Except . . . Darren, I want to tell you this—I can't explain it. He's . . . different from anyone I've ever met. In a lot of ways. I don't know what to think."

Darren looked at her radiant face and shining eyes. She looks like she's in love, he thought. He felt an unexpected pain in his heart. Resolutely, he ignored it. "Well, I guess that accounts for the blush in your cheeks, little girl." Colette smiled almost shyly, but her eyes widened at the note of false heartiness in his voice. Damn, she knows me too well for that shit, he thought.

He pressed on. "Since nobody seems to be able to find this Roger Phillips, let me know if you find out anything. If Mrs. Phillips calls, let me talk to her, okay?"

"I will. But I don't think they could be the same. Roger's not an unusual name, you know. Want some coffee?"

"Sure. Thanks." He opened his *Inquirer* and pretended to read. What he really wanted to do at that moment was to take her in his arms and kiss her until she was weak in the knees and never ever let her go. His knuckles whitened as he reminded himself that that was not an option.

Colette walked out of the office, a troubled look still on her face.

# 20

Roger let the nearly scalding water flow down over his body. The Other and the half-understood impulses that had guided his actions for the past twenty-four hours were gone for now. His mind was his own again and finally he could think things through.

*So, this thing I have, my unknown companion, heals as well as destroys. She was lying next to me and I just touched her and wished I hadn't hurt her. And the bruises and scratches were gone. And that strange memory in the parking lot. Was I the king? Was she my wife?*

*Speaking of wife, what the hell am I doing here? I should be home, with my family, with Wendy. Even though I feel so right with Colette. I know I have never wanted to be with anyone as much as I want her. And it feels good, damn it. I can't remember the last time anything felt this good. Sending Downey straight to hell, finding Colette—it's so good.*

*But it's wrong. Very wrong. It's called arson, murder. Rape and adultery.*

Roger felt the hollowness of hunger in his belly. *Let's go home for breakfast,* he thought. *They're probably worried sick by now.* He was astonished to realize that he had no real desire to see his family. It was as if they were no longer his family, just a group of pleasant acquaintances. Every bit of passion was drained away from them and channeled elsewhere.

He soaped himself slowly and deliberately, cleaning himself thoroughly.

*Maybe I should tell Wendy what's happening to me. Right. And if I do, she'll divorce me and then she'll have me locked up. Yep. Roger finally went off the deep end. The nightmares are for real now.*

*Guess I'll have to kill her. And Bryan and Sarah, too.*

The shampoo bottle fell out of Roger's hand and bounced on the bottom of the tub.

*Where the fuck did that idea come from?*

He was filled with a sense of anticipation such as he had never known. He would be free to experience things he had only dreamed of. Things he had always wanted. The deaths of his family would satisfy this hunger inside. And he would gain power, power to make things happen.

A bluish light shone in his green eyes and his mouth twisted evilly as he grinned.

# 21

Colette returned to the filing cabinets and began to slide the papers into the correct folders. She had been surprised by Darren's reactions while she sat across from him in the office. What she saw disturbed her almost as much as the new questions about Roger did. It was suddenly plain to her that Darren felt a good deal more for her than he was willing to admit. Colette thoroughly enjoyed their affair but she had never thought it would go further than just that—an affair.

Now she looked hard into her own heart. She stared, unseeing, at the sheaf of paper in her hands. Darren was her best friend. He had been ever since she was seventeen and started working at Mama's. He had been kind to her, and fair. She liked the way they worked as a team in the office. After all these years, they were as comfortable with each other as an old couple.

As far as the affair went—well, there was no getting

around the fact that she had seduced him. She hadn't really expected him to take her up on her playful suggestion for making up her lateness. He had never shown anything but a professional interest in her until that moment. Still, it had turned out to be a very pleasant surprise.

She sensed that he was not exactly where he wanted to be. He had never said anything to her, yet she knew that Darren harbored a secret dream. She herself would no more think of deferring a dream than she would of selling her car. Perhaps that was the attraction for him.

He was a passionate and skillful lover, and she had a deep affection for him. It came to her like a thunderclap that perhaps the reason he was resisting her promotion was that he didn't want to lose her. As she considered this idea, Roger's face rose into her mind.

Back to Roger. Obviously Roger was not your average guy. No average guy could do what he had done to her. Choked and raped her, then filled her, completed her, healed her. She was his entirely, at his mercy, and the thought was almost painful.

From deep within her mind, irrational explanations bubbled up. *He was a witch. Or a vampire. Or a fallen angel. Or the devil himself. Was it voodoo or magic or something else?*

*What have I gotten myself into?*

She took a deep breath, trying to steady her nerves. *I can handle him. He's not going to hurt me again, I know it. But what does he want? Is he this missing Roger? What if he is? What* is *he?* Her head began to spin and the sheets of paper rustled in her trembling hands.

"Hey, 'Lette, where's that coffee?" Darren called.

She breathed again. "Oops, I forgot. Coming right up," she called back, relieved to have something else to think about.

# 22

Roger turned up his coat collar against the chill of the spring morning. His head ached dully. He was being pulled along toward his home by a dark impulse he did not understand. *If what I think is going to happen . . . gotta find a way out,* he thought.

Where did this thing come from? He'd been by the fence, doing his rounds and then . . . bam! He was over in Carriage Crossing. And he wasn't alone anymore. He'd been possessed. By something that used to be Mayan, apparently. For Pete's sake. How the hell did a thing like this end up in Aronston? Why pick on him? How did he get so lucky? And why this amazing, terrifying power?

*If I had known, I'd never have let this . . . this Other . . . destroy Downey,* he thought. Just as quickly he thought, *Yes I would. In a heartbeat.* He felt dizzy from the circling in his mind and sat down in the damp grass beside the road. Absently he reached over and began picking violets. He had often come home with a huge handful of violets for Wendy. They were her favorite flowers.

Images flooded Roger's mind again. He saw a thriving village beside a blue lake, set into a green mountain valley. The king he had seen last night walked through the village, among the handsome Mayan inhabitants, who dropped their eyes respectfully as he passed. He wore a long cloak of quetzal feathers, and gold jewelry sparkled in his ears and nose. His body gleamed with sacred oils, which the priests anointed him with every morning.

Then he was sitting atop the pyramid temple, eyes avid as the stone altar dripped with the gore of men and women sacrificed to his terrible hunger. He saw them hacked to death by inches, fingernails and teeth pulled out, beating hearts ripped from their chests while their miserable owners screamed in unimaginable agony—all for his benefit. He watched the slow deaths with enormous satisfaction. The king—Chac Mol, that was his name—used his dark power to incite others to satisfy his needs, cloaking it in the guise of religious sacrifice. The culture became blood-soaked and warlike, a perfect place for a being like Chac Mol.

Then the vision changed from the temple to the bedroom. Roger felt the passion for Xochitl that made Chac Mol commit sacrilege against his own and earn the fear and enmity of the priests. A love that defied even death. He saw the two of them in bed together, happy beyond belief.

Finally, Roger saw three men, the priests, creep up to the couch the king shared with his wife. He saw the moonlight shining on the blade of the curved sword, saw it plunge into his chest, and lift out the still-beating heart. He heard Xochitl screaming as his heart slid into a painted pottery jar. Then darkness, eternal darkness.

A gleam of light. A whiff of fresh air. Eyes and a body were his again. A murderous, frenzied rampage of killing. A pretty girl, her face smashed, dead beneath him as he raped her. Fires burning. A ship. Crewmen falling on one another, wallowing in blood, only to be reduced to grey dust. A spider floating onto a chain link fence. The Downeys and their home incinerating. Roger understood. It was a history. A history of this power that now belonged to him. But the power brought with it a desire to kill, to torture and maim, to burn . . . and to possess forever the love lost centuries ago. At any cost.

Roger's stomach twisted with hunger and horror. The wilting violets fell from his hand. He rose to his feet and began stumbling forward, as if he were being dragged. Now he knew what would happen when he returned home. He was going to sacrifice his own family in the bloodiest way possible. As thousands had been sacrificed before.

The human part of him struggled frantically against this force pulling him onward. He tried to turn and run but his muscles would not obey. Slowly, inexorably, his feet planted themselves one in front of the other. He came within sight of his home. He looked at the pretty, little white Cape Cod with the black shutters and spring blooms around the foundation. He thought of the fifteen happy years he had spent in that house with his wife, watching his children grow, and his heart broke. He wanted to shout, to tell Wendy and Bryan and Sarah all to run for their lives. His throat was sealed. His head blazed with white-hot pain. He was utterly helpless against the hunger of the Other. Worse, he sensed for the first time a part of himself that was actually looking forward to this. The part of him where the nightmares came from. It was developing a will of its own.

"Why?! Why me?" he shouted into the recesses of his own mind.

The words he had spoken to Colette last night came back to him in answer. You are special, Roger. You have been chosen. Their deaths will set you free.

Then he was no longer Roger. The Other overwhelmed him and he was lost for a time.

Roger was an army veteran and a weapons expert, so he had a nice collection of handguns. Since Roger was also a conscientious parent, he kept the guns locked in the shed. He had intended, after the kids were grown, to buy the best gun cabinet he could afford to display his treasures and move them into the family room.

Zombie-like, he unlocked the shed and stepped inside. He picked his way past the lawn mower and the snowblower and various garden tools to a high wooden shelf at the back of the shed. He took down a metal box with a combination padlock on it and opened it. Inside, wrapped in oiled cloth, was a Browning Hi-Power automatic 9mm pistol. It was his favorite, imported from Belgium, and well suited to the occasion. In another cloth there was a silencer. He fitted the silencer to the pistol. Next, he opened another box that contained bullets of various calibers for his guns. He selected the 9mm bullets and filled the clip with thirteen rounds. He slid the clip back into the pistol. Then Roger picked up an eight-inch hunting knife with an inlaid wood handle. He drew his thumb down the blade to test its sharpness. A thin line of blood appeared on the ball of his thumb. Satisfied, he slipped it into his belt. He picked up the Browning, made sure the safety was off, and exited the shed, closing and locking the door behind him.

He walked through the backyard, past the brown rectangle of dirt that would have been the vegetable garden. Clumps of daffodils blossomed around the patio where his wife, Wendy, had planted them years ago. Suddenly a black-and-tan cocker spaniel whizzed around the corner of the house, barking frantically.

"Spunky! How are you, girl?" Roger knelt down on the greening lawn and hugged the jumping, wiggling dog. She licked his face and whined in her excitement at seeing her master. "Good girl. Spunky, sit."

Spunky sat, tongue lolling out in a canine grin.

"Spunky, stay." Roger backed away ten paces from the dog. The Browning came up in his hands.

The dog tilted her head, puzzled.

There was a soft pop. Spunky collapsed, legs and ears in a tangle. The bullet had pierced her brain. Right between her liquid brown eyes, which gazed sorrowfully at Roger even in death. The back of her head was an oozing mess of brains and blood and fur.

Roger bent and picked up the dog's body. He felt a strange,

nauseating mix of pleasure and agony. Holding Spunky in his arms, he approached the back door of his home.


The spring sunshine streamed into the cheerful kitchen. Bryan Phillips sat at the kitchen table, picking at some cold cereal. His back was to the window. He could see his mother on the sofa in the living room, finally sleeping. Down the hall, Sarah's blow-dryer was making its electrical roar as she styled her hair. *She's a basket case, can't eat or sleep, but she's got to have perfect hair,* thought Bryan. *Girls are so weird.*

His mother had called the police last night. A person had to be missing for twenty-four hours before they would file a missing-persons report, they had told her. She'd called the state police in Harrisburg, and they had told her the same thing. Since no one at Mama Angelina's was sure exactly when Roger had disappeared—they only knew he hadn't punched out on the time clock—they had all slept badly, waiting for the twenty-fourth hour. One more would do it, thought Bryan. It was 7:30 now.

*Where could Dad have gone?* he thought for the hundredth time.

The back doorknob turned.

"Dad!" Bryan cried. He jumped up from the table, sloshing his cereal onto the floor. The bowl fell and broke in two, but Bryan never noticed.

Roger let Spunky's stiffening body slide to the floor. He held out his arms.

Bryan was a mature young man of fifteen, merciless on the ice during a hockey game, but tears came to his eyes as he hugged his father close. "Oh, Dad, we were so worried. Man, am I glad to see you!" he said, broken-voiced.

Roger turned his face and rubbed his cheek against Bryan's sandy-colored hair. Bryan felt his father shaking with emotion. He felt something else, too, something frightening. A strange electric charge buzzed through Bryan's body. He tried to draw away, to look at his father's face, but Roger's arms tightened around him. Then Roger thrust him away.

He pulled the knife from his belt and thrust it into his only son's belly. As Bryan flinched back in pain and surprise, Roger pulled out the knife and plunged it back, over and over. Blood spilled out from Bryan's body over the kitchen floor. Bryan's internal organs began to bulge and spill out through the many perforations Roger made with the knife. Bryan tried to speak but could only gurgle helplessly as his life drained away. Roger gazed at the boy's face, the surprised expression permanently frozen there. A pleasant warmth spread outward through Roger's body from the center of his chest.

Roger passed from the kitchen into the living room. He stopped and looked down at Wendy. She was sleeping deeply on the sofa, blue rings of exhaustion under her closed eyes. He brought the pistol handle down sharply on her head, ensuring that she would remain there until he was ready for her. He started toward the bathroom with a sense of anticipation and tears pouring down his cheeks.

Wendy's consciousness swam up through a miasma of pain. She had dreamed that someone was screaming. She realized that she was in the basement, on Roger's workbench. What in the world, she thought. She attempted to get up and discovered she was tied down to the table with lengths of clothesline. She struggled, but the ropes tightened on her wrists and ankles when she did.

"Bryan? Sarah? Where are you?" she called.

No answer. She heard a rhythmic thudding coming from the upstairs bathroom, over and over. A pause. Then Wendy heard water gurgling in the pipes, draining from the bathtub. And a noise that sounded like an animal howling.

"Spunky?" Silence.

"Sarah? What's going on? I'm in the basement."

She heard footsteps, too heavy to be Sarah's, crossing the floor above and then turning, coming down the stairs.

"Bryan? Who's there?" Panic began to overcome her and she struggled hard, heedless of the ropes biting into her.

"It's me, Wendy."

"Roger!? Thank God! Oh, Roger, I'm tied to the work-bench."

"I know." Roger came over and stood in front of her. His clothes and hands were drenched with blood. He had a knife and a pistol in his belt. His face was expressionless.

"Where have you been? What in God's name is going on here?"

Roger's face contorted and he clutched at his temples.

"Answer me!" Wendy's voice was shrill.

"Bryan is dead. He's in the kitchen. I slashed him to rib-bons. I electrocuted Sarah in the bathtub with the blow dryer. Then I took her head and smashed it over and over until the tub was purple with blood and brains. Don't know how many times I told her to drain the water when she was done." An evil, twisted smile spread across his face. "Spunky's gone, too. I shot her between the eyes."

"What?" She stared blankly at him. It was impossible to believe that her loving and faithful husband could even think of such things, much less do them. "Roger, is this some kind of sick joke?" A feeling of foreboding came over her and she knew it wasn't.

"There's this . . . thing, this power that has taken me over . . ." Roger grimaced and doubled over as if something had kicked him. He slowly straightened up and his eyes met Wendy's. They looked different. She realized that they were a piercing blue instead of his usual green.

"Wendy, God knows I never wanted to hurt you or the kids . . . But I must."

Wendy could only lie still on the table. Her arms and legs had turned to jelly and she wanted desperately to throw up. Her mind was as numb as her hands and feet.

Roger stared at his wife. She was paralyzed with disbelief and terror. He reached out for the ropes . . . Suddenly it wasn't Wendy on the bench anymore. It was a girl, not much older than Sarah. She had long, curly, strawberry-blonde hair and was wearing a simple, old-fashioned white nightgown. She had a lovely face, and her eyes were bright with love and anticipation.

A sickening impulse overwhelmed Roger. He balled his

hands up into fists and landed a vicious punch squarely in the center of the girl's face. She recoiled in horror, screaming as the blood poured from her split nose. Suddenly the girl was gone. Wendy lay there, in her gray sweats, tears mixing with the blood on her face. The scream became a terrified whimpering.

He picked up a screwdriver with a long blade. He reached over and jerked Wendy's sweatpants and underwear down to her ankles. She twisted and arched her back, trying to get away from the screwdriver blade. She began screaming in panic.

"Roger, don't! I love you, Roger! Don't do this, please," she babbled.

Roger straightened. His eyes were cold and blue and his mouth had an odd curve to it. He looked at her face for a long moment, genuinely puzzled. "But I need to be free, Wendy. Free of all of you. Your deaths make me free. I need your pain."

He brought the screwdriver down slowly toward her belly. She locked eyes with him, holding his gaze, seeing something there she had never seen in all the years of her marriage. Roger's eyes were blue and evil but she thought she could still see through to the man she had loved. She had to believe that, had to believe she could reach him.

The cold blade of the screwdriver came in contact with her skin and pressed hard. More tears of pain and fear welled into her eyes but she did not drop her gaze. She could feel the blood from her broken nose flowing down the sides of her face and neck. *Stop, Roger, stop,* she mutely begged.

Suddenly Roger's eyes were green again. His mouth straightened and the anticipation left his face. It was replaced by a furious determination.

"*I . . . can't . . . do . . . thissss!*" he roared. He brought his hands up over his head. The house exploded in white-hot flames.


Roger had no idea how he got out of the burning house. Not only got out of the house, but had cleaned up and changed his clothes before he left. Now he was standing on a hill behind the house, concealed in a stand of budding trees, watching the Aronston Fire Company hose down the smoking pit that used to be his home. Tears came again to his eyes.

*Oh my God, what have I done? The only thing I was able to do was to burn the house down before I tortured Wendy to death. They all died so horribly. Sarah, there in the bathtub. And Bryan, disemboweled on the kitchen floor. My son. Even Spunky. They didn't understand that I had no choice. I could only stand by and watch myself do this.*

He screamed out a miserable, inarticulate cry of pain and sat down heavily on the grass. His body was wracked with sobs.

But as quickly as the tears came, they disappeared and a grin slowly spread over his face. He thought of Bryan's surprised face as he lay in a pool of gore. Sarah's once-perfect hair, wet and weedy in the tub as the water turned pink, then red around her. Wendy, half-naked, writhing on the table like an eel. How wonderful it was.

He remembered how the contentment had spread out from the center of his chest. *Well, whoever or whatever you are, you are literally in my heart.* Terror clutched at him as he realized his time was rapidly growing shorter. Soon everything that remained of Roger Phillips would be gone, submerged, or consumed. In its place would be . . . the Other. In the body of Roger Phillips.

He stretched out on the grass to watch the firemen work. Like a wave on a beach, the fear receded as peaceful, pleasant sensations rolled over him again.

He fell asleep, finally, in the warm spring sunshine, a happy smile touching his lips.

# 23

The plant manager tapped on Darren's door. "Ready for me, boss?" asked George Newell. He had a folder under his arm, full of papers that he always brought in for his weekly meeting with Darren.

"Sure, George, have a seat," Darren said, putting his newspaper on the floor next to his briefcase.

George was a big bear of a man, six feet four inches and three hundred and fifty pounds. He was built like the linebacker he used to be in high school. He wore his grizzled hair like he used to in high school, too, back in the early sixties—inch-high stubble all over his head. He had worked for Mama Angelina's for thirty-five years and loved to tell stories about the old days, before Corporate came in with all their big-city ideas on how to run the place. As a matter of fact, George loved to tell stories, period. And of course, editorialize on how he, George, would run the world better.

Today would not be an exception, and Darren resigned

himself to hearing a few before they could get down to business. He drained the rest of his coffee and looked attentively at George.

"Hey, boss, you hear about the fire over in the Carriage Crossing development? The one with all them fancy new homes?"

"No, George. What happened?"

"Personally, I don't see how anyone needs to spend two hundred grand on a damn house. Those things are built out of chewing gum and toothpicks, they all look alike, and what are you going to do in them? Eat, sleep, and crap. Don't need to spend two hundred grand to do that."

"Sure, George. You were going to tell me about the fire?"

"I was getting to that, boss. Anyway, one of those damn tinderboxes just exploded yesterday. Scottie Herr, in the plant, well, you know he's a volunteer fireman, and he said he never seen anything like it. Nothing left but a hole in the ground where the cellar used to be. The neighbors said the owners were home—Downey, I think they were called—Scottie says there wasn't hardly anything left of 'em. Said what was left wasn't pretty. Even the cars in the garage—poof! Just bits of melted metal here and there. The neighbors said that the fire glowed like the sun at noon. Scottie said that even if it was a gas explosion, there'd be stuff here and there, thrown out of the house and all, but man, there was nothing. Strangest thing he ever saw."

Darren's eyes widened a little. "Really, George?"

"Yeah. If you read the *Aronston Clarion* instead of that highbrow city paper, you'd of known. Front page news today. Police have no clues."

"I like my highbrow city paper, George. Gee, that's too bad. Well, what have you got for me today?"

George opened the folder and went over the weekly production figures with Darren. They were both pleased to see that they were on target, which would please Corporate so that they'd stay in New York where they belonged. A shipment of frozen meat had finally arrived.

"Came on that ghost ship they found off Jersey," said George. "Lucky the paperwork was all in order and the ship's owners paid those salvage guys or we'd still be waiting. We'll use that stuff for the meatballs. Keep the fresh for the burgers."

"Sounds good, George. Everything's great and you're doing your usual fine job."

"After all these years I should be able to do my job. Before the Fritzingers sold this plant to those *Noo Yawkers,* I . . ."

Darren's phone buzzed. "Call for you on line two," came Colette's voice through the speaker.

"Okay, George, I guess that's it. Same time next week, eh?"

"You got it, boss." George gathered up his papers and walked out into the plant. Darren picked up the phone.

"Darren Keller here."

"Saved your ass again," Colette said laughingly.

"Thanks 'Lette. Back to work." He hung up the phone and picked up his *Inquirer* again. He leafed through the first section until he found what he was looking for:

## INCENDIARY FIRES PUZZLE HONDURAN POLICE

AP - A string of unusual fires has the Honduran police stymied. They began almost two months ago near the tourist destination of Copan. The fires, which have destroyed several northern Honduran villages and two neighborhoods in Puerto Cortes, are characterized by extreme heat and brightness. Although the fires are deemed to be of a suspicious origin, the police are unable to determine the cause or motive . . .

# 24

Fire Marshal Marcus Turner frowned as he sur-
veyed what was left of the Phillips' home. In all his years as
an arson team investigator he had never encountered fires like
this one and the one yesterday. He had served the Philadelphia
Fire Department for fifteen years before coming to Aronston.
He ran his hand over his close-cropped black hair and shook
his head.

He had seen huge, old brick warehouses, abandoned for
years, set ablaze by thrill-seeking kids or by crackheads. He
had seen row homes torched by angry spouses, sometimes
killing their own kids in the process. He had seen businesses
burn for insurance money. He had investigated strings of fires
set by sick people who had a compulsion. Not to mention all
the fatal fires ignited by careless smoking, faulty wiring, gas
explosions, or just plain stupidity.

After fifteen years and hundreds of fires, he wearied of the
big city and the frantic pace and the piles of unsolved cases.

When he accepted the chief's job for the town of Aronston, he was expecting a barn fire every now and then, an occasional grease fire in a kitchen, and school demonstrations in October for Fire Prevention Week. Hundreds of eager children swarming over his fire trucks seemed peaceful and relaxing after Philadelphia. He wanted no more excitement and no more mysteries. But the smoldering hole in front of him made a mockery of his hopes.

Even a good refinery fire down by the Delaware River couldn't match the utter destruction before him now. Turner had never seen fires that burned so hot and smokeless. Everything was vaporized. They couldn't identify bodies because there weren't any to identify. Furniture, clothing, cars—gone.

"Like a phaser blast from *Star Trek,* huh, Chief?" Scott Herr asked. Turner started, a little surprised that his thoughts could be read so clearly.

"Yeah, Herr, whatever that is," he replied. He was not a sci-fi fan. "Shouldn't you be at work?"

"Got a day off for good behavior. Was going to take my wife's car into the shop. Guess we'll have to do it another time."

"No, go home, Herr. I'll finish up here." Turner needed to do some diagramming and collect material for testing. Scott Herr was one of his best volunteers. Always there when you needed him and always eager to help. But Scottie worried him a little. He was like a little kid at fire scenes. The excitement on his face made Turner worry that he'd do something reckless. Or, worse, that Scottie'd end up as an arsonist himself, setting fires for the pure joy of being able to put them out. Marcus Turner had seen a few of those firemen arsonists in Philly.

"All right, I'm going. Hey, boss, I FedExed that cigarette butt we found in front of the Downey's off to the lab this morning. Told them to do fingerprint and DNA analysis. They said they'd try to have an answer for us on the prints tomorrow."

Turner exploded. "Jesus, Herr, do you know how expensive DNA shit is? What kind of a budget do you think I got? This ain't the OJ case, you know. Not yet, anyway."

He walked over to the pit that used to be the Phillips' basement. His clear, dark brown eyes narrowed against the wisps of smoke as he began collecting ash samples. These would be tested for gasoline or other flammable residues. Next he would sketch the scene and run it through the computer at the station, trying to determine where the fire started and how it burned. Experience told him that it would be a waste of time. From the looks of things, this house and the one in Carriage Circle yesterday had simply spontaneously combusted.

Scott Herr looked contrite. "Sorry, Chief. I just thought that with this being so weird and all that we might need it."

"Aaah, you may be right, Herr. Just next time, ask, okay? Now go take care of your wife."

"Okay, boss, later." Herr left.

"Shit," whispered Turner under his breath. A burgundy sedan pulled up behind the yellow pumper. On the side of the car was stenciled, in Old English-type lettering, *Aronston Clarion*. Two people got out of the car: a small, slender, attractive woman and a young, bearded, bespectacled man, who walked around to the trunk, opened it, and began pulling out cameras and tripods.

"Hi, Chief," the woman sang out as she approached Turner. "Do you have some time for me?"

Not really, thought Turner. "For you, Vicky, anytime," he said, pasting on a grin.

Vicky Collins was the chief reporter and assistant editor for the *Aronston Clarion*. Usually she spent her days rehashing wire stories, doing a police blotter column, recording births, marriages, deaths, and doing fluffy pieces on local events. But on the rare occasions when there was real news in Aronston (usually a petty theft or vandalism, or a barn fire) she had a tendency to come on like a small-town version of Lois Lane. She would wring every drop of news out of a story, and had badgered Turner too often for him to feel anything other than irritation when he saw her. He had played newspaper politics often enough in Philly to know that it was not good to piss off reporters; better to make them your best friends—but he was irritated anyway.

When she got close to the smoking pit that used to be the

Phillips' house, she let slip the reporter's mask for just a few seconds.

"This was the Phillips' *house?*" she said, incredulous.

"It was," said Turner.

"Was . . . were . . . was anyone home when it burned?" She was still stunned by the destruction.

"We don't know, Vicky. Not for sure. There's no way for us to tell right now."

Collins blinked. "There were bodies yesterday. I saw them," she whispered. Then she squared her shoulders. She took out a small tape recorder. The photographer was wandering around the edges of the pit taking pictures. "You be careful now. Don't get close to the edge," warned Turner.

"Chief Turner, does this fire have any relation to the fire yesterday in Carriage Circle?" she said in a professional voice.

"In terms of how the fires burned, yes. Do we know if they were caused by the same thing, no."

"Chief, is there an arsonist on the loose in Aronston?"

Turner patiently answered her questions. Finally, she asked, "In all your years in Philadelphia, have you ever seen any fires like this, and if so, what caused them?"

"No, I have never seen anything like this, but I will find out what, who, and why. And when I do, you'll be the first to know." He grinned at Collins.

She switched off the tape recorder and looked at Turner. Her streaked hair was cut in a short, fashionable layered style that drew attention to her hazel eyes. There was a worry crease between them now.

"God, Marc, I hope you do. This is beginning to scare me. Call me later, okay?" She walked away, turned and waved as she got into the car.

His wide mouth set in a thin line, Marcus Turner decided he'd figure this out if it were the last thing he did. He waved back and watched Vicky Collins drive away. For a few moments he'd almost liked her.

# 25

Roger slowly opened his eyes. He remembered everything.

*Why me?* he wondered again.

As if in answer, a series of images again unspooled inside his head. He saw a sturdy, little boy, about three years old, with strawberry-blond hair. The boy was dressed in old-fashioned clothing. He reached down and picked up a tiger-striped kitten that was playing with its littermates in the grass by the barn. He stroked the small body gently with a chubby hand.

Then the child put one hand on the kitten's head. He began twisting it as if to unscrew it from its body. The kitten was able to get out one pathetic mew before its neck broke with a grating crunch. The little boy threw the kitten down as if it was a broken toy and it lay twitching in the grass. The head hung loosely at a crazy angle from the tiny, furry body. Roger saw the boy grinning down at the kitten's body, an unpleasant, twisted grin on the round baby face.

Roger saw a row of frogs down by the creek, each one impaled on a carefully sharpened stick. They kicked feebly as their jewel-like eyes glazed over. Their skin cracked in the hot sunshine. Again he could see the boy with the cruel smile, just watching the frogs die slowly at the side of the creek.

He saw the same boy as a teenager, drunk, flames lighting up his face. Now the boy was a man, kicking a bloodied and terrified young girl huddled in a corner, cringing away from the blows. The same pretty young girl he had punched in the face a few hours ago.

*What the hell is this?* Roger thought. The images looked like a late-night movie, set in early America. But they also seemed like memories. *What's the connection?* he wondered. *What links some Mayan . . . thing to a Colonial-era sadist? And how do they connect to me?*

Half-formed thoughts sped through his consciousness again. A voice, garbled and indistinct muttered something about a permanent place to stay. A place from which to use power. A compatibility of spirit. A melding of potential, ambition, and desires.

*So, this otherness in me. It likes me. There's something in me that makes it stay. Something even crueler and sicker. Something that was in me—all along.*

*The nightmares I have . . . could they be memories?*

*Please God, help me.*

Roger got up and began walking back toward the town. It was a long dusty walk and the afternoon shadows lengthened as he strode along. It never dawned on him that the police might be looking for him. Fortunately for Roger, they weren't. Not yet.

# 26

Roger glanced at his watch. Four-thirty. Where could he go? He had no home, no job. Well, he could go back to Mama Angelina's and be fired. Get his car anyway, if he could find the keys. Then he'd take Colette home. The idea warmed him as he remembered the previous night.

After they went into her apartment, he'd stripped off Colette's wet and torn clothing. She had lain down on her bed, trembling in anticipation as he lay down next to her. As if to atone for his earlier brutal behavior in the parking lot, he tenderly explored every inch of Colette's body. She moaned in delight, opening herself, surrendering to him completely. Then it was his turn to be pleasured. She kissed him all over, using her lips and tongue to caress and excite. Finally she mounted him, squeezing him with her slim legs, whimpering with exquisite ecstasy as he stroked her pretty breasts and pushed deeper and deeper inside her, where it was dark, hot, silky, and wet. Nothing ever felt so good. He came inside her many times, feeling like he could never have enough of her. He smiled as he remembered.

But even as he saw Colette in his mind, she blurred a little. Another image was superimposed on his mental picture of the beautiful woman on the bed. Her hair became longer and darker and her body shorter and more slender. She had sun-kissed skin and a jade ring in her nose. And the same eager, hungry expression Colette had last night.

*Xochitl,* whispered the distant voice.

The name resonated in his mind. He quickened his pace.

He turned and walked up the driveway that led to the plant. As he approached the office doors, he heard voices. The windows were open to the warm late afternoon breezes.

A man's voice said, "Hey babe, remember me? Had to pass by this burg and thought I'd change your mind for you. Brought you these." There was a rustle of tissue paper, the kind they wrapped flower bouquets in.

"No such luck. Get yourself out of here before I report you to your supervisor," Colette retorted, angrily. There was a soft thud as the flowers landed in the wastebasket.

"I'm an independent. Got no supervisor, unless you want to meet me privately to discuss my conduct." The man laughed and he heard Colette sigh in irritation.

There was a pause. "Look. Read my lips. Not interested, not now, not ever."

"Hey, what's with the image change? You look great, but I loved that little dress you had on the other day. Little being the operative word here." The man laughed again, captivated by his own wit.

Roger's mouth twisted with rage. The rage felt good, like a purifying fire. Again he could hear the Other, whispering half-heard commands into his mind. And then the urge to hurt, to torture and maim, began flowing in his blood. His heart pounded. Again his sense of self slipped away, and the Other took control. His mind began to race, quickly forming a plan.

He turned and saw an idling tractor-trailer with "Davis Trucking" painted on the cab. It was parked in the lot near the loading dock.

*That has to be his,* he thought. Quickly he walked over to

the truck, glancing around to be sure no one was watching. The door was unlocked. A sleeper cab. Good. Moving speedily, yet stealthily, Roger moved around to the dock door. He saw that nobody was in the receiving office. Not too many deliveries came in this late on a Friday afternoon. The paperwork scattered on the desk and the absence of a coffee mug indicated that it was break time. Excellent. But not much time. He walked in, passed through the office and into the plant.

He grabbed a white coat from a peg and put in on. Less conspicuous that way. Roger walked to the back of the plant, where the meat was cut into chunks for processing. On a huge butcher-block table he found what he was looking for. A meat cleaver lay next to a side of beef, its owner apparently also on a break. Roger slipped the cleaver under the coat and darted back outside to the truck. He climbed in and closed the door. He slipped into the narrow bunk in the back, hid among the bunched-up blankets, and waited.

He did not have to wait long. He heard someone whistling as they approached the truck. The door opened, then slammed shut.

"I'll wear her down sooner or later. Then I'll make her beg for it," Dave Davis chuckled under his breath. Suddenly he stopped. The uneasy feeling was back, more intense than ever. The same feeling he'd had when he picked up the load at the marine terminal in South Philly.

*Got to start getting more sleep,* he thought. He released the brake, put the truck in gear, and pressed down on the accelerator.

An unbelievable, searing pain shot through his right shoulder. Blood spurted everywhere, covering the windshield. Davis looked down at the huge gash in his shoulder that nearly severed his right arm. He screamed, but with the cab windows up and the engine on, nobody heard. Nobody heard as the cleaver bit into his groin, castrating him. Finally he was decapitated with one smart blow to the neck. Nobody saw the cleaver flashing behind the gore-smeared windows. In about three minutes, Dave Davis was nothing but chunks of meat and bone and brains.

The truck lurched into gear and began rolling down the driveway. A white-coated, hair-netted woman came out on the loading dock as the truck was pulling away.

"Goddamn it, where the fuck could that thing have gone? Who's got my fucking cleaver?" she shouted.

Suddenly a blinding white explosion came from the truck. The building shook. Windows cracked. A few moments later, people came streaming out from Mama Angelina's. As they did so, there was a second explosion. The blackened meat cleaver flew through the air and landed on the loading dock with a clang, just inches from the woman's foot. She jumped back in terror. Less than a second later, a human arm, skin gray and bubbling, thudded onto the dock. The woman screamed, gibbering with horror.

During the shouting and screaming and confusion, no one saw Roger jump from the passenger door, scurry around the fence, and disappear.

# 27

Hope my Tracy gets here soon. Hasn't been a good day. That damn nurses' aide trying to give me a sponge bath with cold water this morning. Nice start to the day right there. Stupid girl slopped the water all over the bed, too, and then blamed me. Said "Look what you made me do, you old bastard you." She was new, though. Thought I was another senile old goat, like all the other bits of human flotsam locked up in here. Didn't know I still had all my marbles. I looked her right in the eye and said, "I didn't make you spill that water and you know it. Now go and warm that water up or I'll call your supervisor." She sure wasn't expecting that. She warmed up the water, though she wasn't too happy about it. Didn't say another word to me for the rest of the day. Just hope the little bitch stays out of my way. Sorry, Kitty. Guess I'm just too mad to use my vocabulary.

Spent the day looking down in the square. Bunch of kids from the college working like beavers building a stage for

*Shawn's play. One of the most misbegotten ideas for a play I ever heard of. For the life of me I wish I never said anything. Its not like I'm the only one ever knew about Aaron Moyer. It's in the books. You could go to the library and look it up. Even look at the newspapers from back then. They got 'em on microfilm. See a lot worse on TV these days, too. And in the papers.*

*I feel like a witch that cast a spell by accident. Like in that Mickey Mouse movie where everything goes crazy on him. The mops and the buckets dancing around, flooding the house. Now the spell is starting to work and I don't know what it's doing. All I know is I don't like it. I must be going nuts. Nutty as a fruitcake, that's me.*

*And the things I'm seeing. The fires, the dead. No place I recognize and no one I know. None of it making any sense.*

*This godforsaken place finally got to me, I guess. Finally drove me crazy, just like I thought it would. The noise and the smells and the screams. And every other day it seems they're taking another body out of here. Guess my turn is coming soon. I wish Tracy would get here. She always makes me feel better. My dearest Tracy.*

*Great God in Heaven! What was that! An explosion? Rattled my window something fierce. Lucky it didn't break. See if I can get this chair any closer. Come on chair, work, damn you. My God, look at that! A big white fireball over there. Is it Bardwell's?*

*No. Not Bardwell's. Thank goodness. I'd be worried sick about my girl. No, it looks like the meatball place, Mama Angelina's. Looks like the whole damn plant blew up. Odd, don't see much smoke. Just that white flame, kinda like the sun on a real bright day.*

*There go the sirens. Fire trucks on their way. Second time today, too. Couldn't see anything from my window, but I heard the nurses talking about it. Someone's house. Couldn't catch a name. Said the place was totally burned away. Nothing left but the cellar. The Downey place burned like a fireball, too, newspaper said. They thought it might be a gas explosion. Three gas explosions in two days? Hard to believe.*

*Just got a chill down my spine. They say that happens*

*when someone walks on your grave. No, that's not it. It's that I saw this before. I saw this fire. This bright white fire and no smoke. It was only for a second, so I couldn't see where it was, but I know I've seen this fire before. I know it.*

*Nothing natural burns so white and smokeless. Aaron Moyer's come back, come back to kill us all.*

*Now Levi, you stop this nonsense. Aaron's been dead two hundred years and there ain't no such thing as ghosts. It's probably just like they said. Gas explosions. Line must be leaking or something. Or something . . .*

*Tracy girl, get here soon. Please. I don't know why but I'm scared. Real scared.*

# 28

It was after 7:00 P.M. Marcus Turner, Vicky Collins, Darren Keller, and Colette Walls stood a small distance from the black and twisted remains of the truck. Scott Herr and a few other firemen continued to ply their hoses on the steaming metal and rubber. The *Clarion* photographer was busy getting some action shots in the fading light. Turner scowled and pounded his fist into his hand.

"Damn, it just doesn't make sense. Third one of these fires in two days."

"What do you mean, these fires?" Darren asked.

"These super-hot fires. I have two houses that burned down to the ground. Now this. We had to hose this baby down from fifty feet away and even that was too close. Should have been a lot of smoke from the rubber and plastic on the truck, but there was almost no smoke at all. Damn." He looked at Darren. "Sorry. Guess I shouldn't be venting my frustration on you."

Vicky Collins looked at Turner. "Can I quote you on that?" Turner pretended not to hear her.

Darren looked over at the scorched brick, cracked windows, and blistered paint on the side of the building. "'Lette, I'm going to need the name and number of our insurance agent. I'll get him out here over the weekend to assess the damage." His mind was racing. For some reason the *Inquirer* headline popped into his head. Incendiary fires . . .

"Do you know if anyone was in that truck?" asked Collins.

"I think it was the guy from Davis Trucking. He said his name was Dave." Colette shuddered, torn between pity and revulsion.

"Was he delivering anything to you? Anything that might be explosive?" Collins held out her tape recorder.

"He wasn't delivering anything to us. He just . . ." Colette paused for a moment, and then finished. "He just stopped by, I guess."

"He was an asshole who was hitting on my secretary, that's what," Darren said angrily. Colette stared at him, eyebrows raised. "What else he had in that truck, no one knows."

Turner sighed. "According to the witnesses, the cab exploded first, so it wasn't any cargo he had. As far as I can tell now, the trailer was empty. Well, I suppose it's a blessing it happened here in a parking lot and not in the middle of Route 222. He wouldn't have been the only person killed." He began to walk toward the wreck. "We'll have this out of here by tomorrow. Have a good weekend, folks."

Vicky Collins looked at Darren and Colette. "What happened to your employee? The woman who nearly got hit with the knife and the . . . body parts?"

"It was a cleaver, actually. The plant manager, George Newell, took her to the hospital. Her name is Sylvia Herrera. She was pretty shaken up." Darren replied. "Is there anything else you need, Vicky? I need to get back to work."

"If I think of anything, I'll call. Guess I'll head over to the hospital and see if I can talk to George and Sylvia. Colette, I might need to talk to you more about the driver, since you were . . . acquainted with him. Might be a story there. Thanks for your help, and I'll see you later." Vicky went to collect her photographer.

Darren turned to Colette. "Did your car get scorched?"

She grinned shakily. "Nope. There's a reason I park it at the end of the lot. How about yours?"

"It's going to need a new paint job, but other than that it's okay. Did you see Sylvia's car?"

"Melted, just about. It was only ten feet from the truck when it exploded."

Darren looked at Colette. He said, slowly, "There was another car, too, that got burned badly. A white sedan. I think it belongs to our AWOL night guard." He watched her closely, gauging her reaction.

Colette sighed, then shrugged. "Poor Sylvia," she murmured.

"She was screaming hysterically. I wonder if she's stopped yet."

"For heaven's sake, Darren, don't you think you'd be a little upset if you nearly got your foot cut off with a meat cleaver and then clobbered by a severed arm?" She raised an eyebrow and met his gaze. "You're a little upset yourself. I heard what you said about Dave Davis."

"Sorry, 'Lette. But the guy was definitely an obnoxious prick, and it would have gotten worse. Where'd you find that loser, anyway?"

"Same place I found you." She stuck her tongue out at him and Darren laughed.

"Friends again?" he asked, trying to sound casual.

Colette grinned. "Absolutely. I need all the friends I can get." A small chill in the pit of her stomach reminded her that her statement was a little too true.

Darren offered his arm to her. "Let's go and I'll help you get that insurance information. It's been a hell of a week." She took his arm and hugged it, and they walked back inside the main office.

**29**

Tracy ran into the ElderCare Center. She was
late because the police had traffic detoured around Mama Angelina's, and it was a real mess. A real mess for Aronston,
anyway. Not only was there the usual amount of traffic, but
the out-of-towners were beginning to arrive for the Founders'
Days festivities. And of course every other street in Aronston
was one-way, going the wrong way. A ten-minute drive took
Tracy forty minutes, including the stop at the Coffeeteria, one
of the new espresso bars that opened up in the last year. She
had almost forgotten that she promised Pop-Pop some good
coffee.

She slowed down just long enough to glare at the receptionist, who was filing her nails noisily and looking bored and
sullen. Excuse the world for expecting you to work for a living,
thought Tracy as she pressed the elevator button.

Tracy had always been ambitious. As a child she was fear-
less and competitive. She tagged along with the older chil-

dren. She played baseball and touch football with them. She rode her bike as fast and far as they did. She swam in the deep parts of the creek like they did. On the rare occasions when she couldn't keep up, she learned from her defeats. Then she tried again with renewed effort.

She worked hard to be one of the brightest at school. She was valedictorian of her senior class and a formidable lacrosse player, taking her team to the championship. She went to Drexel University in Philadelphia with the idea of becoming an engineer.

She fell in love with the city. Independence Mall. The wonderful restaurants. The rich history. Society Hill with its beautifully preserved colonial homes. The vitality of the open-air Italian Market in South Philly. The stately elegance of Chestnut Hill. She even loved the Mummers with their jangly string-band music and their satin, sequins, and feathers.

She switched her major to business, hoping to find a job in the city and make it her home. But when she came home for the summer, after receiving her B.A. degree, she saw how frail Levi was becoming. She knew she would have to decide soon whether to go back to Philly or stay in Aronston with her Pop-Pop.

She adored her great-grandfather. He was her cheering section and her confidante when she was younger, consoling her when she couldn't run as fast or play as hard as the big kids, when they called her a twerp and told her to go home. As she grew older, they remained close. She loved to listen to his stories of the "olden times," and she knew he loved to tell them to her. Pop-Pop was the constant in her life. Her parents' marriage cooled considerably and her father was frequently absent. Rather than stay home and listen to her mother's bitter rantings, she escaped to Pop-Pop's warm old house full of old photos and books, and dusty curiosities he would tell her about, and she let him fuss over her as if she were a rare treasure. He became a surrogate father to her. Best of all, he was not afraid to show Tracy how much he loved her, and she enjoyed taking care of him as he grew feeble. There was always enough time for him.

As much as she loved Philadelphia, when it came to her

Pop-Pop there really was no choice. Tracy took a job at Bardwell's as an assistant manager. She vowed to make top management by her thirty-fifth birthday. She bought a tiny old house in the historic district and furnished it in a style that would have pleased Emma Bardwell immensely.

Tracy was not a beauty, but she was elegant. She had her mother's dark eyes and hair, and a sense of true style. She did not lack for dates, but she had no time for romance. Work and Pop-Pop were the only commitments she was willing to make.

As soon as she entered Levi's room, she knew something was wrong. Levi sat in his usual spot by the window, but his face was pale and drawn. The evening sun lit up his profile in red-gold light and made him look as though he'd aged ten years since yesterday. Tracy's heart ached for him.

"Hey, Pop-Pop. Got your coffee here," she said softly so as not to startle him.

Levi turned and looked at her. He smiled wanly.

"My Tracy. Come here and hug your old Pop-Pop." His voice was quavering. He held out his arms to her.

She leaned down and gave him a bear hug. "Why, Pop-Pop! You're so cold! Let me get you another blanket. You shouldn't be sitting next to that window when you're cold like this." Tracy bustled around the room scolding Levi, getting blankets and taking the lids off the coffee cups, which were still hot, and gave one to Levi. She rested on the arm of the wheelchair and smiled down at her Pop-Pop.

"There. That'll warm you up."

Levi looked at the coffee and then up at Tracy. He had a teasing gleam in his eye and looked like her Pop-Pop again and not some confused old man. "Little girl, this isn't one of those fancy 'chino coffees, is it?"

Tracy laughed. "Nope. Plain old coffee with cream. Real cream, too, not that powdered junk. I have the fancy coffee. A mocha latte. You just don't know what you're missing, Pop-Pop."

"If it ain't broke, I ain't fixing it. I like my coffee just like this. And this is real good, Tracy. Thanks, honey." He took a big sip of coffee and patted Tracy's arm gently. "Guess the fire made you late, Tracy girl?"

Tracy nodded. "What a mess by Mama's. A truck blew up or something. The plant's okay, mostly, from what I hear. Driver was killed, blown apart, they say. Someone on the loading dock almost got conked by an arm or a leg."

"Did you hear about the fire this morning?" asked Levi, casually.

Tracy nodded again. "It's so weird, Pop-Pop. We were just talking about him last night. It was Roger Phillips' house. Nobody knows for sure if anyone was home when it happened because the house was totally destroyed. But Roger, Wendy, and the kids are all missing. I found out Roger's been missing since last night."

Tracy sighed. She really liked Roger and knew how unfair Bardwell's was to him. Guilt at her own part in Roger's dismissal pinched at her, also. Now that Downey was dead, she thought of calling Roger, to see if he was interested in coming back to Bardwell's. Too late now, she thought. She sighed again.

Levi felt the same strong chill down his spine he felt when thinking about Aaron's ghost. For a moment the room dissolved and he saw Tracy sitting across from Roger at a table. In a restaurant, it looked like. She was laughing. Then Roger's face subtly changed and it was the cruel face of Aaron Moyer, his icy eyes looking his precious great-granddaughter up and down. Then he was back in his own room, with the scent of coffee and Tracy's perfume in his nose.

Fear rose up in his throat like bile, sour and burning. He needed to warn Tracy.

"Honey, I promised you I wouldn't talk crazy tonight, but you listen to me. I have a feeling Roger isn't dead. He'll turn up real soon. When he does, make sure you steer clear. Promise me?"

Tracy frowned. "Pop-Pop, what makes you say that? Besides, I'm over thirty. I can handle just about anything, thank you." She looked at Levi and saw how fragile he looked. His bony, blue-veined hands were wrapped around the coffee cup as though it was the only warmth left in the world. They shook a little as he raised the cup to his lips. The skin on his face was like a crumpled paper bag draped over his skull, and so thin she could see the veins just under the skin. He's only trying to protect me, she thought. He's the one who needs protection.

She stroked his hair, still thick, soft and white as snow. "Don't worry about me, okay? There are younger heads than yours to do all this worrying," she said tenderly. "I love you, Pop-Pop. Even if you are a little nuts. I kind of always thought you were anyway." She kissed the top of his head and grinned down at him.

Levi grinned back. "You weren't so sane yourself, little girl. I remember you and the rope swing over the creek. You'd come running down the hill that led down from the house in your bathing suit, all arms and legs and hair flying, screaming like a banshee. Then you'd leap for that swing and go flying out over the water and splash! Into the creek you'd go. Your cousins were all scared to do it, but not you. And you were only seven years old." He shook his head and chuckled at the memory. "Your great-grandma used to say you had nine lives, just like a cat. And you weren't afraid of anything."

Tracy laughed, too, and put her arms around Levi's neck. It was good to sit with someone you loved and remember when life was simple, she thought. Everything was a big adventure, and the world was your playground. Especially when you were seven years old and afraid of nothing.

"Guess I got it from you, Pop-Pop. You aren't afraid of anything, either, are you?"

Levi was silent.

# 30

Byron Mirkowski walked slowly up Chestnut Street on his way home from Mama Angelina's. He was frightened badly by the explosions and the fire, and then fascinated by the efficiency of the firemen as they worked on the blazing truck. Scottie Herr let him come closer than anyone else to watch.

"You stay right there, Byron. This is a hot one. And don't get in anyone's way."

"I won't, Scottie." He stood and watched until steam no longer rose from the melted and twisted wreckage. Then he decided it was time to go home.

Home was a room in a boardinghouse at the other end of town. Byron walked three miles in each direction every day. But tonight was special because of the fair. He could smell the hot grease from the french fry and funnel cake trailers. There was the delicate fruit-and-sugar scent of cotton candy and the artificial buttery smell of popcorn. Byron's mouth watered.

He reached into his pocket and felt for his money. Today was payday. George Newell took him to the bank at lunchtime and helped him fill out the deposit slip. The tellers all knew Byron and said hello to him, even though Friday lunch hour was their busiest time all week. The one who took his check gave him a lollipop.

"Thank you," said Byron politely.

"There now, Byron. Twenty, forty, sixty, eighty, one hundred. Don't spend it all in one place," she said, smiling.

Byron didn't quite understand what she meant, but he smiled back. "See you next week. 'Bye."

His parents were professors at Gretna College. They married when they were both in their late thirties and were surprised and delighted to discover that they would have a child. They dreamed of raising an intellectual and artistic prodigy, even selecting the name of a famous poet for their boy.

Byron turned out to be a boy with a kind and gentle disposition but one who would never progress beyond a third-grade level. His parents were bitterly disappointed. They were unable to enjoy their son's small gifts at all and regarded his mild retardation as a crushing blow. Finally, finding it impossible to cope with him, or more accurately, their feelings about him, they sent him off to the Aronston County Boys Home at the earliest possible age. Their visits to Byron became fewer and farther between.

Byron did not miss them much. He knew that somehow he had managed to let them down in a big way, and they had not shown him any real tenderness since he was very young. Better to forget about them and play with his new friends. He was naturally a cheerful little boy, and he endeared himself to the teachers and attendants at the home. Even his schoolmates accepted him. New boys might come and try to bully Byron, but they soon found themselves beaten to a pulp by the other students.

For most of his life, people were kind and patient with him and he responded with loyalty and affection. Instances of cruelty always left him bewildered and uncomprehending. His landlady, Miss Helen, tried to explain that there were always a few bad apples out there and that he mustn't let it bother him. But it was so hard to forget the leering faces, stinging words, and nasty laughter of those who hurt him.

At the street fair, Byron moved along with the crowd on the grassy median of Chestnut Street, enjoying it all. The food smells, the high-pitched, happy sound of children, the calls of the hucksters at the concessions, and the music the band was playing in the old bandshell near the town square. On the other side of the square there were rides for the children, including pony rides. Along the edges of the square were craft booths, selling colorful quilts, handcrafted jewelry, stained glass and pottery, and many other beautiful and impractical things.

Byron stopped at a food truck. He bought a hot dog and french fries and sat down on the curb to eat them. A little girl with tousled blonde hair walked up to him and smiled.

"Look what my daddy won for me!" She held out a bright purple stuffed poodle that looked as though it would not survive a week before it fell apart.

"That's really nice," Byron said in his slow way. "Can I see it?"

The girl thought it over. "I guess so. For a minute."

Byron took it from her and looked it over. "This is really nice," he said again and handed it back to her. He smiled at her eager little face with blue cotton candy sugar all over it.

"Ashley!! There you are! Hey, Byron, how's it going?" Mel Ehst, who worked on the grinders at Mama's, smiled at them. "Taking care of my little runaway for me?"

"She showed me her dog," said Byron.

Ashley giggled. "Byron's a funny name," she said. "Maybe I'll name my doggie Byron."

Mel choked back a laugh and frowned, trying to look sternly at his daughter. "The first thing you have to do, Ash, is not take off like that. You have to stay with me or I'll give your doggie back to the man at the booth. The second thing is, don't talk to strangers. Ever. You're almost five years old and you know better. You're just lucky I know Byron here from work or I'd . . . I'd . . ." Mel tried to think of a dire threat. But his daughter already knew how to manage him.

"Oh, Daddy, let's go to the side across the square. Please? I want to ride the pony again, and you have to walk next to me." Ashley smiled up at her father.

Mel sighed. "Oh, okay, Ash. Geez, you are spoiled." He grinned and picked her up and put her on his shoulders.

" 'Bye, Mr. Byron. Say bye to my doggie, Byron."

" 'Bye," said Byron dutifully.

"See you Monday, Byron," Mel said and off they went into the crowd.

Byron finished his dinner and bought some cotton candy. He sat back down on the curb and admired the hundreds of colorful Chinese lanterns strung into the trees along Chestnut Street and through the square, illuminating the fair with their soft light. He watched the people go by, laughing and looking and buying. A clown meandered through the crowd, giving balloons to the children. Another one was blowing up long, skinny balloons and twisting them into animal shapes. Byron stared, fascinated, as a few quick twists produced a bunny or a dog or a giraffe. The music swelled around him. The recent rash of fires didn't seem to have scared anyone off, as there was a good crowd of both tourists and local people promenading along the street.

He finished his cotton candy, got up and began walking toward the square. A voice stopped him.

"Hey, buddy, over here. Three balls for fifty cents. Win a prize for your lady friend."

Byron looked over. He saw a trailer with three big painted targets in it. Each target had a hole in the center. Surrounding the targets was a profusion of brightly colored plush animals, all with take-me-home expressions embroidered on their faces. A bored concessionaire was seated at one end of the trailer. He flicked his cigarette and gestured at him. "Yeah, you. Come on over. Three balls for fifty cents."

Byron ambled over. "What do I win?"

"Three balls in the target wins one of these." He indicated the stuffed animals strung up along the back of the trailer. Byron noticed a purple dog like the one Ashley Ehst had.

"Maybe Miss Helen would like that purple dog," Byron said slowly.

"You betcha she would, buddy." The huckster, a fat, bald man in a dirty T-shirt, pulled three baseballs out from under the counter and laid them on the counter. "That's fifty cents."

Byron fumbled in his pocket, pulling out a fistful of change. He put it all on the counter and carefully counted out fifty cents. The huckster's eyes widened as he realized that Byron might not have all the lights on upstairs. Then he licked his lips.

"C'mon, buddy. Do it for Miss Helen."

Byron threw the first ball awkwardly. It missed the target hole and bounced onto the floor.

"Could that be for practice?" Byron asked, timidly.

"Nope. Gotta get all three in for the big prize."

Byron threw the other two and got one in. "Hey, I did one!" he said, delightedly.

"Try again, try again. I know Miss Helen would love that dog." The huckster's tone was so earnest, he almost believed himself.

Byron did try. Finally, triumphant and ten dollars poorer, he tucked the purple dog under his arm and walked across the square. He thought he might show Ashley that he had a purple doggie, too. For Miss Helen. But he had lost track of the time. It was late now, the music from the bandshell was rock n' roll, and the fairgoers now were mostly teenagers.

Byron did not see the group of four teenage boys who were watching him struggle to win the dog. They whispered to each other, snickered nastily, and began to follow Byron up Chestnut Street.

The kiddie rides were nearly empty, and the patient ponies were given the rest of the night off. Byron watched them munch their hard-earned hay. Since there were no children around, he decided to go back to the square and sit down. Maybe Mel and Ashley would pass by. He'd watch for them.

He turned around and found his path blocked by the boys. He tried to go around them but they kept moving in front of him.

"Hey, you're the town retard, aren't you?" one boy asked, tauntingly.

Byron felt a clutch of fear. He'd seen that sneering expression too many times. He stopped and gripped Miss Helen's dog tightly.

The boys smelled Byron's fear. "Yeah, he's a retard. A retard with his toy dog." A second boy hawked and spat. The glob of snot landed inches from Byron's feet.

"I won this dog for Miss Helen," Byron said. His voice quivered a little.

"Ain't that sweet. The retard's got a girlfriend."

"What kind of girl would want to fool around with a moron like you? You're a lying sack of shit."

"He's a pervert, man. Probably likes to play with little girls."

"Go away!" cried Byron. "Let me alone!" He was trying not to cry. His knees began to tremble.

"Make us, retard." They closed ranks and moved toward him, threateningly.

"Y'know, my kid sister might like that dog. Maybe we should take it from him."

"Yeah, and maybe his wallet, too." They laughed and moved closer to the terrified Byron. One boy was smoking a cigarette. He blew a mouthful of acrid smoke into Byron's pale, sweating face. "Then we can beat the shit out of him for being a pervert."

"Shit, man, who needs a fuckin' reason to beat up a retard?" They laughed.

Byron looked around wildly, trying to escape. Tears were blurring his vision. Then a voice came from behind him and made him jump.

"Evening, Byron." Byron spun around to see Police Chief Eddie Haas strolling up the median behind him. Chief

Haas was a big, burly, heavyset man who was always smiling. Behind the easy smile was a good cop.

He had lived in Aronston all his life and knew almost everyone in town. During Founders' Days he enjoyed patrolling the street fair himself instead of sitting behind his desk at the police station. It was a chance to say hello to everyone, as well as an excuse to get out and walk around. The extra police presence didn't hurt, either. Right now it appeared that there were four young punks who needed to be taught a lesson.

He looked the boys up and down for a few long seconds, as their threatening swaggers suddenly turned into nervous posing. They tried to keep looking tough and failed utterly. Eddie Haas pulled out his nightstick and tapped his palm with it gently. He took a few steps toward the group.

"Lester Murphy, I think your mother wants you. That goes for you other boys, too." His eyes narrowed. "Think I'll have to give your mothers a call, let them know what you've been up to tonight. By the way, Rodney Guydish, does your mother know you're smoking?" The boys stood mute. Chief Haas smiled. "Run along home now. I don't want to see you back here tonight." The boys backed up a few paces, then scattered like leaves in the wind.

Eddie Haas chuckled. "I know Mrs. Murphy's gonna let young Lester have what for. Think the other folks will, too." He turned to Byron. "Are you okay? Those are a mean bunch of boys. Not bad, just mean and cowardly. Punks."

Byron wiped his eyes with the dog. Little bits of purple fuzz stuck to his face. He was too frightened and hurt to speak. Eddie put his nightstick away and sighed. Damn kids, picking on a guy like Byron Mirkowski, he thought. Let me catch them again and . . .

"Hey, Byron. You know, it's kinda late. Bet Miss Helen's worrying about you. How about if I have Officer Schutter give you a ride home in a real police car?"

Byron nodded silently. Eddie said "Okay, c'mon with me," and walked Byron up to a cruiser parked on the Gretna Road.

Officer Schutter was happy to oblige and tried to engage

Byron in conversation, but Byron remained silent. Finally, they pulled up to a big old farmhouse. An elderly, arthritic woman opened the door. Byron jumped out of the car, ran over to her, put his head on her bony old shoulder, and cried and cried as she patted his back and murmured comforting words.

# 31

It was nearly 7:30 P.M. Roger pulled his clothes out of Colette's dryer and put them on. They felt warm and fresh against his skin. No trace of bloodstains anywhere. Roger looked at the box of detergent on top of the dryer. Damn, this stuff is good, he thought. Maybe I should write the manufacturer. *Dear Soap Company, I'm a serial killer and there's nothing like your product to remove those messy bloodstains. . . .*

He guessed that Colette would have to stay late tonight and help her boss take care of the mess at Mama's. After igniting the truck, he hurried back to her apartment, knowing he had to get cleaned up before she saw him. His face, hair, and clothes had been encrusted with blood and body fluids from Dave Davis' corpse. One of the hazards of dismembering a body in a small, confined space. He had stripped naked, thrown the clothes in the washing machine, and then taken a long shower. Now he was ready for her.

It was the first time since the Downey fire that killing had been such a pleasure, a hands-on job, up close and real personal. It had been thoroughly satisfying to hear Dave Davis scream in pain, to bury the cleaver deep in his groin. How wonderful to know that Davis knew he was castrated. The oversexed bastard died a eunuch. Roger grinned with his new, cruel grin.

This time, he felt no pangs of regret or revulsion.

He walked into the living room, with its white walls, dark hardwood floor, and restored brick-and-wrought-iron fireplace. Colette had furnished it with Persian rugs and Victorian-style furniture. There were masses of silk flowers in huge gilded vases on the tables and mantel. In the round turret alcove she had placed a small settee, upholstered in a burgundy jacquard fabric and loaded with tasseled pillows. The effect was rich and warm and feminine, just like her.

Roger sat down among the pillows and gazed out the window, watching for the Corvette.

From his vantage point he could see down the street almost to the town square. The trees were just beginning to leaf out, so his view was relatively clear. He had driven through this section of Aronston hundreds of times but never seen it from this angle. The view was pretty in the fading light. The Victorian homes lining the street, with lights shining yellow in the windows, looked like something out of a Norman Rockwell painting. He could see lilacs and ornamental cherry trees in bloom. The breeze sent hundreds of tiny pink petals from the cherry blossoms flying through the air like snowflakes.

He could hear the sounds of the street fair half a block down on Chestnut Street. The old bandshell was host to several local bands during the fair, playing everything from ragtime to rock. Right now it was big band music. Roger found himself humming along with "Take the A Train." People strolled by the house on their way to the fair, their excited children laughing and giggling. He could hear the hucksters calling the fathers and boyfriends over to the chance games, playing on their hopes of being a bit of a hero in their loved ones' eyes.

Roger looked at the yellow lights and the black silhouettes

of buildings against the indigo sky. Then he closed his eyes and listened. The fair sounds gradually seemed to swell into a roar of voices, some angry, some horrified, some screaming. Roger's eyes flew open. The view wavered, then dissolved in front of Roger's eyes. He gasped. He saw a crowd, dressed in the fashion of two hundred years ago. He could see a gallows, with two bodies swinging from the ropes, writhing in agony, their feet kicking the air frantically. He leaped to his feet. Then he heard footsteps coming up the stairs and Colette's key in the lock. The vision disappeared. Roger took a deep breath and steadied his nerves.

Colette came in, her blue eyes alight with happiness at seeing him there.

"Hi there, you," she said.

"Hi, honey, how was your day?" Roger replied in a bantering tone.

"Oh, fine. Except for a truck blowing up in the parking lot." She came over to him and hugged him. She felt that strange electricity Roger possessed. It made her feel warm and excited.

"Tell me all about it." His lips met hers.

It wasn't until much later that Colette realized that a normal person would have been shocked and curious about the accident. A normal person would have asked her lots of questions, not taken her off to bed as if nothing had happened. But then, Roger was not a normal man.

Colette turned lazily to Roger. She felt utterly sated, like a cat dozing on a sunny windowsill after lapping up a saucer of milk. She pulled the sheet up over her body and propped her head on her elbow. The happy sounds of the street fair drifted in through the open window. She smelled french fries and hot dogs. She remembered that she had not had dinner for two nights running now. Yet, she was not hungry. Neither, apparently, was Roger.

Roger lay on his back, eyes closed. Never had he felt so satisfied, so happy. This Other had given him so much. He had power beyond his wildest dreams. He could kill with impunity. Anyone who crossed him would die, and painfully.

Nobody could refuse him anything he wanted. He could just take it.

He was in love with the most wonderful woman he had ever seen, and he knew she returned his love. She belonged wholly to him. The world belonged to him. Which was absolutely as it should be.

Stop, he thought. Hang on to yourself. This happiness, this peace, belongs to the Other. It's not Roger. Don't let this thing win. Remember Wendy and Bryan and Sarah.

Colette stroked his tousled, reddish hair. She knew she had to ask him some questions, and she feared the answers. I don't want to know, she thought. All I know is that he pleases me. Like nothing else, ever. And he's familiar, somehow. I've known him all my life. Even longer. And I love him. I *need* him.

Roger turned to her. He read the troubled expression on her face.

"You want to know, don't you?"

"Yes," she whispered and hung her head. She felt ashamed of her fear, ashamed of her lack of faith in him. Yet she had to know.

Roger said nothing. He took her hands in his and placed them over his heart. She felt the rhythmic pulse against her palms. Her mind shattered like glass into hundreds of images, like fragments of dreams. An ancient Mayan village. A king named Chac Mol. Sacrifices on a tall, stepped pyramid. Blood and screams of agony. Smoke writhing toward the sky. A beautiful woman named Xochitl, painted red with cinnabar and with eyes like hers. Chac Mol declaring his love in front of the entire city. An intense, romantic passion. Happiness beyond anything she had ever known. Murder . . . horrible deaths in the night. The end of everything . . . until now.

Roger watched closely as her eyes went blank, turning inward. Roger felt her trembling, then shaking violently as the memories flooded her brain. He watched the expression on her face change from fear to wonder to happiness to horror. With a tremendous wrench, she pulled away and sat up, facing him. Her eyes were her own again. They filled with tears as she looked at him.

"Oh my God . . . oh my God. . . ."

She got up and fled into the bathroom.

Roger heard her lock the door behind her, then the hiss of the shower as she turned it on and stepped in. Twenty minutes later, she came back into the bedroom, her hair wrapped in a towel. Her skin was pink from the scalding hot water she had used. She had tried to scrub the memories away, but could not. She sat down on the edge of the bed.

She looked at him silently for a long time, her expression a mix of anger and fear. Finally she spoke.

"I'm not Xochitl, okay? I'm Colette Walls. I live in the twentieth century, in a little town called Aronston in the middle of nowhere. You are not some king from a dead civilization. Your name is Roger Phillips. Your family is looking for you. And most of all, human sacrifice is called murder these days." Her voice was rising. "I know you won't hurt me—but I don't understand the power you have, and I can't, I won't be part of it. Not anymore."

Roger took her hand. He felt the energy flow from him. Colette abruptly stopped talking. She lay down on the bed, next to him. Her body relaxed and curled into his. He put his arm around her, under her neck. The part of him that was still human inside him struggled for voice.

"You will never be a part of this. I wouldn't let you." Roger shuddered. Colette sat up quickly and looked at him, surprised. In a choked voice he said, "Colette . . . we will find a way . . . we will beat this . . ." His body arched in pain and then he was still.

"Roger?" Colette asked anxiously.

"Sleep, my love," Roger said in an entirely different voice. His hand passed over her damp, uncombed hair and she lay down again, snuggling close to the warmth of his body. Her eyelids fluttered and closed, like a child's. Within moments she was in a deep sleep. Roger watched her for a long time before he too finally fell asleep.

# 32

Roger awoke to hear Colette cursing softly in the bathroom. He got up and went in to see what she was doing. She was wearing a dark blue silk robe and trying to get a comb through her tangled, slept-on-wrong hair.

"Good morning?" he said with a smile.

"Damn it to hell, why did you let me fall asleep with my hair wet?" Her mouth was set in an annoyed line as she sprayed conditioner on a particularly bad snarl and attacked it again with her comb.

"Sorry. It won't happen again. Look, about last night . . ."

"I don't want to discuss it now," she retorted. "At least, not until I've had my coffee. Would you mind?"

Roger wrapped a towel around his waist and padded out to the kitchen. He rummaged around until he found coffee and filters. Colette's kitchen was sparsely equipped. Apparently she didn't eat at home much. However, she did have a nice

coffeemaker. And there was fresh half-and-half in the refrigerator.

Roger poured the water into the coffeemaker and turned it
on. In a few moments, the wonderful aroma of brewing coffee filled the apartment.

Colette emerged from the bathroom, her frazzled hair tied
back loosely with a wide white ribbon, muttering something
about dealing with it later.

"Smells good, Roger." She smiled. "I'm sorry I snapped at
you."

"Understandable," said Roger. He poured two cups and
handed one to her.

"Hey, this is good coffee," she said after a sip. "I didn't
know they had coffee, or coffeemakers, a zillion years ago."
She smiled faintly at the feeble joke.

"Something tells me you want to talk," said Roger.

She sighed deeply. "First, let me tell you what I think and
you tell me if I'm right. You are Roger Phillips, long-lost security guard. Somehow you've been possessed by this Mayan
god or king or whatever it is. And this thing thinks I'm his
long-lost wife. Now the question is, what next? Other than we
both go to the loony bin?"

Roger studied her in silence for a few moments. Obviously
she was unaware that he had killed his family and his former
boss. All she had seen were the Mayan visions. Finally he
spoke.

"That's about right. There's two of us in here, Colette."

"Well, what do we do? Call Ghostbusters? An exorcist?"
She took a long sip of her coffee. "Plus there's an added attraction. I'm in love with you, but the question is, which
one?" She began to laugh, but not her usual infectious laugh.
It was a high-pitched, almost hysterical sound.

Roger reached out to hold her. She shied away. "No, don't
touch me. Strange things happen to me when you touch me. I
need to think clearly."

"Look, 'Lette . . ."

"Don't call me that," she said irritably. "Only Darren is allowed to call me 'Lette."

"Who's Darren? Darren Keller? The GM at Mama's?"

"The one and only," she replied. She could not conceal a small smile.

Roger felt a twinge of jealousy. His face darkened. Colette leaned back against the counter. She frowned back at him.

"Knock it off. He's my boss and my friend."

Roger was almost certain that Darren meant more to Colette that just a friend, but decided to let it go. For now. He said, "Well, as I was going to say, I'll go out this morning. That will give you some space to decide what you want to do. When I come back, we can talk some more."

"That's probably a good idea." She sighed. Without thinking, she reached out and patted his arm. "What was that you said last night about fighting this?"

Her vision clouded. It was a warm night and she was swimming naked in a lake. The full moon shone down on the lake, making the still surface gleam like a mirror. The trees and mountains surrounding the lake were bathed in the eerie, beautiful light. She took a deep breath of warm, fragrant air and dipped down under the water, swimming like a seal in the blackness.

The cool dark water refreshed and energized her. When she came up for another breath of air she noticed, as if it had always been so, that her skin was dark and her coal-black hair grew past her waist. She lay back into the wet coolness and let her hair float up around her like seaweed. She felt as if she belonged to this lake, to this night, and to this starry, moonlit sky. She sighed contentedly.

A movement on the lakeshore caught her eye. A man was waiting for her at the water's edge. Chac Mol from the dream she saw last night. Her heart beat faster with anticipation. She waded ashore, feeling the gentle breezes on her skin, silver rivulets of water streaming from her hair and her breasts, flowing down her thighs.

She reached up and took his face in her hands. He wrapped his arms around her and kissed her, over and over, as they stood on the soft grass of the lakeshore. She was enveloped by his love, fulfilled by his passion. She had never felt more alive than she did at this moment. She was totally, ecstatically, happy.

The man whispered, "Xochitl, my beautiful Xochitl."

She wrapped her arms around his neck and kissed him deeply. "You are my love, my god, my husband," she breathed back. They stood, embracing each other by the lake, for what seemed like hours.

When Colette came back to herself, she was standing alone in the middle of her kitchen. Her robe and the white ribbon she had tied her hair with were on the floor. As she bent to pick them up, a smooth, glossy curtain of silky, tangle-free hair fell over her face.

She felt utterly bereft and empty. "Come back, oh, come back," she cried into the silence of the lonely apartment. Then she shook her head and sighed deeply.

"Better yet, don't. Ever."

She wrapped her arms tightly around herself.

# 33

Marcus Turner sat at his desk in the Aronston Fire Company building. From the exterior, the firehouse was a lovely old 1880's-era red brick building, just a few blocks from the town square and carefully preserved according to Emma Bardwell's exacting standards. On the inside, it was a nightmare.

Although the building had been well maintained, it had never really been upgraded since they wired it for electricity. The walls had so many layers of paint that the fine details of the carved molding were obscured. The place was also noisy, lacking anything like carpeting or curtains to absorb sound. When the fire bells rang, the clanging was deafening. Turner had seen worse in Philadelphia, but that didn't make it any easier when he was trying to concentrate. At least the pumpers and the hook-and-ladder trucks were relatively new.

He slowly and carefully entered data into his laptop computer, cursing the mismatch between his big clumsy fingers and the tiny cramped keyboard. He had borrowed a state-of-the-art animation program from the Harrisburg Fire Department, hoping that a pattern would emerge from the three fires—how they burned, what they burned, a diagram of each site. He knew in his gut that he was dealing with arson on a level he had never seen before, but at this point he would consider anything.

As he finished entering the data, a Federal Express driver came in, envelope tucked under his arm.

"Didn't think I'd find anyone here on a Saturday. How're you doing, Chief?"

"Hanging in. You got something for me there?"

"Yepper." He handed Turner the envelope and a signature pad. "Had a hard time getting here, what with all the streets blocked off for the parade. And with all the one-way streets I felt like a fucking rat in a maze."

"Well, man, least it's only once a year."

"I tell you, the streets in this town can drive you nuts."

Turner was in no mood to listen to complaints this morning. He could have come up with a few of his own. He handed back the signature pad. "Nice talking to you, but I gotta get back to work here."

"No problem. Later."

When the driver had left, Turner opened the envelope. It was the fingerprint report from the crime lab. DNA tests would take a week or two.

Turner read aloud to himself. "Fingerprints belong to one Roger Phillips, U.S. Army, 82nd Airborne, honorable discharge, served Desert Storm in reserves 1990-91. Wife, two children, currently employed as security for Mama Angelina's Specialty Meats, Aronston, PA. No criminal record. Hmmm . . ."

The Phillips house was the one that burned yesterday. No way to determine if Roger had died in the flames or not. No one had seen him since he left for work on Wednesday. His car had been in the lot at Mama's since then. It had been melted to scrap metal yesterday in the truck fire. The Downey home had burned early Thursday morning. Carriage Circle was a couple of miles from Mama's, all the way over at the other end of town. How'd a cigarette butt get all the way over there? Unless Roger Phillips was the arsonist. But where was Roger Phillips? Why would he burn the Downey home, and his own? And there was the matter of the truck fire.

Turner decided it was time to give Police Chief Eddie Haas a call.

# 34

Darren got out of his car and gently shut the door so as not to awaken the rest of his family. Since there was no home delivery of the *Inquirer* in Aronston, Darren picked up the paper at the local 7-Eleven. During the week he stopped on his way to work, but on Saturday and Sunday he had to make a special trip. This morning, he returned home not only with the *Inquirer,* but with the *Clarion* and a box of doughnuts as well.

When they were younger, Corrine and Katelyn looked forward to their Saturday doughnuts all week, and when Darren came home they would dive for the box as though they were starving, and emerge sticky with powdered sugar and glaze all over their small hands and faces. Darren would sit at the kitchen table, drink his coffee, and read the paper while they ate their doughnuts. It was a small family ritual that Darren had always made time for, no matter how busy he was with school and work.

Now that his girls were teenagers, the doughnut ritual had become fraught with angst. They worried about gaining weight. Would the sugar and oil in the doughnuts make their faces break out? Dad, don't you know that doughnuts are terrible for your cholesterol? Still, Darren continued to bring them home. Most of the time they went stale and were thrown away, but he cherished the rare occasions when his daughters would deign to eat them with him.

Corrine was sitting at the kitchen table when he came home. She had a banana and a glass of orange juice in front of her.

"Hey, Pops," she said, smiling. She was her father's daughter in many ways, the most obvious one being her looks. She was slender but wiry. Her wavy chestnut hair spilled down her back, and she had hazel eyes that crinkled at the corners when she grinned. She wore braces on her teeth, which was the only difference between her expectant smile and her father's. She was wearing a white terry bathrobe over a T-shirt and was barefoot. Right now she had that warm, slightly confused look people have when they have just awakened.

Darren thought she was beautiful.

"Hey yourself, Queenie. I brought you some doughnuts." He put them on the table. Queenie was his special name for her. He had called her that since she was a toddler, trying to pronounce "Corrine" with her baby lisp.

"Eeeew, gross. Dad, they are sooo bad for you." She rolled her eyes and took a big bite of her banana.

"You've got a meet today. You'll work it off. Eat one for your old Pops." He poured himself a cup of coffee and sat down at the table with her.

She looked at him and made a face. Darren grinned. "You love them and you know it. Come on, just one."

"Well, okay. But only because I have a meet today." She picked out a powdered-sugar doughnut, handling it as though it were radioactive waste. Darren pretended to be absorbed in his paper. He didn't miss the look of satisfaction on her face after she took the first bite. Bananas don't make her look like that, he thought. They also don't give her a powdered-sugar moustache. As much as he wanted to laugh, he kept his face still. He knew that if he looked at her or said anything, the moment would be spoiled and she'd probably never touch a doughnut again.

"Can I have the sports section?" she asked with her mouth full. "Then I want to read about what's up with Founders' Days for tomorrow. Christy and I are going to watch the play. Too bad I have to miss the parade today."

Darren handed her the *Clarion.* "Forgot to ask you how the street fair was last night."

"Oh, it was okay. Kind of babyish, really. It was lots more fun when I went with you and you won stuff for me and Katie. I still have the stuffed monkey you won me when I was six." Darren grinned inwardly, enormously pleased with her almost offhand remark.

"Let's see," she said, leafing through the pages." I want to see if there's anything about our meet today. If we win, we have a chance at the state championship. Mom says you're going to come."

"I hope so, Queenie. We had a fire at the plant yesterday and I have to meet with the insurance appraiser."

"Yeah, I heard. A truck exploded or something."

"Read the front page and you'll know all about it." The front page was covered with photographs of the blazing truck. There was also one of the remains of the Phillips' home. Wonder what happened to Roger Phillips? Darren thought. We never did find out. And I never found out if Roger Phillips is Colette's Roger. Finding that his thoughts were leading in an uncomfortable direction, he turned back to his *Inquirer.*

Corrine rummaged through the sections on the table, looking for something interesting. When she thought Darren wasn't watching, she took another doughnut.

"Hey, Pops, look at this. We're studying them in school."

Darren looked. There was a feature article in the *Inquirer* on the artifacts unearthed by the ill-fated Los Naranjos archaeology team. There was a color photograph of a wonderfully intact pottery jar painted with Mayan glyphs and pictures. Next to it was a small jade ring.

"The Mayans were really cool. They had writing and

astronomy and calendars and stuff while Europe was in the
Dark Ages. This Los Naranjos site was in Honduras. I guess
that jar thing was a jewelry box, huh? Neat."

Darren was instantly interested. "Let me read that when
you finish, Queenie."

Katelyn came downstairs, yawning. "Eeewwww, I can't
believe you *ate* those fried hockey pucks," she said to Corrine. "Hi, Pops," she added as an afterthought.

"Open your mouth any wider and I'll shove one in," said
Corrine, embarrassed at having been caught with powdered
sugar on her face.

"There are some hockey pucks for you too, Katie. Now
stop bickering or you'll wake up your mother."

"Gross," Katelyn said by way of a thank-you. She padded
over to the refrigerator and poured herself a glass of orange
juice. She had dark hair, like her mother's, cut short, and was
small boned and fine-featured. Darren could not see any of
himself in his youngest daughter. She sat down at the table,
humming the "Hallelujah Chorus."

"Is that what you're singing in choir?" asked Darren.

Katelyn looked at him as if he were stupid. There's nothing like the contempt of a teenage girl, thought Darren. "Of
course, Pops," she said. She might just as well have said
"Duh".

"You sound like a sick cat," said Corrine, eating her third
doughnut. As long as she'd been caught, she figured she
might as well enjoy herself.

"Yeah, and you look like a pig," Katelyn retorted.

"That's it!" said Darren. "If you two are going to go at it,
I'm going to the den and read."

"I gotta take my shower anyway, Pops. Here's the paper."
Corrine went upstairs, ignoring the grunts and oinks from her
little sister. Darren glared at Katelyn, gathered up the newspapers, and retired to his den. He knew that after he left, Katelyn would eat a doughnut or two herself. That's why he'd
gotten the glazed ones for her.

He opened up the *Inquirer* to the Los Naranjos article and
began to read.

# 35

Shawn Williams looked over the hastily constructed stage in the middle of Aronston's town square, with the gallows set off to one side. His students were frantically scrambling around, putting the last touches on the stage for the evening's premier performance of *The Devil's Own*.

"Where do you plan to hide that contraption during the first two acts?" he asked the student director. He pointed at the gallows, which was stage right at the moment.

"Behind the stage? The backdrops will hide most of it, and then we can bring it around for Act Three," replied the young girl.

"All right, Kim, it's your show," said Shawn. He looked at the cast members, all Gretna theater students, who were watching him, ready to get to work. He rubbed his hands together. "Okay, people, let's run through Act Two, Scene Two. Remember, Sherry, he's going to knock your teeth out. You are absolutely shocked and terrified. Try to scream like you mean it. And Matt, you are evil personified. No mercy." He clapped his hands and the actors scurried to their places. Kim nodded, and the rehearsal began.

Shawn could hear the sound of the parade coming down the Harrisburg Pike West. The Aronston High School marching band was playing a Disney medley.

"Not too shabby for a high school band," he said to himself.

He turned and looked across the square for a few minutes, watching through the crowd lining the street.

He saw the baton twirlers, wearing their sequin-studded costumes, prance up the street in front of the band. Behind the band were floats that the local Boy Scout and Girl Scout troops had put together. Each float had a theme for Founders' Days Community Pride, Working Together, Keeping It Clean. The floats were pulled up the street by cars driven by the scouts' parents. The troop members rode proudly on the floats, smiling and waving at their friends and families.

Shawn grinned and waved back.

There was a piercing screech of tires. A battered ten-year-old blue sedan pulled up on the side of the square nearest to where he was standing.

"Professor Williams, the playbills just came from the printer," a lanky boy shouted from the hastily parked car.

"About freakin' time," he replied and walked over to the car. He opened the back door and pulled a box off the back-seat. It was heavier than he expected and he lost his grip. The lid of the box opened and sheets of folded paper flew everywhere.

*"Oh, shit!"* yelled Shawn, and he began scrambling around grabbing playbills before they could blow away completely. A tall man who was passing by stopped to help and gathered up quite a few before walking over to Shawn with them.

"I sure do appreciate this," he said, looking up at the good Samaritan. He paused and frowned. I've seen this face before, he thought. "Do I know you? You look familiar."

Roger Phillips smiled. "No, I don't think we've met. What's going on here?"

"This is where we're going to put on the play for Founders' Days. You know, *The Devil's Own*? You just rescued our playbills. I'm Shawn Williams, author of the play."

"Pleased to meet you," replied Roger. "*The Devil's Own*, eh? What does the devil have to do with our beautiful town?"

"There's a folk legend that Aaron Moyer, the man this town is named after, was the devil's son. Look." Shawn opened the playbill. There was a brief summary of Aaron Moyer's story and a reproduction of the engraving from Levi's book. "This guy's father was the son of one of the founders of Aronston . . ." His voice trailed off as he stared at Roger.

"Holy jeez, you look just like him!" The resemblance was remarkable. The same handsome features, thick fair hair and full-cut mouth. If it wasn't for the antique clothing Aaron was wearing, they could be twins. The only difference was that Roger's mouth did not have the cruel twist Aaron's had. "Are you related to him or something? This is too weird."

Roger stared at the picture. It was as if it were a mirror. The resemblance was just too good. Was it possible that he was descended from the devil?

It explained a lot of things that had been happening to him in the past thirty-six hours.

The devil's own. The devil. He broke out in a cold sweat. Suddenly he knew somehow that Aaron Moyer was alive and living in him, along with the Other. He recalled the "memories"—the kitten, the burning barn, the girl bleeding and moaning from his fists. And then there were the Mayan memories, too—the sacrifices, tortures, ritual disembowelment on the pyramid altar.

Aaron and the Other. They were working together, soulmates, kindred spirits. Working in him and through him. Becoming him. Drowning Roger Phillips out.

"My God," echoed Roger. "I must be. Guess I am," he stammered.

Shawn was still alternately glancing at the playbill and then at Roger's face. "But this is wonderful! A relative of Aaron Moyer! A look-alike, too! Come on, let me introduce you to my students. They'll be thrilled. Maybe we could even get you a walk-on in the play if you'd like, being as how you're Aaron's great-great-great-whatever you are. What did you say your name was?" He turned to Roger.

Roger was gone.

The Corvette pulled up to the gated fire road. Colette shut off the engine and got out, pulling a backpack over her shoulders. She was dressed in jeans and a sweatshirt and hiking boots. She set off, striding up the fire road into the woods.

The trees had a soft green haze on their branches as the new leaves were emerging. Along the path were white, purple and yellow violets. It was a gorgeous spring day, and Colette felt her spirits lift. Finally.

She had found it impossible to stay in her apartment after Roger left. The sense of bereavement without him had been crushing. She felt as though she had an arm or a leg missing. She had gazed out the window for a while, curled up on her red settee.

Damn it, I wish I knew what to do, she had thought. Roger is dangerous, like the devil, and if I had any sense I'd tell him never to come near me again, ever. But I love him. Or part of me loves him. I know he loves me and that he'd never ever hurt me. Is this Xochitl woman part of me? Did Roger leave me here on purpose, so that I'd feel this way? Totally empty? Lonely and confused? She began to feel headachy, trying to sort it all out.

She decided she'd try cleaning, working over her well-kept apartment as though it were a pigsty. Each dust mote became an enemy to vanquish. Then the phone had started ringing.

She let her answering machine pick up. "Hi, this is Vicky from the *Clarion*. I'm working on some sidebar pieces for tomorrow's edition and I'd like to ask you some more questions about your relationship with Dave Davis. Were you dating, what was he like, things like that. I promise not to get too personal." Vicky chuckled reassuringly. "Call me back before three if you can. 'Bye."

Ugh, thought Colette. Back to work. The Disney medley from the parade passing by two blocks down came to her ears.

She smiled sardonically as she mentally contrasted the whole-someness of Uncle Walt with the sinister mess she found her-self in. She toyed with the idea of walking down to see the parade, but feared she might run into Roger. As much as his absence hurt her, she knew she had to sort out her emotions on her own.

The phone rang again. "Hi 'Lette, it's Darren. Can you meet me at the office at four-thirty tomorrow? Chris Fein from the insurance company is going to be there and look over the damage. You don't have to call back unless you can't make it. See you then."

Colette ran to pick up the phone, but stopped. As much as she wanted to talk to someone normal, someone who was a friend, she feared Darren would hear something in her voice and know she was in trouble. How could she possibly tell him what was going on? He'd think she'd gone insane. Perhaps I am insane, she thought. She pushed her fingers up through her hair.

The walls of the apartment began closing in on her. The pain in her heart was crushing. She had to get out of the apart-ment, get away from these spinning thoughts and this insan-ity that was sucking her in like quicksand. She pulled on her hiking boots, threw trail mix and a bottle of water into her backpack, and started down the stairs. The sound of a door slamming behind her made her jump.

"Hey, Colette," came a friendly voice from the top of the stairs. It was Lee Hsiang, the third-floor resident. She smiled with relief. Lee was refreshingly normal.

"Hey, Lee. How's it going at school?" Lee was a Gretna student and aspiring professor and/or novelist.

"Pretty good, Colette. You going up to the parade? I thought I'd take a look and get some fresh air. Got finals next week and I am sick of studying." His round face broke into an infectious grin.

Colette shook her head. "Nope. I need some exercise so I thought I'd take a hike."

"Hey, who's the redheaded guy I saw this morning leaving your place?" Lee's grin became a sly smile. "He looks like he's a good match for you."

Lee liked to tease her, and Colette usually laughed along with him. This time Lee's words echoed in her mind . . . A good match for you. A pang went through her, as sharp as a knife. She could feel it in every fiber of her being. In a moment it was gone.

Lee saw her face change. "Are you okay, Colette? Did I say something wrong?"

No, she thought. She descended the porch stairs and turned to Lee.

"Have a good time at the parade. See you later," she called and got into her car.

He watched her go, a puzzled expression on his face.

She turned up Gretna Road North and sped down the back roads, windows wide open to the cool spring air, feeling the wind in her hair. Now, as she hiked up the hill, she felt more rational and self-possessed. More like Colette the living woman and not some long-dead Mayan princess. She breathed deeply, feeling her lungs fill with the fresh air, enjoying the sensation of breathing.

As her thoughts stopped their crazy spinning, her common sense returned from its two-day vacation. She *had* to get Roger out of her life. He was not human. He was beyond human. And she had a feeling that he was not exactly looking to save the world. Not that he was a creep or anything. Just slightly weird and a little sinister.

She had to get him out before she got deeper into something she could not control. Before he took her over and turned her into Xochitl. Or something else. But she had never felt this way about anyone, ever. He had become a part of her.

"Geez louise," she said to herself. Here she was, Miss Live-Free-Or-Die, feeling like her life would be over without Roger. Yes, life will be over without a guy who thinks he's King of the Mayans. You sure picked a winner this time, girl. She stopped and remembered how she felt when he touched her, the rush of feeling that enveloped every sense she had. The ecstasy, the fullness, the complete and unending joy. How could she live the rest of her life without ever feeling that way again? Impossible.

Stop it now, she told herself. Roger is more than you or

anyone else can handle. You're in way too deep, girl, she thought. He's got to go, even if it hurts. The question is, how to do it?

After all, the man has powers I don't understand. I really don't think he'll just ride off into the sunset if I tell him to. I'm not sure why, but I think he could get really ugly if he thinks I've hurt him in some way. It's something I sensed when I saw those visions last night. There's a potential for violence beyond . . . but even so, I can't believe he'd hurt me. He loves me.

She pondered as she strode along, feeling her courage strengthen with every step.

"Aronston Police."

"Yo, Ed. Marc here."

Eddie Haas chuckled. "Hey, Turner, whassup? What can I do you for today?"

"You know anything about a guy named Roger Phillips?"

"Yeah, I do. His wife called here Wednesday. Said he hadn't come home from work and nobody knew where he was. I told her there was a twenty-four hour waiting period before we could file a missing persons report. Never heard back from her. Guess the fire . . ." His voice trailed off for a moment. "Anyway, I also know Roger personally. His kid plays . . . played hockey with mine. Nice guy. Veteran and all. Why you asking?"

"I found a cigarette butt with his prints on it at the fire scene in Carriage Circle. Just got the report back today."

"The Downeys. Right. Real early Wednesday morning. Hmmm . . . Well, I know Roger didn't get along real well with Downey when he worked for him but then he got the job at Mama Angelina's and he seemed okay. You know if he was home when the fire hit his house?"

"Man, the place was vaporized. Nothing was left. Maybe some bone fragments. No way of knowing for a few weeks, anyway."

"I'll tell you off the record, this Downey guy was a real snot-nose asshole who thought the world owed him. His wife was the same. They used to call here when their neighbors had parties and ream us out for letting them make noise. But I can't see Roger Phillips as an arsonist. Or a murderer. Oh well, in this line of work there's always surprises." Eddie Haas sighed.

Turner's brow furrowed. It was the closest thing to a suspect he had at this point. And the guy could very likely be dead. "Listen, Ed, can we go on the assumption that Phillips might still be alive? Can you ask your guys to watch for him, put out an APB or something? I think if he *is* still alive, we should ask him a few questions."

Haas echoed Turner's thoughts. "Guess it's the closest thing we got to a suspect, huh? I'll get on it for you, no problem."

"Do me a favor? I bet Vicky Collins is calling you five times a day on this. Don't tell her. I don't want to scare Phillips away if he's still around."

Eddie Haas snorted. "Bitch is a pain in the ass all right. Just doing her job, but geez . . . You got it, Marc. Will let you know what we find."

"Thanks, bro." Turner hung up the phone. Just gotta be patient, he thought.

## 36

Vicky Collins was the full-time reporter and assistant editor for the *Clarion*. Most of her days were filled with rehashing wire stories, making sure births, deaths, and marriages were published, police blotter tidbits, weather reports—in short, tailoring the newspaper to suit its small-town audience.

As a girl, growing up in Harrisburg, she had dreamed of being the next Margaret Bourke-White. Her favorite day-dream even now was accepting the Pulitzer Prize for her incisive, insightful reporting.

In her senior year of high school, William Collins stepped between her and her dream. Bill was tall and handsome and the captain of the football team. He found himself drawn to this petite, lively, intelligent, and ambitious girl who sat next to him in social studies class. It was a classic case of opposites attracting. Vicky was immensely flattered by Bill's attentions. She found herself receiving an entirely different type of edu-

cation in the backseat of Bill's car. Three weeks before graduation, she discovered she was pregnant. Bill and Vicky were
married that summer at their parents' insistence.

Instead of beginning college in the fall, like their friends
did, they took childbirth classes. Bill got a job at Bardwell's
Chocolates and they bought a two-bedroom bungalow in
Aronston with a loan from their families. The following January Vicky gave birth to a healthy baby boy who was the
image of his father.

Bill never really forgave Vicky for getting pregnant and, in
his view, forcing him to get married. Over the years, as he was
promoted to middle management at Bardwell's, he nursed his
resentments. After a time, he imagined that she had entrapped
him. Vicky had derailed an almost certain college football
career and a possible shot at the NFL. If not for her, he could
have been wealthy and famous. He began to drink heavily and
fall into bed with women who understood him.

Vicky decided she had no time for resentments and that it
was up to her to make the best of a bad situation. When Ryan
entered preschool, she took a part-time job at the *Clarion* typing up classified ads. She made no secret of her ambitions and
worked hard at the paper. It wasn't exactly the *New York
Times* but it would have to do. Her work and her attitude won
her a reporter's job after a few years. Bill Collins and his
anger became irrelevant to her. He was reduced to background noise, someone that occasionally appeared in her bed.
Weeks would go by without Vicky and Bill having more than
five minutes' conversation.

The *Clarion* was never going to win a Pulitzer. Neither
was Vicky Collins. She had come to accept that. She liked
Aronston and decided to remain, even when Bill Collins finally divorced her for his much younger and less ambitious
secretary, quit his job at Bardwell's, and took off for Seattle.
It also helped that Ryan was happy in Aronston and that it was
a peaceful place.

But right now Vicky was intensely excited. A real live
story in her little town. She sat at her desk at the *Clarion*,
notes and tapes and photographs scattered all over her desk,
typing into her word processor for dear life. She was putting

together a four-page spread for the Sunday edition. And she thought it would be her best work ever.

She had cobbled together a history of the major fires in Aronston—mostly barn fires, except for the time the Cross Keys Tavern burned down, killing three men, but that was a hundred years ago. She had a scholarly sounding article on the methods of arson investigation, featuring extensive quotes from Chief Turner. As far as any criminal investigation, Police Chief Haas said he had no suspects, so nothing to write about there. Damn it, it would have been perfect to have a police story to go with the arson story.

Now for human interest stuff. She had prepared flowery, sorrowful obituary pieces for the Downeys, detailing what a credit to the community they had been. She had gotten a few comments from the neighbors referring to their unfriendly and rude behavior, but decided it wasn't right to speak ill of the dead. At least not in their obituary. She almost cried at the pathos of her own prose.

She also prepared a piece on the Phillips family, even though it hadn't been confirmed yet that they perished in the fire. The contributions of the family, the children's achievements in school, what a loss to Aronston the Phillipses were. She grew misty again when she wrote about the abrupt end to Bryan and Sarah's future. So much promise, now a memory. She sighed, then smiled with satisfaction. My readers will be in tears, she thought. And I just love it.

Now, if only Colette Walls would call her back. She thought a budding romance cut short by untimely death would be a gripping story. Or perhaps the driver was a menacing stalker preying on a pretty young woman, who was rescued from almost certain harm by a mysterious act of God. But first she needed to get the story and a few quotes from Colette. Deadlines were looming. She did not want to save it for Monday's edition.

She decided to call one more time. This time, the phone was answered by a male voice, breathless and hoarse. "Colette? Is that you?"

"No, this is Vicky Collins from the *Clarion.* May I leave a message for her?"

Click went the phone in her ear.

"How rude! I wonder who that was?" she murmured to herself.

Her article would have to wait till Monday.

"Damn it!" she said, and stamped her foot.


Roger hung up the phone with a bang. His legs were trembling under him as he stood, so he slowly sat down on the floor and held his head in his hands. He was absolutely terrified. The crumpled playbill with the story of Aaron Moyer fell to the floor next to him.

He had wandered through Aronston, lost in the crowd of visitors, his mind reeling. Obviously I must be descended from this wife-beating psycho, he thought. The face is a dead giveaway. Is that why I was chosen? Chosen to receive an ancient power I never asked for?

Again the half-thoughts, hard for him to read, flowed through the back of his mind. He sensed not just a potential fulfilled, but even enhanced. The brutal madness of Aaron Moyer was now linked with the forces that drove Chac Mol. Rage and hate now had unlimited powers, contained in the hapless body of Roger Phillips. And all Roger could do was stand by and watch. He tried, with what remained of his own mind, to figure out a way to fight it. Turning himself in would be useless, even if the forces aligned in him let him. Through him, they could just vaporize wherever he was locked up. Suicide was an option, but again, he'd have to get past his unwanted companions. They had already made it plain that they were in control. Within a very few hours his humanity would be useless to them and therefore eliminated.

The worst part was, he found himself enjoying all this occasionally. It was as if he had entered one of his nightmares and found that it wasn't so bad after all. In fact, it was a delightful place. After forty-odd years he was finally where he was meant to be. There was a deep, complete satisfaction in watching others die in pain. There was the cleansing and purifying power of bright white fire. And the prospect of bringing his Xochitl back, to continue the journey so rudely interrupted by a bunch of jealous and stupid priests, made him smile.

After a time he, too, felt the apartment too confining. He walked back up to the town square. He kept to the rear of the stage area, wanting to avoid that playwright and his annoying introductions. The gallows had been moved behind the stage, awaiting their moment in Act III, Scene Five.

His head began to ache painfully. His eyes were suddenly sensitive to the sunlight. He kept his head down, hoping no one would recognize him as he cut close by the gallows.

A babble of strange and ominous voices rose up around him. He stopped and looked up. He was standing in a crowd of people, all dressed in the clothing of two centuries ago. They were eagerly watching something behind him. He turned around. Upon the gallows behind the stage stood two young men, feet and hands bound, nooses around their necks. They stared over the heads of the crowd, erect and proud.

A minister walked across the platform to the men. "Do you have any last words?"

"No, Reverend. We said our piece. Let's get it over with."

"Mark and Thomas Reifsnyder, I commend you to God. May He have mercy upon your souls." With an awkward pat on each man's back, the minister slowly left the platform and stood behind another man, who was swaying a little as his hand rested on a lever. The man picked up two black silk hoods, staggered over, and fumbled them onto the Reifsnyder boys' heads. Roger saw them turn their heads away from him, grimacing as the curtain of black silk hid their faces. The smell of whiskey reached Roger. My God, he's blind drunk, Roger thought. The hangman returned to his lever.

The trapdoor opened and the men fell through, then were jerked up sharply by their necks. The crowd moaned. The moan died down to a whisper, then suddenly increased in volume. Women began screaming. Instead of hanging lifeless, the bodies were arching and writhing like fish on a hook. Mark Reifsnyder kicked free of the rope around his feet and began doing a macabre dance in midair. The hood fell from Thomas Reifsnyder's head, revealing his purple face, bulging eyes, and swollen tongue. His face contorted horribly in soundless agony.

Roger was alternately sickened and fascinated by the scene before him. He felt renewed by the emotion from the dying brothers and the revolted crowd. The cries of the crowd became a high-pitched shriek. A foul stench filled his nostrils. He looked at the people around him.

Their faces were gray as ash. Pieces of flesh began dropping from their faces and hands. Their eyes seemed to melt and the liquid streamed down over the exposed bones of their skulls. Their chests and bellies burst with a ghastly wet sound like ripping wet rags, and rotted, blackened organs tumbled out onto the ground. Still the shrieking continued.

An icy clutch of panic sealed Roger's throat. He looked over at the gallows. The Reifsnyder boys were covered with their own body wastes, struggling more feebly now. Roger nearly fell down, as though he had been struck. On the gallows, where the minister had stood, was a Mayan priest. It was one of the men who had dragged Xochitl up the side of the pyramid. He was with Chac Mol on the altar when he took Xochitl to be his wife. He had frowned and whispered "Sacrilege!" with the others on the pyramid. And he was the one who had driven the knife into his king's chest thousands of years ago.

He was dressed in jade and gold, with a feathered headdress. His body was painted with cinnabar. He stared down at Roger, unblinkingly. In his right hand was a black-bladed obsidian sword, in his left a red, painted pottery jar. Slowly he raised the sword and pointed it at Roger. Then he used the sword to gesture at the jar. His face was set and determined. Roger was transfixed by his resolute stare. He felt like a deer in the headlights of an oncoming car.

What? thought Roger. What's happening here? The panic began to flow into his veins.

"Roger? Roger Phillips? Is that you?"

Roger wheeled around and looked into the dark and elegant face of Tracy Faber. He hadn't seen her since Downey fired him. He could only stare at her, open mouthed with fear.

"Roger, what is it? Are you okay? Did I scare you? I'm sorry . . ." She reached out to touch his arm, concerned.

Roger turned and fled at top speed. He didn't hear Tracy call, "Wait, Roger, wait . . ." All he wanted was to run, to hide from the scene of carnage in the square and the priest demanding death.

He realized that even in this world, thousands of years later, he still had enemies. Part of him was frightened.

But a small part of him rejoiced.

# 37

There now. Nice and comfy next to my window, with my cup of tea. Damn, when did lemons get to be so hard to squeeze? Hope my Tracy gets here soon. She called and said she's antiquing today and she'd stop in. Girl should stop buying all that old furniture and stuff and start saving for her old age. Don't think she'll ever marry. Too independent and hardheaded. Wants to be the boss before she'll be someone's wife. Women's Lib messed everything up. But if she were married, she'd have no time for me. Don't know what I'd do without her. She takes good care of me.

Nobody else in the family comes around like she does. Oh, they all have lives of their own. Jobs, kids, school, Little League, soccer, town meetings. Always a reason why I don't see 'em but maybe once, twice a month or so. They bring me a plant, or some candy, stay for about fifteen or twenty minutes and then they're gone. They don't want to hear the same old stories again. And they sure don't want to hear what I have to say about this godforsaken place. Must make 'em feel guilty, I guess. But I suppose they must hate coming here, too. Can't say as I blame 'em, but I feel pretty lonesome.

Quit whining, you old fool. Won't do me any good to have a long face when she comes. Let's see what those kids are doing down there with that stage. Think I can just about see Shawn down there, ordering those kids around. Must be rehearsing for tomorrow. Hmph. That boy should get a haircut. Looks like a damn hippie. I can remember when he wasn't Mr. Big Deal Playwright, Aronston's claim to fame. No, he was just a jug-eared, freckle-faced kid who played with little Phil out in the barn.

Thing behind the stage there looks like a gallows. Must be going to reenact the Reifsnyders getting hanged. Now why anyone'd want to see that, I don't know. Wonder how they'll do it so no one gets hurt. There's a man down there near the gallows. Redheaded. Too old to be a student. Must be some tourist, coming to see what's what. Should wait for the play 'stead of trying to figure it out now. He sort of looks familiar. Hmmm . . .

Hold on. My eyes are going on me. Must be these glasses. Thought I saw a bunch of people . . . Hellfire and damnation! There are a bunch of people. Weren't there a second ago. Where'd they come from? And there, on the gallows. What the hell is that? The Reifsnyders? Can't be. Must be rehearsing. Looks like they all got costumes on. But Shawn and the kids are on the other side of the stage. Let me clean my specs here.

Damn good job, though. The audience looks real authentic. Clothing of the time and all. Still, it's godawful. Can't imagine how anyone ever thought watching people die was fun. Shawn, you young snot, I don't care how successful you are, this is not wholesome entertainment. For anyone. What's that? They opened the trapdoors! You idiots, they're strangling! Got to tell them at the nurse's desk. Send someone down to rescue them . . . Wait.

Levi, you're losing what's left of your mind. Look at those people. I can see them so clear, like I'm right there. Like I have a telescope. They've turned into rotten things, guts and bones hanging out. Oh my God. And that . . . that must be *them. Mark and Thomas Reifsnyder. My God, my God. Look at them. Look at their faces. Horrible, horrible. Why can't I look away?*

*And that fellow on the platform. Looks like some kind of Indian or something. Feathers on his head. Got a sword of some kind. What the hell, there weren't any Indians around for the hanging. No Indian I ever heard tell of had a sword, either. I can't believe what I'm seeing. Know it's not one of those damn premonitions. Premonitions are for the future, not the past. Or I must be senile. No other explanation.*

*Now they're gone. Like a dream. A real bad dream. But I'm not dreaming this time. I'm wide-awake. Look at that red-headed man down there. Running as if the devil were after him. The devil . . . Could it be? Did he see it, too? And that woman standing there. Is that Tracy? Looks like her. Oh, lit-tle girl, you run, too. Run away from that place. Run, damn it!!*

*God, I hate being an old man. Can't do anything about nothing. Can't tell anyone either or they'll dope me up for sure. I won't spend the rest of my miserable life doped up and drooling, having to wear diapers and be spoon-fed like the other living dead around here. Curse me for an old fool. And curse you, too, Aaron Moyer. Don't you hurt my Tracy.*

When Tracy entered Levi's room a few minutes later, he was still pounding his fists on the arms of his wheelchair. Tears were running down his cheeks, flowing like melted sil-ver in the grooves and furrows of his face.

# 38

Byron Mirkowski sat and stared blankly at the television.

"I hate Saturdays," he said. His voice was petulant, like a little boy's.

He lived in a room he rented from Helen Bauman, an elderly woman who lived in a big, dilapidated, old farmhouse on the west side of Aronston. At one time it had been a beautiful place, with a wide porch running on three sides and tall narrow windows. Now the house was in dire need of paint and upgraded plumbing and heating. The porch roof groaned under the weight of a badly overgrown wisteria vine. Out in back of the house, the empty barn had a crazy tilt to it and appeared to be in imminent danger of collapse.

"I was born in this house and so help me God I will die in this house," she told her nieces and nephews. No cozy retirement for her. So she took in boarders to help keep the place running.

He called Helen Bauman Miss Helen—in fact, everyone did—and he loved her with the devotion of a Labrador retriever. In return, she kept his rent low, helped him take care of his money, and watched over him in a grandmotherly sort of way. The Professors Mirkowski had moved to Florida a long time ago. It never occurred to Byron to visit them, and they did not offer to invite him. His contact with his mother and father was limited to birthday and Christmas cards. So Helen was the closest thing to family Byron had. And Helen had never married, preferring her independence to any man she had ever met. So Byron became the son she never had.

It was a satisfying arrangement for both of them.

Byron had worked for Mama Angelina's since he was eighteen. He loved cleaning the big steel machines, scrubbing them down with disinfectant and polishing them until he could see his face in them. He kept the floors meticulously clean, dusted and vacuumed the offices, and tended the grounds. In the spring and summer he would plant flowers in the patch of lawn in front of the offices. He also liked his coworkers. Everyone was friendly and kind, and they all appreciated his hard work. Byron put in twelve-hour days and more. He enjoyed the activity and the people at the plant so much that he would forget to go home. Patiently Darren Keller explained to him over and over that he wouldn't get paid for unnecessary overtime. And he had to take weekends off. The plant was closed from midnight Friday till 7:00 A.M. Monday. Byron either didn't listen or didn't understand. In desperation, Darren called Miss Helen.

Miss Helen solved the problem by giving Byron more to do around the house. She had him mow the lawn, weed the flowerbeds, and taught him how to do small plumbing and painting jobs. She let him know, lovingly, that she needed him at home with her for evenings and weekends.

For a few years she took him to the movies every Saturday afternoon. And of course they went together to special events such as Founders' Days. The two of them were seen together in Aronston so often that they became a couple, in people's minds.

But as she grew older and increasingly feeble, she was no

longer able to drive. Even short walks tired her. Byron did not even ask if she would take him to the parade or to the play. He knew better. So, on this beautiful spring day, Byron remained inside with her, watching TV while Miss Helen knitted a sweater with her gnarled old hands.

Upstairs Byron could hear the rhythmic thumping of a boom box. One of Miss Helen's boarders was a graduate student at Gretna College. He always played his radio a little too loudly while he worked on his thesis. If Byron listened very closely, he could hear the snores of the third boarder, a man who worked as an orderly at the ElderCare Center on the third shift.

Miss Helen would occasionally find empty bottles of Canadian Club in the trash when the orderly was at work. Miss Helen said it was none of her business as long as he didn't make it her business. He made no trouble and paid his rent on time. However, she kept her most prized possessions (there weren't many) under lock and key, and watched him carefully. Miss Helen was arthritic and frail, but her eyes and mind were sharp as ever.

Byron shifted restlessly in his chair. Miss Helen looked up from her knitting and peered over the top of her glasses at him.

"Need something to do, Byron?" she asked.

"Yes, Miss Helen. I finished cuttin' the grass and I raked all the leaves out of the flowerbeds. You got some pretty daffies an' tulips out by the barn."

"Would you like to go to the store for me?"

"Sure, Miss Helen," Byron replied. His face lit up with a childlike smile. Then it quickly faded. Miss Helen thought she knew why.

"Now don't you go fretting over last night. Those boys were just bad apples, is all."

Byron's eyes filled with tears again. "They called me a retard, Miss Helen," Byron said in a quivering, hurt voice. "They were going to take the doggie I won for you."

Miss Helen cast an affectionate glance over at a chair by the fireplace. The garish purple dog was proudly seated in the center of the chair, propped up with a few throw pillows.

"Byron, dear heart, they didn't know you. Anyone who knows you knows you are not a retard. Whatever that means. Remember, sticks and stones may break my bones, but names will never hurt me." She peered at Byron again. "You were so sweet to bring me that dog. How about if I give you some extra money for a candy bar? Would you like that?"

"Yes, Miss Helen." Byron smiled.

She got up slowly and hobbled over to the old-fashioned secretary desk and listed a few items in her spidery handwriting. She handed it to Byron.

"Read it back to me, now. I want to make sure you know what to get."

Byron read slowly, his lips moving silently. Then he looked up at Miss Helen.

"It says here to get one quart of milk, one pound of butter, one package of bacon, one lettuce, and a candy bar."

Miss Helen handed him some money. "Very good. We'll have BLTs for dinner, you and I. Then, when it gets dark, we can sit on the porch and watch the fireworks from over at Cumberland Park."

"A BLT is a bacon and lettuce and tomato sandwich, right? I like tomatoes."

"Yes, Byron, you do." She smiled.

"And I like fireworks, too. They're so pretty."

"Run along now." She gestured at the door. "Shoo, shoo."

Byron put the money in his pocket and left.

Miss Helen watched him go, smiling. It usually took Byron several hours to go to the store and back. He would walk down by the Swatara Creek and skip stones on the water, just like a little boy. He would meet people from Mama's on the street and chat with them. He would have a long conversation with Mr. Jenkins, who ran the small grocery a mile away, where Byron was headed. And he would come back happy and tired, which was what Miss Helen wanted.

"That'll keep you busy awhile," she murmured, and returned to her knitting.

# 39

The Aronston High School gymnasium was decorated with a huge painted banner that read "Go Lionesses!
On to the States!" The gym floor was covered with thick gray
mats. The uneven parallel bars, the balance beam, and the
vault were set up on one side of the gym, while the other side
was reserved for floor exercises. Slender, leotard-clad girls,
their hair pinned tightly to their heads, their hands chalky, and
their faces pinched with nervousness lined up by the equipment, preparing to do their best. The bleachers were full of
their relatives and friends.

Three-minute pieces of classical and jazz music blared as
the competitors did floor exercises. There was a constant low
hum of conversation in the bleachers, punctuated by an occasional sigh of disappointment or shout of triumph as proud
parents watched their daughters perform. Darren Keller
watched Corrine Keller dust her hands with chalk and wipe

them on her legs, square her narrow shoulders, and walk up to the uneven parallel bars.

Her wavy hair was pulled hard back from her face and coiled into a knot at the nape of her neck. Her burgundy-and-gold leotard fit her thin, muscular frame like a second skin. The dark lipstick she was wearing made her face look even paler, and from his seat in the bleachers Darren could see the lines of concentration around her mouth.

Go for it, Queenie, he thought.

Andrea was sitting next to him, tensely watching Corrine. She let go the breath she was holding as Corrine gracefully and successfully mounted the bars and began her gravity-defying routine.

"Doughnuts didn't slow her down any," Darren chuckled, half to himself.

"Really, Darren, don't you think they're getting too old for that? I always end up throwing most of them away," said Andrea, a little irritably.

Darren turned to look at Andrea. She knew the Saturday doughnuts were a father-daughter ritual. They had been for years. He opened his mouth to reply, and then snapped it closed again.

A thought came to him, a fundamental, seismic thought, and his world shook violently.

With the force of a deadly earthquake he finally realized that all he had ever been to Andrea was a means to an end. He had never been anything else to her. Never. He had given up the career he had wanted in order to become the husband she had wanted. He had provided the home she had wanted, and the daughters she had wanted. Their life was solid, respectable, and middle class. No rock 'n' roll animals allowed.

The cool, analytical mind he had once found so intriguing concealed a heartless ambition. Andrea wanted life on her terms only. Neat, clean, tranquil, and safe. And she had done a damned good job convincing him that it was what he wanted, too. Well, not anymore. The blood began to pound in his temples. A fury like nothing he had ever felt kindled in his brain.

He wasn't certain if he was angry with her for manipulating him all these years or at himself for allowing it. No matter.

"Damn it, Andrea, that's it!" Darren exploded. "I've had it with your shit!"

Andrea turned to him, openmouthed, as Corrine stuck a perfect dismount with a resounding thud on the mat. She raised her arms up over her head and bowed right and left. Her eyes met Darren's, and she grinned. He grinned back and waved.

"Now what brought that on? I missed the dismount!" hissed Andrea.

"Just this; I'm really sick of doing it your way all the time. I'm going to try living my life the way I want to, not the way you want me to." His voice rose a little with anger.

"I have no idea what you're talking about," said Andrea, coldly. She was absolutely furious, he could tell. Whether for yelling at her in public or for finally figuring her out, he didn't know. But heaven forbid he make a public scene. "And keep your voice down."

Darren grinned wickedly at her. For a fleeting moment Colette's laughing face flashed before his eyes. In a loud voice he said, "Sure, you do, Andrea. Just think about it. I'm on to you now, baby. You are a manipulative, ice-cold bitch. And I am sick of your shit!" He fairly roared out the last two sentences.

With more noise than was necessary, Darren stomped down from the bleachers and moved toward the sidelines where Corrine was toweling off. Apparently she had heard him in the stands—her expression was a perfect mixture of curiosity, embarrassment, and pride.

What's with that, Pops? she mouthed at him.

He grinned at his daughter, and he left Andrea staring straight ahead, lips pressed together in a thin line, while the other parents stared and whispered.

**40**

Marcus Turner pressed the button that closed the garage door and entered his house. A large, black Newfoundland dog lumbered through the kitchen toward him, planted its front paws on his shoulders, and covered his face with slobbery kisses.

"Yo, Cindy, knock it off!" But he reached around the dog's massive head and rumpled her ears. Cindy plopped her paws back down on the floor while Turner wiped his face with his sleeve. He went over to the sink to get her some fresh cold water. Then a beer for himself.

Cindy was short for Cinders. She was a gift from Turner's girlfriend, Ashara. The woman was drop-dead gorgeous, but not awfully bright sometimes. She had seen Cindy in a pet shop window and bought her on impulse as a gift for Turner. She knew absolutely nothing about Newfoundlands and how big they get. All she knew was that Cindy was black and cute and cuddly.

"Girl, what the hell am I going to do with a goddamn puppy?" was his reaction when Ashara presented him with Cindy. Ashara's liquid, amber eyes filled with tears.

"Marcus, I thought you'd like her. See how cute she is? She'll keep you warm for me when I'm in New York on assignments." Ashara picked Cindy up and hid her face in Cindy's fuzzy puppy coat. Cindy squirmed and whined to be put down, which Ashara did. She waddled over to Turner, sat down at his feet, and looked up at him expectantly, as if to say, "Well? Are you going to keep me or what?"

Turner found himself trapped between a beautiful woman's tears and a puppy's endearing charm. "Okay, okay. I'll keep her. I'll keep her. Ashara, don't cry, honey." He wrapped his arms around her. Satisfied, Cindy began chewing on a corner of the carpet.

Ashara was an aspiring model and actress, and she spent a lot of time in New York and occasionally away on assignments. Since Turner was stuck caring for the puppy, it was only logical that the puppy became devoted to him. Much to his surprise, he became equally devoted to her. He tried to explain it once to his friend Jay Stanley, who was on the police force.

"Stan, man, Cindy don't bitch or complain. She listens to me. She don't want to go to fancy restaurants or go dancing or have me buy her stuff. She just wants to hang with me. So what if she slobbers? She's cool, man."

"Shit, Turner, you are just a fool for that dog. She's getting huge. What is she, part moose or something? You better find a farmer someplace who'll take her, 'cause your landlord sure as shit ain't gonna let you keep no moose at your place."

Turner knew Stanley was right. He began, quietly, looking for another job that would take him out of the city. He was already sick of the city, and Cindy became another reason for leaving Philadelphia.

She was a very good reason for taking the job in Aronston. There was a lot of space to run, some nice roads to walk down, a life in the country. When he arrived in Aronston, Turner rented a two-bedroom house with a fenced backyard. When Turner went to work, he left the back door ajar. Cindy would push the storm door open with her head when she wanted to go out, and use her paws to claw it open when she wanted to come back in. Her sheer size made Turner confident about leaving the house unlocked. He knew burglars didn't like to mess with big dogs.

"Burglars have no more brains than Ashara does," he said to Cindy once, tousling her ears. "And you got more brains than most people."

Cindy kissed him with her big pink tongue, covering the side of his face with dog spittle. He didn't mind.

His relationship with Ashara did not survive the move. When Philadelphia was only a two-hour train ride away, it was easy for her to come down to see Turner, or for him to spend weekends up in New York. But now it was a lot harder to get together. Ashara wanted to pursue her career, and she did not own a car, so she needed to be close to New York. So they parted with the usual lets-be-good-friends and lets-get-together-real-soons and forgot about each other. Much to his surprise, Turner found that he didn't really miss her all that much.

Jay Stanley had thought he was crazy. "Marcus, man, Ashara is gorgeous. She's been in *Sports Illustrated,* in *Vogue.* You are out of your tiny mind to let her get away like that. Why don't you take a job in New York if you don't like it here? Instead of someplace west of Nowhere Land? Ashara is to die for, man." Stanley looked quizzically at Turner. Suddenly he burst out laughing.

"It's the damn dog, ain't it? You're taking a job in the country so's the dog will have a place to run around. You are a bigger fool than I thought, choosing your stinkin' dog over a babe like Ashara." Stanley had chuckled over that for days. Turner smiled and said nothing. What Stanley didn't know was that Cindy was a more intelligent and affectionate companion than Ashara ever would be.

Marcus Turner had no regrets. He took a long pull from the cold bottle of beer and rubbed Cindy's flanks absently as he thought about Roger Phillips and the mysterious fires.

"Hope we get a quiet night tonight, girl," he said to the

dog. "I didn't bring you all the way out here to be this busy."
Cindy looked expectantly into her master's dark eyes and
barked. "Okay, okay. Let's walk."

Cindy went over by the door and waited as Turner finished his beer and picked up his coat. Just then the phone
rang. Cindy sighed and lay down by the door.

"Yo," said Turner into the phone.

"Hey, bro! How's it going in Nowhere Land?"

"Shit, if it ain't the Stan Man. How you doin'?"

"That's Mr. Jay Stanley, Philadelphia police detective, to
you, Marko. They promoted me."

"Shit," Turner said again by way of congratulations.

"Listen, Mark, got something here that might be of interest to you. I heard about those fires you got out there."

"Tell me about them," replied Turner, furrowing his
brow.

"Well, Coast Guard towed a ship in here the other day.
Nobody aboard, cargo intact. The Customs boys let the
cargo out. Yours truly inspected the ship to confirm that
there was no criminal evidence. Nothing on board, except
for these piles of ash here and there."

"Ash?" Turner was immediately interested. "On a ship?"

"Yep. Did some analysis. Human."

"No shit," Turner whistled low into the phone.

"Is that the only word you know? Anyway, some of
the cargo was shipped up your way. Davis Freight was
the hauler. Frozen meat for some place called Mama
Angelina's."

"No chance anyone stowed away? Some psycho maybe?"

"Nope," Jay Stanley said. "I know it probably ain't anything, but just thought you should know."

"Thanks, man. Come up and visit so I can buy you a
beer."

"Yeah, next time I feel like taking a two-hour drive I'll
head up there." Stanley snorted.

"Later." Turner hung up the phone. "Ready, Cindy?" He
snapped the leash onto the eager dog and they walked out
into the late afternoon sunshine. He stopped suddenly. Davis

Freight . . . Dave Davis. The truck that exploded and the driver that died.

Cinders pulled on the leash. "Okay, girl, I'm coming. But what's the connection?"

Turner was lost in thought for the rest of the walk.

# 41

The plastic bag rattled as Colette tipped her head back and shook the last of the trail mix into her mouth. She was perched on a big, sun-warmed boulder on top of a hill. She could see the entire town below her through the greening trees. She twisted her hair up and held it against the back of her head so the breeze could cool her neck.

*It looks like a postcard,* she thought. So pretty and peaceful. She could see the Victorian houses that radiated out from the town square, the busy swaths of the Harrisburg Pike, both east and west, cutting through the center of town. The steeples of the churches shone golden in the slanting afternoon sun. If she looked eastward, she could see the big houses give way to newer, smaller, more contemporary ones. On the edge of town she could see the huge, rambling complex of buildings that housed Bardwell's Chocolates. She could see the big banner announcing Founders' Days.

Nestled on the ridge of hills above Aronston, she could see

the pretty bungalows and low stone buildings of Gretna Village and the college. Several white gazebos marked where the art shops and ice cream parlors were.

Closer to Swatara Creek, she could make out the low brick building that was Mama Angelina's. On the other side of the creek, up on a rise, were the new, elegant homes of Carriage Court. Turning her eyes west, the town again gave way to rolling farmland. The fields were dotted with tiny black-and-white patches that were cows grazing on the fresh young grass.

She let the view sink in, breathing deeply of the earthy spring air. *This is reality, girl. Not some bizarre dream given to you by the devil.* With a sigh, she let her hair fall and slid off the rock. *Time to go home,* she thought, and began making her way down the trail. She figured Roger would be there. She was determined to have it out with him immediately, before he could change her mind. She knew all too well that he could. Her eyes pricked with tears, and she wiped them away almost angrily with the back of her hand.

*You just had to fall in love with the guy, didn't you? Eighteen zillion men in this world and you end up as the leading-lady in Exorcist, Part Twenty-three.* She wiped her eyes again and set her mouth in a straight line. *I won't cry. I won't.*

She found herself wondering if a garlic necklace or a crucifix would help stave off Roger, like some vampire in a folk-tale. "Maybe a stake through his heart," she said out loud with a brave chuckle. Then she shuddered.

Colette was not far from the truth.

Roger was stretched out on the Victorian-style sofa in Colette's living room, eyes closed. The sofa was slippery and hard and not very comfortable. His heart had finally stopped pounding, but the scene in the town square kept rising up before him—the putrid bodies of the crowd, the grotesque death of the Reifsnyders, the Mayan priest pointing the sword at him. *What does it all mean?* he asked himself. *How does it all fit together?*

Someone or something was after him. More than one

something. He recalled the priests in the night, cutting Chac Mol's heart out. But why? Because he took Xochitl as a wife instead of a sacrifice?

A clear thought cut through the radio-static buzz that had become the background noise in his mind. *Of course. My enemies pursue me beyond death. Because I took what was mine to take. And to cherish. And they were small and fearful men.*

The clarity faded and Roger could hear nothing but the buzzing.

He remembered the Reifsnyder boys. Still looking to avenge their sister and their own death two hundred years later? They want to kill Aaron twice?

Roger laughed suddenly and heartily. He felt a rush of confidence. *They can't kill me. Not now. And when I finally join with Xochitl . . . I mean Colette . . .*

The apartment door opened.

Colette dropped her backpack down by the door and walked to the center of the living room. Roger sat up on the sofa and looked at her. She looked flushed and tired, but her gaze was level and there was a determined look on her face.

Without speaking a word to him, she crossed her arms in front of her and stood still, staring down at him.

He looked up at her. Their eyes locked. Colette noticed that Roger's green eyes had a strange cold blue cast to them. Roger could feel the power of his own gaze pushing against the determination in hers. She swayed slightly and dropped her eyes.

"You have to leave here. Now. I . . . can't be with you anymore." She trembled a little with the effort it cost her to say those words. Roger lay unmoving on the sofa, staring at her. His eyes bored into her, weakening her resolve. She squared her shoulders.

"If you won't go, I'll . . . I'll call the police," she said emphatically. She lifted her eyes to his again, challenging him. The expression on her face stirred a memory. Of an equally angry, equally strong woman being dragged up the temple steps.

Roger got to his feet. "Don't come near me," she warned.

She quickly moved to the fireplace and picked up the poker, tightening her fingers around it.

"I don't have to," he said. Slowly he raised his arm and pointed at her.

Colette trembled, but she did not let go of the poker. A tide of images and emotions began rising inside her. She began chanting under her breath, "My name is Colette, my name is Colette," over and over like a mantra. Suddenly Xochitl stood before her, her turquoise-blue eyes staring into Colette's. Xochitl spoke, in a musical voice.

"I love him."

"Your time is past," replied Colette. "I have my own life."

"I died with him."

Xochitl's image dissolved. Colette saw the priests, gathered around the body of the slain Chac Mol. His heart slid off the sharp, smooth obsidian blade into a pottery jar. Xochitl stood nearby, head held high, awaiting her fate. The head priest turned to her and stopped for a moment. He bowed his head for a moment, in respect to her rank and to her dignity. Then he lunged forward and plunged the sword into her lower belly. Xochitl shuddered under the force of the blow but did not cry out or fall. The priest twisted the blade upward, then ripped up with all his force, through entrails, heart and bone, all the way up to her neck. A sickening wet tearing and crunching sound, along with the priest's grunts of effort as he pulled on the blade, were the only sounds in the room.

Then he pulled out the sword, raising it high over his head, and watched her now-lifeless body topple backward onto the floor. Her insides erupted from her opened torso in a geyser of blood. Her blue eyes, still open, gazed tranquilly at the ceiling. The room filled with the metallic scent of blood and the smell of stomach, bowel, and bladder contents—the stench of death.

The priest stepped forward and bent down over Xochitl. He reached out and tore the jade ring from her nose with a jerk of his arm, and dropped it into the jar with Chac Mol's heart. One of the priests clapped a lid over the mouth of the jar and quickly sealed it with pitch from a small pot.

Nausea swept over Colette. She heard Xochitl's voice again.

"They burned our bodies on the temple altar to please the gods. In a room deep inside the temple they buried his heart with my ring. Now he wants to me to live again. As he is living."

"I am Colette. I don't want to be you. I won't live your life for you."

"My love, my god, he wants me by his side."

"I am not you. He is not Chac Mol. Look at him."

Colette closed her eyes tightly and opened them again. Xochitl had disappeared. Roger still stood before her, in a trance-like state, pointing at her. She raised the poker in a sweeping motion and brought it down, hard, on Roger's shoulder. It bounced off his shoulder and came down on the coffee table, smashing a vase of calla lilies. Roger grimaced with pain. The grimace became a snarl.

Roger dropped his arm and lunged for her. Quickly she stepped back, toward the kitchen, holding the poker like a sword. She pushed the sofa at him with her foot, parrying and thrusting as Roger tried to dodge around it. Finally he leaped over it, knocking it on its back, and reached out to touch her.

"Out! Out!" she shouted. "Go back where you came from!" She pointed the poker at his throat. She knew that she was fighting for her life, and the thought exhilarated her. She was beyond fear. Roger grabbed the poker and Colette pushed it at him and let go. The unexpected move knocked Roger off balance, and he crashed into a glass-fronted curio cabinet. Colette wheeled around into the kitchen, opened a drawer, and took out a butcher knife.

A knock sounded at the door. "Colette? Are you okay?" It was Lee Hsiang. The noise from the fight had brought him down from the third floor.

"Lee! Call nine-one-one!" Colette shouted, watching Roger get up out of the shattered glass in front of the cabinet. Blood poured down his face and neck from several cuts on his head. He got to his feet, his eyes wild with pain, fear, and something Colette had never seen before. In his hand was a six-inch shard of glass. The light from the kitchen made rain-bows along the sharp edges.

Lee opened the door and stepped into the room, his eyes taking in the broken glass and porcelain, the tumbled furniture, the bloodied Roger and the knife-wielding Colette.

"What the hell is going on here?" he said.

"Lee! Get out of here!" Colette shrieked.

In three steps Roger was in front of Lee. With a single quick motion, he slit Lee's throat with the glass blade, then placed his hands on either side of Lee's head. Lee's mouth opened to scream, but no sound came from the severed windpipe. Lee's body convulsed as Roger drew out his life force. Roger took his hands away, and Lee collapsed, drowning in his own blood.

Roger extended his arm and dropped the glass into the pool of blood. Then he turned and looked at the horrified, mute Colette. He grinned at her, his mouth twisting into a strange and cruel grin. As she watched, the blood from Roger's wounds stopped flowing. The cuts closed up and healed over. He passed his hands over his face and neck and they were clean. Then he turned to Lee's body. He pointed his finger at it. With a white-hot flash and a sound like a gunshot, Lee's body was nothing but a pile of gray ash on the scorched hardwood floor.

He turned back to Colette. She brought up the knife and brandished it. The twisted smile came back and his newly blue eyes glittered.

"I'll leave you again to consider your options," he said in a strange, cold voice. "The next time I see you, you will become mine. Or you will die." He smiled slightly. "See you later," he said, and laughed. Colette did not reply. She held her ground, watching him intently.

Roger turned and left. She heard the door downstairs slam behind him. She dropped the knife and ran to her own door. The ash that used to be Lee crunched under her boots and she shuddered. She locked the door. She turned and pressed her back hard against it, shaking and gasping for breath.

# 42

Roger Phillips stood on the porch of Colette's home. The sun was just setting and the sky was streaked with fiery pinks and golds, cool lilacs and mauves. Vapor trails crisscrossed the patches of color, glowing white or gold depending on where they were in the sky. The venerable maple trees along the street thrust their black branches up toward the blazing sky, the new leaves just bumps along the naked limbs. As Roger gazed at the sky through the branches, he had the impression that the sky was cracking into thousands of tiny incandescent pieces, hanging suspended for a moment before crashing down at his feet.

Aaron's cruel smile left Roger's face. So much had happened in the last several hours. He needed a chance to go off and think it all through, to plan a course of action. He stepped down off the porch and walked up toward the town.

Colette was stronger than he had anticipated. It was not

going to be easy for her to accept Xochitl. But she would,
sooner or later.

What if she won't accept?

Then she dies. Painfully.

Roger's humanity was losing ground more and more rapidly to the forces that possessed him. However, he had enough
left to think, *Not if I can help it.*

One of Tracy Faber's loves was antiquing. Aronston had a
few good shops at which Tracy was a regular customer. She
had spent the afternoon, after leaving Levi napping in his
wheelchair, in Rennie's Collectibles, discussing the merits of
a nineteenth-century Chippendale highboy and a lusterware
sugar bowl and cream pitcher with Veronica Newton, the
owner of Rennie's. She purchased the lusterware, but she had
a suspicion that the highboy was not genuine. Veronica had
tried to prove to Tracy that it was indeed a Chippendale, but
Tracy had an instinctive feeling that it wasn't. Finally, after
poring over several antique books, Veronica ruefully con-
cluded that Tracy might be right.

"Sorry, Veronica. I just had a feeling. Hope you're not mad
at me."

Veronica was not angry. She couldn't afford to get angry
with a good customer like Tracy Faber. Besides, she could sell
the highboy at a good price to a tourist or a less discriminat-
ing collector.

Now it was time to head home. Tracy set the carefully
wrapped lusterware on the front seat of her blue Ford pickup
and started off. She tried to picture how her new acquisition
would look in her china closet, but another image kept in-
truding on her thoughts.

She could not get Roger Phillips' face out of her mind. The
utter fear and horror etched on his features haunted her. *Perhaps it was the shock of losing his home and probably his
family, too,* she thought. *I wish I hadn't scared him so.*

As she drove up a pretty, tree-lined street toward the town
square, she saw a familiar figure walking on the right side of

the street. It looked like she might have a chance to make it up to him after all.

She pulled alongside and stopped her pickup truck.

"Roger? Do you need a ride?" she called.

Roger turned, smiled, and waved.

"Sure, Trace," he said cheerfully. He walked around and got into the truck. She waited until he was safely in, then started down the street.

"God, Roger, I am so sorry I scared you earlier. I didn't mean to. Let me buy you some coffee or something, catch up on things, okay?"

"Coffee sounds great, Trace. I'm sorry I ran off like that. Got a lot on my mind these days."

"I guess you do. Roger, I heard about your house. Was it your family, too?"

"Yes," said Roger, very low.

Tracy said nothing, but reached over and squeezed his hand. Roger looked over at her face. Her brown eyes were full of pity and concern. She had been a good boss and a good friend, until Downey had come along and made her choose between her friend and her job.

Dark thoughts began pushing into his mind. Resolutely he forced them back and returned Tracy's squeeze.

"I'll be all right, Tracy. Thanks." He picked up the kraft paper bundle next to him. "What's this? More stuff for your museum?"

Tracy laughed. "It's lusterware from the turn of the century, and you'd better not drop it."

She pulled up and parked her truck in front of the Coffee-teria. She turned to Roger again and looked hard at him.

"You know, it's funny. My great-grandpa Levi said he had a feeling you didn't die in the fire. He's been having lots of strange feelings lately. Thinks he might be going crazy. I thought he might be, too. But now it looks to me like he might be getting to be psychic in his old age. Wait till I tell him he was right about you. I know it will make him feel better."

"Maybe," Roger replied. He grinned wolfishly.

# 43

The brilliant sunset went unnoticed by Darren Keller. The den echoed with discordant piano chords. He was experimenting with a jazz piece he was writing. He had come home from the gymnastics meet and gone straight to his den without speaking to Andrea, and promptly lost himself in the intricacies of composing. He did not realize how rapidly the room was darkening.

The door opened. "Hey, Pops, turn on the light," said Corrine. She flopped down in the big recliner and watched him.

Darren turned on the old brass lamp that sat atop the piano and illuminated the keyboard. He smiled at his eldest daughter.

"Congratulations again, Queenie. Great job today. Bet you can't wait to get to Pittsburgh in a couple of weeks."

"Yeah, it's cool. Dad, what's with you and Mom?"

Darren sighed. "Hard to explain. I guess I just lost my temper."

"Mom said you threw a major shit fit over the doughnuts."

"Watch your mouth, little girl." Darren frowned at her. Then he paused and said, thoughtfully, "If your mother said that, then she missed the point. Totally."

Corrine rocked back and forth in the chair, slowly. Her eyes met his, and she smiled. "I kind of thought she did. You don't get weird over stuff like that."

He looked at his daughter. She had taken her second shower of the day and her wavy hair was still wet, making dark spots on the shoulders of her T-shirt. Her jeans were ripped at the knees and her feet were bare. Corrine never wore shoes if she had a choice.

"I'm glad you washed that dark lipstick off. It made you look too much older," he said lightly.

"Hey, I'm only three years younger than Mom was when she met you."

"Don't remind me," he said. "I'm already having a bad day."

Corrine chuckled.

He patted the piano bench. "Come here, Queenie." She sat next to him and he wrapped his arms around her, pressing his cheek against her damp, sweet-smelling hair. She hugged him back. They embraced silently for a minute.

"Pops, is being married hard?" Corrine asked softly.

"Yes, little girl, it is. You have to give up a lot and make compromises." Too many sometimes, he added silently. Then he switched back to the fatherly mode. "But if you love someone, you make it work."

"Like you gave up the band?" she asked, guessing his thoughts.

"Yes." Darren sighed again and tightened his arms around her.

"Ow, Pops!" She shrugged off her father's arms and straightened up. Then she grinned at him. "I love you, too."

The door opened again. Andrea stood in the doorway. Her eyes glittered with anger, belying the false smile she wore. "You two are thick as thieves," she said, a little too coldly. "Dinner's ready."

"Oooh, I smell sauerkraut. My favorite! In France they call

it *choucroute garni*." Corrine bounced up from the piano
bench. Darren rose in time to hear Katelyn say, "Mommm! I
hate sauerkraut!"

Darren turned off the light and went in to dinner.

# 44

Police Chief Eddie Haas walked carefully around the disordered room, making detailed notes in a little black leather-bound notebook. Colette sat on her window seat and watched him attentively. She appeared calm and collected, but her mind was spinning like a squirrel in a cage.

Officer Schutter was collecting ash samples and placing them in an evidence bag. He kept glancing over at Colette. She could see him watching her and sighed inwardly. *He's trying to decide if I'm drunk or on drugs or just plain crazy,* she thought. *I would think I was crazy, too.*

A new thought occurred to her. *What if they think I did it? What if they lock me up in jail, or worse, in the loony ward of the hospital?* She crossed her arms and held them tightly to suppress a shudder.

But she couldn't fight Roger alone. She doubted the cops could either, but the more people that knew about him the better. *Look on the bright side,* she thought grimly. *If they lock*

*me up, I'll be safe. Maybe. God, please don't make me be*
*sorry I called 911, she prayed.*

Chief Haas and Officer Schutter had arrived within minutes of her call. Colette had not touched a thing, except to
put the knife she had used to defend herself back in the
drawer. She told them about her acquaintance with Roger
from the beginning. She left out the parts about the rape, the
visions, and the apparitions. The less said about that the better, she decided.

The smashed and overturned furniture, the gray ash, and
huge scorch mark on the floor mutely corroborated her story.
To say that Eddie Haas was skeptical would be an understate-
ment. However, Eddie Haas knew of one person who would
be very interested in knowing that Roger Phillips was still
alive.

"Tell me again, Miss Walls. When did you first meet Roger
Phillips?"

"I . . . well, I guess I must have met him a few months ago
when he interviewed for the night guard's job at Mama's. If
you mean, when did I become . . . personally involved with
him, it was Thursday night."

"Thursday night, okay. And everything was fine until
tonight?"

"Yes," said Colette. Sort of, she thought.

"And tonight you asked him to leave, and he wouldn't, so
you had a fight."

"Yes," she said again.

"And Lee Hsiang from upstairs tried to break it up and
Roger Phillips used some kind of force or something to burn
him to ash right here?" Chief Haas pointed to the blackened
area of the floor. He stared at her with a slightly incredulous
look. Officer Schutter could not repress a derisive snort. Colette stood up.

"Yes. Look, I don't expect you to believe me, at least not
right away, but it's the truth." She met his eyes with a level
blue gaze.

They all say that, thought Eddie Haas. Yet, in all his years
of police work, he had never heard such a farfetched story delivered so gravely and earnestly as Colette Walls had. There's

three possibilities here, he thought. She's a terrific liar. She's nuts. Or she's telling the truth. Even though his rational mind told him her story couldn't be true, his gut told him she was speaking the truth, as far as she knew. And his gut had years of experience. He decided to try her a little.

"Miss Walls. Did you know Roger Phillips' house burned down yesterday morning?"

"No." Colette's eyes widened a little.

Chief Haas's eyebrows rose. "You mean he didn't tell you?"

"We didn't discuss it, no," she responded.

"Did you know his wife and children are missing and presumed dead?"

Colette shook her head. "I knew he had a wife who was looking for him Thursday night. My boss, Darren Keller, and I talked about it in the plant yesterday morning. Honestly, I didn't think about it again until just now. Roger and I don't talk a great deal, if you get my drift." She sat back down and crossed her legs. Even in jeans, hiking boots, and a loose black sweatshirt, she was beautiful.

Chief Haas got the drift. "You don't read the papers?"

"Sorry, I don't."

"Geez, these fires are all anyone talks about. Hard to believe you didn't know."

"Chief Haas, yesterday we had one of those fires at Mama's. A truck blew up in the parking lot. The driver was killed and the plant damaged. I came home late and Roger was here. We didn't read a paper or watch TV." She sighed.

"This morning I got up and went for a walk in the woods. Then I came home and . . . well, you heard about the rest. So yes, I do know about the fires. I just didn't know about Roger's family." She shook her head. Stay strong, she told herself.

Chief Haas decided she was telling the truth about Roger's family. As for the rest . . . "Officer Schutter and I have to collect evidence, Miss Walls, dust for fingerprints and traces of blood, photograph the scene. You understand, I may have to take you down to the station for more questioning."

"I'm staying right here. I feel safer with you around.

Would you two like something to drink? Ice water?" She smiled.

"Sure," they said. "May I make a phone call? " asked Chief Haas.

It was Colette's turn to say "Sure." She turned and went into the kitchen. Officer Schutter followed her. Chief Haas heard their voices as Office Schutter engaged Colette in some idle chitchat about Founders' Days. He frowned and rubbed his forehead. With all the extra shit going on for the goddamn Founders' Days, we have to deal with this science-fiction crap, thought Chief Haas. What else could it be? People just don't get vaporized.

But . . . a fire big enough to scorch the floor like that should have left some soot and smoke behind. Hell, the entire building should reek of smoke. And there was no doubt that there had been a fight in here. And Colette Walls was either telling the truth or a psychopathic murderer with some kind of laser gun.

There's got to be a logical explanation of all this, he thought.

His cop's mind couldn't think of one. Yet.

He picked up the phone and dialed Turner's number.

# 45

Tracy Faber and Roger Phillips faced each other across the table. Tracy curved her hands around her coffee cup as she spoke.

". . . so that's what's been going on at Bardwell's. You know the company is sending a funeral arrangement for Downey? Usually the coworkers chip in and send one from the department. Well, they collected nothing. Zip, zero, nada. God, that man was hated." Tracy shook her head and looked at Roger. Behind the counter, the cappuccino steamer let out a long rude noise, as if in agreement.

Tracy took a deep swallow of coffee. It tasted really good. It felt good, too, to sit here in this clean warm place, full of light oak tables and dark green ferns, recessed lighting fixtures, huge copper machines behind the counter giving off the delectable fragrance of brewing coffee and spices. It was very good to talk with an old friend.

Roger stretched out his legs and leaned back in his chair, as if savoring the moment.

Tracy watched him over the rim of her coffee mug. *He looks different somehow,* she thought. *His mouth has a twist to it . . . I don't like it. And his eyes look like glacier ice, really cold. Well, I guess if I lost my family I'd look different, too. But not like Roger.*

Roger saw her staring at him and grinned at her. Now he looked more like the old Roger. Tracy returned the grin, a little relieved.

"I haven't seen you look like that in a long time," she said. Her face lit up suddenly as an idea came to her. "Look. Now that old Lemonhead Downey is gone, why don't you come back? I can set up a meeting, show that you were practically framed out of a job. Lots of people still miss you, Roger. Including some of your customers. What do you say?"

"That sounds great, Tracy. But first I need a place to live and some new clothes. I lost everything . . ." His voice trailed off.

Tracy's heart turned over with pity. It was on the tip of her tongue to ask him to stay at her place. But some deep, indefinable instinct warned her not to. Roger was a good man and a good friend and he had indeed lost everything. Yet the cold look in his eyes a few seconds ago had unsettled her.

Pop-Pop's words suddenly came into her mind. He had known, somehow, that Roger was still alive. And that Roger was trouble. *That weird expression he gets really creeps me out.* Pop-Pop never was wrong about much.

Besides, her strict Italian mother would have a fit if she found out Roger was staying at her house. *A strange man in my house? That's one fight with Mom I don't want to have,* she thought.

She decided she could lend him some cash. Just to tide him over. And she remembered an errand she still had to run.

"I've heard of a place on the end of town where there's a lady who takes in boarders—students and such. I can give you a lift there and I'll lend—lend, mind you—some money. Just until you get your job back." She spoke as if it were a certainty. Roger chuckled at her confidence.

"I know exactly where you're talking about. Miss Helen's. The janitor at Mama's lives there."

"I just don't think you should be all alone right now and Miss Helen's is cheaper than a motel. She'll take care of you." Tracy smiled at Roger, then felt a chill go down her spine. Roger's eyes had gone flat and cold again. *Those are not the eyes of a grieving man,* she thought. *They look more like the eyes of a mass murderer or something.* She curled her hands around her cup as Levi had done last night, feeling the lingering warmth.

"Do you want some more coffee or shall we go?" asked Roger. The pleasant moment was over. His heart felt like a heavy black fog was moving in around it. The low-grade static was beginning to buzz at the edges of his consciousness.

"Let's roll on out," said Tracy. "Enrico is probably dying for his dinner." Enrico was Tracy's spoiled white Persian cat.

They finished their coffee and left. Out in the truck Tracy turned to him and grinned. "It will be so good to have you back at Bardwell's. You're such a nice guy."

Roger grinned noncommittally. "Thanks, Trace," was all he said.

The truck turned and headed west.

# 46

Vicky Collins walked into her kitchen. The savory aroma of chicken and tomatoes, onions and garlic, greeted her. Her seventeen year-old son Ryan was standing at the stove stirring something in a big pot.

"Hey, Mom. How's it going?"

"It goes," Vicky sighed. Ryan was exactly like his father at seventeen—tall, dark, and handsome, with a straight nose and gorgeous white teeth. Vicky remembered how Bill Collins had made her weak in the knees once upon a time. She looked fondly at her son. Ryan may have his father's looks, she thought, but he's a one-hundred-percent better person than Bill will ever be.

"What's for dinner, Ry?" she asked. "It smells wonderful."

"Chicken Marengo. I got the recipe out of an old cookbook. Says it was served to Napoleon."

"Well then, it's good enough for me," Vicky laughed. She picked up the cookbook Ryan was using and turned it to see the cover. "I think your dad and I got this for a wedding gift. I also think I never used it."

"Someone has to cook around here or we'll starve."

Vicky put her arm around her boy. "Thanks, honey. I love your cooking."

"Only because it isn't yours."

Vicky laughed again and turned on the police scanner radio. She had finished the Sunday articles and sent them to Layout before she left the *Clarion* offices. She wished she could have gotten an interview with that Walls woman, but there was always tomorrow. In the meantime, she was pleased with what would be all over the front page Sunday morning. No need to rely on the wire services this week.

She busied herself in the little kitchen, setting the table and pouring iced tea for Ryan and herself. Ryan ladled the steaming cassoulet onto two plates.

"Dinner is served, madame," he joked to his mother. With exaggerated gestures, he pulled out her chair, bowing low and theatrically.

"Why, thank you, sir," grinned Vicky. She sat down daintily in the chair and allowed Ryan to push her in.

"So, Mom, what's the latest on the fires?" Ryan placed her plate in front of her and sat down himself.

"Well, Ry, there's not a whole lot. No new clues, no new fires today. I spent the day writing up the Sunday articles. Eddie and Marc have promised to call if there's any new developments."

"I bet you called them about five times today." Ryan grinned at her. "They know they'd better call you or you'll get them out of bed or something."

"Or something?" Vicky looked quizzically at her son. "What's 'or something'? And I'm not that bad."

"Oh yes you are, Mom. You know it, too. You're like a bloodhound when you're on a story. And you know what 'or something' is. I'm not a kid anymore."

"Well, you're my kid and you worry me sometimes. Ryan, this is delicious." She gestured at her plate with her fork. They ate in silence for a few moments.

The police radio crackled. Vicky and Ryan both turned to listen.

**47**

Byron Mirkowski plodded slowly along the river toward home. The fading sunset made deep gold, rose, and blue patterns appear on the rippling surface of the Swatara. He thought they were pretty.

Byron had had a busy afternoon. He had stopped to watch a Little League game being played in the park. He liked to watch the children in their bright T-shirts and caps play as their families cheered them on. When the team in the blue shirts won, Byron cheered, too, though he would have been just as happy if the team in the yellow shirts won.

He continued on his way toward the town, where he ran into George Newell on the street. George detained Byron for forty-five minutes while he told Byron about what had happened at the hospital last night.

"Sylvia was sitting there in emergency just screaming and screaming. I couldn't get her to stop. Thought about giving her a good slap across the mouth, but you can't do that kind of stuff these days. She'd sue me for something or other."

Byron nodded. *Sylvia'd be pretty mad if George slapped her,* he thought.

"Anyway, finally, after she's been screaming like a god-damn fire siren for half an hour the nurse calls us back and gives her a shot of something. Bang! She was out like a light. Fell asleep on my shoulder. She's a big girl, too. Felt like I couldn't breathe. Goddamn hospitals. I mean, here's this woman having hysterics and they make us wait for half an hour to give her just a little shot. Then it's another forty-five minutes for the doctor to come in, look her over, and tell me she's okay. Geez Louise, Byron, lemme tell you. You can frickin' bleed to death before a doctor will come over and tell you you're dead. I tell you, if I was in charge . . ."

Finally, George ran out of ideas on how to save the health care system and decided to go check out the street fair. He asked Byron if he'd like to go, but Byron said good-bye and walked down the street to Mr. Jenkins' store. *George sure is smart,* Byron thought. *Wish I could think like that.*

Byron pushed open the door and a bell tinkled. Jenkins' Groceries was an old-fashioned grocery store, a survivor from a time prior to strip malls and supermarkets. The ceiling was high and made of embossed tin, which had dimmed to a dark gray with time. Ceiling fans were suspended at intervals. In the summer, they spun lazily and provided the only form of air conditioning in the store.

The wooden shelves that ran along the walls were high and dark with age. The counter was real marble. And the cash register was brass, polished to a bright gleam every Saturday night. There were a few concessions to modern times: the floor was linoleum, there were refrigerated cases and a freezer, and the center of the store had metal shelves running down the aisle. Still, the store was clean and had plenty of charm to delight the occasional tourist who stopped in for a soda or a newspaper or Tylenol.

"Hello, Byron," said Mr. Jenkins. Harold Jenkins was the third generation of Jenkinses in Aronston to run the little grocery store. He was in his sixties now, bald and rotund. He still wore an apron over a dress shirt and tie every workday. He still enjoyed coming to work every day. His wife Crystal, however, was tired of the Pennsylvania winters. She wanted him to sell the store and move to Florida. She wanted to buy a condominium near her sister's place in Delray Beach.

Harold Jenkins wasn't ready to retire yet. He loved Aronston and felt connected to the town as he was connected to nothing else. He loved having people he'd known all his life come by and chat for a while. Besides, Crystal's sister Janie was a bitch on wheels and the last place he wanted to be was within walking distance of her. Of course, he'd never explained this to Crystal, but he had told everyone else who would listen.

He had a soft spot for Byron. Harold had known Byron ever since he moved in with Miss Helen. Byron's childlike simplicity was charming and he enjoyed his life thoroughly, which was more than most people did. Harold found talking to Byron refreshing, because Byron was a good listener and did not try to tell Harold how to run his life. Plus Byron was never in a hurry. Too many people were in too much of a hurry these days, in Harold's opinion.

"Hi, Mr. Jenkins. Miss Helen gave me a list of stuff for you." Byron pulled the list out of his pocket. "She needs milk, butter, lettuce, and bacon. And a candy bar." He handed Harold the list.

"Now, that candy would be for you, right? Why don't you pick one out and I'll get the other things bagged up for you." He bustled around the store, filling a bag with the items on the list, while Byron stood spellbound in front of the candy rack. Harold knew it would take at least ten minutes for Byron to make up his mind. He also picked out a small vanilla cream soda for Byron. He waited patiently behind the counter until Byron carefully selected a Bardwell's Trufflicious Bar and put it next to the register.

"Here's a little something to wash it down with, Byron. No charge." Mr. Jenkins handed Byron the soda. Byron's round face broke into a grin.

"Thanks, Mr. Jenkins. You sure are nice." Byron opened the soda and took a big gulp. He was thirsty.

"That'll be six twenty-seven." Byron fished around in his pockets until he found the bills Miss Helen had given him. He laid them out on the counter and, after some thought, handed a five and two ones to Harold Jenkins. He put the other two ones back in his pocket. Harold rang up the amount on the big brass register and handed Byron back three pennies, two dimes, and two quarters. Byron studied the coins carefully.

"Twenty-seven cents plus seventy-three cents equals one dollar," he announced proudly. He put the coins in his pocket and unwrapped his candy.

"What'cha been up to today, Byron?" Harold asked.

Byron told him. The two friends chatted for nearly an hour, with a few interruptions for business, until Harold looked out the front window and saw the sun low in the sky.

"Better head on home now, Byron. Getting late. Miss Helen will be worried about you. Hey, you going to Cumberland Park tonight? See the fireworks?"

"No. Miss Helen and me can see 'em from the porch."

"You be careful on that porch, now. Got some rotten boards there."

"I know. 'Bye, Mr. Jenkins. Thanks for the soda. Don't move to Florida."

"No, Byron, I won't," laughed Harold. "Just don't tell Mrs. Jenkins, okay?"

"Okay, I won't." Byron walked slowly out the door, carrying the bag of groceries.

He ambled in his usual leisurely fashion back toward Miss Helen's, along the Swatara, throwing rocks occasionally, and watching the sunset colors on the ripples. He listened to the birds singing their late afternoon songs. He watched a turtle swim in the creek, just the tiny rocklike head above the water as it moved slowly upstream. Finally he came to the road and turned left toward Miss Helen's.

He was still about half a mile from the house when it exploded into flames.

# 48

Tracy stopped the truck at the end of the driveway. She turned to Roger. "I'll call you Monday night and let you know what's going on," she said. As Roger opened the door to get out, she pressed four twenties into his hand and kissed him on the cheek. "Let me know if there's anything else I can do. I mean it." Then she was gone, the blue truck heading back toward Aronston.

Roger approached the house, his feet crunching on the gravel driveway. He could see the black silhouette of the house against the fading reds and oranges and blues of the magnificent sunset. A light glowed dimly downstairs, and one other upstairs. For some unfathomable reason, Roger thought the tired-looking old house was familiar. A sense of foreboding filled him.

The feeling of being Roger again, the comfortable feeling that had filled him when he was with Tracy in the coffee bar, was fading very quickly. Something was very homelike, and very wrong, about this place.

Miss Helen leaned on her cane and peeked out the window. It was getting late, and she was concerned about Byron. She heard the noise of the truck and thought perhaps someone had given Byron a ride back home. She opened the door before he could knock.

"Can I help you?" she asked. She looked over the tall red-headed man with her sharp blue eyes, sizing him up. He seemed a bit nervous, but harmless enough.

Roger spoke. "Hi. I'm Roger Phillips. I understand you have rooms to rent, and I was wondering if you had one for me." He forced a smile. Get a grip, he thought. It's only a house.

"Come in, Mr. Phillips." She closed the door behind them. "Come into the kitchen, young man, and I'll see what I can do." Roger followed her as she hobbled slowly down the dimly lit and slightly dusty hallway into a big country kitchen with a fireplace at one end. In the center of the kitchen was an old trestle table with twelve unmatched chairs of varying ages. She motioned for Roger to sit down. "Would you like something to drink?" she asked.

"No, thanks," he said. He looked around the kitchen. He knew beyond a doubt that he had been here before. His dark mood deepened.

Miss Helen looked at him. "Phillips, you said? Are you related to the Phillipses who . . . whose house burned the other day? It was in the paper."

"That was my house," said Roger. "I . . . wasn't home when the fire broke out. But my family was."

"Oh dear, how dreadful. I'm so sorry, Mr. Phillips. Of course I have a room for you. It's on the third floor. It gets rather cold up there in the winter, I'm afraid, but you'll have the entire floor to yourself. There's a half-bath up there and you can use the second-floor bathroom when you need to bathe. I charge fifty dollars a week, paid in advance of course, and you have kitchen privileges. The house rules are no visitors beyond the first floor, and none after nine o'clock, and you are expected to clean up after yourself. This is not a hotel and I am too old to be a maid. Let's see, what else? Oh, there's a washer and dryer in the basement you may use, but bring your own soap." She peered at him over her glasses. "Will it do, Mr. Phillips?"

Roger clenched his hands under the table. The sense of familiarity, yet being unable to remember, was unnerving. He forced a smile. "This house . . . it seems like it must have a history, it's so old. Can you tell me about it, Mrs. Bauman?"

Miss Helen was a little startled. None of her boarders had ever expressed an interest in the farmhouse, except when the quirks of an aging house might interfere with their comforts. Then she smiled, showing yellowed and stained teeth. A few were missing.

"Why, yes, Mr. Phillips," she said, very pleased. "Do call me Miss Helen. Everyone does. Let me see, now." She paused a few moments to collect her thoughts. "This house was built in 1801 by Ezekiel Moyer. He was one of the original settlers in this area. He built the house for his son Aaron, for whom the town is named, and Aaron's wife Zipporiah. Aaron was murdered not long after they moved in, and the house was sold to . . ."

Roger no longer heard her. He looked over by the fire-place. Something was moving. A figure slowly and painfully struggled to its feet, turned, and looked at him. A girl. Her lips were split, and the blood flowed down over her chin. Her left eye was swelling and turning purple. Roger could see that, even with gore smeared all over her face, she was very pretty. Or at least she had been pretty until someone had broken her nose a few times, bruised up her face, and done other un-speakable things to her.

*Good God,* he thought. *I've seen her before. She was the girl in the basement—the girl who turned into Wendy. The girl I punched . . .*

She was dressed in a long plain dress and apron, stained with blood, and her cap had fallen down onto her neck, re-vealing thick, curly, strawberry-blonde hair. Her eyes widened with recognition, and then terror. She began to scream, pierc-ingly, like a terrified child.

"Aaron! No! Please, Aaron, go away!" The screams became shrieks, incoherent and deafening in their hysteria.

Roger looked over at Miss Helen. She continued talking as if nothing were wrong. "Then my father came to Aronston when he was just a boy and his parents bought . . ."

"Do you hear that?" Roger interrupted. The shrieking was pulsing in his ears like the howl of a fighter jet's afterburners.

"Hear what, Mr. Phillips?"

"That . . . that noise!"

"I don't hear anything. But then I am a little deaf these days." She pronounced it deef, in the old-fashioned way. She listened for a moment. A far-off pop came to her. "Oh. You must mean the sound of the fireworks over in Cumberland Park. They're just starting, I suppose." She glanced over at Roger.

"Mr. Phillips, are you all right? You look pale."

Roger's mouth twisted. His eyes darkened. The high-pitched sound beat against him like hammering fists, again and again. Suddenly he could stand it no more.

"Stop that yowling, you stupid cunt!" he roared and raised his arms over his head.

The old wooden house shook to its very foundations as flames tore up three stories and roared out of the roof. For a few moment Miss Helen's screams were even louder than the girl's. Then the screams were gone, and Miss Helen's eyes stared out of her charred face at Roger with the same gray-filmed expression Downey's had had. He pushed his chair back from the table and got up. Miss Helen's corpse slid out of her chair and onto the blazing floor.

Tongues of flame circled around Roger, licking at him as he walked through the kitchen and opened the side door. He made his way to the ramshackle barn and stood in the shadowy doorway, facing the house.

The shrieking had stopped. No sound now but the roar and crackle of the fire. It seemed peaceful to Roger after all the screaming and shrieking, and he watched the fire burn. The fire's light played over a face that was no longer his, but coming to resemble more and more the long-dead Aaron Moyer, as he had looked so many years ago while watching his father's barn burn.

# 49

Glad this day is just about done. Nurse will be in here in about twenty minutes to help me get to bed. Tuck me in and all that. Hope it's that nice nurse Alison. She's a real sweet girl. Always has a smile on her face.

Been one hell of a day. My Tracy's all upset now. Wants me to see the doctor. Tells me she'll call herself on Monday. Couldn't talk her out of it, damn it. Maybe I'll call her tomorrow and see if she's changed her mind.

It's so hard to be seeing all these things and being afraid to tell anyone. Afraid that no one will believe me. Kitty understood. She always believed in me. Because she did, I just couldn't tell her about the last one, the creature eating her alive. I knew she'd give up all hope if I told her. Hope—that's what keeps us going, keeps us alive.

Nobody's going to believe an old man who says he saw a hanging in the square, with naked Indians to boot. But I saw what I saw. Wish I knew what it meant.

*Another thing I don't understand. Been thinking of Helen
Bauman since Tracy left. Haven't seen Helen in years. Know
she's not dead though, because I haven't seen her obituary.
Feisty girl, Helen is. Angel of Death is going to have to drag
her kicking and screaming all the way to the Promised Land.*

*Wonder how she's doing? And that boarder of hers? The
slow fellow . . . Brian? Myron? Can't remember now. Nice
young man though.*

*It's getting dark out there. Kitty used to call this an indigo
sky. Fireworks will be starting pretty soon. Could go into the
lounge and look out the window to watch them. Windows face
west there. But they'll have all the lights up bright in there
and the TV blasting some drivel and the ones who can will
want to make conversation that makes no sense. Think I'd
rather stay here with my indigo sky. Seen enough fireworks in
my time anyway.*

*I must be dreaming again. Thought I saw Helen's house.
On fire. That strange white-hot fire I saw yesterday at the
meatball place. I can't see Helen's house from here. She's on
the west side of town.*

*But I can see it. Whole house is blazing. White flames
shooting out the windows. No smoke, just bright white light.
The boarder fellow is running around outside the house crying for Helen. God almighty, she's inside! Oh dear God,
Helen.*

*There go the sirens. And the trucks. Ain't no dream, I
guess. Damnation, Helen, I wasn't ready to read your obituary. Not today.*

*Levi, you'd best stop bawling or Nurse Alison will be in
here with a needle for you.*

Cursing under his breath, Marcus Turner opened the back
passenger door of his Jeep Cherokee. Cindy hopped in and lay
down on the seat, panting a little with excitement.

"Goddamn it, Cindy, another fucking fire. Bet it's our mystery arsonist again. Damn it to hell." He turned on the flashing lights on the roof and flew down the road. Cindy put her
head up to the window, making nose prints on it. "Geez,

Cindy, I just cleaned the car. Don't drool all over everything."
Cindy ignored him.

He had just hung up the phone with Eddie Haas when the call came. Eddie's news had been Twilight-Zone material, but at least Roger Phillips was alive and in the area.

"Whaddya mean, Roger Phillips burned some guy to ashes? With his hands? C'mon, Ed, you must be joking."

"I tell you, Marc, that's what the lady says. I'm standing in her apartment right next to the burns on the floor. No smoke smell, just burns. Plus there's this weird gray ash. Mark, I can't believe her, but I can't shake her. And before you ask, no, she's not drunk and she doesn't seem like she's nuts. She's as calm and collected as you or me."

"Shit," said Turner softly.

"She's a suspect, obviously, but my gut tells me she's not the perp. And with these crazy fires, I'd have to say I'm starting to believe that anything is possible." Eddie sighed. "Well, at least Phillips is still around. And Miss Walls here said the last thing he said to her was that he'll be back. And that I do believe. I'll be increasing patrols in town. We'll find the guy. Even if I have to call the state cops in on it."

"Thanks for clueing me in, Ed. I'll let you know if I hear anything."

Turner hung up the phone. It rang again immediately. Five minutes later he was in the Jeep with Cindy, heading toward the west end of Aronston.

# 50

The trucks were already at the scene when Turner arrived. He jumped out of the Jeep and let Cindy out.

"Stay, Cindy." Cindy sat down next to the Jeep. She would remain there until called or until Turner came back. He took a coat and helmet off the nearest fire truck and put it on as he approached the wreckage. The house had collapsed and it looked like an immense Halloween bonfire in the middle of the yard. Charred and twisted wood reared black and broken against the dancing white and yellow flames. Sparks were flying everywhere, but there was very little smoke. The heat was searingly intense. Behind the wreck of the house, in the distance, fireworks bloomed and sparkled and fizzled away in the clear night sky. Turner could faintly hear the booming over the hiss and pop of the fiery pile in front of him. Most of the firefighters were hosing down the remains, but he noticed Scott Herr plying a hose on the barn roof, trying to keep it from igniting.

"Hey, boss," Scott yelled over the noise of the fire and the roaring hiss of the water from the hose. "You missed a hell of a show. House went up like the Fourth of July."

"Anybody in there?"

Scott pointed with his chin over to the left. Turner noticed a man slowly walking toward them through the flickering shadows. Tears were running down his cheeks.

"Miss Helen was in there," Byron mumbled between sobs.

"Who? Do you live here?" asked Turner.

"Sure he does. This is Byron Mirkowski. Works with me over at Mama's," Scott said.

Byron had begun to run down the road when he saw the house burst into flames. He got there about five minutes before the fire trucks did. He had circled the house frantically, looking for Miss Helen, only to be beaten back by the heat. The firefighters had found him standing in the yard, calling for Miss Helen in a broken, childlike voice. He was still clutching the bag from Jenkins' Store.

"How do you know Miss Helen was in there, Byron?" Scott asked gently. Byron's tears moved him.

"I was coming home from town. I got these groceries here for Miss Helen. We were going to have BLTs for dinner. That's bacon and lettuce and tomatoes. I was up the road and the house just . . ." Byron gestured with his hands. The swinging motion tore the bag in Byron's left hand and the contents spilled onto the grass. Byron went on as he knelt to pick up the butter and the bacon. "Miss Helen don't walk too good. She was probably waiting for me. I don't see her anywhere so I guess she was in there." Byron began to sob again as he slowly stood up.

"Was anyone else in the house? Do you know?" Turner put his hand on Byron's shoulder.

"Well, I don't see Danny's car so I guess he's out. Danny, he's got a girlfriend he goes to see up at the college sometimes. And Joey likes to go to Victor's on Saturday nights." Victor's was a bar in town. "But Joey has to walk up there. He don't have a license. He said they took it away from him. He said he got a DUI. I don't know what that means."

"So we don't know if Joey was there or not?"

Byron's face lit up suddenly. "Well, he might be in the barn. I saw someone go into the barn from the house as I was running up the road. Maybe Joey went in there to hide."

"Watch the barn, Scott," shouted Turner. He wheeled around and began sprinting back to the Jeep. He had to get hold of Eddie Haas. Now.

The gravel sprayed out from under his feet as he ran. He could see the Jeep and Cindy sitting next to it, patiently waiting to be released from his command. A pair of headlights came down the driveway toward him and temporarily blinded him. He stopped in his tracks, squinting at the light. The car crunched to a halt and Eddie Haas got out, pulling on his leather jacket.

"Man, am I glad to see you," Turner panted.

"Heard on the police radio what was going on and thought I'd come down and check up on you," Eddie said with a grin.

"Ed, listen. A guy who lives here saw a man heading into the barn right after the fire broke out. I have a hunch it could be our man Phillips." Turner's face was alive with excitement. "Damn, I want that sonofabitch."

"Marcus, Marcus," chided Eddie. "Slow down, all right? Let's just check out the barn now." Eddie patted himself down, locating his gun and cartridges, and they turned to head back to the barn.

Another pair of headlights came down the driveway a little too fast. The car skidded on the gravel and stopped just inches from Eddie Haas's fender. The doors were flung open and Vicky and Ryan Collins scrambled out of the car. Ryan had a Minolta 35mm camera around his neck.

"Ryan, go take some pictures of the fire before they put it out. Marc, Ed, what can you tell me about this?" Vicky called to them.

"Stay put, Vicky. We have something to check out here. We'll be back," Eddie responded.

The hell I will, thought Vicky. She followed them down to the barn at a discreet distance.

# 51

"So that's what happened to Lee," Colette
Walls explained to the McDevitts. She wiped her eyes and
nose on her sweatshirt sleeve.

Jason and Emily McDevitt were speechless. They had
come home from dinner and a movie, their regular Saturday
night date, to find a police car parked in front of the house.
They rushed upstairs. Eddie Haas was just leaving.

"What's going on here?" Jason demanded.

"Hi, folks. It's all right for now. I've gotta run but Colette
will tell you what happened. Be careful, okay?" Chief Haas's
boots thumped down the stairs and he was gone. Half an hour
later, Officer Schutter would leave in a hurry, carrying a big
briefcase full of evidence samples.

Jason and Emily looked at Colette, who was shaky now
that the police were gone. Tears flowed down her cheeks
while she was explaining how Lee had tried to be a hero and
ended up burned to a crisp for his bravery.

Almost automatically Colette had started cleaning up while she talked, and the McDevitts pitched in. Jason, who was stocky and strongly built, righted the sofa as if it were a doll's toy, while Emily held the dustpan for Colette to sweep glass into.

There was a long uncomfortable silence. They could hear sirens wailing in the distance.

Finally Jason spoke. "Colette, you know your story's kind . . . well, kind of hard to believe." He looked at the scorched floor. It was going to take a lot of time and possibly a lot of money to restore the floor to its original shape. He saw the gray ash on the floor. "I mean, a guy with some kind of superpowers just blasts Lee away and burns the floor. You didn't, like, just have a wastebasket fire or something?" Jason was trying to be polite but he was certain Colette had to be lying.

Emily spoke. "Colette, I'll be honest. When I first saw the cops here, I thought maybe your boyfriend had gotten out of control. I mean, you've always been a good tenant and paid your rent and stuff, but I did worry about that last guy that went in and out of your place. The redheaded guy. He was a little weird." She shook her head slowly and looked at the marks on the floor. "Don't give anyone else a key again, okay?"

"You got it. But this . . . Lee dead . . . I mean, this isn't just some creep acting out."

"Oh, come on, Emily," Jason said, exasperated. "There was some kind of accident here and Colette's making up some story so she won't have to pay for the fucking repair. Probably some insurance scam or something." Jason glared at Colette, who just looked at them, too tired and drained to defend herself.

"Jason, why would the cops come for a fire? The fire department should be here, not the cops. And why would she be so upset? And anyway, look at the ceiling. There'd be a smoke smudge from a fire hot enough to scorch the floor so much. There's no smoke damage anywhere in here. It hardly even smells like smoke. Whatever happened was not a fire. Use your brains, honey."

"Thanks, Emily," murmured Colette.

"Sherlock McDevitt," said Jason, a little derisively. "Guess it was Martians, then, huh?" He bent down and ran his fingers through the ash on the floor. He brought his fingers up to his face and sniffed.

"Smells weird. More like burned food than burned wood." Unthinkingly, he touched his tongue to his index finger.

A gurgling sound made him raise his eyes to Colette. She was deathly pale. She raised her hands to her mouth and sprinted down the hall to the bathroom. A moment later he heard retching sounds.

His eyes met Emily's. She was staring at him, open-mouthed. "What?" he asked, irritated.

Emily whispered, "If what she said was true, you just ate Lee."

Jason looked stunned for a moment. Then, shaking his hand as if it was burning, he ran into the kitchen and turned on the water. He grabbed the dishwashing liquid that was on the sink and began washing his hands furiously. He used almost half the bottle. A few moments later Emily heard the sounds of spitting and gargling. She followed Jason into the kitchen. He had his face under the faucet, running the water into his mouth and over his tongue. Cold sweat beaded his brow and his shirt front was soaked with water. She waited until he was finished and then handed him a paper towel to wipe his face and hands.

"Elementary, my dear Watson, eh?" she said, half-smiling.

Colette came back into the kitchen, still pale but looking a little better. "Jason. Emily. The last thing Roger said to me is that he'll be back. It's me he's after but you guys . . . please be careful. Like Chief Haas said. Don't get in the way, okay?"

Jason straightened a little and blotted his shirt. "Tomorrow we'll get the locks changed. I'll put a bolt in the entry door so that anyone trying to get in will have to break the glass. In the meantime, I'll drag the bench off the porch and put it in front of the door. Anyone trying to sneak in will trip over it." He shuddered. He could still taste the dry, chemical salt taste of the ash. "God, Colette, I still can't believe it."

Emily went to Colette and put her arms around her, hugging her close. Since Emily was short and plump, Colette had to bend down a little to return the hug. "Do you want to stay with us tonight?" Emily whispered. Jason nodded in silent assent.

Colette smiled wanly. "No, thanks, guys. I'll be okay. I think it'll be all right. They'll find him."

"Okay, Colette, if that's what you want. We'll be right downstairs if you need anything." Emily took Jason's arm and they walked downstairs. Colette closed and locked the door behind them. She finished cleaning up all the broken glass and porcelain. Then she washed the scorched area of the floor, scrubbing away all traces of the gray ash. She dumped the bucket of dirty, soapy water down the toilet and flushed.

"Sorry, Lee," she whispered. "You deserved better." *I'll have to get Jason and Emily to let me into his apartment,* she thought. *Someone has to tell his family. Not that they'll believe me either.*

*God, I wish it wasn't true. I wish it was a big lie. Better yet, a bad dream, and I'd wake up and be late for work as usual.*

She did not stop cleaning until the room looked perfect again, except for the missing vase, the broken curio cabinet, and the black mark on the floor. She surveyed the room for a few moments. Then she dragged the settee out of the window nook and put it in front of her door. She checked all the windows to make sure they were locked. She left the living room light on.

She took the knife out of the kitchen drawer. She went back into the bathroom to shower, taking the knife in with her. She listened intently for any sounds over the hissing water. She scrubbed herself clean, dried herself, and braided her damp hair. She got into bed and slid the knife under her pillow.

Finally, exhausted, she sank into a restless, fitful sleep.

The McDevitts didn't sleep at all. They lay awake in bed, holding hands, thinking of the possibilities. Thinking of their treasured house in flames. With them inside.

# 52

Roger Phillips stepped back into the shadows inside the barn. It smelled like musty hay and mildewed, rotting leather inside. He could see the firelight through the chinks in the walls. Sprays of water from the hose spewed through the cracks, and he could hear the drip of water leaking through the roof. He moved gingerly in the darkness, not knowing if he would trip over an ancient pitchfork or fall through a floorboard.

He saw two men approaching the barn. One of them held a flashlight. It was plain that they were searching for him. He considered running, but it seemed unlikely that he would get away if he ran. There were just too many people around.

Trying to hide in this decrepit barn had its own dangers. Still, he really didn't want to be taken into custody.

The memory of an event at an archaeology dig in Honduras came into his mind. Roger smiled in the darkness.

"Well, let's be friendly," he said, and chuckled to himself.

He took his hands out of his pockets and sauntered out of the shadows and through the door. He brought his hands up as he approached Haas and Turner.

Eddie Haas saw Roger emerge from the barn. He drew his gun with his free hand and played the flashlight in Roger's eyes. Roger put his hands up to shield his eyes, turning his head away from the beam.

"Stop right where you are," called Eddie in a warning voice.

"Hello, gentlemen." Roger spoke in a curiously formal and cool tone.

"Hello, Roger. It's Eddie."

"I know."

"Roger, we've been looking for you."

"I know that, too, Eddie."

The coolness in Roger's voice took Eddie aback. Something's wrong here, he thought. This is not the same guy who watches his kid play hockey with my kid.

"You want to take a little ride with me down to the station, answer a few questions about the fires and such?" Eddie lowered the flashlight. He decided not to mention Colette Walls just yet.

"Sure, Eddie. Anything for a friend," said Roger. He began walking toward Turner and Haas. Then he stopped. "Am I under arrest?" he asked.

"Not yet, Roger," Eddie said. He motioned to Roger to keep walking up toward the police car.

Turner could not resist. "Should you be under arrest, Roger?" he said, remembering the Downeys' charred and reeking bodies. There was an edge to his voice.

"I think not," said Roger. As he drew in front of Turner and Haas, he glanced briefly at them. His eyes were cold and opaque, his mouth almost sneering.

Vicky Collins had been following about twenty paces behind Turner and Haas. She watched the man emerge from the barn with intense interest. She switched on her tape recorder and spoke.

"A man comes out of the barn, bearded, dark jacket. Hands at his sides. Relaxed. Chief Haas is apparently going to take him in." She held out the tape recorder to catch what Turner, Haas, and Roger were saying.

At that moment the fire, which had been dying down, blazed up suddenly. Roger's face was brightly illuminated. His eyes met hers for a moment. The expression of raw menace froze her like an arctic blast. Fear hit her hard, like a punch in the solar plexus. As if he could read her mind, he smiled wolfishly at her. Her throat closed and she dropped her eyes.

At the same moment there was a loud bang about a half-mile away. The sky was illuminated with Founders' Days fireworks from Cumberland Park. They burst into flaming gold-and-red glory behind what was left of the Bauman house.

Roger raised his arm and pointed almost casually at Eddie Haas. Eddie jumped in the air like a startled cat. Then he whirled around, pulled out his pistol, and pointed it at Turner.

Vicky found her voice again. "Marc!" It was a screech of terror.

Turner looked up at Vicky's white face, her panicked eyes focused on Roger Phillips. He glanced over at Eddie and saw the muzzle of a gun pointed at his heart. Terror seized him and he stepped back and away from Eddie.

"Man, what are you doing?!" Eddie's face was as blank and smooth as a sleeping child's. Turner continued backing away slowly, never taking his eyes off Haas.

Roger Phillips continued walking up to the cars. He moved as carelessly as if he were strolling down the beach on a summer afternoon. The firefighters kept hosing down the fire. Ryan Collins was snapping pictures. Vicky Collins was staring, rooted to the spot in an agony of fright.

Then Eddie Haas fired, the bullet whistling past Turner's left ear. Turner spun around and began to run in a zigzag pattern as several more bullets were fired. He saw Cindy on her feet, alert and tense. Fearing she might get hurt, he called, "Cindy . . . Aaagh!" A bullet grazed his arm. It felt like a red-hot hornet's sting, but Turner kept running toward the cars, silently thanking God for the thick protection of a firefighter's coat.

The fireworks were booming and cracking, making it hard

to figure out what were gunshots and what were fireworks. The sky shimmered and sparkled overhead.

The firefighters, seeing Turner running for dear life, dropped their hoses and ran toward Haas. Vicky Collins was too paralyzed with fright to move. A huge black shape, faster then all of them, whizzed past the fleeing Turner, who wheeled around and shouted "No!" It darted through the running forms and hurled itself at Eddie Haas, knocking him flat. Then it stood over the inert form of the chief, panting.

Turner heard the thump of Eddie's body as it hit the ground. He stopped running. "All right, Cindy! Good girl! Cindy, stay!" he yelled. He jogged back to the small crowd coming up to surround Chief Haas and Cinders. As he approached he heard a soft pop. Vicky Collins screamed, once.

Voices and questions swirled around them, rising with fright.

"What the fuck happened?"

"Is he crazy or what? Why'd he do that?"

"Damned if I know. Did someone get the gun?"

"Vicky. Are you okay? Are you hit?"

Turner pushed through to the center of the circle. Cindy had not moved since she had been told to stay. She wagged her tail expectantly when she saw Turner's face. He knelt and hugged the dog gratefully.

"Guess I should have named you Lassie, huh, girl?" he crooned softly to her. Then he bent down over Eddie Haas and picked up the flashlight.

Chief Haas had apparently brought the gun up and into his mouth after Cindy knocked him down. He had fired. The .38 slug had come up through the roof of his mouth and blasted through his left sinus, blown out his left eye and exited through the top of his forehead. His right eye was open and empty, staring out at nothing.

Turner shone the light on Haas's face. His jaw dropped in horror. He took in the shattered face, gray brain tissue and jellied bits of eye and blood and white bone everywhere, and the eerily vacant remaining eye. The sight transfixed him for a second or two. Then he abruptly shut off the light. But not before everyone else saw Haas's blasted face.

A couple of the firefighters lurched off a few paces and vomited. The rest just stared, pasty-faced and aghast at what had happened. Vicky Collins appeared shell-shocked. Turner stood up shakily and put his hand on her arm. She turned to face him, but her eyes were glazed and empty.

"You okay there Vicky?" Turner asked, loudly. He shook her arm.

She stared past Turner, unseeing, watching images in her mind. "I saw the whole thing," she whispered. "The man from the barn kind of pointed at Eddie and he just . . . He was trying to kill you, Mark. Then when Cindy knocked him down, he shot himself like it was nothing. Mark, that man from the barn is evil. I saw his face. He's evil, I tell you."

Turner had temporarily forgotten all about Roger Phillips. He quickly looked around the scene. "Phillips? Yo, Phillips!" he yelled.

Roger was nowhere to be seen.

"Damn!" cried Turner. "Damn it to hell!" Tears of frustration, fear, and sorrow for his good friend Eddie welled up in his eyes. Cindy nosed his shoulder and whined softly. He put his face against her neck and leaned against his dog, motionless except for his heaving shoulders.

Ryan Collins came up and put his arms around his mother. She began to sob, softly at first but then louder and louder. Ryan led her to the car and drove away, leaving Marcus Turner and his men to handle the mess that used to be Eddie Haas, and to finish putting out the fire that destroyed Aaron Moyer's home.

# 53

Darren Keller hummed a few bars of Lovin' Spoonful's "Daydream" as he paid for his newspaper and coffee at the 7-Eleven. The clerk smiled at the old tune as she took his money.

"What a gorgeous day!" he said aloud to himself as he got back into his car. It was late morning, and the sun shone down brightly. There was a cacophony of birdsong echoing in the Sunday quiet. The air smelled fresh and clean as a newly washed pillowcase, and Darren took in the faint sweet fragrance of spring flowers. He'd decided to go into the office, as his home was not a pleasant place to be right now.

Andrea, after giving him the silent treatment last evening, had made a point of making up the bed in the guest room. She spent the night in there. A night's sleep did not improve her mood. Darren had never seen her this angry, and he wondered whether she was upset about the tiff at Corrine's meet or mortified at having been caught after all these years. He decided that he didn't care enough to try and find out.

Katelyn took her mother's side and was more than usually bratty. Corrine, his good girl, tried to stay above all the currents and eddies of tension in the house. Finally she could stand it no longer and went off to her best friend's house.

Darren saw no reason to hang around and be a target for Andrea's thinly veiled barbs. He decided to go to Mama's even though the insurance guy was not due until 4:30 P.M. At least he could read the paper in peace and have some solitude in which to consider his next move.

As much as he'd hoped to succeed in the music business, he'd never been one to be rash or impulsive. He'd seen too many bad decisions made on the spur of the moment by young and impatient musicians. What happened when you signed the wrong contract at the wrong time was never good.

"Maybe that's why I like people who do take risks," he said to himself, thinking of Colette. He considered opening his heart to her. In all the time they had spent making love to each other in his office, neither had ever said anything about feelings or emotions. Darren wouldn't, and Colette . . . Darren sighed.

Maybe she didn't have any feelings for him. Maybe he was just a contact sport for her. If that was the case, then he really didn't want to know for sure. But then, she knew he was married. And she was very discreet. Maybe she did care, a little.

But of course there was the mysterious Roger. Darren sighed again as he remembered how Colette had looked on Friday, with her eyes shining and cheeks glowing. *For all I know, she's already engaged to this Roger guy,* he thought.

*I shouldn't say anything. Who knows how this is all going to turn out? Let's deal with the priority stuff first. Like cooling off before I call my lawyer. There's a lot at stake here.*

Still, it was hard to resist thinking about her. He decided to let his mind run with it while he drove along the way to Mama's. After all . . . He began whistling.

• • •

When Darren pulled into the parking lot, he could see the damage to the plant much more clearly. The remains of the truck were gone, and the mess of melted metal that had been Sylvia's car. But the brick that had faced the explosion was blackened. The aluminum siding that covered the soffit and fascia on that side was warped and sagging, its paint burned off. Near the loading dock he could see what was left of a white sedan, windows blown out, charred roof sagging, melted tires puddled on the asphalt. The car that used to be Roger Phillips'.

Darren's brow furrowed. He felt, somehow, that Roger had to be involved in these bizarre fires. But how? He pondered for a few moments, and then sighed. Guess I've been reading too many Agatha Christies lately, he thought.

Darren got out of his car. He ran his hand over the bubbled paint on the door and noticed the cracking rubber gasket that sealed the windows. Next good rain and the car will leak like a sieve, he thought. He took a step toward the back of the minivan to check the other windows when a movement, reflected in the dark-tinted glass windows, startled him. The hair on the back of his neck rose.

He spun around to look, gravel spattering under his heel. Byron was kneeling by the walkway to the office, planting white petunias and yellow marigolds in the earthen strip that ran alongside. Darren smiled ruefully. Hell, I should have known it'd be Byron, he thought. All these strange happenings around here are making me paranoid.

Byron looked up and waved a dirty trowel at Darren. "Hi, Mr. Keller," he called.

Darren returned the wave. "Byron, you shouldn't be here on such a beautiful day. You should be at home taking care of Miss Helen." Darren shook his head as he approached Byron.

Byron's eyes immediately filled. "Ain't got a home no more, Mr. Keller. Miss Helen's house burned down last night. She was in it. I was coming home from the store. Scottie came and helped put out the fire. Afterwards he asked me where did I want to go. I couldn't think of any other place so I said here and Scottie dropped me off." Byron dropped his chin to his chest. Two huge tears rolled down his cheeks.

Darren was speechless. He knelt down next to Byron and put his arm around Byron's shoulders. They were silent for a few moments. Then the roar of a powerful, finely tuned engine resounded down the street, echoing off the walls of Mama Angelina's.

"Miss Walls is comin'," said Byron, sniffling.

Colette's Corvette, shining candy-apple red in the bright sunshine, pulled into the parking lot. Out of force of habit, she parked down at the end of the lot. She got out of her car and waved to Darren and Byron. Sensing something was wrong, she strode toward them quickly.

She was wearing khaki shorts and a white polo shirt. Her wavy hair flowed over her shoulders as she pushed her sunglasses on top of her head. Darren stared for her for a moment, unable to quell the sudden surge of happiness he felt, just looking at her, then quickly rearranged his features for Byron's sake.

"What is it?" she asked.

Byron's eyes filled up with tears again. "My house burned down last night and Miss Helen burned up inside it."

Colette's blood froze in her veins. Darren saw her face go white and still. Then she quickly bent down over the sorrowing Byron, patting his back and murmuring comforting sounds. After a while she said, "Do you want to come inside? I'll make some coffee and we can talk for a while."

Byron wiped his eyes on his sleeve. "No thanks, Miss Walls. I want to get these here flowers planted before they get thirsty. They're pretty, aren't they?"

"Yes, they sure are. Well, you come on in when you're ready." She got to her feet and looked at Darren. "Good thing I came early. Why are you here so early, anyway?

"I was going to ask you the same question, but now I have another one. Why did you look like that when Byron mentioned the fire?" They walked up to the door and Darren opened it, holding it for Colette.

"Oh, I had some things I wanted to work on. Payroll, quarterly taxes, and stuff. The number stuff is always easier when there aren't any interruptions." She smiled at him, just a touch too brightly.

Darren knew she was ignoring his question. He had never known her to be afraid of anything, but something had her scared. On a hunch, he asked, "How's Roger?" He kept his voice light.

Colette said slowly, "I don't know. I haven't seen him since last night."

He was determined to find out what was going on with her, but when he saw the blankets on the reception area couch, he knew now was not the time.

"We have to find someplace for Byron to stay. He can't live here," Darren said. "No matter how much he'd like to."

Colette looked thoughtful. "Well, when he comes in, I'll talk to him. I know he must have someone he can stay with. But I can't blame him for coming here. Mama's has always been another home to him." Darren helped her fold the blankets and put them away in the coat closet. He watched her walk over to her desk and turn on her computer, ready to work.

Darren turned and went into his office. "Whatever your secret is, 'Lette, I'll find out. We'll solve this together," he muttered.

He opened up the Sunday *Inquirer.* His eyes widened.

## U. OF PENNSYLVANIA MUSEUM ROBBED

One of the most interesting artifacts brought back from the Los Naranjos site excavated by the late Dr. Paul Crane was stolen late yesterday, according to museum officials. A richly painted pottery jar was missing as of 7:00 P.M. Saturday. There was no sign of forced entry into the museum, and the glass case that housed the artifacts was undisturbed. A jade ring, found with the jar, was left in the case, along with several other objects from the ill-fated archaeology expedition. Detectives are searching for clues . . .

# 54

Roger Phillips slowly opened his eyes, then closed them quickly. A beam of brilliant sunlight poured in through one of the chinks in the barn wall and onto his face. He stretched out lazily on his bed of musty hay and smiled as the acrid smell of burned wood came to him on the breeze.

His escape last night had been laughably easy. While Marcus Turner had been running around like a headless chicken until his hero dog came to the rescue, Roger had just kept walking in a circle, behind the burning house and back to the barn. Once inside, he had carefully made his way to the back, where he had found a pile of old hay. It was dry enough, and Roger had curled down into it, sure that they wouldn't search the barn.

They didn't. Between the fire and the corpse of Chief Haas and Turner's bullet-grazed arm, the Aronston police had more than enough to do. Good, thorough police work was forgotten in this time of confusion and grief. When Turner explained that Phillips had come out of the barn and was last seen walking toward the road, nobody thought to look in the barn again. Not that anyone really wanted to, either. The walls were angled crazily on the old stone foundation, and the roof smoldered in several places in spite of Scott Herr's hosedown. The place was a deathtrap. Only a crazy person would hide in there a second time.

Roger had fallen asleep, half-buried in the hay, before they left. He had slept very well. Now he sat up, rubbed his eyes, and yawned. He knew that today would be his last day in Aronston. Too many people were too interested in him. But he had unfinished business with Colette.

Today she would join him and become his Xochitl, his eternal love. Or she would die. He felt a stab in his heart at the thought of killing her, of crushing out her vital spark of joy and life. But if she would not become one with him . . . He smiled slightly and shrugged his shoulders. This made him realize that his clothing was full of hay and that he was very thirsty. He needed to find some water.

He made his way through the back of the barn so as not to be seen from the road. He squeezed out through two broken boards and spotted what looked like the remains of a springhouse near a stand of trees at a point midway between the house and barn. He peered around the corner of the barn. No one was there. Just the pitiful blackened remains of the house. He moved quickly to the springhouse.

The old, rotted wooden door broke away in his hand as he lifted it up. He looked down a flight of seven well-worn stone steps, stained green with moss and algae, and saw a pool of still, black water. He descended the steps, knelt down, put his face into the water, and drank deeply. The water was icy cold and utterly delicious.

Roger took off his jacket and shirt and splashed handfuls of water over his upper body, which was itchy from sleeping in the hay. He gasped at the shock of the cold water on his skin. He thrust his face deep into the black pool, holding his breath for almost a minute. Then he dressed, waiting for the water's surface to become smooth again. He looked back down into the water. The reflection was more Aaron Moyer than Roger Phillips. His eyes looked strange and flat. His mouth had an unsavory curve to it. Roger blinked hard but the reflection remained unchanged.

The small bit of him that was still Roger was quickly overcome by an intense grief. *I'm dying by inches. My family is gone, my home is gone, my life is gone. Now I don't even look like myself anymore. I figure I've got maybe another twenty-four hours before I'm swallowed up, gone forever.* A tear ran down his cheek. Then he gathered himself as well as he could. He thought, *A lot can happen in twenty-four hours. I'm going to find a way to end this if I can.*

If Roger had been looking into the spring while he was thinking, he would have seen his own face return for a few fleeting moments. The mouth uncurled and his eyes were warm and green. Then he remembered that he still needed to attend to Colette. The cruel twist returned to his mouth as he smiled.

He left the springhouse and began walking east, back toward Aronston.

# 55

Marcus Turner grunted as sat down on the sofa. He swallowed a painkiller, washing it down with ice water. He rested his bullet-grazed left arm on a stack of pillows and put an ice pack on the bandages. The emergency room doctor had told him it was a fairly minor wound, gave him some antibiotic ointment and some pills for the pain, and left it to a nurse to clean up and bandage his arm. The doctor had been very businesslike with him, but Turner saw the stress lines around her eyes and mouth. He knew she had come to him after she'd seen Eddie Haas.

"Guess even doctors can get grossed out, huh, Cindy?" he asked the dozing Newfoundland, curled up on a worn, fake fur rug by the fireplace. Cindy stretched out on the rug, grumbled, and went back to sleep.

*Maybe it was only a minor wound, but man, did it hurt,* thought Turner. He picked up Eddie Haas' notebook to read over his notes from last night. Before leaving the fire scene last night he had spoken to Eddie's second-in-command, Adam Schutter. Turner had filled him in on all the details about Roger Phillips as Schutter coordinated the ambulance, the coroner, and ordered more frequent police patrols of Aronston. Schutter kept wiping his eyes on his sleeve.

"God, Eddie. God, am I gonna miss you." Schutter blew his nose. "Mark, man, anything you want. Anything I can do, just let me know."

"Let me have Eddie's notebook, plus anything else you boys have on the call he took. Eddie came here to talk to me about it, but he . . . died before he could say anything."

"It was that Phillips guy all right. A woman named Colette Walls ID'd him as the killer of her neighbor. It was real weird, she claimed he'd been zapped—you'll read about it in the notes. So then Eddie came up here to tell you about it and now he's . . . gone."

Now it was Turner's turn to wipe his eyes. "I want to find out more about Phillips. I'm pretty sure he's our arsonist." Turner hesitated a moment, and then went on. "You know, Vicky Collins swears that Roger Phillips made Eddie start shooting. She says she saw Phillips point or something and then all hell broke loose. Then she saw Eddie put the gun in his mouth. You know what's weird, Adam? I almost believe her." Turner swallowed hard.

Schutter was silent for a few moments. Finally he spoke, slowly and thoughtfully. "You know, Marc, I kinda have to believe her, too. Eddie was a happy guy. Two boys he was real proud of. Loved his wife. Sanest person I ever met. No reason for him to go postal at all, especially not to you, Marc. He thought you were a great guy. No, I gotta believe something made him do it. Person has to be totally fucked to do murder and suicide. Eddie ain't like that . . . .wasn't like that." Schutter puffed out his cheeks and blew a sigh. "Well, let's get you over to the hospital and get your arm checked out."

"I'm riding with Eddie," Turner had said. And he did, staring at the bloody sheet covering Haas's face in the back of the ambulance. The ambulance siren screamed as it sped up the Harrisburg Pike East on the way to the hospital. The streetlights flickered through the heavily tinted glass, making pale eerie shadows on the red-stained whiteness. Turner picked up Haas's cold, rubbery hand and held it in his own until it was warmed. It felt alive again. Turner whispered, "I'll get him, Ed. I'll get him for us both." He could have sworn that Haas' hand tightened on his.

The ambulance careened around the corner, heading up the last block to the hospital. The sheet fell away from Eddie Haas's face. Eddie's right eye, the only thing intact in his blown-apart face, stared intently into Turner's. Turner could not repress a shudder.

Now, in the sunlit security of his own living room, Turner remembered the eye and muttered, "I'll get the sonofabitch," and opened Haas's notebook. The codeine in the pills made his eyelids heavy, and he rubbed his eyes with his right hand.

Five minutes later, Marcus Turner and Cinders were both dozing in the Sunday peace and quiet.

# 56

Darren emerged from his office with a sheaf of papers. He saw Colette staring blankly at the posters on the wall.

"'Lette, are you okay?"

She turned to him and smiled wanly. "I'm all right. Just thinking."

Darren looked at her. Suddenly he said, "Look, 'Lette, my wife's working this afternoon and my girls are off with their friends. Why don't you come over and we can have some lunch and talk? Just talk?"

Colette looked relieved at the idea of having something, anything, to take her mind off whatever it was that was troubling her. "Sure, Darren. Sounds good. I'll go tell Byron where we'll be and we'll get him a sandwich or something. Poor man."

Darren nodded in agreement. After Colette returned with Byron's lunch order, they left together in Darren's minivan.

The silence between them lay thick and heavy. Colette was deeply concerned by Byron's story. She wanted to tell Darren everything and to hide in his arms but feared he'd think she was crazy. For his part, Darren was weighing whether to tell Colette what was in his heart. He, too, was wondering if she'd think he was nuts.

"A pearl of great price," Colette murmured to herself.

"What?" asked Darren, startled.

Colette looked at Darren. "A friend like you," she said, gazing at him levelly.

Darren saw the seriousness on her face. He took a deep breath and said, "As long as we're talking about jewels, I think your price is far above rubies." He smiled.

She grinned back at him. It felt good to be with each other.

When they entered the house, Colette looked at the immaculate, picture-perfect décor, smiled and said nothing. Darren ushered her into the den. Scribbled-over staff papers were scattered everywhere. A stack of newspapers was on the floor. The bookcases were jumbled like a rummage sale. Darren quickly drew the curtains to hide the dust.

"Now this looks like you," she said, grinning. "What a beautiful piano!"

"Make yourself comfortable and I'll get us a glass of wine," he said, feeling oddly formal with her. It was the first time he had ever seen her out of the office, except at the company picnics and they didn't count. He found a bottle of Chablis in the refrigerator and poured it into two of Andrea's best crystal wineglasses.

When he came back into the den, Colette had slipped off her shoes and was curled up in the big recliner looking over some of his music sheets.

"Thanks," she said as he handed her the wine. "I didn't know you wrote music. Would you play something for me?"

Since there was no other seat in the room, Darren sat down at the piano bench. "What would you like to hear?"

"I don't know. Whatever."

He gazed at her, his light brown eyes soft. In the big chair and the dim light Colette looked fragile and lost. He had never seen her look so vulnerable. Almost unconsciously he began to play "Love is the Answer" and was immediately lost in the music. He had never played it so well. In a fine clear baritone he began to sing:

> *And when you feel afraid, love one another*
> *When you've lost your way, love one another*
> *When you're all alone, love one another*
> *When you're far from home, love one another*
> *When you're down and out, love one another*
> *All your hope's run out, love one another*
> *When you need a friend, love one another*
> *When you're near the end, love, we got to love*
> *We got to love one another*

When he finished the song, it felt like he had awakened from a dream. He looked over at Colette again. She was staring at him, blue eyes wide with surprise.

"That was wonderful, Darren. I had no idea," she whispered.

"I didn't either," he admitted. "And I don't usually sing it."

"What was that? I know I've heard it before."

"An old Todd Rundgren song. 'Love Is the Answer.' I used to play it when I worked with a band years ago."

Colette smiled at her wineglass and ran her finger around the rim. "So, you used to be a rock-and-roll wild man. What happened?"

Darren shrugged. "I decided I wasn't good enough to make a living at it. I met Andrea and got a real job at Mama's. Went to school and worked hard and here I am."

Colette raised an eyebrow, as if she didn't quite believe his story. She unfolded herself and got up, walked over to the piano, and leaned on it. "Here you are," she agreed softly.

"Look," said Darren. "This is me seventeen years ago." He handed Colette the photograph.

She looked at it and laughed. "I never would have guessed that was you. Well, maybe. I've seen that expression on your face." She pointed to the other band members. "What happened to the rest of them?" she asked.

Darren took the picture from her. "What happened to

Myth? Let's see. Laurie lives in Reading now. She has six
kids and weighs about two hundred pounds. Ed went to L.A.
ten years ago and I haven't heard from him since. Tommy was
killed in a car accident a few years ago." He fell silent, staring at the picture as if it were a window back in time.

Colette said lightly, "I bet you were a lot better than you
think you were," and then looked at Darren's expression. She
realized, with the force of a revelation, that this was the dream
Darren had lost so long ago. He probably was really good, she
thought, and something happened to make him quit.

She walked over to him, bent down, and kissed his cheek.
"I'm sorry," she whispered. Darren understood.

"It's hard to explain to a nonmusician, 'Lette." Darren's
voice was low. "All I can say is, once the music is in your
soul, it's there forever. No matter how hard you try to forget
it." Darren stared down at the piano keys.

Colette placed her hand on his shoulder and was silent for
a moment. She looked at the overstuffed, untidy bookcases. In
an effort to make conversation, she asked, "Have you really
read all these mystery novels?"

"Yes, and there's a real-life one going on right now in
Aronston. Your Roger is a part of it somehow."

"I know," she said in a low voice. She sat down next to him
on the bench. Darren picked up her hand and held it.

"Listen, 'Lette, I've been thinking. There were strange
murders and fires in Honduras six weeks or so ago. We got a
shipment from Honduras three days ago and now we are having the same strange fires here. People are dying in these
fires. Whatever is causing this came with the meat."

"But what, Darren? The meat passed inspection. Besides,
how could a meat shipment have anything to do with fires?"

"I don't know. Think. Tell me about Roger."

Colette sighed deeply. Slowly, haltingly, she told Darren
the entire tale. How she'd met Roger. How he had raped her,
hurt her, and then healed her. How he knew things about her.
How he made her feel. About the strange power she could
sense within him.

She told him about the Mayan visions. The king and the
captive princess. How Roger was possessed by the spirit of

the king, and she was supposed to be the princess. How Roger was able to make her see the memories of thousands of years ago. How she could feel that she was becoming Xochitl more and more, each time Roger touched her.

She told him how she had felt safe, secure, and adored when she was with Roger, but deeply troubled and empty when he was not there. And how, finally, he threatened her when she found the courage to resist him. She also told him about Lee's murder and how Lee's body had burst into intense white flame.

"Darren, I know it all sounds crazy. I don't expect that you'll believe me. I do know that he's . . . not human. I know he's the one starting the fires. I saw him kill Lee and burn him to ash. I hate being afraid, but I *am* afraid. Of him and of this . . . power he has over me." She blinked back tears.

Darren squeezed her hand tightly. "'Lette, I'm afraid for you. There were some archaeologists who were murdered in Honduras about four months ago. They were working at an old Mayan village site. Then there was a string of unexplained fires. Then . . . nothing until a few days ago. At the archaeology site they found a jar, empty, and right next to it a ring. Maybe whatever's in Roger came from there." He got up and pulled out the photograph of the artifacts from yesterday's newspapers stacked next to the chair. Colette looked at the picture and gasped with shock.

"Darren . . . this ring . . . the woman, the Mayan princess in the visions, the one who's supposed to be me, she wears this ring in her nose. I *know* this is it. Dear God." She lifted her eyes to Darren's, her face pale.

Darren took her hands again and folded them into his. "Please tell me you'll be careful. Don't see this guy again. Keep your door locked. Call the police if you suspect anything. Or call me. Call me anyway. 'Lette, I . . . I worry about you, okay?" He could not say what was really in his heart. *Damn it,* he thought. *I sound like her father, not her lover. Why can't I tell her?*

Colette looked at Darren's face. *He really is in love with me,* she thought. She pulled her hands free and touched his face. Their eyes locked for a long moment. Her eyes widened a little. *I love you, too,* she thought, amazed at the realization.

Darren dropped his eyes and cleared his throat. "Well, guess I'd better make us something to eat." He started to get up but Colette stopped him.

"Wait a second. I have something to tell you," she murmured. She drew his face down to hers and kissed him, tenderly, with her heart on her lips. He pulled her close to him and returned the kiss. Then they broke apart. Darren held her face in his hands, studying her eyes. Then he grinned impishly at her.

"Ham and cheese okay with you, 'Lette?"

Colette laughed for the first time in what felt like years. It felt wonderful to laugh. "Sounds good. Let me help."

Hand in hand, they walked into the kitchen.

Darren remembered that the jar was missing. No sign of a break-in at the museum. Suddenly he had a powerful sense that Colette was in terrible danger. More than either of them knew.

# 57

Roger had retraced Byron's path of the previous day, wanting to keep off the main roads as much as possible. He did not fear the police but didn't want a confrontation if it could be avoided. It would only waste time. Still, in order to reach Colette's apartment, he would have to walk through the town.

Aronston was packed with Founders' Days tourists. As expected, the news of a brand-new play by Shawn Williams had brought a tidal wave of people into town. The cute little restaurants had huge lines of hungry people waiting for brunch. The artsy boutiques and antique stores that lined the streets around the town square were ringing up record sales. Roger walked quickly and purposefully, like a man on a mission, and blended into the groups of people chatting on the sidewalks or gazing into windows. Once he saw a passing patrol car and turned down an alley until it was gone.

He still needed to cross the square to get to High Street,

where Colette's house was. He pushed back the memory of yesterday's horrible vision. *Soon I will be beyond their reach,* he thought. *I'm almost there.* He began to cut through the square.

The town square was already thronged with theater fans trying to get the best vantage point for the play. Roger moved quickly, threading his way through the crowd. Suddenly he tripped over something and fell heavily, landing on his chest.

He groaned in pain. He was sprawled out on the brick walkway. His shins were scraped and bleeding. His ribs hurt sharply when he breathed. He rolled on his side to see what he had tripped over.

It was a large rectangular stone, carved with Mayan glyphs. A god-figure was grimacing at him, tongue extended, eyes wild with blood lust. He felt something at his back. Slowly and painfully Roger struggled to his feet and turned.

Behind him was the gallows upon which Mark and Tom Reifsnyder had died so gruesomely. On the platform adjoining the gallows was the altar that had stood atop the pyramid in the visions. The gray stone was stained with rivulets of human blood and gore. It seemed to glow in the bright sunlight.

The Reifsnyders' bodies were still dangling from the nooses, faces bloated and purple, clothes stained. But their eyes were open, staring at him. Next to them stood the Mayan priest, his face an echo of the god-figure carved on the stone behind him.

Roger heard a faint rustle behind him. He spun around again and saw the gallows crowd from yesterday. Their clothing had rotted away in places, and sickly gray-green skin hung from their bones like rags. Some had their inner organs exposed, leaking pus and thick black fluid onto the ground. One woman was nursing a skeletal, blue-black infant at her shriveled breast. The stench was overpowering.

They stared balefully at Roger with rheumy yellow eyes. He stared back, terror rising in his throat. As if they were a single entity, they took a step toward him. Roger stepped back behind the carved rock. He turned to look at the priest.

Without taking his eyes from Roger, the priest stepped in front of the swaying, staring bodies of Mark and Thomas Reifsnyder. His right hand clutched a gleaming, black-bladed sword. The priest stood absolutely still for several moments. Roger could feel the eyes of the ghoulish men and women behind him, staring. Roger held his breath. The silence pressed down on him like warm, sultry summer air, overhung by the stench of death.

With a single swift motion that broke the spell as thunder breaks a humid afternoon, the priest whirled and sliced his sword through the ropes swinging taut from the gallows. The Reifsnyders' bodies fell to the ground with a sickening thud. Roger sucked in his breath and then gasped as the brothers sat up, stared unblinkingly at him, and then rose to their feet.

Their swollen, mottled faces and bulging bloody eyes contorted weirdly in a mask of hatred and rage. Like the crowd before, their mouths opened as one.

"Aaron," they croaked, their voices rough and indistinct from the nooses still tight around their throats.

Behind Roger the crowd echoed "Aaron" in perfect unison, the name rising and falling as if on the breeze. The priest pointed his sword at Roger. The Reifsnyder brothers and the crowd stepped slowly and deliberately toward Roger, closing ranks.

Roger spun in panic, saw a gap between the desiccated bodies and ran. He pushed through the people, their odor filling his lungs and making him want to retch. One man spat at him as he shoved past, a brown-black gob of foul stuff that burned Roger's cheek like pure acid. He kept running, through the square, across the Harrisburg Pike, dodging cars that honked angrily at him.

"Jesus, asshole, what the fuck are you on?" one driver shouted out the window as Roger leaped over the hood of his car, twisted to evade another, and finally made it across the street. He turned and looked over his shoulder for a moment.

## 58

The staff at the ElderCare Center, not wishing to completely miss the Founders' Days closing festivities, decided that it would be nice to take the patients that were able to go outside out to enjoy this gorgeous spring day. That way, patients and staff could enjoy the crowds and at least some of the play. All patients who were not bedridden or completely lost to Alzheimer's dementia were duly bundled up and taken out to the sidewalk along the Harrisburg Pike. Levi Faber was one of the last patients to be wheeled out in his chair.

Levi was in one of the moods he fell into occasionally, usually on days when Tracy was not expected. On those days he let the despair of the ElderCare Center and the indignity of his situation get to him. After all, he had nothing to look forward to except his cup of tea. Added to that was all the unpleasantness of the last few days.

"Not so fast, young man!" he snapped at the orderly who was pushing his chair.

"Relax, Mr. Faber," said the orderly, good-naturedly. "Lemme find you a good spot here so you can see what's going on." The orderly was a Gretna College student who worked at the ElderCare Center part-time. He was rather fond of Levi, even when Levi was behaving like an old curmudgeon.

"In the sun, young man, in the sun. My bones are chilled."

"You spend too much time sitting by that drafty window, that's why. Should go into the lounge once in while, watch some TV. Nice and warm in there."

"No thank you. I got my window and my radio and that suits me just fine," Levi replied irritably. Damn fool thing, hauling us all out here, he thought. I can see everything just fine from my window. Besides, by the time they get us all back in it'll be too late for my tea. High point of my day anymore. Fools, all of them.

"Well, okay, if that's how you want it. Here, this is a good spot. You have a good view of the stage here, and it's nice and sunny. Now don't go anyplace. I've got to go back and get some more of your friends." The orderly parked Levi's chair in a sunny spot near the edge of the sidewalk, set the brake, and left.

Even Levi's bad temper could not resist the golden sunshine and sweet clean air. He closed his eyes and tipped his face into the light, feeling it warm his skin. He breathed deeply.

He had been badly troubled last night. He knew before he even got his copy of the *Clarion,* with its late-breaking story, that the Bauman place was gone and Helen was dead. He had called Tracy that morning to ask her not to call the doctor. She began talking about the Bauman fire.

"I can't believe it, Pop-Pop. I was just there not an hour before the fire. I had to drop Roger Phillips off at her house. I don't know what to say. I guess she never had a chance once the fire broke out." Tracy's voice was shaky.

"Who did you say? Who did you drop off?" Levi's voice scaled up with apprehension.

"Roger Phillips. Oh! Pop-Pop, you were right about him. He did survive. He wasn't home when his own house burned. But now he's missing again. Maybe he died in this fire."

"No, young lady, he didn't die in the fire last night. I'd bet my life on it. Tracy Faber, I thought I told you to stay away from him. There's something wrong about him and I . . . and I'm not sure what it is." Levi thought he did know, but he also knew that Tracy would hang up on him if he dared to suggest that Roger Phillips was possessed by the soul of Aaron Moyer.

He could hear the frown in her voice when she replied. "Pop-Pop, he's perfectly fine. A little shaken up, maybe, but so would I be if I lost my family. We went for coffee and I took him out to Miss Helen's because he needed a place to stay. I was going to see about getting him his job back." Yet he could also hear a little doubt in her voice, as if she wasn't quite sure about Roger. She was a smart girl, Tracy was, he had thought. Didn't need a rocket scientist to figure out that two fires involving the same guy meant trouble. In the silence, he heard her sigh and knew she'd figured it out, too.

"Tracy, listen to your Pop-Pop. Are you listening?"

"Yes, Pop-Pop. I'm not a little girl anymore. I can make . . ."

"Was I right about Roger Phillips?" he interrupted.

"Yes."

"All right then, missy. If you never do anything else for me again, stay away from him. Don't get him his job back. Don't see him again. Don't even talk to him on the telephone." Levi put all the force he could muster into his old-man's voice.

Tracy sighed deeply. "Okay, okay. I'll do it for you, Pop-Pop. I love you."

"I love you, too, little girl."

He had hung up the phone, worried and unhappy. Until now, in the warm sunshine, which beamed down on his aged face like a benediction. He slowly opened his eyes and sighed contentedly.

For a moment, he thought he was dreaming again. Then, abruptly, he knew he wasn't.

Aaron Moyer himself, alive as could be, was shoving his way through the crowds lining the sidewalk. He had a look of abject terror on his face. But the mouth, the full, soft-lipped mouth, had that unmistakable evil turn to it. He was coming directly toward Levi.

Without stopping to think, Levi fumbled with the brake that held his chair in place. He released it and smartly turned the chair and wheeled it into Aaron Moyer's path.

Roger stopped for a moment in front of the determined old man. He was startled by the steely expression on Levi's face, the look of recognition.

"Stay out of my way," he cried and tried to push around Levi.

Levi's arm shot out and clutched Roger's arm with a strong, viselike grip. His bony fingers dug deeply into Roger's flesh.

"Thought I told you to stay out of *my* way, Aaron Moyer," he hissed. Levi could feel a strange electrical tingle traveling up his arm, but was too angry to think about it.

*This is no ghost that's got me,* thought Roger. *This is a real person. And he knows who I am. He knows . . .*

Roger shook his arm violently and pushed Levi away, hard. Levi lost his grip on Roger's arm and the wheelchair careened toward the curb. The chair went over the curb with a thump and spilled Levi out into the street. Levi's head hit the curb, and his fragile, century-old skull cracked as delicately and irrevocably as an eggshell.

As the people hurried to Levi's side, the oldest citizen of Aronston was already dead. Roger sprinted down the Harrisburg Pike. He did not look back.


Marcus Turner awoke from his codeine doze with a start. "Man, how long was I out?" He craned his neck to look at the clock over the mantel. An hour and a half had passed.

"Cindy, don't let me sleep like that. I've got work to do." Cindy thumped her tail on the floor but didn't stir from her patch of sunshine on the floor. Turner opened Haas's notebook to the last written page. He carefully deciphered the black scrawled notes, muttering as he read.

"Colette Walls. High Street, second floor. Assault, murder. Broken furniture. Scorched floor, quantity of gray ash . . ."

Gray ash. He remembered Jay Stanley's phone call. Gray ash on the ship. Human ash. A twinge of apprehension ran up his spine.

"Lee Hsiang missing, resides third floor of building. C. Walls states one Roger Phillips burned Hsiang into dust. Walls. Phillips stated that he will be back. Walls obvious suspect *but* don't think she did it. No evidence."

Marcus Turner felt the same deep dread that Darren Keller had felt an hour earlier. Something was going to happen soon, and it wasn't going to be good. He decided to get dressed and go talk to Colette Walls himself.

"She's the key, Cin," he said to his dog.

He got a tail thump in response.

# 59

Winded and terrified after his one-and-a-half mile sprint, Roger Phillips saw the nondescript, fire-damaged building housing Mama Angelina's Specialty Meats ahead on his right. Without glancing back, he ran into the parking lot and back behind the plant to the loading dock. The door to the receiving office was open to the warm afternoon breezes. Roger noticed without emotion the remains of his car, as if it were a relic of another life. He raced up the steps and into the office, slamming the door behind him. He leaned against Scott Herr's desk and panted, drawing in great gulps of air, tasting the raw-meat-and-disinfectant smell that lingered in the manufacturing area of the plant.

He looked on the wall and saw the key to the receiving office door hanging on its labeled hook. He quickly picked it up and locked the door.

"Now what?" he said aloud. "How do you hide from a bunch of corpses who want to kill you?" His heart still thudded in his chest at a jackhammer pace. The fear clutched at his stomach like an iron claw. Every nerve in his body was stretched taut. Gotta chill, gotta think, get ready to do battle. He tried to remember his training in the 82$^{nd}$ Airborne, but that, too, seemed like a distant memory from another life. He stood facing the door, waiting for his mind to clear and form a plan.

"Hey, Mr. Phillips!" exclaimed a voice behind him.

Roger nearly jumped out of his skin. He wheeled around and saw Byron Mirkowski grinning at him.

"Lots of people wanted to know where you were. I'm glad you came back." Byron's grin faded as he looked at Roger's wild eyes and strangely altered face. "Are you okay? I'm sorry for scarin' you." Roger stared and said nothing. Byron began to shift his weight uncomfortably.

"Did you know my house burned down? Miss Helen got burned down, too." Byron sniffled. "Miss Walls said she'd find a place for me to live 'cause I can't live here. Mr. Keller said."

Roger found his voice. "Colette Walls? Is Colette here?"

"No, she an' Mr. Keller went to get some lunch. They should be back pretty soon now. They were going to bring me some. I think Mr. Keller might be kinda mad at you. You forgot to punch out on the clock when you left." Byron looked again at Roger's face. "You look different. But you didn't shave your beard or nothing. Scottie Herr looked real different when he shaved his."

Roger was smiling, Aaron's smile. A plan was finally forming in his brain. "No, Byron, I think Mr. Keller won't be mad at me. It's going to be okay."

Byron smiled back. "If you say so, Mr. Phillips."

**60**

Colette Walls and Darren Keller pulled up to Mama Angelina's. The ride back to the plant had been almost as silent as the ride to Darren's house. But this time they had each been sorting out their thoughts.

Darren had not yet told Colette of the argument with Andrea and of his emerging plans for the rest of his life. He was satisfied with the feeling that his 'Lette would be there with him. Colette, for her part, was a little bewildered to realize just how much she had felt for Darren. On this gorgeous spring day, full of promise, it was easy to believe that anything was possible. Even a future together.

Colette picked up the bag containing a sandwich and soda for Byron. "I'll just take this back to Byron and then I'll get to work," she said.

"Okay, 'Lette. Chris Nein should be here in an hour and a half or so. Maybe I'll give him a call and see if he can make it sooner." Darren and Colette smiled at each other, a private sharing, and then Colette passed through the double doors and down the hall to the plant.

"Byron? I've got your lunch here." Colette called, her voice echoing in the empty plant. The coolness of the air in the plant made her shiver.

No answer.

"Byron?" she called again. Out of the corner of her eye she detected a small movement behind the long row of shiny meat-grinding machines. She turned and began walking toward the machines.

As she approached the last machine, she saw a pool of blood on the floor. It was fresh, and the smell of copper came to her. Quickly she took the last few steps and rounded the corner behind the machines. She stopped short and gasped with fear.

A strangely altered Roger stood there, hands in pockets, grinning at her. Byron's corpse lay at his feet, with its throat torn out. The head was nearly severed. Pieces of white fibrous trachea, shreds of muscle tissue and chunks of vein and artery like black spaghetti were scattered around the body. A surprised expression was on the face, and the sightless eyes gazed up at the ceiling. Blood trickled from the torn veins of Byron's throat.

Colette took two steps backward, never taking her eyes from Roger's. She stifled the revulsion creeping up in her throat and the terror freezing the blood in her veins. The best defense is a good offense, she thought. Got to stay cool. She took a deep breath.

"Why, Roger? What did Byron ever do to you?" She was grateful that her own voice sounded strong and challenging.

Roger's grin widened, and he looked unspeakably evil. "He was going to answer you when you called. I couldn't let him do that. So I tore out his throat with my bare hands. Easy enough, and rather fun, actually." He took his blood-smeared hands out of his pockets and held them out to her as if to hug her.

"I wanted to surprise you. And you are surprised, aren't you, my love?"

Colette's fear was suddenly overcome by anger. It heated

her blood and fired her courage. "I wouldn't call it surprised, exactly. Not by a long shot." She looked down at Byron's corpse—an innocent victim in every sense of the word—and back up at Roger.

"Give up. Turn yourself in to the police. Maybe they can help you. Think, Roger. You killed your own family and the couple over in Carriage Court. You killed my neighbor, you incinerated a nice old lady, and now a harmless man is dead. You can't go on like this. Please, Roger. I know you're in there. You told me you were going to fight this . . . whatever it is. Fight, damn you!"

Roger's face changed a little. For a moment Colette saw the mouth straighten and the green eyes soften, the cold blueness gone from them.

"Help me, Colette!" It was a whisper.

Then his face hardened again and the mouth twisted. He stared icily into her eyes.

"You forgot the trucker," he said. "But I'm not surprised." He threw back his head and laughed.

Colette's eyes darted around, looking for some kind of weapon. If I can just make it to the back, she thought. That's where the cleavers and knives are.

She spun around and began to run. Her foot splashed in the oily slick that was Byron's congealing blood. She stumbled, unable to overcome her horror. Roger's quick steps came up behind her. She twisted to face him and fell on her back.

"Don't touch me or I'll . . . or else!" she panted. She raised herself up a little, like a crab, and moved away from Roger. He watched her for a moment, smiling a little, then moved toward her. She lashed out with her left foot, aiming at his crotch. Deftly he caught her foot and pulled her in towards him. He leaned over, seized her shoulders and brought her to her feet.

His face was inches from hers. "Give up, Colette. You belong to me. You have belonged to me all through time and you will belong to me through eternity."

"No. Xochitl doesn't want me. That vision last night? She went away when I told her what a monster you were. She wants to be with the man she loves, not some cruel inhuman thing. Let me go!" She struggled, but Roger's fingers tightened painfully on her shoulders. She was too close to him to get in a good kick.

" 'Lette? What's going on here?" came Darren's voice.

Colette was seized by panic. She knew Roger would kill Darren, as surely as he had killed Lee. And Byron. And all the others. And that she could not allow to happen. "Darren! Go back! Call the police! Please, please, don't come in here!" Colette screamed desperately. She squirmed and stomped down hard on Roger's insteps. He did not seem to feel her at all. His attention was focused on Darren's approaching figure.

Darren stared, aghast at what he saw. Colette, her legs smeared with blood, being held against her will by someone vaguely familiar. With a shock, he realized it had to be Roger Phillips.

"Phillips? Is that you? Let her go!"

"So this is Darren Keller. Your good friend Darren. Your knight in shining armor. Is he what's keeping you from me?" Roger hissed into Colette's face, his skin reddening with jealousy and anger.

With a seemingly superhuman effort, Colette freed herself from Roger's grip. She ran a few steps toward Darren, pressed her hands on his chest, and began pushing him backwards toward the door. Her face pale and drawn, she summoned every ounce of earnestness she possessed.

"Darren, listen to me. Go back. Leave now. Call the police. Please just *go*. I'm begging you!" She was yanked back and away from Darren. Roger's arm encircled her neck, cutting off her voice. His other arm wrapped around her waist. He stared coldly at Darren, using the fiercely struggling Colette as a shield.

"She belongs to me, Keller. This is between us. Perhaps you had better take her advice and go—" He roared with pain. Colette twisted away from him, her mouth red with blood. Roger gazed at his arm, at the place where she had bitten him. She spat and wiped her chin, then remembered the cleavers. She ran toward the back of the plant, past the huge freezer room and the steamers for the meatballs. As she ran, she heard the sounds of punches being thrown behind her.

*Got to hurry or Roger will* . . . She could not bear to finish the thought.

Finally she saw the long tables and the butchering tools all hanging neat and sharpened on the back wall. She grabbed a twelve-inch knife. The light glinted on the razor-sharp blade. She took down a cleaver with her other hand, spun around and ran back.

The throbbing rumble of machinery exploded into her brain. Someone had turned on the grinders.

## 61

Marcus Turner pulled up in front of the Victorian home with its shining brass mailboxes, tall narrow windows, and etched-glass front door. In front were a man and a woman. The man was working on the door, and the woman was planting marigolds around the latticework beneath the porch. They both looked haggard and worried.

Turner got out of the car. "Excuse me," he called. "I'm looking for Colette Walls?"

The man's eyes narrowed. "And who are you?" he asked, coldly. The woman looked up, her face pale with fear and exhaustion.

Turner walked up to Jason McDevitt, badge and ID in hand. "I'm Marcus Turner, the fire marshal. I'd like to ask Colette a few questions about Roger Phillips."

Jason and Emily exchanged glances. "Do you know where Roger Phillips is?" asked Emily.

"No, but I think Miss Walls might. Either that, or he's going to come looking for her."

"That's what Colette said he'd do," said Emily. "Why are you interested if you're the fire marshal here? Where's Ed Haas?"

Turner bowed his head. "Dead," he said simply. Jason and Emily gasped. Turner continued. "Guess you didn't see the paper. Last night the Bauman place burned down. I was there with my people while Eddie was talking to Miss Walls. Eddie drove out to find me and tell me that there was a connection between these fires and Phillips. While he was there, something happened. He shot himself."

With a deep sigh, he continued. "Look, please tell me if you know where Colette Walls is. She may be in danger."

Jason and Emily looked at each other again. Finally Emily spoke. "I saw her a couple of hours ago. She said she was going into work. She works at Mama Angelina's."

"I know," said Turner. He looked at them both. "Well, guess I'd better be going. Hey, why aren't you going up to see the play?"

"We don't feel very festive right now. One of our tenants was killed last night," Jason said, his voice low.

Emily shuddered. "The last thing I want to see right now is more death, more pain."

"That's right. God, I'm sorry." Turner shook his head, then straightened up and lifted his chin. "We're going to get this guy, I promise you." He tried to project a confidence he didn't quite feel.

Emily reached out and took his big brown hands into her small, plump, dirt-streaked ones.

"Good luck, Chief Turner. Good luck," she said earnestly, looking into his face.

Turner smiled down at her. Then he withdrew his hands from hers and turned back to the Jeep. He sped away without another word.

**62**

Nearly frantic with apprehension, Colette tightened her grip on the knife and the cleaver and sped toward the grinders. Darren and Roger were struggling near the conveyor belt, and Darren was no match for Roger and his devil-given powers. Colette surmised that they were trying to push each other into the grinder.

She took careful aim and threw the cleaver at Roger with all her strength. Roger saw it coming out of the corner of his eye and ducked. It narrowly missed his head. In that split second, while the cleaver distracted him, Darren was able to land a punch directly on Roger's jaw. His head snapped back and he fell to the floor. He raised himself up and looked at Darren and Colette with a bewildered expression. Colette noticed that his eyes were green again and his mouth softened. She pressed her advantage.

She knelt down beside him and held his head in her hands. She felt no strange galvanic charge. Roger's face contorted, a last struggle with the force that had overwhelmed him from the start.

In an urgent, low voice she said, "Roger, Roger. Stay with us. Help us fight. We can do it. Please, Roger. Hang in there."

His eyes began to flicker, green to blue, an eerie sight that chilled Colette. In a choked voice, he said "Can't . . . fight . . . Colette . . . it's the heart . . . get the heart . . ." Roger's voice trailed off and he closed his eyes for a moment.

In that moment, Colette felt her skin begin to tingle with that familiar, wonderful, evil sensation. She quickly put Roger's head down and backed off. She went to Darren, whose face was bloodied and bruised.

"Darren, I want you to *leave now*!" She used the same urgent tone she had used to Roger. She gazed at his face. "Please, Darren. Go."

Darren returned her gaze. His eyes had a tender expression she had never seen before.

"No," he said simply. "Not without you, 'Lette."

Colette felt someone grab her arm and send her spinning and crashing to the floor. She slid through the greasy slick of congealed blood and came within inches of Byron's astonished, dead face.

She hastily got back up on her feet and turned around. As she did, she heard a terrible scream and a ghastly, sickening crunch.

Colette looked and then fell again to her knees. Roger had pushed Darren headfirst up the conveyor belt. The grinders had crushed his head. Chunks of brain slowly slid off the blades and onto the floor. Red arterial blood still spurted from his mangled neck. His body was twitching reflexively and bizarrely, like a fish on a spear. Roger grinned, surveying Darren's body.

Colette was so stunned by the sight of Darren, so horribly mangled, that she could not move.

*His last words were 'Not without you, 'Lette.' His last words to me.*

The will to fight abruptly left Colette. The exhilarating adrenaline rush was gone. She felt alone and exhausted. Tears burned in her eyes. She looked down at the knife she still

clutched in her right hand. She heard footsteps and knew
Roger was coming for her. Quickly she turned the knife and
pointed it at her belly. *I've lost,* she thought dully. *Lost everything. Not without you* . . . She gripped the knife tightly,
readying herself for death.

A roar of terror and anger stopped her. She blinked the
tears from her eyes and looked up. An incredible sight greeted
her. She saw a mob of rotten and desiccated corpses lurching
drunkenly, yet in perfect step with one another, into the plant.
The Mayan priest she recognized from the vision led them,
walking beside two men with ropes around their necks. Their
faces were purple and black and bloated. Between them
walked an old man, dressed in a plaid flannel workshirt and
khakis. His face was stern and set, and a trickle of blood ran
down his cheek from his temple.

Roger was standing about a foot from Colette, riveted to
the floor with horror. He had been reaching for her hands, to
pull the knife away, when the nightmare mob had entered the
room.

"Aaron," moaned the crowd.

"Who's Aaron?" Colette said. She struggled to her feet and
stepped quickly away from the paralyzed Roger.

The two strangled men moved forward and grabbed Roger
by the arms. He struggled briefly and then was still. A wave
of rotten stench rolled over Colette, and she fought the urge to
vomit. The priest approached her. His face was impassive, his
eyes like isinglass, black and depthless. He pointed with his
menacing black sword at the knife in her hand and then at
Roger's chest. Roger swayed in the grip of the men and
opened his eyes. They were blue and cold.

"Xochitl, no," he whispered.

Rage rushed through Colette, galvanizing her nerveless
muscles. She glanced up at Darren's headless body, now lying
still on the conveyor belt. She thought of Lee Hsiang and of
Byron and of all the others who had died. She remembered
Roger's words to her. *The heart . . . It's the heart.*

A cracked, old-man's voice called to her. "Do it now, little
girl. *Now!*"

She plunged the knife into Roger's chest with all her strength.

An earsplitting, unearthly scream made Colette flinch as it resounded in the plant. She placed both hands on the knife and pushed up and to the left with all her strength, slicing through bone and blood and tissue. The priest stepped forward and placed his hands into Roger's open chest. He ripped out the still-beating heart and held it over his head for all to see.

A sigh rippled through the crowd like wind on a wheatfield. The priest then bent down and picked up a beautiful pottery jar. It had Mayan glyphs and images painted on it depicting a fierce battle. The priest dropped the heart into the jar and pressed the lid down tightly. Then he handed it to Colette and bowed.

Roger's corpse suddenly burst into white-hot flames. In an instant, there was nothing left but powdery gray ash. The priest, the two men, and the crowd sighed again. The old man grinned at her. "Nicely done, young lady," he said.

As Colette watched, they began to fade before her eyes, watching her as they slowly dissolved into the light and shadows of the plant. She looked down at the jar she was holding and recognized it as the one from the paper Darren had showed her. It felt heavy in her hands.

"Jesus Christ," said a low voice behind her.

Colette jumped. She wheeled around and saw Marcus Turner, his eyes round and staring, gun drawn and pointed at where the crowd had been standing.

"How long have you been here?" she asked.

"I came in just as you were about to stab yourself. Phillips was running toward you, reaching for the knife. Guess he wanted to kill you himself. Then this . . . these . . . God, I don't know what they were . . . came in. I was ready to shoot Phillips, and then my fingers were frozen. My whole body was frozen. What in God's name was that?" Turner kept staring at the pile of ash.

"I'm not sure," said Colette. All her well-managed emotions suddenly surged up in her throat—rage, pain, a crushing sense of loss, and loneliness. It was as if her heart had burst inside her chest. She swayed a little and said, her voice scaling up with hysteria, "All I know for sure is that Byron Mirkowski is dead, and Darren Keller is dead, and Roger Phillips is dead, and God knows who else and I . . . I'm still here and I don't know why. Why?" she screamed into the silence.

Turner put his arm around her as she burst into heaving, rib-shaking sobs, clutching the jar. They stood there for several minutes with only the harsh sound of Colette's sobs echoing in the empty room.

Then they heard a voice calling. "Darren? Darren Keller? Helloooo . . . anyone here?

Turner turned to Colette, who managed to say, "It's Chris Nein, our insurance man."

Turner thought a moment. "Lose the jar and try to calm down. I'll call Schutter down at the police station. And deal with this Nein guy for now."

"Should I tell them the truth?"

"Yes, but leave out those . . . things. Roger Phillips came here to kill you. He killed Keller and Mirkowski and was going to kill you. You stabbed him in self-defense. He just kind of spontaneously combusted. I saw that part, so I'll back you up."

They heard footsteps coming down the corridor to the plant. "Go," said Turner. Colette moved toward the back of the plant. She couldn't think of anything else to do with the jar, so she opened the freezer-room door and put it on a shelf. She closed the door and heard Turner say to Chris Nein, "Don't come any farther. There's been a double murder here and the police have to investigate." She heard Chris gurgle unintelligibly, and then the sound of retching.

She stepped into the ladies' room and washed her face. She took huge wads of paper towels and washed the blood off her skin. Her shoes and clothing were soaked and smeared in blood. Her shorts stuck to her legs, and the copper smell was overwhelming. She felt bile rising in her throat and fought it back. She stared at her haggard face in the mirror and remembered that Darren was dead.

"Why?" she whispered to herself. Her eyes filled with tears again.

Then Colette heard the sound of police sirens through the plant walls. She wiped her eyes on the back of her hand, squared her shoulders, pushed her hair back, and walked out of the plant into the offices. She did not even glance at the stiffening corpses of Byron and Darren, nor at the ash pile that was Roger.

## 63

Colette tossed restlessly in her bed. She had not slept well since—well, since before she'd met Roger. The police always had more questions for her, and she occasionally had an unreasonable fear that somehow they'd think she did the murders. But Marcus Turner stubbornly corroborated her story, so there really wasn't anything they could do.

She had seen today's *Clarion,* with its front-page, full-color photos of Darren's grieving family at his graveside. She had sent flowers but did not attend the funeral. His wife, Andrea, she noted, was doing a small-town Jackie Kennedy imitation. So cool, calm, and dignified, yet grieving. The daughters, especially the eldest one, seemed much more genuinely affected. The tear-stained face of Corrine Keller touched Colette.

"I wish I could tell you that I loved your father, too," Colette had said to the picture.

Don Klauss from Corporate in New York was coming

tomorrow to fill in for Darren until they found a replacement. He had hinted that perhaps she might like to try for the job, probably because she was the only surviving member of the front office staff. Spending the rest of her life at Mama's was the last thing she wanted to do. She knew she had to leave Aronston. Finally and for good.

Moonlight filtered in through the curtains. It was a full moon on a warm, cloudless May night. A breeze parted the curtains just enough to let a shaft of moonbeam fall on the Mayan jar on Colette's bureau. In the silver light it glowed eerily, as if lit from within, a grayish-green luminescence. Colette lay in bed and stared at it.

When the police were through with their questions on that first terrible day, she had gone out through the back of the plant, retrieved the jar from the freezer, and brought it home. She didn't know why, exactly. The Mayan priest had handed it to her, so there must be a reason for her to have it.

Though why anyone would think she'd want Roger's heart was beyond her.

Evil, evil. It lives inside that jar, she thought. Memories flooded over her—her own memories this time. Of Roger and how he had made her feel. Of Darren and how she'd found out too late how much he loved her. Darren's eyes just before he died. And here she was, alone, her life blasted as surely as if burned by Roger's white-hot fires.

She was overcome by an urgent feeling that she needed to get rid of the jar and its contents. Immediately. She leaped out of bed and pulled on her robe. Grabbing the jar, she ran down the stairs and out to the backyard. There was a wooden shed building in the backyard, painted to match the house. Emily McDevitt even had windowboxes fastened to the shed windows. Colette opened the shed door. The moonlight was bright enough for her to find a shovel in the dim interior of the shed.

She picked up the shovel and began to run, barefoot, with the jar tucked securely under her arm. She ran up to the Harrisburg Pike East and turned at the end of the block. She ran down past the town square until she saw the hulking dark outline of the First Evangelical Church of Aronston come into

view. It had been built in the late 1800's on the site of the old
Mennonite meetinghouse. There was a small, old cemetery in
the half lot next door to it. An ornate, Victorian-era cast-iron
fence surrounded the cemetery. Colette pushed open the rusty
iron gate and walked into the graveyard.

Trees and fence cast bizarre curling shadow patterns on the
old untended graves. Colette stopped at the first headstone she
came to. It was badly weathered, but in the crystalline moonlight she could just make out the name "Moyer." The name
meant nothing to her. She placed the jar on the grass and
began to dig in front of the headstone, pushing on the shovel
with her bare foot, heedless of the pain. All she wanted to do
was to dig down as far as she could and bury the jar so that no
one would ever find it again. *Let Roger's heart rot in darkness,* she thought.

She had dug down about three feet when she stopped to
rest. Most of the lettering on the headstone was hidden behind
the pile of earth and sod she had made. She leaned on the
shovel, panting, and pushed her hair out of her face, leaving a
dirty smear on her forehead. She looked at the silvery head-
stones and monuments all around her, the bright surfaces and
inky shadows giving them a surreal, haunted quality. A breeze
came up, bringing the scent of lilac to Colette and cooling her
sweating body. She sighed, gripped the shovel, and prepared
to dig again.

A white light shot up out of the newly dug hole. Colette
jumped back, tightening her hold on the shovel.

God, what is it now? she thought.

As she watched, a figure began to form within the light,
becoming darker and more substantial. Colette glanced over
at the jar on the grass, half-believing Roger must have something to do with this. She raised the shovel menacingly as
something stepped out of the light.

Xochitl stepped regally and gracefully forward, her blue
eyes fixed on Colette's. She extended her hands to Colette.

She wants the jar, thought Colette. She dropped the shovel,
bent down and picked it up off the ground, never taking her
eyes from Xochitl. She hesitated for a moment, wondering if
perhaps this was a mistake. Perhaps Xochitl would find a way

to release this evil again. Colette stared hard at Xochitl's face, trying to read what was there.

*I love him. Let me rest with him. Forever.*

Xochitl's words sounded inside Colette's head. She knew then that she had no reason to fear. Xochitl would keep the jar, and its contents safe. Hesitantly, she held out the jar toward the light.

Xochitl reached out and took the jar from Colette. Then she reached out her left hand as if to offer something to Colette. Colette tentatively reached out her hand, palm upward, not knowing what to expect. Xochitl dropped something smooth and hard into Colette's palm. Then Xochitl, the jar, and the light disappeared as abruptly as it had come.

Colette blinked several times, temporarily blinded. Her eyes finally readjusted to the night. She opened her right hand and looked down into her palm. It was the jade ring. The one Xochitl wore in her nose. A promise . . . and a thank-you, thought Colette. She slipped it onto her little finger. It fit perfectly. It felt warm, as if she had always worn it.

She bent down to pick up the shovel she had dropped. She gasped and sat down heavily on the grass. The hole she had dug was gone. The sod was undisturbed. Numbly she lifted her eyes to the headstone and read it:

MOYER
AARON EZEKIEL

1784–1802

*Beloved Son of Ezekiel and Leah Moyer*

The smell of lilacs came to her again. Suddenly she was bone-weary and wanted nothing more than to sleep. She got up from the ground, putting her hand on the headstone to help herself up. A faint, electric feeling passed into her body. The same kind of feeling that happened when Roger touched her. Her eyes widened and she leaped backward.

She grabbed the shovel and held it in front of her. She backed away slowly, her eyes fixed on the headstone. In the moonlight it seemed to glow from within, the same gray phosphorescence that had emanated from the pottery jar on her bureau. When she was about ten paces from the cemetery gate, she spun around and ran for dear life back toward her house.

She flung the shovel into the shed, raced up the stairs, locked her door behind her, and fell into bed, heedless of her dirty feet, hands, and face. She lay awake, trembling, for a long time. Slowly, however, a peace and calm descended on her and she slept deeply and dreamlessly for the first time in weeks.

The next day, the *Philadelphia Inquirer* reported that another of the Los Naranjos artifacts was missing from the University's museum. As before, there was no sign of forced entry and no suspects. Colette did not read the *Inquirer,* and Darren was dead, so she never knew that the jade ring she was wearing on her left little finger was missing from the museum.

# 64

Marcus Turner sat at his desk. The window was open and he was staring out at the spring day, trying not to think about Eddie and Roger Phillips and the unbelievable scene at Mama's. He had brought Cindy into work with him—he had a sudden aversion to being alone—and he could hear her snoring softly, stretched out in front of his desk. The door downstairs creaked open and the sound made him jump. Cindy lifted her head and looked expectantly over at the old mahogany staircase.

"Yoo-hoo! Anyone home?" The lilting, feminine voice echoed in the old fire company building.

"Yo, Vicky. Up here," called Marcus. He was too numb to feel the usual irritation that being cornered by Vicky Collins produced. He listened to her footsteps as she ascended the stairs.

She smiled when she saw him at his desk. He noticed that she looked tired and washed out. Maybe it was the black suit she had on. She had been covering a lot of funerals these past few days. Cindy lumbered over to Vicky and rubbed up against her by way of greeting and nudged Vicky's hand to be petted.

"Knock it off, Cin," Turner said. "You'll get the lady's nice suit all covered with dog hair."

Vicky chuckled as she patted Cindy's silky head. "It's okay, it's a black suit. Black dog hair won't show. How are you, Marc?" She sat down in the old, hard wooden chair next to his desk.

Turner rocked back in his own chair. "Hangin' in, Vicky. Just hangin'." He noticed that she was not carrying her usual tape recorder or even a notebook. "What brings you here today?"

Vicky sighed. "I just came from a memorial service for the Phillips children. Marc, I feel as if I'll go crazy if I have to cover one more funeral. There have been too many lately. Too damn many." Tears welled up in her eyes. She pulled a lace-trimmed handkerchief from her pocket and dabbed at her eyes, careful not to smudge her makeup. Turner remembered the Keller funeral yesterday and the heartbroken, racking sobs of Corrine Keller.

"I don't think you came here just to tell me about another funeral. What's really on your mind, Vicky?"

Vicky leaned forward in her chair. "Marc, what *really* happened at Mama Angelina's Sunday? I read the police report. Spontaneous combustion? Come on, Mark. That's something out of science fiction, for God's sake." She looked at him earnestly. "This is strictly off the record. I'd really like to know."

Turner leaned his elbows on his desk and matched his fingertips. He rested his chin on his thumbs and slid his eyes over at Vicky. "Why do you think I'm hiding something? Why don't you think I told the whole story?"

"Because I was there at the Bauman place on Saturday and I saw Roger Phillips do something, what I don't know, that made Eddie Haas go berserk and start firing at you. You were lucky he didn't kill you. He was a damn good shot. And if it hadn't been for your dog . . ." They both glanced over at Cindy, who had gone back to sleep in the middle of the room.

"Then, when Cindy knocked him down, he put the gun in his mouth as cool as you please and bang! And Roger Phillips just walked off into the night." She paused and took a deep breath. "So, Marc, you see that I have a hard time believing that Colette Walls just stabbed him in self defense like an ordinary guy. After all, he had just murdered two fairly young and healthy men. In horrible ways. You think I believe he let Colette just walk up to him and stab him? There was barely a bruise on her. And then he just bursts into flames? Come on!"

Marcus sat up and looked Vicky Collins straight in the eyes. "I saw what I saw and I reported what I saw. Phillips leaned over Colette Walls and she stabbed him. Right in the chest. He staggered back and then he burned. End of story. You saw the murder scene, the ash pile."

He thought of Jay Stanley and the ash piles on the *Empreza*. "Maybe this magic you saw Phillips do to Haas is what made his body burn. I don't know. All I know is what I saw, and that's all I have to say. On or off the record."

Vicky's eyes narrowed as she looked at him. "You are not telling the truth, Marcus, and I know it." After a few moments, she let out a sigh. "But I'm too tired right now to care. I'll find out someday what really happened, and what really caused all the fires and murders. With or without you."

*Maybe I'll get my Pulitzer after all,* she thought. *Or at least a fat book contract.*

Marcus shrugged. "Vicky, go ahead and try. It's a free country, First Amendment and all that shit. But my story stands. And if you go making a pest of yourself—well, why would you want to spoil such a beautiful friendship, huh?" He stared coldly back at her. Then he relented a little. "Maybe some things are better left alone. Some things are just not for us to understand. That's why we have a God."

Vicky wanted to retort that knowledge and understanding was her business but decided not to. Her resolve to find out everything was unshaken, but she saw the wisdom in retaining Marcus' good will. At least for now.

She smiled, professionally. "I guess you're right, Marc. Well, I'll shove off. Deadlines and stuff. It never ends."

"Nope, never does. See you later, Vicky." He rose as she left, then sat down again.

After a few moments, he said to Cindy, "She'd never believe me anyway. And neither would anyone else. Only Colette and I believe it. And you, 'cause you don't know any better."

Cindy thumped her tail and went back to sleep.

# 65

The red pickup truck rumbled and lurched up the rocky track into Alta, Colorado. The September sun cast slanting, afternoon shadows over the weathered, crumbling buildings of the ghost town. The truck stopped and a woman swung out of the cab. She was dressed in hiking boots, jeans, and a flannel shirt. She ran her hands through her short, dark blonde hair.

Colette surveyed the deserted remains of the town. Alta was a mining town, founded in 1877 and had finally been abandoned in the 1940s. What an eerie, godforsaken place, she thought. My tour groups will love it. She lifted her canteen up to her lips and drank deeply of the cool water. She was still not quite used to the thin mountain air and felt a little lightheaded.

She looked up at the snowcapped, purplish-gray Rockies and breathed deeply. She walked over to what had been a saloon and sat down on the rickety steps.

She finger-combed her short, almost punkette, hair again—she'd had it cut off when she began her new life—and sighed. The lonesome, dilapidated quality of the buildings made her feel forlorn and sad.

When the investigation into the murders was finished, Colette had sold her Corvette and most of her furniture and bought the truck. She drove west to Denver, Colorado and found an apartment and a job as a tour guide for Rocky Mountain Adventures. She found the sheer physical work of shepherding tourists on rock-climbing and camping expeditions left her little time to think. Which was good.

But now, sitting in the middle of this slightly creepy place, where so many dreams had been born and then died hard, she thought of the rolling green hills around Aronston. She remembered the way it felt to go speeding through the hills in the 'Vette, windows open and hair flying. And she remembered the wild life she left behind. She remembered Roger and Darren . . . and quickly shook her head. *I don't want to think about them. I don't want to think about any of it.* She absently twisted the jade ring she wore on her left little finger. The ring had never left her finger since she had first put it on one night last May. Colette had come to regard it as a talisman, an amulet to ward off evil.

Since coming to Colorado, Colette had been alone. This was purely her choice and she liked it that way, most of the time. She had become very sensitive to the uses and abuses of all sorts of power. Including the power of personal attraction. Until she learned how and when to use her powers for the best, she decided not to use them at all. She threw away her makeup and her little dresses and lived a very simple and spartan life. She learned how to cook and ate healthily, read good books, and went to bed early. She lost weight and discovered muscles she never knew she had. Her face became tanned and freckled, which was very becoming to her.

No one else had seen her bedroom except for Athena, her cat. She had found Athena drowning in a drainage ditch during a solitary hike. She had scrambled down the side of the ditch, waded into the mucky canal, and fished the cat out by the scruff of the neck. After she had gotten the cat home and cleaned it up, she had discovered that it was female, black and tan and white tiger-striped, with a funny black mask around her eyes that made her look very wise. Hence the name Athena.

Athena was nice to come home to, but Colette had had a few bad nights. She had a new, full life, but the old one had left an aching, empty space behind, like the gutted logs in her fireplace. And the memories were too awful to contemplate. So she immersed herself in work and in Athena and in exploring the huge beauty of Colorado.

She bent down to re-lace her hiking boot. The wind picked up a bit, whistling weirdly around the buildings and stirring up dust devils. Suddenly the sound of a piano playing burst out of the saloon behind her. She started and looked over her shoulder at the door.

"A piano? Here? No way!" she said out loud to her boot.

She scrambled to her feet and turned around. The saloon windows were shuttered with rotting plywood sheets. The door was shut and locked. She had seen no sign that anyone else was here in Alta but her. Yet the piano continued playing. A familiar song, too. She tried to remember what it was, but her mind was too busy to focus.

She walked across the porch to the door and pushed gently on it with her left hand. It sprang open, silently, as if the hinges had been oiled yesterday. She blinked at the darkness inside, took a step in, and waited for her eyes to adjust.

Inside there was nothing but a broken, cobwebbed piano with keys missing, and a long bar on the opposite wall. The broken mirror behind the bar was filmed with dust. The place smelled as though no one had been inside for fifty years. Colette looked at the piano. Her blood ran cold as she realized it was playing by itself. It sounded as sweet and tuneful as Darren's antique piano back in Aronston. She realized with a start that the piano was playing "Love is the Answer." The song Darren had played for her just an hour before he died.

I'm hallucinating, she thought. There's no such thing as ghosts. Snap out of it, girl. She shook her head, hard, trying to clear the sound away.

A movement to her left caught her eye. She looked. A man

was standing next to the bar. Panic tried to clutch at her throat, but she willed it away. Then recognition shot through her like a bolt of lightning.

"Darren?" she whispered into the dimness, her eyes wide with disbelief.

Darren leaned on the bar, one foot on the dusty tarnished brass rail, gazing at her with his soft hazel eyes. He was dressed in a T-shirt and jeans, Top-Siders and no socks. His face slowly broke into a happy, expectant grin, as if he were pleased to see her and wanted to hear about what she was doing these days. It was the smile from the photograph on the piano. She was suddenly conscious of her short tousled hair and her unmade-up face and her thinner, muscular body. Don't be stupid, she said to herself.

"Hi, Darren," she said softly. Hesitantly, she approached him, her heart thudding in her chest.

"Hey, 'Lette," he replied. His grin widened and he held out his hand. She took it. It felt cold but solid. *I never thought I'd see you again,* thought Colette.

"You okay?" Colette asked in a trembling voice. Her voice echoed in the empty room. As Colette looked at Darren's smiling face, she heard the words, sung by a rich female voice:

> *Light of the world*
> *Shine on me*
> *Love is the answer*
> *Shine on us all*
> *Set us free*
> *Love is the answer*

Darren picked up her hand and saw the jade ring on her finger. His eyes met hers and she knew he remembered where it came from. He turned her hand over and kissed her palm, then pulled her close and kissed her. She closed her eyes and felt hot tears roll down her cheeks and the sweet taste of Darren's kiss on her lips. She felt safe and warm in his embrace. She wrapped her arms around . . . nothing.

The music stopped. She opened her eyes. Darren was

gone. She felt a sharp pang stab through her heart. She whirled and looked wildly around the room. The place was empty, the piano beyond repair. "Oh, Darren. Come back!" she cried piteously into the darkness. She began to sob like a child. "Not without you, Darren. Please. Not without you."

A warm, comforting feeling stole around her shoulders like a strong arm. It led her gently out of the saloon, and the door shut and locked behind her. She walked back out to the wide dirt path that passed as a street. She knew beyond doubt that she was not alone. She was not without Darren. She would be okay.

Colette wiped the tears off her cheeks with the palms of her shaking hands. She shook her head again, then suddenly grinned impishly. She blew a kiss into the air. "I love you!" she shouted at the top of her lungs. She listened to the echo bounce back to her three or four times. She smiled, satisfied, and strode back to her truck. The mountain shadows plunged Alta into twilight as the pickup left it far behind.

New York Times bestselling author

# MICHAEL MARSHALL

## THE STRAW MEN

0-515-13427-9

Three seemingly unrelated events are the
first signs of an unimaginable network of fear that will
lead one unlikely hero to a chilling confrontation with
The Straw Men. No one knows what they want—or
why they kill. But they must be stopped.

## THE UPRIGHT MAN

0-515-13638-7

Ward Hopkins is afraid. He's seen something dreadful
in the high plains of the Columbia River. It's sent him
fleeing cross country, forever running. And in his wake,
one by one, people are dying.
Something's following Ward Hopkins.

Coming September 2005

## BLOOD OF ANGELS

The thrilling conclusion to the Straw Men trilogy.

**Available wherever books are sold or at
www.penguin.com**

J006

# BESTSELLING AUTHOR
# MATTHEW COSTELLO

# Unidentified

**As inexplicable terrors erupt across the globe, humanity's only hope of survival lies with those who are willing to enter the source—a house where time, space, and reality have given way to something else.**

**"TRULY TWISTED."
—PETER STRAUB**

**"COSTELLO WRITES WITH POWER AND PATHOS."
—PUBLISHERS WEEKLY**

**Available wherever books are sold or at
www.penguin.com**